THE AZTEC
TREASURE-HOUSE

THE AZTEC TREASURE-HOUSE

A Romance of Contemporaneous Antiquity

THOMAS ALLIBONE JANVIER

A LOST RACE NOVEL

TO C. A. J.

A LOST RACE NOVEL

Published by Wildside Press, LLC
www.wildsidebooks.com

Who'd hear great marvels told—
Come listen now!
Who longs for hidden gold—
Come listen now!
Who joys in well-fought fights,
Who yearns for wondrous sights,
Who pants for strange delights—
Come listen now!

For here are marvels told
To listen to!
Here tales of hidden gold
To listen to!
Here gallant men wage fights,
Here pass most wondrous sights,
Here's that which ear delights
To listen to!

PROLOGUE

"God sends nuts to them who have no teeth:" which ancient Spanish proverb of contrariety comes strongly to mind as I set myself to this writing.

By nature am I a studious, book-loving man, having a strong liking for quiet and orderliness. Yet in me also is a strain that urges me, even along ways which are both rough and dangerous, to get beyond book-knowledge, and to examine for myself the abstractions of thought and the concretions of men and things out of the consideration whereof books are made. And I hold that it is because I have thus sought for truth in its original sources, instead of resting content with what passes for truth, being detached fragments of fact which other men have found and have cut and polished to suit themselves, that I have gathered to myself more of it, and in its rude yet perfect native crystals, than has come into the possession of any other modern investigator. In making which strong assertion I am not moved by idle vanity, but by a just and reasonable conception of the intrinsic merit of my own achievement: as will be universally admitted when I publish the great work, now almost ready for the press, upon which, in preparatory study and in convincing discovery, I have been for the past ten years engaged. For I speak well within bounds when I declare that a complete revolution in all existing conceptions of American archæology and ethnology will be wrought when *Pre-Columbian Conditions on the Continent of North America*, by Professor Thomas Palgrave, Ph.D. (Leipsic), is given to the world.

Upon this work I say that I have been engaged for ten years. Rather should I say that I have been engaged upon it for forty years; for its germs were implanted in me when I was a child of but six years old. Before my intelligence at all could grasp the meaning of what I read, my imagination was fired by reading in the pages of Stephens of the wonders which that eminent explorer discovered in Yucatan; and my mind then was made up that I would follow in his footsteps, and in the end go far beyond him, until I should reveal the whole history of the marvellous race whose mighty works he found, but of whose genesis he could only feebly surmise. And this resolve of the child became the dominant purpose of the man. In my college life at Harvard, and in my university life at Leipsic, my studies were directed chiefly to this end. Especially did I devote myself to the acquisition of languages, and to gaining a sound knowledge of the principles of those departments of archæology and ethnology which related to the great work that I had in view. Later, during the ten years that I occupied (as I believe usefully and acceptably) the Chair of Topical Linguistics in the University of Michigan, all the time that I properly could take from my professorial duties was given exclusively to the study of the languages of the indigenous races of Mexico, and to what little was to be found in books concerning their social organization and mode of life, and to the broad subject of Mexican antiquities. By correspondence I became acquainted with the most eminent Mexican archæologists—the lamented Orozco y Berra, Icazbalceta, Chavero, and the philologists Pimentel and Peñafiel; and I had the honor to know personally the American archæologist Bandelier, the surpassing scientific value of whose researches among the primitive peoples of Mexico places his work above all praise. And by the study of the writings of these great scholars, and of all writings thereto cognate, my own knowledge steadily grew; until at last I felt myself strong enough to begin the investigations on my own account for which I had sought by all these years of patient preparation fittingly to pave the way.

But inasmuch as my life until a short time since has been wholly that of a scholar, and wholly has been passed in quiet ways, I truly have had no teeth at all for the proper cracking of the nuts which have come to me in the course of the surprising adventures that I have now set myself to narrate. For in the course of these adventures (necessarily, yet sorely against my will) I have been thrust by force of circumstances into many imminent and prodigious perils; much time that I gladly would have devoted to peaceful, fruitful study I have been compelled to employ in rude and profitless (except that my life was saved by it) battling with savages; and—what most of all has pained me—many curious and interesting skulls that I gladly would have added entire to my collection of crania, I have been driven in self-defence to ruin irreparably with my own hands.

All of which diversities of my likings and my happenings will appear in due order, as I tell in the following pages of the strange and wonderful things which befell me—in company with Rayburn and Young and Fray Antonio and the boy Pablo—in our search after and finding of the great treasure that was hidden, in a curiously secret place among the Mexican mountains more than a thousand years ago, by Chaltzantzin, the third of the Aztec kings.

CHAPTER I

FRAY ANTONIO

My heart was light within me as I stood on the steamer's deck in the cool gray of an October morning and saw out across the dark green sea and the dusky, brownish stretch of coast country the snow-crowned peak of Orizaba glinting in the first rays of the rising sun. And presently, as the sun rose higher, all the tropic region of the coast and the brown walls of Vera Cruz and of its outpost fort of San Juan de Ulua were flooded with brilliant light—which sudden and glorious outburst of radiant splendor seemed to me to be charged with a bright promise of my own success.

And still lighter was my heart, a week later, when I found myself established in the beautiful city of Morelia, and ready to begin actively the work for which I had been preparing myself—at first unconsciously, but for ten years past consciously and carefully—almost all my life long.

Morelia, I had decided, was the best base for the operations that I was about to undertake. My main purpose was to search for the remnants of primitive civilization among the more isolated of the native Indian tribes; and out of the fragments thus found, pieced together with what more I could glean from the early ecclesiastical and civil records, to recreate, so far as this was possible, the fabric that was destroyed by the Spanish conquerors. Nowhere could my investigations be conducted to better advantage than in the State of Michoacan (of which State the city of Morelia is the capital) and in the adjacent State of Jalisco; for in this region tribes still exist which never have been, reduced to more than nominal subjection, and which, maintain to a great extent their primitive customs and their primitive faith, though curiously mingling with this latter many Christian observances. Indeed, the independence of the Indians of these parts is so notable that the proverb "Free as Jalisco" is current throughout Mexico. Moreover, Morelia is a city rich in ancient records. The archives of the Franciscan province, that has its centre here extend back to the year 1531; those of the Bishopric of Michoacan to the year 1538; and those of the Colegio de San Nicolás to the year 1540;

while in the recently founded Museo Michoacano already has been collected a rich store of archæological material. In a word, there was no place in all Mexico where my studies and my investigations could be pursued to such advantage as they could be pursued here.

From a fellow-archæologist in the City of Mexico I brought a letter of introduction to the director of the Museo, the learned Dr. Nicolás Leon; and so cordially was this letter worded, and so cordially was it received, that within the day of my coming into that strange city I found myself in the midst of friends. At once their hearts and their houses were opened to me, and they gave me with a warm enthusiasm the benefit of their knowledge and of their active assistance forwarding the work that I had in hand.

In the quiet retirement of the Museo I opened to that one of its members to whom the director especially had commended me, Don Rafael Moreno, the purposes which I had in view, and the means by which I hoped to accomplish them. "Surely," I said, "among the free Indians in the mountains hereabouts much may be found—in customs, in tone of thought, in religion—that has remained unchanged since the time of the conquest."

Don Rafael nodded. "Fray Antonio has said as much," he observed, thoughtfully.

"And as your own distinguished countryman, Señor Orozco y Berra, has pointed out," I continued, "many dark places in primitive history may be made clear, many illusions may be dispelled, and many deeply interesting truths may be gathered by one who will go among these Indians, lending himself to their mode of life, and will note accurately what he thus learns from sources wholly original."

"Fray Antonio has professed the same belief," Don Rafael answered. "But that his love is greater for the saving of heathen souls than for the advancement of antiquarian knowledge, he long ago would have done what you now propose to do. He has done much towards gathering a portion of the information that you seek, even as it is."

"And who is this Fray Antonio, señor?"

"He is the man who of all men can give you the wisest help in your present need. We see but little of him here at the Museo, though he is one of our most honored members, for his time is devoted so wholly to the godly work to which he has given himself that but little remains to him to use in other ways. He is a monk, vowed to the Rule of St. Francis. As you know, since the promulgation of the Laws of the Reform, monks are not permitted in our country to live in communities; but, with only a few exceptions, the conventual churches which have not be secularized still are administered by members of the religious orders to which they formerly belonged. Fray Antonio has the charge of the church of San Francisco—over by the market-place, you know—and virtually is a parish priest. He is a religious enthusiast. In God's service he gives himself no rest. The common people here, since his loving labors are among them while the pestilence of small-pox raged, reverently believe him to be a saint; and those of a higher class, who know what heroic work he did in that dreadful time, and who see how perfectly his life conforms to the principles which he professes, and how like is the spirit of holiness that animates him to that of the sainted men who founded the order to which he belongs, are disposed to hold a like opinion. Truly, it is by the especial grace of God that men like Fray Antonio are permitted at times to dwell upon this sinful earth."

Don Rafael spoke with a depth of feeling and a reverence of tone that gave his strong words still greater strength and deeper meaning. After that moment's pause he resumed: "But that which is of most interest to you, señor, is the knowledge that Fray Antonio has gained of our native Indians during his ministrations among them. It is the dearest wish of his heart to carry to these heathen souls the saving grace of Christianity, and for the accomplishment of this good purpose he makes many journeys into the mountains; ministering in the chapels which his zeal has founded in the Indian towns, and striving earnestly by his preaching of God's word to bring these far-wandered sheep into the Christian fold. Very often his life has been in most imminent peril, for the idolatrous priests of the mountain tribes hate him with a most bitter hatred because of the inroads which his mild creed is making upon the cruel creed which they uphold. Yet is he careless of the danger to which he exposes himself; and there be those who believe, such is the temerity with which he manifests his zeal, that he rather seeks than shuns a martyr's crown."

Again Don Rafael paused, and again was it evident that deep feelings moved him as he spoke of the holy life of this most holy man. "You will thus understand, señor," he went on, "that Fray Antonio of all men is best fitted by his knowledge of the ways of these mountain Indians to advise you touching your going among them and studying them. You cannot do better than confer with him at once. It is but a step to the church of San Francisco. Let us go."

What Don Rafael had said had opened new horizons to me, and I was stirred by strange feelings as we passed out together from the shady silence of the Museo into the bright silence of the streets: for Morelia is a quiet city, wherein at all times is gentleness and rest. For priests in general, and for Mexican priests in particular, I had entertained always a profound contempt; but now, from an impartial source, I had heard of a Mexican priest whose life-springs seemed to be the soul-stirring impulses of the thirteenth century; who was devoted in soul and in body to the service of God and of his fellow-men; in whom, in a word, the seraphic spirit of St. Francis of Assisi seemed to live again. But by this way coming to such tangible evidence of the survival in the present time of forces which were born into the world six hundred years ago, my thoughts took a natural turn to my own especial interests; and, by perhaps not over-strong analogy, I reasoned that if this monk still lived so closely to the letter and to the spirit of the Rule that St. Francis, six centuries back, gave to his order, most reasonably might I hope to find still quick something of the life that was in full vigor in Mexico only a little more than half that many centuries ago.

We turned off from the Calle Principal by the little old church of La Cruz, and passed onward across the market-place, where buying and selling went on languidly, and where a drowsy hum of talk made a rhythmic setting to a scene that seemed to my unaccustomed eyes less a bit of real life than a bit lifted bodily from an opera. Facing the market-place was the ancient church; and the change was a pleasant one, from the vivid sunlight and warmth of the streets to its cool, shadowy interior: where the only sign of life was a single old woman, her head muffled in her *rebozo*, praying her way along the Stations of the Cross. For more than two hundred and fifty years had prayer been made and praise been offered here; and as I thought of the many generations who here had ministered and worshipped—though evil hearts in plenty, no doubt, both within and without the chancel there had been—it seemed to me that some portion of the subtle essence of all the soul-longings for heavenly help and guidance that here had been breathed forth, by men and women truly struggling against the sinful forces at work in the world, had entered into the very fabric of that ancient church, and so had sanctified it.

We crossed to the eastern end of the church, where was a low door-way, closed by a heavy wooden door that was studded with rough iron nails and ornamented with rudely finished iron-work; pushing which door open briskly, as one having the assured right of entry there, Don Rafael courteously stood aside and motioned to me to enter the sacristy.

From the shadowy church I passed at a step into a small vaulted room brilliant with the sunlight that poured into it through a broad window that faced the south. Just where this flood of sunshine fell upon the flagged floor, rising from a base of stone steps built up in a pyramidal form, was a large cross of some dark wood, on which was the life-size figure of the crucified Christ; and there, on the bare stone pavement before this emblem of his faith, his face, on which the sunlight fell full, turned upward towards the holy image, and his arms raised in supplication, clad in his Franciscan habit, of which the hood had fallen back, knelt Fray Antonio; and upon his pale, holy face, that the rich sunlight glorified, was an expression so seraphic, so entranced, that it seemed as though to his fervent gaze the very gates of heaven must be open, and all the splendors and glories and majesties of paradise revealed.

It is as I thus first saw Fray Antonio—verily a saint kneeling before the cross—that I strive to think of him always. Yet even when that other and darker, but surely more glorious, picture of him rises before my mind I am not disconsolate; for at such times the thought possesses me—coming to me clearly and vehemently, as though from a strongly impelled force without myself—that what he prayed for at the moment when I beheld him was that which God granted to him in the end.

Some men being thus broken in upon while in the very act of communing with Heaven would have been distressed and ill at ease—as I assuredly was because I had so interrupted him. But to Fray Antonio, as I truly believe, communion with Heaven was so entirely a part of his daily life that our sudden entry in nowise ruffled him. After a moment, that he might recall his thoughts within himself and so to earth again, he arose from his knees, and with a grave, simple grace came forward to greet us. He was not more than eight-and-twenty years old, and he was slightly built and thin—not emaciated, but lean with the wholesome leanness of one who strove to keep his body in the careful order of a machine of which much work was required. His face still had in it the soft roundness and tenderness of youth, that accorded well with its expression of gracious sweetness; but there was a firmness about the fine, strong chin, and in the set of the delicate lips, that showed a reserve of masterful strength. And most of all did this strength shine forth from his eyes; which, truly, though at this first sight of him I did not perceive it fully, were the most wonderful eyes that ever I have seen. As I then beheld them I thought them black; but they really were a dark blue, and so were in keeping with his fair skin and hair. Yet that which gave them so strong an individuality was less their changing color than the marvellous way in which their expression changed with every change of feeling of the soul that animated them. When I first saw them, turned up towards heaven, they seemed to speak a heavenly language full of love; and when I saw them last, stern, but shining with the exultant light of joy triumphant, they fairly hurled the wrath of outraged Heaven against the conquered powers of hell. And I can give no adequate conception of the love that shone forth from them when pitying sympathy for human sorrow, or even for the pain which brute beasts suffered, touched that most tender heart for which they spoke in tones richer and fuller than the tones of words.

Don Rafael, standing without the door that he had opened in order that I might precede him, did not perceive that we had interrupted Fray Antonio in his prayers; and began, therefore, in the lively manner natural to him, when I had been in due form presented as an American archæologist come to Mexico to pursue my studies of its primitive inhabitants, to commend the undertaking that I had in hand, and to ask of Fray Antonio the aid in prosecuting it that he so well could give.

Perhaps it was that Fray Antonio understood how wholly my heart already had gone out to him—assuredly, later, there was such close sympathy between us that our thoughts would go and come to each other without need for words—and so was disposed in some instinctive way to join his purposes with mine; but, be this as it may, before Don Rafael well could finish the explanation of my wishes, Fray Antonio had comprehended what I desired, and had promised to give me his aid.

"The señor already has a book-knowledge of our native tongues. That is well. The speaking knowledge will come easily. He shall have the boy Pablo for his servant. A good boy is Pablo. With him he can talk in the Nahua dialect—which is the most important, for it is sprung most directly from the ancient stock. And I will arrange that the señor shall live for a time in the mountains—it will be a hard life, I fear—at Santa María and at San Andrés, in which villages he can gain a mouth-mastery of both Otomí and Tarascan. A little time must be given to all this—some months, no doubt. But the señor, who already has studied through ten years, will understand the needfulness of this short discipline. To a true student study in itself is a delight—still more that study which makes the realization of a long-cherished purpose possible. The señor, I know, reads Spanish, since so perfectly he speaks it"—this with a gracious movement of the hands and a courteous inclination of the body that enhanced the value of the compliment—"but does the señor read with ease our ancient Spanish script?"

"I have never attempted it," I answered. "But as I can read easily the old printed Spanish, I suppose," I added, a little airily, "that I shall have no great difficulty in reading the old script also."

Fray Antonio smiled a little as he glanced at Don Rafael, who smiled also, and as he turned out his hands, answered: "Perhaps. But it is not quite the same as print, as the señor will know when he tries. But it makes no difference; for what is most interesting in our archives I shall be glad—and so also will be Don Rafael—to aid him in reading.

"You must know, señor," he went on, dropping his formal mode of address as his interest in the subject augmented, and as his feeling towards me grew warmer, "that many precious documents are here preserved. So early as the year 1536 this western region was erected into a Custodia, distinct from the Province of the Santo Evangelio of Mexico; and from that time onward letters and reports relating to the work done by the missionaries of our order among the heathen have been here received. In truth, I doubt not that many historic treasures are hidden here. In modern times, during the last hundred years or more, but little thought has been given to the care of these old papers—which are so precious to such as Don Rafael and yourself because of their antiquarian value, and which are still more precious to me because they tell of the sowing among the heathen of the seed of God's own Word. It is probable that they have not been at all examined into since our learned brothers Pablo de Beaumont and Alonzo de la Rea were busy with the writing of their chronicles of this Province—and the labors of these brothers ended more than two hundred and fifty years ago. In the little time that I myself can give to such matters I already have found many manuscripts which cast new and curious light upon the strange people who dwelt here in Mexico before the Spaniards came. Some of these I will send for your examination, for they will prepare you for the work you have in contemplation by giving you useful knowledge of primitive modes of life and tones of faith and phases of thought. And while you are in the mountains, at Santa María and San Andrés, I will make further searches in our archives, and what I find you shall see upon your return.

"With your permission, señores, I must now go about my work. Don Rafael knows that I am much too ready to forget my work in talk of ancient matters. It is a weakness with me—this love for the study of antiquity—that I struggle against, but that seems rather to increase upon me than to be overcome. This afternoon, señor, I will send a few of the ancient manuscripts to you. And so—until we meet again."

CHAPTER II

THE CACIQUE'S SECRET

Fray Antonio punctually fulfilled his promise in regard to the manuscripts, and I had but to glance at them in order to understand the smile that he had interchanged with Don Rafael when I so airily had expressed my confidence in my ability to read them. To say that I more easily could read Hebrew is not to the purpose, for I can read Hebrew very well; but it is precisely to the purpose to say that I could not read them at all! What with the curious, involved formation of the several letters, the extraordinary abbreviations, the antique spelling, the strange forms of expression, and the use of obsolete words I could not make sense of so much as a single line. Yet when, being forced into inglorious surrender, I carried the manuscripts to the Museo, and appealed to Don Rafael for assistance, he read to me in fluent Spanish all that I had found so utterly incomprehensible. "It is only a knack," he explained. "A little time and patience are required at first, but then all comes easily." But Don Rafael did here injustice to his own scholarship. More than a little time and patience have I since given to the study of ancient Spanish script, and I am even yet very far from being an expert in the reading of it.

In regard to the other promise that Fray Antonio made me—that he would send me a servant who also would serve as a practical instructor in the Nahua, or Aztec, dialect—he was equally punctual. While I was taking, in my bedroom, my first breakfast of bread and coffee the morning following my visit to the church of San Francisco, I heard a faint sound of music; but whether it was loud music at a distance or very soft music near at hand I could not tell. Presently I perceived that the musician was feeling about among the notes for the sabre song from *La Grande Duchesse*—selections from which semi-obsolete opera, as I then remembered, had been played by the military band on the plaza the evening before. Gradually the playing grew more assured; until it ended in an accurate and spirited rendering of the air. With this triumph, the volume of the sound increased greatly; and from its tones I inferred that the instrument was a concertina, and that whoever played it was in the inner court-yard of the hotel.

Suddenly, in the midst of the music, there sounded—and this sound unmistakably came from the hotel court-yard—the prodigious braying of an ass; and accompanying this came the soft sound of bare feet hurrying away down the passage from near my door.

I opened the door and looked out, but the passage was empty. The gallery overlooked the court-yard, and stepping to the edge of the low stone railing, I beheld a sight that I never recall without a feeling of warm tenderness. Almost directly beneath me stood a small gray ass, a very delicately shaped and perfect little animal, with a coat of most extraordinary length and fuzziness, and with ears of a truly prodigious size. His head was raised, and his great ears were pricked forward in a fashion which indicated that he was most intently listening; and upon his face was an expression of such benevolent sweetness, joined to such thoughtfulness and meditative wisdom, that in my heart (which is very open to affection for his gentle kind) there sprung up in a moment a real love for him. Suddenly he lowered his head, and turned eagerly his regard towards the corner of the court-yard where descended the stair-way from the gallery on which I stood; and from this quarter came towards him a smiling, pleasant-faced Indian lad of eighteen or twenty years old, whose dress was a cotton shirt and cotton trousers, whose feet were bare, and on whose head was a battered hat of straw. And as the ass saw the boy, he strained at the cord that tethered him and gave another mighty bray.

"Dost thou call me, Wise One?" said the boy, speaking in Spanish. "Truly this Señor Americano is a lazy señor, that he rises so late, and keeps us waiting for his coming so long. But patience, Wise One. The Padre says that he is a good gentleman, in whose service we shall be treated as though we were kings. No doubt I now can buy my rain-coat. And thou, Wise One—thou shalt have beans!"

And being by this time come to the ass, the boy enfolded in his arms the creature's fuzzy head and gently stroked its preternaturally long ears. And the ass, for its part, responded to the caress by rubbing its head against the boy's breast and by most energetically twitching its scrag of a tail. Thus for a little time these friends manifested for each other their affection; and then the boy seated himself on the pavement beside the ass and drew forth from his pocket a large mouth-organ—on which he went to work with such a will that all the court-yard rang with the strains of Offenbach's music.

It was plain from what he had said that this was the boy whom

Fray Antonio had promised to send to me; and notwithstanding his uncomplimentary comments upon my laziness, I had taken already a strong liking to him. I waited until he had played through the sabre song again—to which, as it seemed to me, the ass listened with a slightly critical yet pleased attention—and then I hailed him.

"The lazy Señor Americano is awake at last, Pablo," I called. "Come up hither, and we will talk about the buying of thy rain-coat, and about the buying of the Wise One's beans."

The boy jumped up as though a spring had been let loose beneath him, and his shame and confusion were so great that I was sorry enough that I had made my little joke upon him.

"It is all right, my child," I said, quickly, and with all the kindness that I could put into my tones. "Thou wert talking to the Wise One, not to me—and I have forgotten all that I heard. Thou art come from Fray Antonio?"

"Yes, señor," he answered; and as he saw by my smiling that no harm had been done, he also smiled; and so honest and kindly was the lad's face that I liked him more and more.

"Patience for yet a little longer, Wise One," he said, turning to the ass, who gravely wagged his ears in answer. And then the boy came up the stair to the gallery, and so we went to my room that I might have talk with him.

It was not much that Pablo had to tell about himself. He was a Guadalajara lad, born in the Indian suburb of Mexicalcingo—as his musical taste might have told me had I known more of Mexico—who had drifted out into the world to seek his fortune. His capital was the ass—so wise an ass that he had named him El Sabio. "He knows each word that I speak to him, señor," said Pablo, earnestly. "And when he hears, even a long way off, the music that I make upon the little instrument, he know that it is from me that the music comes, and calls to me. And he loves me, señor, as though he were my brother; and he knows that with the same tenderness I also love him. It was the good Padre who gave him to me. God rest and bless him always!" This pious wish, I inferred, related not to the ass but to Fray Antonio.

"And how dost thou live, Pablo?" I asked.

"By bringing water from the Spring of the Holy Children, señor. It is two leagues away, the Ojo de los Santos Niños, and El Sabio and I make thither two journeys daily. We bring back each time four jars of water, which we sell here in the city—for it is very good, sweet water—at three *tlacos* the jar. You see, I make a great deal of money, señor—three *reales* a day! If it were not for one single thing, I should soon be rich."

That riches could be acquired rapidly on a basis of about twenty-seven cents, in our currency, a day struck me as a novel notion. But I inquired, gravely: "And this one thing that hinders thee from getting rich, Pablo, what is it?"

"It is that I eat so much, señor," Pablo answered, ruefully. "Truly it seems as though this belly of mine never could be filled. I try valiantly to eat little and so to save my money; but my belly cries out for more and yet more food—and so my money goes. Although I make so much, I can scarcely save a *medio* in a whole week, when what El Sabio must have and what I must have is paid for. And I am trying so hard to save just now, for before the next rainy season comes I want to own a rain-coat. But for a good one I must pay seven *reales*. The price is vast."

"What is a rain-coat, Pablo?"

"The señor does not know? That is strange. It is a coat woven of palm leaves, so that all over one it is as a thatch that the rain cannot come through. What I was saying just now to El Sabio—" Pablo stopped suddenly, and turned aside from me in a shamefaced way, as he remembered what he also had said to El Sabio about my laziness.

"—Was that out of the wages I am to pay thee thou canst save enough money to buy thy coat with," I said, quickly, wishing to rid him of his confusion. And then we fell to talking of what these wages should be, and of how he was to help me to gain a speaking knowledge of his native tongue—for so far we had spoken Spanish together— and of what in general would be his duties as my servant. That El Sabio could be anything but a part of the contract seemed never to cross Pablo's mind; and so presently our terms were concluded, and I found myself occupying the responsible relation of master to a mouth-organ playing boy and an extraordinarily wise ass. It was arranged that both of these dependants of mine should accompany me in my expedition to the Indian villages; and to clinch our bargain I gave Pablo the seven *reales* wherewith to buy his rain-coat on the spot.

I was a little surprised, two days later, when we started from Morelia on our journey into the mountains to the westward, to find that Pablo had not bought his much-desired garment; though, to be sure, as the rainy season still was a long way off, there was no need for it. He hesitated a little when I questioned him about it, and then, in a very apologetic tone, said: "Perhaps the señor will forgive me for doing so ill with his money. But indeed I could not help it. There is an old man, his name is Juan, señor, who has been very good to me many times. He has given me things to put into this wretchedly big belly of mine; and when I broke one of my jars he lent me the money to buy another with, and would take from me again only what the jar cost and no more. Just now this old many is sick—it is rheumatism, señor—and he has no money at all, and he and his wife have not much to eat, and I know what pain that is. And so—and so—Will the señor forgive me? I do not need the rain-coat now, the señor understands. And so I gave Juan the seven *reales*, which he will pay me when he gets well and works again; and should he die and not pay me—Does the señor know what I have been thinking? It is that rain-coats really are not very needful things, after all. Without them one gets wet, it is true; but then one soon gets dry again. But truly"—and there was a sudden catching in Pablo's throat that was very like a sob—"truly I did want one."

When Pablo had told this little story I did not wonder at the esteem in which Fray Antonio held him, and from that time onward he had a very warm place in my heart. And I may say that but for his too great devotion to his mouth-organ—for that boy never could hear a new tune but that he needs must go at once to practising it upon his beloved "instrumentito" until he had mastered it—he was the best servant that man ever had. And within his gentle nature was a core of very gallant fearlessness. In the times of danger which we shared together later, excepting only Rayburn, not one of us stood face to face and foot to foot with death with a steadier or a calmer bravery; for in all his composition there did not seem to be one single fibre that could be made to thrill in unison with fear. Of his qualities as a servant I had a good trial during the two months that we were together in the mountains—in which time I got enough working knowledge of the Indian dialects to make effective the knowledge that I had gained from books—and I was amazed by the quickness that he manifested in apprehending and in supplying my wants and in understanding my ways.

As to making any serious study of Indian customs—save only those of the most open and well-known sort—in this short time, I soon perceived that the case was quite hopeless. Coming from Fray Antonio, whose benevolent ministrations among them had won their friendship, the Indians treated me with a great respect and showed me every kindness. But I presently began to suspect, and this later grew to be conviction, that because my credentials came from a Christian priest I was thrust away all the more resolutely from knowledge of their inner life. What I then began to learn, and what I learned more fully later, convinced me that these Indians curiously veneered with Christian practices their native heathen faith; manifesting a certain superstitious reverence for the Christian rites and ceremonies, yet giving sincere worship only to their heathen gods. It was something to have arrived at this odd discovery, but it tended only to show me how difficult was the task that I had set myself of prying into the secrets of the Indians' inner life.

Indeed, but for an accident, I should have returned to Morelia no wiser, practically, than when I left it; but by that turn of chance fortune most wonderfully favored me, and with far-reaching consequences. It was on the last afternoon of my stay in the village of Santa María; and the beginning of my good-luck was that I succeeded in walking out upon the mountain-side alone. My walk had a decided purpose in it, for each time that I had tried to go in this direction one or another of the Indians had been quickly upon my heels with some civil excuse about the danger of falling among the rocks for leading me another way. How I thus succeeded at last in escaping from so many watchful eyes I cannot say, but luck was with me, and I went on undisturbed. The sharply sloping mountain-side, very wild and rugged, was strewn with great fragments of rock which had fallen from the heights above, and which, lying there for ages beneath the trees, had come to be moss-grown and half hidden by bushes and fallen leaves. In the dim light that filtered through the branches, walking in so uncertain a place was attended with a good deal of danger; for not only was there a likelihood of falls leading to broken legs, but broken necks also were an easy possibility by the chance of a slip upon the mossy edge of one or another of the many ledges, followed by a spin through the air ending suddenly upon the jagged rocks below. Indeed, so ticklish did I find my way that I began to think that the Indians had spoken no more than the simple truth in warning me against such dangers, and that I had better turn again while light remained to bring me back in safety; and just as I had reached this wise conclusion my feet slid suddenly from under me on the very edge of one of the ledges, and over I went into the depth below.

Fortunately I fell not more than a dozen feet or so, and my fall was broken by a friendly bed of leaves and moss. When I got to my feet again, in a moment, I found myself in a narrow cleft in the rocks, and I was surprised to see that through this cleft ran a well-worn path. All thought of the danger that I had just escaped from so narrowly was banished form my mind instantly as I made this discovery; and full of the exciting hope that I was about to find something which the Indians most earnestly desired to conceal, I went rapidly and easily onward in the direction that I had been pressing towards with so much difficulty along the rocky mountain-side. The course of this sunken path, I soon perceived, was partly natural and partly artificial. It went on through clefts such as the one that I had fallen into, and through devious ways where the fragments of fallen rock, some of them great masses weighing many tons, had been piled upon each other in most natural confusion, so as to leave a narrow passage in their depths. And all this had been done in a long-past time, for the rocks were thickly coated with moss; and in one place, where a water-course crossed the path, were smoothed by water in a way that only centuries could have accomplished. So cleverly was the concealment effected, the way so narrow and so irregular, that I verily believe an army might have scoured that mountain-side and never found the path at all, save by such accident as had brought me into it.

For half a mile or more I went on in the waning light, my heart throbbing with the excitement of it all, and so came out at last upon a vast jutting promontory of rock that was thrust forth from the mountain's face eastwardly. Here was an open space of an acre or more, in the centre of which was a low, altar-like structure of stone. At the end of the narrow path, being still within its shelter, I stopped to make a careful survey of the ground before me; for I realized that in what I was doing Death stood close at my elbow, and that, unless I acted warily, he surely would have me in his grasp. Coming out of the shadows of the woods and the deeper shadows of the sunken path to this wide open space, where the light of the brilliant sunset was reflected strongly from masses of rosy clouds over all the eastern sky, I could see clearly. In the midst of the opening, not far from the edge of the stupendous precipice, where the bare rock dropped sheer down a thousand feet or more, was a huge bowlder that had been cut and squared with ineffective tools into the rude semblance of a mighty altar. The well-worn path along which I had come told the rest of the story. Here was the temple, having for its roof the great arch of heaven, in which the Indians, whom the gentle Fray Antonio believed to be such good Christians, truly worshipped their true gods; even as here their fathers had worshipped before them in the very dawning of the ancient past.

A tremor of joy went through me as I realized what I had found. Here was positive proof of what I had strongly but not surely hoped for. The Aztec faith truly was still a living faith; and it followed almost certainly that, could I but penetrate the mystery with which it was hedged about so carefully by them still faithful to it, I would find all that I sought—of living customs, of coherent traditions— wherewith to exhibit clearly to the world of the nineteenth century the wonderful social and religious structure that the Spaniards of the sixteenth century had blotted out, but had not destroyed. What my fellow-archæologists had accomplished in Syria, in Egypt, in Greece, was nothing to what I could thus accomplish in Mexico. At the best, Smith, Rawlinson, Schliemann, had done no more than stir the dust above the surface of dead antiquity; but I was about to bring the past freshly and brightly into the very midst of the present, and to make antiquity once more alive!

As I stood there in the dusk of the narrow pathway, while the joy that was in my heart swelled it almost to bursting, there came to my ears the low moaning of one in pain. The faint, uncertain sound seemed to come from the direction of the great stone altar. To discover myself in that place to any of the Indians, I knew would end my archæological ambition very summarily; yet was I moved by a natural desire to aid whoever thus was hurting and suffering. I stood irresolute a moment, and then, as the moaning came to me again, I went out boldly into the open space, and crossed it to where the altar was. As I rounded the great stone I saw a very grievous sight: an old man lying upon the bare rock, a great gash in his forehead from which the blood had flowed down over his face and breast, making him a most ghastly object to look upon; and there was about him a certain limpness that told of many broken bones. He turned his head at the sound of my footsteps, but it was plain that the blood flowing into his eyes had blinded him, and that he could not see me. He made a feeble motion to clear his eyes, but dropped his partly raised arm suddenly and with a moan of pain. I recognized him at a glance. He was the Cacique, the chief, and also, as I had shrewdly guessed, the priest of the village—the very last person whom I would have desired to meet in that place.

"Ah, thou art come to me at last, Benito!" he said, speaking in a low and broken voice. "I have been praying to our gods that they would send thee to me—for my death has come, and it is needful that the one secret still hidden from thee, my successor, should be told. I was on the altar's top, and thence I fell."

I perceived in what the Cacique said that there was hope for me. He could not see me, and he evidently believed that I was the second chief of the village, Benito—an Indian who had talked much with me, and the tones of whose voice I knew well. Doubtless my clumsy attempt to simulate the Indian's speech would have been detected quickly under other circumstances, but the Cacique believed that no other man could have come to him in that place; and his whole body was wrung with torturing pains, and he was in the very article of death. And so it was, my prudence leading me to speak few and simple words, and my good-luck still standing by me, he never guessed whose hands in his last moments ministered to him.

As I raised his head a little and rested it upon my knee, he spoke again, very feebly and brokenly: "On my breast is the bag of akin. In it is the Priest-Captain's token, and the paper that shows the way to where the stronghold of our race remains. Only with me abides this secret, for I am of the ancient house, as thou art also, whence sprung of old our priests and kings. Only when the sign that I have told thee of—but telling thee not its meaning—comes from heaven, is the token to be sent, and with it the call for aid. Once, as thou knowest, that sign came, and the messenger, our own ancestor, departed. But there was anger then against us among the gods, and they suffered not his message to be delivered, and he himself was slain. Yet was the token preserved to us, and yet again the sign from heaven will come. And then—thou knowest—" But here a shiver of pain went through him, and his speech gave place to agonizing moans. When he spoke again his words were but a whisper. "Lay me—in front of—the altar," he said. "Now is the end."

"But the sign? What is it? And where is the stronghold?" I cried eagerly; forgetting in the intense excitement of this strange disclosure my need for reticence, and forgetting even to disguise my voice. But my imprudence cost me nothing. Even as I spoke another shiver went through the Cacique's body; and as there came from his lips, thereafter forever to be silent, a sound, half moan, half gasp, his soul went out from him, and he was at rest.

When a little calmness had returned to me, I took from his breast the bag of skin—stained darkly where his blood had flowed upon it—and then tenderly and reverently lifted his poor mangled body and laid it before the altar. And so I came back along the hidden path, safely and unperceived, to the village: leaving the dead Cacique there in the solemn solitude of that great mountain-top, whereon the dusk of night was gathering, alone in death before the altar of his gods.

CHAPTER III

THE MONK'S MANUSCRIPT

When Pablo and I started, the day following, upon our return to Morelia, the village of Santa María was overcast with mourning. The Cacique was dead, they told us; had fallen among the rocks on the mountain-side, being an old man and feeble, and so was killed. And I was expressly charged with a message to the good Padre, begging him to hasten to Santa María that the dead man might have Christian burial. I confess that I found this request, though I promised faithfully to comply with it, highly amusing; for I knew beyond the possibility of a doubt that if ever a man died a most earnest and devout heathen it was this same Cacique for whom Christian burial was sought; and I felt an assured conviction that when the services of the Church over him were ended—and whatever good was to be had for him from them secured—he would be buried fittingly with all the fulness of his own heathen rites. But this matter, lying in what I already perceived to be the very wide region between the avowed faith and the hidden faith of the Indians, was no concern of mine; yet I longed, as only a thoroughly earnest archæologist could long, to be a witness of the funeral ceremony in which Fray Antonio most conspicuously would not take part. As this was hopelessly impossible—for only by very slow advances, if ever, could I reach again by considerate investigation the point that in a moment I had reached by chance—I came away from Santa María reluctantly, yet greatly elated by the discovery that I had made.

So jealous was I in guarding the strange legacy that the Cacique had bequeathed to me that not until I was safe back in Morelia, in my room at the hotel, with the door locked behind me, did I venture to examine it. The bag, about six inches square, tightly sewed on all four of its sides, was made of snake-skin, and was provided with a loop of snake-skin so that it might be hung from the neck upon the breast like a scapulary. My hands trembled as I cut the delicate stitching of maguey fibre, and then drew forth a mass of several thicknesses of coarse gray-brown paper, also made of the maguey, such as the ancient Aztecs used. Being unfolded, I had before me a sheet nearly two feet square, on which was painted in dull colors a curious winding procession of figures and symbols. My knowledge of such matters being then but scant, I could tell only that this was a record, at once historical and geographical, of a tribal migration; and I saw at a glance that it was unlike either of the famous picture-writings which record the migration of the Aztecs from Culhuacan to the Valley of Mexico, and then about that valley until their final settlement in Tenochtitlan. I was reasonably confident, indeed, that this record differed from all existing codices; and I was filled with what I hope will be looked upon as a pardonable pride at having discovered, within three months of my coming to Mexico, this unique and inestimable treasure.

My natural desire was to carry my precious codex at once to Don Rafael, that I might have the benefit of his superior knowledge in studying it (for he had continued very intelligently the investigation of Aztec picture-writing that was so well begun by the late Señor Ramirez), and also that I might enjoy his sympathetic enjoyment of my discovery. As I raised the bag, that I might replace in it the refolded paper—which I already saw heralded to the world as the Codex Palgravius, and reproduced in fac-simile in *Pre-Columbian Conditions on the Continent of North America*—some glittering object dropped out of it and fell with a jingling sound upon the stone floor. When I examined eagerly this fresh treasure I found that it was a disk of gold, about the size and thickness of a Mexican silver dollar, on which a curious figure was rudely engraved. The engraving obviously represented an Aztec name-device, the like of which, in the ancient picture-writings, distinguish one from another the several generations of a line of kings. This name-device was strange to me; but, as I have said, I had not at that time studied carefully the Aztec picture-writings, and there were many names of kings which I would not then have recognized. But that the gold disk was the token concerning the meaning of which the dying Cacique had given so strange a hint, I felt assured.

Being still further gladdened by this fresh discovery, I carried my treasures at once to the Museo; and Don Rafael's enthusiasm over them was as hearty as I could desire. Being so deeply learned in such matters, he was able in the course of a single afternoon to arrive at much of the meaning of my codex; and his rendering of it showed that it possessed a very extraordinary historical value. In the Codex Boturini, as is well known, are several important lapses that neither that eminent scholar, nor any other archæologist whose conclusions can be considered trustworthy, has been able to supply. All that reasonably can be imagined concerning these breaks is that the historian of the Aztec migration deliberately omitted certain facts from his pictured history. The astonishing discovery that Don Rafael made in regard to my codex was that it unquestionably supplied the facts concealed in one of the longest of these unaccountable blanks. This was not a mere guess on his part, but a demonstrable certainty. On a fac-simile of the Codex Boturini he bade me observe attentively the pictures which preceded and which followed the break in question; and then he showed me that these same pictures were the beginning and the ending of my own codex—obviously put there so that this secret record might be inserted accurately into the public record of the wanderings of the Aztec tribe.

Further, the geographical facts set forth in the Codex Boturini having been very solidly established, it was easy to determine approximately the part of Mexico to which the beginning and the end of my codex referred. But the migration here recorded was a very long one, and all that Don Rafael could say with certainty concerning it was that it told of far journeyings into the west and north. He was much puzzled, moreover, by a picture that occurred about the middle of the codex, and that seemed to be intended to represent a walled city among mountains. To my mind this picture tallied well with what the dying Cacique had told me touching the hidden stronghold of his race. But Don Rafael attached very little importance to the Cacique's words; and on archæological grounds maintained that a walled city was an impossibility in primitive Mexico—for while walls were built in plenty by the primitive Mexicans, and still are to be found in many places, no mention of a walled city is made by the early chroniclers, and of such a city there never has been found the slightest trace.

In regard to the engraved disk of gold, Don Rafael said at once and positively that it represented a name-device which never had been figured in any known Aztec writing; and he was of the opinion—being led thereto by consideration of certain delicate peculiarities of the figure which were too subtle for my uninstructed apprehension to grasp—that the name here symbolized was that of a ruler who was both priest and king. That the piece of gold was found associated with picture-writing unquestionably belonging to the theocratic period lent additional color to this assumption. The sum of our conclusions, therefore, was that we had here the name-device of a priest-king who had ruled the Aztec tribe during some portion of the first migration. And, assuming that he had lived during the period to which my codex referred, and accepting the system of dates tentatively adopted by Señor Ramirez, we even fixed the ninth century of our era as the period in which he had lived and ruled.

During two whole days Don Rafael and I worked together over these matters in the Museo; and it was not until our investigations were ended—so far, at least, as investigations could be said to be ended while yet no definite conclusions were reached—that my thoughts reverted to Fray Antonio, and to the requirement of courtesy that I should report to him the result of my course of study in the Indian tongues. It is but justice to myself to add that, knowing him to be gone to Santa María to attend to the Cacique's burial, I had temporarily dismissed this matter from my mind.

But when I was come to the Church of San Francisco—carrying with me the Codex Palgravius and the engraved disk of gold, in both of which I knew that he would take a keen interest—I had no immediate opportunity of exhibiting to him my treasures.

As I pushed open the sacristy door, when I had knocked upon it and he had called me to enter, he came towards me at once in excitement so eager that his face was all lit up by it; and almost before I could greet him he exclaimed: "You are most happily come, my friend. At this very moment I was about to send for you; for I have found that which will stir your heart even as it has stirred mine. Yet perhaps," and he spoke more gravely, "it will not stir your heart in the same way that mine is stirred by it—for if I can but find the key that will unlock the whole of the mystery that here partly is revealed, I see before me such opportunity to garner the Lord's vintage as comes but seldom to His servants in these later ages of the world."

So strange was Fray Antonio's manner, and so wayward seemed his speech, that I was half inclined to think his religious enthusiasm fairly had landed him in religious madness; which thought must have found utterance in my look of doubtfulness, for he smiled kindly at me, and in a quieter tone went on:

"My wits still are with me, Don Tomas; though I do not wonder at your thinking that I have lost them. Sit down here and listen to the story of my discovery; and when it is ended you will perceive that I very well may be excited by it and still be sane."

Being assured by this calmer speech that Fray Antonio had not taken leave of his senses, I made a weak disclaimer, that he smilingly accepted, of my too clearly expressed doubts in that direction; and so seated myself to listen.

"You know, señor," he began, "that common report has declared that beneath this Church of San Francisco is a secret passage that extends under the city and has its exit in the outlying meadow-lands. I may confide in you frankly that this passage does exist, and that I, in common with all members of my Order who have dwelt here, know precisely where its entrance is and where its outlet. These matters need not be exposed, for they are not essential to my purpose. But you must know that in the midst of this passage I found on the day preceding your return from the mountains a little room of which the door was so well concealed that my finding it was the merest accident. And in the room, with other things which need not here be named, I found a chest in which are certain ancient papers of which I have been long in search. In the archives are frequent references to these papers—they are of much importance to our Order—but as with all my search I never could discover them, I had decided in my mind that in one or another of the troublous periods that our Church has passed through they had been destroyed. It is plain to me now that in one of these periods of danger they were hidden in this safe place.

"Some of these papers, dealing with mere matters of history, you will have pleasure in examining in due time. But that which I shall show you now, and which has so excited me that you not unnaturally thought that I had gone mad over it, has got among the rest, as I verily believe, by simple accident. Among the books and papers in the chest was a parchment case on which was written 'Mission of Santa Marta,' and the date '1531.' Within it were some loose sheets of paper on which were records of Indian baptisms, as is evident by the strange mixing of Christian and of heathen names. Plainly, this was the register of some mission station of our Order in that far-back time. But as I pried into the case more closely, I found, within a double fold of the parchment—yet not as though intentionally hidden, but rather as though there placed for temporary safety—a sealed letter directed to the blessed Fray Juan de Zumárraga, who was of our Order, and who, as you know, was the first bishop of our holy Church in this New Spain. As I drew forth the letter, the seal, that time had loosened, fell away and left it open in my hand. That this letter never until now has been read I am altogether confident, for the prodigy of which it tells would have made so great a stir that ample record of it would have been preserved. Nor is it difficult to account for the way in which it missed coming to the eye for which it was intended. In that early time many and many of our Order, going out to preach God's Word among the barbarians, came happily to that end which is the happiest end attainable in God's service: a blessed martyrdom." Fray Antonio's voice trembled with deep feeling as he spoke, and I remembered that Don Rafael had told me that this good brother, it was believed, himself longed for a death so glorious. "And being thus slain," Fray Antonio in a moment continued, "the mission stations which they had established were left desolate, with what they held—save such few things as might be cared for by the savage murderers—remaining there within them. In later times, as the conquering Spaniards overspread the land, many of these stations were found, with nothing to tell save nameless bones of those who had died there that God's will might be done.

"It is my conjecture, therefore, that this parchment case was found—how many years after the death of him who owned it, who can tell?—in one of the many stations that the savages thus ravaged; that the soldiers, or whoever may have found it, brought it hither, the nearest important abiding-place of our Order; and that, being carelessly examined, it was carelessly thrown aside when found to contain, apparently, only the little record of the work which our dead brother accomplished before God granted him his crown of earthly martyrdom and so made quick his way to heaven. Had the letter ever reached that 'first hand' for which the writer says he waits to send it by, it assuredly would have come to the knowledge of the gold-loving Spanish conquerors, and armies would have gone forth to answer it. But our dead brother, having written it and placed it in this fold of the parchment for safety until the chance to send it southward should come, was cut off from life suddenly; and so, of the prodigious marvel of which knowledge had so strangely come to him, only this mute and hidden record remained."

"But the letter itself?" I asked, with more energy than politeness. "What *is* the story that it contains? What is this mystery? Tell me of it first, and then explain as much as you please afterwards."

Fray Antonio smiled at me kindly. "Ah, you too are becoming

excited," he said. "But, truly, it is not fair that I should thus have kept you waiting. Indeed, I am so full of it all that I forgot that as yet you know nothing. Come out with me into the court-yard, where the light is stronger—for the writing is very faint and pale—and I will read you this letter in which so wonderful a story is set forth."

Together we passed out through a little door in the rear of the sacristy into what had been the inner and smaller cloister court-yard of the old convent—a lovely place in which a fountain set in a quaint stone basin sparkled, and where warm sunshine fell upon the rippling water and upon beds of sweet-smelling flowers. And here it was, standing among the flowers in the sunshine, beside the quaint fountain, that Fray Antonio read to me the letter—that in this strange fashion had come to us from a hand dead for much more than three centuries, and that yet brought to us two a vital message that wholly was to shape our destinies.

CHAPTER IV

MONTEZUMA'S MESSENGER

The letter was without date, but, being addressed to the Bishop Zumárraga, the phrase that occurred in it—"this New Spain, wherein, Very Reverend Father, you have labored in God's service this year and more past"—showed that 1530 was the year in which it was written. As to place, there practically was no clew at all. The writer referred repeatedly to "this mission of Santa Marta, in the Chichimeca country"—but the mission had perished utterly but a little while after it was founded; and at that period the term Chichimeca country was used by the Spaniards in speaking of any part of Mexico where wild Indians were.

Being shorn of a portion of its pious verbiage, and somewhat modernized in style, the ancient Spanish of this letter contained in effect these English words:

"Very Reverend Father,—This present letter will be sent forward to you by the first hand by which it may be hence transmitted; and in your wisdom, with God's grace also guiding you, I doubt not that you will take measures for sending missionaries of our Order to the great company of the heathen whose whereabouts I am to disclose to you. And also, no doubt—keeping the matter secret from the pestilent Oidores of the Audiencia—you will communicate this strange matter through safe channels to our lord the King: that with our missionaries an army may go forth, and that so the great treasure of which I give tidings may be wrested from the heathen to be used for God's glory and the enriching of our lord the King.

"Know, Very Reverend Father, that a month since, I being then abroad from this mission of Santa Marta, preaching God's word in a certain village of the Chichimecas that is five leagues to the northward, was so strengthened by God's grace that many of the heathen professed our holy faith and were baptized. And of these was one who among that tribe was held a captive. Which captive, as I found, was of the nation that dwelt in Tenochtitlan before our great captain, Don Fernando Cortés, reduced that city to submission. But little of earthly life remained to this poor captive when I, unworthily but happily, opened to him the way to life glorious and eternal; for in the fight that happened when he was captured—of which fight he alone of all his companions had survived—he was sorely wounded; and though in time his wounds had healed he remained but a weakly man, and the service to which his captors forced him was hard. So it was that I had but little more than time to put him in the way leading to heaven before his spirit gladly forsook its weary body and went thence from earth.

"That he truly was a convert to our holy faith I am well assured, by the signs of a spirit meet for repentance which he showed in his own person; and still more by his strong longing, most earnestly expressed, that this same glorious faith of freedom should be preached to a certain great company of his people, whereof he most secretly told me, who still remain bound in the bondage of idolatry. And it is what he told me of these, Very Reverend Father, and of the marvellous hidden city wherein they dwell, and of the mighty treasure which there they guard, that I desire now to bring to your private knowledge, before it shall be known of by the Oidores, and through you to our lord the King. Here now is the whole of the mystery that he recited:

"In very ancient times, he said, his people came forth from seven caves which are in the western region of this continent, and wandered long in search of an abiding-place. And in the course of ages it came to pass that a certain wise king ruled over them to whom was given the gift of prophecy. Which king, by name Chaltzantzin, foretold that in the later ages there should come an army of fair and bearded men from the eastward, who would prevail over the people of his race: slaying many, and making of the remainder slaves. Being sorely troubled by thought of what he thus foresaw, he set himself to provide a source of strength whereon his descendants in that later time might draw in the hour of their peril—and so save themselves from cruel death and from yet crueler slavery. To which end, in a certain great valley that lies securely hidden among the mountains of this continent, he caused to be built a walled city; and this city he then peopled with the very bravest and strongest of his race. And he made for those dwelling there a perpetual law that commanded that all such as showed themselves when come to maturity to be weak or malformed in body, or coward of heart, then should be put to death; to the end that their natural increase ever should be of the same stout stuff as themselves, and also that there might be no lack of victims for the sacrifices which are acceptable to their barbarous gods. And thus he provided that in the time of need there should be here a strong army of valiant warriors, ready to come forth to fight against the fair-faced bearded men, and by conquering them to save safe the land.

"And yet more provision did King Chaltzantzin make for the strengthening and the saving of his race in the later ages. Within this walled city of Culhuacan he caused to be builded a great treasure-house, wherein he garnered such store of riches as never was gathered together in one place since the beginning of the world. And his order was that if even the power of the army which should go forth from that city sufficed not to conquer the foreign foemen, then should this vast treasure be used to buy his people's ransom, that they might not perish nor be enslaved.

"Having set all which great matters in order, King Chaltzantzin came forth from the Valley of Aztlan, leaving behind him the noble colony that he had there founded; and so with his people wandered vagrant—even as their gods had commanded that they should go until by a sign from heaven they should be shown where was to be their lasting home. And that the fulfilling of his purpose might be made the more sure, he brought his people forth from that valley by most perilous passes and through strait ways so that they might not return thither; and that they who remained might not follow, he closed the way behind him with mighty bars.

"In the fulness of time this wise king died, and others reigned in his stead; and at last the ages of wandering of the Aztec tribe were ended by the sign coming from heaven whereby they knew that the Valley of Anahuac was to be their abiding home. There built they the city of Tenochtitlan: which city the valiant captain, Don Fernando Cortés, conquered this short time since—and by conquest of it verified precisely the prophecy that King Chaltzantzin uttered in very ancient times.

"But the captive Indian told me, further, that before the coming of the Spaniards there was seen the sign of warning that King Chaltzantzin had promised should tell when the danger that he had so well prepared for should be near; which sign was the going out of the sacred fire that the priests guarded on a certain high hill. Meantime, all knowledge of their brethren hidden in the Valley of Aztlan for their help in time of peril was lost to the Aztec tribe in dim tradition;

for the King had commanded, in order that his people might not fall into weakness through trusting in the strength of others for protection, that no open record of the colony that he had founded should be preserved. Therefore was this matter a secret known only to a few priests whose blood was of the royal line; in whose keeping, also, was the token that King Chaltzantzin had commanded should be sent to the walled city of Culhuacan when its warriors were to be called forth, and a map whereby the way thither was made plain. And so it was that, when the sacred fire ceased burning, the priests were alert for the threatened danger; and when the landing of the Spaniards—'fair-faced and bearded men, coming for the eastward'—was known to them, they warned their king, Montezuma, that the prophecy was fulfilled, and that the time for sending for the army and the treasure had come.

"For the bearer of this message was chosen a priest of the blood royal, with whom went also a younger priest, his son. And with these went a guard, whereof the captive Indian was one, that they might be carried in safety through the region where the wild Indians were. But the valor of the guard was useless, for the wild Indians set upon them in such prodigious numbers—in a place not far from where is this present mission of Santa Marta—that all of the company, save only this single Indian who was wounded and made captive, was overpowered and slain. Yet among the slain, the Indian said, was not found the body of the priest's son; nor was there found on the priest's body the token that he had been the bearer of, nor the map that showed the way. For a time the Indian had hoped that the younger priest had escaped out of the fight alive, and had carried to them who dwelt in the walled city of Culhuacan the message of summons; but as the years went onward and nothing came of it, this hope had died within his heart.

"This, Very Reverend Father, is the strange story told me by this Indian; who spoke with the urgent sincerity of one devout in the Christian faith who knew by sensible perception that his death was near at hand. Eagerly he begged that to these Gentiles, his brethren by blood, might be sent in their secret fastnesses the blessed Word whereby they would be delivered from the chains of their idolatry into the freedom of Christian grace. And, surely, the treasure that they ward very well may be wrested from these heathen that it may be used in part in this land in God's service, and that in part it may go to the just enriching of our lord the King.

"Nor is the matter one that is difficult of accomplishment. For a token which shall give us the right of entry into this walled city of Culhuacan we need only the Word of God and a sufficient force of men well armed with swords and matchlocks. Nor is it any bar to our quest that the map showing the way thither has been lost. The Indian told me that this way is so plainly marked that one who had found it could not lose it again. For at spaces of not more than a league or two apart, upon flat places of the rock convenient for such purpose, was cut the same figure that the token of summons had engraved upon it; and, with this, an arrow pointing towards where the next carving would be found: and so these signs went onward, the heathen priest had told him, even to the very entrance of the Valley of Aztlan. And that this matter might be made sure to me, he led me to a spot but a league to the westward of this mission of Santa Marta and there showed me one of these signs, with the pointing arrow carved also on the rock beside it—of all of which the drawing here made is an indifferent good copy. And by that guiding arrow we went onward to another like carving at a little less than two leagues away to the northward. Therefore, Very Reverend Father, I, of my own knowledge, am a witness to a part, at least, of the truth of what that Indian told. And with all my heart do I add mine own entreaty to his simple pleadings for the salvation of the souls of his brethren; and also do I venture to entreat that among those who go to carry the Word of God to this hidden heathen host I may be one; so that I, though all unworthy of such honor, shall have a part in rendering to God so glorious a service.

"The more urgently do I ask this favor because here, in this mission of Santa Marta, it is but too clear to me that I am laboring in a barren field. Some hundreds of the heathen I have indeed baptized; but among all these who have professed our Christian faith scarce a score show outward and visible signs of a true regeneration. Many, I am sadly sure, still practise in secret their old idolatry—and find little more than mere amusement in the rites of our most holy Church. When they tire of this novelty, which, in the case of folk of such light natures no doubt will be in a little while, they will return openly to their idolatry; and it probably may happen that they then will sacrifice me to their heathen gods. That, in one way or another, they do intend to kill me, and that soon, I feel quite sure. I am but twenty-three years old, Very Reverend Father; and that is an early time in life to end it. No doubt, also, in killing me they will use torture. And I long fervently to live, not only for the pleasure of it, but also that I may do good service to God, and to our Father Saint Francis, by saving many heathen souls. Therefore I beg that when the army marches to the reduction of this hidden city that I may be one of our brethren who will go with it, to hold by tender preaching of God's goodness and mercy such heathen as may remain alive after our soldiers shall have conquered that city with the sword.

"I commend you, Very Reverend Father, to the care of Our Lord in all things, and pray that he may guard your most illustrious and very reverend person, and protect you in all matters of your temporal and spiritual estate. And I am the least worthy of your servants,

Francisco de los Angeles."

"Of a truth," said Fray Antonio, as he ceased reading, "this brother of mine adhered closely to the truth when he subscribed himself the least worthy of the bishop's servants. Were it not here in his own hand, I should refuse to believe that one of our Order at that time in New Spain had any thought of saving his own life when God's work was to be done."

For myself, I must own that my heart was deeply touched by the very humanity of this poor Brother Francisco's cry for help that came up out of the dead depths of the past; and that was the more keen and pitiful because the cruel death at the hands of the barbarous Indians that he so dreaded assuredly had overtaken him. His could not have been a strong nature, and it was the weaker because of his youth; but, after all, it was the nature that God had given him, and there must have been a strain of strength in it, else he never would have braved the dangers which overcame him in the end. And he was "but twenty-three years old"!

Yet when I sought to lead Fray Antonio's mind to such consideration of the matter he replied, sternly: "This weak brother failed in his duty. To him God gave an opportunity to die gloriously for the Faith; but, instead of accepting that noble reward joyfully, his strongest wish was that he might find a way by which he might escape alive. Had all professors of the Christian creed so conducted themselves, that creed long since would have perished from off the earth. *Semen est sanguis Christianorum* is well said of Tertullian the Carthaginian, and, later, of the blessed Saint Jerome."

As Fray Antonio thus spoke he so drew up his slight figure, and in his sweet voice was a ring of such commanding sternness, that he was for the moment transformed. Here was a man wholly different from the gentle scholar whom I had already learned to love. In the glimpse that I thus had of his underlying character I saw vivified again the spirit of the early Christian Church; and I understood, as I never had understood before, of what stuff they were made who heard pronounced upon them the sentence, "To the lions!" and joyfully accepted their cruel fate, defiant of what man might do to them because of the perfection of their faith in the merciful forgiveness and upholding steadfastness of their Christian God.

But in a moment a look of sadness and regret came into Fray Antonio's face, and he added, sorrowfully: "God forgive me for thus judging my brother, who long since was judged! Who can say that when the hour of trial came he did not meet his death as bravely as any martyr of them all? And who can say," he went on, but speaking softly, as one communing with his own soul, "how I myself—But God gives strength." And then he ceased to speak aloud, but his lips moved silently as though in prayer. As I close my eyes I see him again as clearly as I saw him then—standing beside the old stone fountain, amid the flowers, in the gladness of the bright sunshine; in his eyes a strange, far-away look, as though the future for a moment had been opened to him; and on his strong, fine face a sternly resolute expression, which yet was softened by the traits which were so strong within him of holiness and gentleness and love. I cannot know what Fray Antonio prayed for, there in the old convent garden; but I can guess, and I am well persuaded that his prayer was heard. Truly, I think that it was something more than chance that led us thus at first to talk, not of the wonder that was in Brother Francisco's letter, but of Brother Francisco himself and of his end.

And then the subject-matter in chief of the letter claimed our attention. In itself this was sufficiently marvellous; but what increased the marvel of it was the conviction, strong within us both, that if the hidden city of Culhuacan ever had existed at all it existed still. Our belief was so entirely logical that, assuming the truth of the story told by the Indian captive, it admitted nowhere of a doubt. That the city had been hidden for a long period, through at least several hundreds of years, from the Aztecs themselves, and that no knowledge of it had been conveyed to them by wild Indians who had come by chance upon the valley wherein it was, was evidence enough of the security of its concealment. There was nothing surprising, consequently, in the fact that the Spaniards had not discovered it when they first overran Mexico, nor that it had remained unknown to the Mexicans of modern times. As is well known, there are to this day prodigious areas in Mexico which remain utterly unexplored. In the region west of Tampico; in the north-western States of Sinaloa, Durango, and Sonora; or in the far southern States of Oajaca and Chiapas, a valley as great as that in which the City of Mexico now stands might lie utterly hidden and unknown. And if, as the Indian's narrative implied, this particular valley had been selected deliberately because it was so hidden and so inaccessible, and if the described precautions had been taken to isolate its inhabitants, it very well might have continued to be lost in its deep concealment through an almost infinite range of years. That it never had been found since the Spaniards came into Mexico we were absolutely certain, for the outcry over so great a wonder would have echoed throughout the whole of the civilized world. Finally, in the name of the city, Culhuacan, we had a substantial fact which connected the extraordinary story that had come to us so strangely with matters within our own knowledge. For this name not only is given in the Aztec traditions as that of the sacred spot in which their god Huitzilopochtli spoke to them, but survives until this present day in the name of the village that lies at the foot of the sacred mountain, in the Valley of Mexico, called by the Aztecs the Hill of Huitzachtla, and by the Spaniards the Hill of the Star—on which, at the end of each cycle of fifty-two years, the sacred fire was renewed. Surely it was no accident that had caused the name Culhuacan to be given to this village on this sacred spot; rather must it have been so named by the elect few to whom the secret was known as a perpetual reminder to them of the reserve of men and treasure upon which they could draw should danger threaten their country and their gods.

"No doubt," said Fray Antonio, "what is here told of a secret record, known only to the priests, supplies one of the lapses in the pictured history of the Aztec migration; but as we know not which break in the history is thus filled in, we have no clew whatever as to the whereabouts of this hidden place. Nor have we any clew as to the whereabouts of the mission of Santa Marta, whence we might go onward, guided by the carvings upon the rocks, until we found at last the place we sought. The mission of Santa Marta, where my brother Francisco long ago ministered, might have been anywhere in all Mexico; and being so small a mission, and enduring for so short a period, it is not likely that any record of it anywhere has been preserved. Had we but the map and the token of which my brother writes, our way would be clear; without these guides it well may be a toilsome way and long. Yet do I know," Fray Antonio continued, earnestly, "that I shall find this hidden city. In my soul is a strong and glad conviction that God has called me to the most glorious work of carrying to the heathen dwelling there the message of His saving love. He has worked one miracle already to call me to this duty; in His own good time and way I doubt not that He will work another miracle by which I may be set in the way of its accomplishment."

As Fray Antonio spoke of the map of the Aztec migration, a hope came into my heart that, as I considered it, seemed surely to be a certainty. In the excitement of listening to this strange letter—concerning which not the least strange matter was, that between the writing and the reading of it had passed three hundred and fifty years—I had forgotten my own discoveries, and that my purpose was to show him the pictured paper and the curious piece of gold. But as he spoke of the migration this matter was called to my mind suddenly; and then in an instant the conviction thrilled through me that the clew which would lead us to the hidden city was in my possession.

"God already has worked that other miracle," I cried, joyfully. "Here is the token, and here is the map that shows the way!" and, so speaking, I opened the snake-skin bag that I had taken from the breast of the dead Cacique and drew forth its precious contents.

For myself, I needed no additional proof that here was all that was needful to guide us to the hidden city. Yet was I glad that in so grave a matter we should have added to absolute conviction the weight of absolute proof. And this we had most clearly; for Fray Antonio, cooler than I, compared the drawing in the letter with the engraving upon the piece of gold, and found the two to be essentially identical, save that the engraving lacked the sign of the arrow pointing the way.

"And now," I cried, enthusiastically, "for such discoveries in archæology as the world has never known!"

"And now," said Fray Antonio, speaking slowly and reverently, "for such glorious work in God's service as has been granted but rarely to man to do!"

CHAPTER V

THE ENGINEER AND THE LOST-FREIGHT MAN

That the weight of a strange destiny was pressing upon us, neither Fray Antonio nor I for a moment doubted. It was something more than chance, we believed, that had brought us together, and that thereafter, by such extraordinary means, had put into our hands, in places far asunder, yet at almost precisely the same moment, these two ancient papers; either of which, alone, would have been meaningless; but the two of which, together, pointed clearly the way to a discovery so wonderful that the like of it was not to be found in all the history of the world.

At the moment that I comprehended how great an adventure was before me, and what honorable fame I was like to get out of it, I determined that I would keep the whole matter secret from my fellow-archæologists until I could tell them, not what I intended doing, but what I actually had done—for I had no desire to divide with any one the honors that fairly would be mine when I published to the world the result of my investigation of this hidden community that had survived, uncontaminated, from prehistoric times. Having this strong desire within me, it was with great pleasure that I acceded to Fray Antonio's request that our project of discovery should not be published abroad. His motive for secrecy, as I presently perceived, was bred of the one single strain of human weakness that ever I found in him. Even as I was determined that no other archæologist should share with me the honor of discovering this primitive community, so was Fray Antonio determined that to him alone should belong the glory of carrying into that region of dense heathen darkness the radiant splendor of the Christian faith. If this were sin on his part, it certainly was a sin that he shared with many saints long since in Paradise. Even the blessed Saint Francis himself, when, at the Council of Mats, he portioned out among his followers the heathen world that they might preach everywhere Christianity, reserved for himself Syria and Egypt; in the hope that in one or the other of those countries he might crown his labors by suffering a glorious martyrdom. And perhaps in this matter Fray Antonio was not unmindful of the example set him by the great founder of the Order to which he belonged.

But while we were thus firmly decided to keep to ourselves the honors that so great an archæological discovery and so great a Christian conquest must bring to us severally, we perceived that it would not be the part of prudence to essay our adventure without any companions at all. Some portion of the country through which we were to pass we knew to be frequented by very dangerous tribes of Indians, against the assaults of which two lonely men—neither of whom had any knowledge whatever of the art of war—could make but a poor stand. And even should we escape the wild Indians, we knew that we might get into many evil straits in which our lives might be ended, yet through which a larger company might pass in safety. And for my own part, I must confess that I had a strong desire to have with me some of my own countrymen. For the gallantry of the Mexicans, which gallantry has been proved a thousand times, I have the highest respect; yet is it a natural feeling among Anglo-Saxons that when it comes to facing dangers in which death looms largely, and especially when it comes to a few men against a company of savages, and standing back to back and fighting to the very last, Anglo-Saxon hearts are found to be the stanchest, and Anglo-Saxon backs to be the stoutest which can be thus ranged together. But in our own case I did not at all see whence such an Anglo-Saxon contingent was to be obtained.

We had been talking over this matter of a fighting force one after-noon in Fray Antonio's sacristy—where our many colloquies were held, for we moved with a thoughtful deliberation in setting agoing our adventure—and we had come almost to the determination of organizing a little force of Otomí Indians, and calling upon two brave young gentlemen of Fray Antonio's acquaintance to join us as lieu-tenants. Although I was willing to adopt this plan, since no other was open to us, I was far from fancying it; both for the reason which I have already named, and also for the reason—and this Fray Antonio admitted was not without foundation in probability—that our young allies would be more than likely, by their indiscreet disclosures, to make our purpose fully known. Therefore, it was in no very pleasant frame of mind, our conference being ended, that I returned to my hotel.

As I entered the hotel court-yard I heard the sound of Pablo's mouth-organ, and with this much laughter and some talk in English;

and as I fairly caught sight of the merrymakers, I heard said, in most execrable Spanish, "Here's a *medio* for another tune, my boy; and if you'll make the donkey dance again to it, I'll give you a *real*."

That I might see what was going forward without interrupting it, I stepped behind one of the stone pillars that upheld the gallery; and for all that my mind was in no mood for laughter just then, I could not but fall to laughing at what I saw.

Over on the far side of the court-yard, with Pablo and El Sabio, were two men whose type was so unmistakable that I should have known them for Americans had I met them in the moon. One was a tall, wiry fellow, with a vast reach of arm, and a depth of chest and width of shoulders which allowed what powerful engines those long arms of his were when he set them in motion. His face was nearly covered by a heavy black beard, and his projecting forehead and his resolute black eyes under it gave him a look of great energy and force. The other was short and thick-set, with a big round head stockily upheld on a thick neck, and with a good-humored face, which, being clean-shaven, was chiefly notable for the breadth and the square-ness of the jaws. He had merry blue eyes, and his crown—he was holding his battered Derby hat in his hand—was as bare as a billiard ball. Below timber-line, as he himself expressed it, he had a brush of close-cut sandy-red hair. I had encountered both of these men when I first came to Morelia, and during two or three weeks I had seen a good deal of them, for we had met daily at our meals; and the more that I had seen of them the better was I disposed to like them. The tall man was Rayburn, a civil engineer in charge of construction on the advanced line of the new railway; the other was Young, the lost-freight agent of the railroad company—whose duty, for which his keen quickness peculiarly well fitted him, was that of looking up freight which had gone astray in transit. Both of those men had lived long in rough and dangerous regions, and both—as I then instinc-tively believed, and as I came later to know fully—were as true and as stanch and as brave as ever men could be.

What they were laughing at, there in the court-yard, was an extraordinary performance in which the performers were Pablo and El Sabio. With a grin all over the parts of his face not engaged in the operation of his mouth-organ, Pablo was rendering on that instru-ment a highly Mexicanized version of one of the airs from *Pinafore* that he had just acquired from hearing Young whistle it. To this music, with a most pained yet determined expression, the Wise One was lifting his feet and swaying his body and nodding his head in a sort of accompaniment, his movements being directed by the waving of Pablo's disengaged hand. The long ears of this unfortunate little donkey wagged in remonstrance against the unreasonable motions demanded of his unlucky legs, and every now and then he would twitch viciously his fuzzy scrap of a tail; but his master was inexorable, and it was not until Pablo's own desire to laugh became so strong that he no longer could play the mouth-organ that El Sabio was given rest. As he ended his dancing I must say that there was on El Sabio's face as fine an expression of contempt as the face of a donkey ever wore.

"Hello, Professor!" Young called out, as he caught sight of me, "have you given up antiquities an' gone into th' circus business? This outfit that you've got here will make your fortune when you get it back into th' States. If you don't want to run it yourself, I'll run it for you on th' shares; an' I guess Rayburn'll be glad t' go along as clown. He'd make a good clown, Rayburn would. You see, we're both of us out of work, an' both lookin' for a job."

"What do you mean by being out of work?" I asked, when I had shaken hands with them. "What's become of the railroad?"

"Oh, th' railroad's got into one of its periodical bust-ups," Young answered. "A row among the bondholders, an' construction stopped, an' working expenses reduced, an' pretty much all hands bounced, from th' president down. I guess Rayburn an' I can stand th' racket, though, if th' company can. I've been wantin' t' get out of this damned Greaser country for a good while, an' I guess now I've got my chance. I must say, though, I wish it had come a little less sudden, for I haven't anything in particular in sight over in God's country, an' Rayburn hasn't either. So if you want to start your circus we're ready for you right away. Where did you get that boy-an'-donkey outfit from, anyway? They're just daisies, both of 'em an' no mistake!"

"I don't know that you can count on me for a clown, Professor," Rayburn said, "but I might go along as door-keeper, or something of that sort. But I don't believe that Young and I will need to go into the circus business. We are out of work, that's a fact; but the company has done the square thing by us—paid us up in full to the end of next month and fitted us out with passes to St. Louis. We're all right. Young is heading straight for home, but I rather think that I'll take a turn around the country and see what the civilized parts of it look like. Ever since I came down here, nearly, I've been at work in the wilds. I want to see some of the old temples and things too. You can put me up to that, Professor. Where's a good ruin to begin on?"

From the moment that I laid eyes on these two men, as I came into the court-yard, my mind was made up that I would do my best to induce them to join with Fray Antonio and me in our search for the hidden city; and I had listened very gladly to what they told me, for it showed me that I should not have to ask them to abandon profitable work in order to join in our doubtful enterprise. So we talked lightly about the circus and other indifferent matters for a while; and then we had a lively supper together at La Soledad (which always seemed to me a very original name for a restaurant), and then I brought them to my room to smoke their cigars.

It was while they were in the comfortable frame of mind that is begotten of a good meal and subsequent good tobacco—over there in Morelia we smoked the Tepic cigars, which are excellent—that I opened to them the great project that I had in hand. I told them frankly the whole story: of my strange adventure in the Indian village, of the paper and the gold token which the Cacique unwittingly had given me, of the letter that Fray Antonio had found, and of how our joint discoveries set us clearly in the way of finding an Aztec community that certainly had existed unchanged, save for such changes as had been developed within itself, since a time long anterior to the Spanish conquest of Mexico. I dwelt with enthusiasm, and I think forcibly, upon the inestimable gain to the science of archæology that would result from the investigations that we intended to make; and I touched also upon the scientific value that would attach to a careful and accurate description of the effect produced upon this primitive community by Fray Antonio's preaching; for this would be, as I pointed out, the first occasion in the history of the world when a record would be made, from the stand-point of the unprejudiced ethnologist, of the reception accorded by a heathen people to the doctrine of Christianity. In a word, I presented the case most glowingly—so glowingly, in fact, that my own heart was quite fired by it—and ended by urging them earnestly to join us in a work that promised so greatly to increase the sum of human knowledge touching the most interesting subjects that can be presented to the consideration of the human mind. And I am pained to state that I discovered, when I finished my appeal, that

Young was sound asleep!

Rayburn did not go to sleep, and he did take a certain amount of interest in what I said, but I was discouraged by his very obvious failure to respond to my enthusiasm.

"You see, Professor," he said, "the fact of the matter is that I can't spare the time. I might take a month or two, but you seem to think that a year is the least time in which any substantial results can he accomplished. I can't give a year, or anything like a year, to what, so far as I am concerned, will be sheer idleness. I've got a mother and sister at home on Cape Cod who depend on me for a living, and I must get to work again. You see, there is glory enough in all this, and glory that I should like to have a share in; but glory is a luxury that I can't afford. I've got to go to work at something that has money in it."

The sound of Rayburn's voice had the effect on Young of waking him up. He listened, in a sleepily approving way, to Rayburn's practical comment, and then, giving a prodigious yawn, added, on his own account: "Yes, that's about the size of it. We're neither of us here for our health, Professor; what we're after is spot cash. If there was any money in your scheme I'd take a hand in it quick enough; but as there isn't—Well, not this evening, Professor; some other evening."

"No money in it!" I answered. "Why, haven't I told you that there is stored in this hidden city the greatest treasure that ever was brought into one place since the world began?"

"No, I'll be damned if you have!" Young replied, with great energy and promptness. "Not a word, unless it was while I was asleep. What's he said about a treasure, Rayburn? I'm awake now, an' I'll keep awake if there's anything like that to be talked about."

"You certainly haven't said anything about a treasure so far, Professor," Rayburn said. "I'd like to hear about it myself. If there is a treasure-hunting expedition mixed up with this scientific expedition of yours, that puts a new face on the whole matter. I can't afford the luxury of scientific investigation pure and simple, but if there is money in it too, that is quite another thing. So tell us about your prospect, Professor, and if the surface indications are good you can count on me to go in."

I confess that I was a trifle disappointed upon finding how eagerly these young men sought information in regard to a matter that I considered so unimportant that I had forgotten even to mention it. But I reflected that, after all, the motive by which they were induced to join in our adventure was immaterial, while our need for the strength that their joining in it would give us was so pressing that upon gaining them for allies very likely depended our eventual success. Being moved by which considerations, I dilated upon the magnitude of the hidden treasure with such vehemence that presently their eyes were flashing, and the blood had so mounted into their brains that their very foreheads were ruddy and their breath came short. And I must confess that my own pulses beat quicker and harder as I talked on. Of this treasure I had not before thought at all, being so thoroughly taken up with the scientific side of the discovery that I hoped to accomplish; but now I was moved profoundly by thoughts of what I could do for the advancement of science had I practically limitless wealth at my command. And especially was I thrilled by the thought of the magnificent form in which my own magnificent discoveries could be given to the world. Compared with my *Pre-Columbian Conditions on the Continent of North America*, Lord Kingsborough's great work, both in form and in substance, would sink into hopeless insignificance. And in all that I said of the vastness of the hidden treasure I felt certain that I was keeping well within the bounds of truth, for I had the positive assurance that in the Aztec treasure-house in that hidden valley the ransom of a nation was stored.

"Will you go with us?" I asked, when I had brought my glowing description to an end.

"Well, I should smile, Professor," was Young's characteristic answer.

"You can count me in now, and no mistake!" said Rayburn, and added, "By Jove, Palgrave, I mean to take a part of my share and buy the whole of Cape Cod!"

And so the make-up of our party was decided upon. Fray Antonio joined it for the love of God; I joined it for the love of science; and Young and Rayburn joined it for the love of gold. In regard to the boy Pablo, he could not strictly be said to have joined it at all. He simply went along.

CHAPTER VI

THE KING'S SYMBOL

Fray Antonio was well pleased when I told him of the stout contingent that I had secured; and when he had seen Rayburn and Young, and had talked with them—though his talk with Young did not amount to much, for Young's Spanish was abominable—he was as thoroughly satisfied as I was that for our purposes we could not possibly have found two better men.

In the course of this conference we made short work of our preparations for departure. Rayburn's experience in fitting out engineering parties had given him precisely the knowledge required for putting our own little party promptly and effectively in the field; and in this matter, and in all practical matters connected with the expedition, he took the lead. He and Young already possessed the regulation frontier outfit of arms—a Winchester rifle and a big revolver—which they increased by another big revolver apiece; and I armed myself similarly with a pair of revolvers and a Winchester: concerning the use that I should make of which, in case need for using them arose, I had very grave doubts indeed. Fray Antonio declined to carry any arms at all; and after he had accidentally discharged one of my pistols, which he had picked up to examine, so that the ball went singing by my ear and actually cut through the brim of Young's hat, there was a general disposition to admit that the less this godly man had to do with carnal weapons the safer would it be for all the rest of us. Young's hat was a battered Derby, and about as unsuitable a hat for wear in Mexico as possibly could be found; but for some unknown reason he was very much attached to that hat, and he was so wroth over having a hole shot through it in that unprovoked sort of way that he manifested a decided coolness towards Fray Antonio for several days.

In the matter of armament, the happiest member of our party was Pablo. He was a handy boy, and when he had demonstrated his ability to manage a revolver by doing some very creditable shooting with mine (at mark that I had stuck up in the corral, in order that I might gain ease in the use of this unknown weapon), I delighted him inexpressibly by buying him a pistol for his very own. I think that

Pablo, upon becoming the possessor of that revolver, at once grew two inches taller. The way that he strutted as he wore it, and his eager thrusting forward of his left hip, so that this gallant piece of warlike furniture might be the most conspicuous part of him, were a joy to witness. For a time his mouth-organ was entirely neglected; and coming quietly into the corral one day, I found him engaged in exhibiting the revolver to El Sabio; who regarded it with a slightly bored expression that I do not think Pablo took in good part.

Rayburn decided that our expedition could be made more effectively with a small force than with a large one. He argued that unless we took into the Indian country a really powerful body of men, we would be safer with a very few: for a few of us would feel keenly the necessity of keeping constantly on guard; could be more easily managed and held together in running away; and in case a fight was forced upon us we would fight more steadily because each of us would know surely that he could rely upon the support of all the rest. Which reasoning we perceived to be so sound that we promptly accepted it.

Rayburn added to our company, therefore, only three men: two Otomí Indians of whom Fray Antonio gave a good account, and Dennis Kearney, who had served as axeman on the recently disbanded engineering corps. He was a merry soul, this Dennis, with a stock of Irish melodies in his head that would have made the fortune of an old-time minstrel. He and Pablo took to each other at once—though, since neither of them spoke a word of the other's language, music was their only channel of communication—and Pablo presently presented us with a rendering on his mouth-organ, from a strictly Mexican stand-point, of "Rory O'More" that quite took our breaths away. While Pablo played, Dennis would stand by with his head cocked on one side, and with an air of attention as closely critical as that which El Sabio himself exhibited; and when Pablo went wrong, as he invariably did in his attempted *bravura* passages, Dennis would stop him with a wave of his hand, and an "Aisy now, me darlint! That's good enough Mexican, but it ain't good Irish at all, at all," and then would show him what good Irish was by singing "Rory O'More" in a fashion which made the old stone arches ring with a volume of music that could have given odds to an entire brass band. Poor Dennis! Only the other day I heard an organ-grinder grinding forth "Rory O'More," and the memory of the last time I heard Dennis sing that song, and of what heroic stuff that merry-hearted rough fellow then showed himself to be made, came suddenly over me, and there was a choking in my throat, and my eyes were full of tears.

Well, it was a good thing—or a bad thing, as you please to put it—that we could not see far into the future that morning when we packed our mules in the corral of the hotel, and set out upon the march that was to lead us through such perilous passages before we reached its end.

That I might fill to the brim the cup of Pablo's happiness—for my conscience pricked me a little that I suffered him to go with us—I had bought him the rain-coat of palm leaves for which his heart so long had pined. What with this and his revolver, and the delight of going upon a journey (for he had very fully developed that love of travel which is so strong in his race), his wits seemed to be completely addled with joy. He insisted upon putting on his absurd rain-coat at once; and he did so many foolish things that even El Sabio looked at him reproachfully—this was when he tried to place on that small donkey's back some of the heavy pack-stuff destined for the back of one of the big mules—and we got along much better with his room, as he presently enabled us to do, than we did with his company. When the time for starting came, we had quite a hunt for him; and we might not have found him at all had we not been guided by the sound of music to the sequestered spot to which he had retired in order to give vent to his pent-up feelings by playing on his mouth-organ "Pop goes the weasel"—an air that Young had been whistling that morning and that had mightily taken Pablo's fancy.

We made rather an imposing cavalcade as we filed forth from the great gate of the hotel, and took our way along the Calle Nacional, the principal street of the city, towards the Garita del Poniente. Fray Antonio and I rode first; then came Rayburn and Young, followed by Dennis Kearney; then the two pack-mules, beside which walked the two Otomí Indians; and closing the procession came Pablo, wearing his rain-coat, with his revolver strapped outside of it, and riding El Sabio with a dignity that would have done honor to the Viceroy himself. Pablo certainly was in the nature of an anti-climax; but I would not have told him so for the world. Fray Antonio wore the habit of his Order, this privilege having been specially granted to him by the Governor of the State as a safeguard for all his expeditions among the Indians. It was understood, indeed, that he now was going forth on one of his missionary visits among the mountain tribes, and simply rode with us, so far as our ways should lie together, for greater security. I had announced that I was going among the Indians again in order to increase my knowledge of their manners and customs; and Rayburn—to whom the rest of the party was supposed to belong— had stated that he was taking the field in order to make a new reconnaissance along the line of the projected railway. It was in order to maintain these several fictions that we went out by the western gate, and that we continued for two days our march westward before turning to our true course.

Of our progress during the ensuing fortnight it is not necessary that I should speak, for beyond the ordinary incidents of travel no adventures befell us. During this period we went forward steadily and rapidly; and at the end of it we had covered more than three hundred miles, and had come close to where—supposing our rendering of the Aztec map to be correct, and that we had rightly collated it with the dead monk's letter—the mission of Santa Marta had stood three centuries and a half before. There was no possibility that any trace of this mission would be found; but every rock that we came to was most eagerly scrutinized, for on any one of them might we find the King's symbol engraved.

For two or three days we had been travelling through a region very wild and desolate. Far away along the western horizon rose a range of mountains whose bare peaks cut a jagged line along the sky. The country between us and these far-away mountains was made up of many parallel ranges of rocky hills; which ranges were separated by broad, shallow valleys, where cactus and sage-brush covered the dry ground thickly; and the only trees that broke this dreary monotony were pita-palms, the most dismal thing in all created nature to which the name of a tree ever has been given by man. There was no trail, and travelling through this tangle of briers was very difficult. All of Rayburn's skill, which long practice had developed to a high degree, was required to enable us to pick a way through so thorny a wilderness. At times the Indians with their *machetes*, and Dennis with his axe, had to cut a path for us; and despite all our care, our own hands were cut and torn, and the legs of our poor beasts were red with blood.

The deadly dryness of this arid waste added to our discomfort. A strong dry wind blew steadily from the north, building up out of fine dust which was over all the surface of the baked ground little whirlwinds—*remolinos*, as the Mexicans call them—which went dancing down the valleys as though they were ghostly things; and occasionally, when one of these struck us, we were covered with a prickly dust that fairly burned our skins. What water we got was to be had only by digging in the *arroyos* which traversed the centre of each valley longitudinally; and although this water always was muddy, and had a strongly alkaline taste, it is the only thing that I remember with pleasure in all that weary laud. Of animal life there was nothing to be seen, save a-plenty of rattlesnakes; and a few great buzzards which wheeled above us from time to time as though with the intention of keeping track of us until we should fall down and die of thirst and weariness, and they should be able to feast upon us at their ease.

At the end of the third day of this dreary travelling we had come close to the great western range of mountains, and our camp that night was made in the mouth of a little valley that opened from among the foot-hills. The night before we had made a dry camp, and for the whole of the twenty-four hours we had had but a pint of water apiece. Pablo, I am sure, had given half of his own scant allowance to El Sabio. The other animals—it was all that we could do for them—had only their dusty mouths and nostrils wiped out with a wet sponge. They were pitiable objects, with their bleeding legs, their haggard eyes, their out-hanging tongues, and their quivering flanks. As Fray Antonio unsaddled his horse I saw that there were tears in his eyes; but the rest of us, I fear, were too thoughtful of our own misery to feel much sorrow for the misery of our beasts.

I suppose that a man must suffer the lack of it, as we then did, in order to know how precious a thing water is. And to give some notion of its preciousness to those who not only are free at any time to drink their fill of it, but even can fill bath-tubs with it, and feel the joy of it on their bare bodies whenever they are so minded, I will say that when a little digging gave us that night as much water as we wanted, our joy was far greater than it would have been had we there found the hidden city of which we were in search.

Our well was sunk in the broad sandy bottom of the *arroyo*, in the midst of a narrow and delectably grassy valley between two foot-hills. And the abundance and the sweetness of the water, as well as the presence of grass, showed us that but a little way up this valley there must be an open stream. We drank, and our beasts drank, until all of our skins were nigh to bursting; and the abundance of water was so great that we even could wash the dust at last from our parched faces and necks and arms; and much like raw beef our skins looked when our washing was ended, and the stinging of them was as though we had been whipped with nettles. It was our intention now to leave the plains and to march along the edge of the foot-hills parallel with the main range, otherwise we should not have ventured thus to wash ourselves. In a region where alkali dust is in the air, washing is to be shunned; for each time that the skin is cleaned the new deposit of dust takes a deeper biting hold.

It was rather that we might escape the misery of further travel on the arid plains than because we had any strong hopes of thus finding the way of which we were in search that we had decided to change our line of march. Young had begun openly to express his contempt for the Aztec map, and in the hearts of all of us had sprung up some doubts as to its trustworthiness as a guide. After all, it was not in the least a map in the true meaning of the word; and that it should show us rightly our way depended not only upon our having interpreted correctly its curious symbolism, but also upon the correctness of the interpretation that Mexican archæologists had given to the map of the first Aztec migration—of which map, as we believed, our map was a reserved and secret part. If either interpretation were wrong, then we might be hundreds of miles distant from the region in which the way marked by gravings of the King's symbol should be sought.

Four or five hours of daylight still remained to us after we had dug our well, and with the delicious water flowing into it had satisfied our thirst; but we had no intention of going farther that day. We had no need to hobble the animals, for they could be trusted to stay near the water-hole while they feasted on the grass, and we needed food and rest quite as much as they did. Young and Dennis together got us up a famous meal, and when it was ended we lighted our pipes and held a sort of council of war. That we might talk the more freely, in both English and Spanish, we drew away a little from where the two Otomí Indians and Pablo were stretched out upon the grass together; and we bade Dennis take a look around the shoulder of the first hill, so that we might know something of what our way would be like when we started in the morning; for we were not as yet ready that the minor members of the expedition should know the purpose that we had in mind. We had decided that when, by the finding of the course indicated by the gravings of the King's symbol, our quest fairly had a beginning, being no longer a matter of mere hope and conjecture, we then would give Dennis and Pablo and the two Indians some notion of what we intended doing; with the option of deciding for themselves whether or not they would have a part in it. And the thought never once occurred to our minds that circumstances might arise of such a nature that neither they nor we would have any choice in the matter at all.

As we consulted together we had spread out before us a map of Mexico, and with this the map that the Cacique had given me, and a copy of the map showing the great Aztec march. Yet the more that we councilled the less could we come to any reasonable conclusion as to what was best for us to do. As nearly as we could tell from the strange guides that we needs must be led by, we had beaten thoroughly the region where once the mission of Santa Marta was; and not a trace of the gravings on the rocks had we found. To go over this region again, searching still more minutely, was too great an undertaking even to be thought of; and yet the only alternative to this painful course seemed to be that we should abandon our search altogether; in short, we were completely at sea.

"What _I_ think," said Young, "is that that old dead monk, an' that old dead Cacique, have set up a job on us. They're both of 'em lyin' like fiddlers; that's what's th' matter with _them_. There ain't any hidden city, or hidden treasure, or hidden damn anything; it's all a fraud from beginnin' t' end. I vote t' pull up stakes an' go home."

A cool refreshing wind was beginning to sweep down to us from the mountains; but it was blowing only in puffs as yet, for the night would not be upon us for several hours. Borne faintly and fitfully upon this uncertain wind came to us the strains of "Rory O'More"; with which melody, as we inferred, Dennis was beguiling his solitude while he explored the route that we were to take the next day. Pablo, sitting comfortably on the grass, his back propped against the back of El Sabio, also caught the sound; and straightway began to play an accompaniment on his mouth-organ to Dennis's distant singing. The strains gradually grew louder, showing that Dennis was returning; but when they stopped suddenly we thought that he had only tired of the sound of his own voice, or, perhaps, did not think anything about the matter at all.

But when a sound of hurried, irregular steps came down the wind to us, we all were on our feet in a moment and had our arms ready, for it was evident that Dennis was running from something; and the danger was likely to be a serious one, for running was not at all in Dennis's line. We wondered why he did not call out; but the explanation of his silence was plain enough, ten seconds later, as he came around the shoulder of the hill, staggered in among us, and fell on the grass at our feet—with the blood streaming from his mouth and nostrils, and with an arrow clear through his breast.

"Indians!" he gasped, with an effort that brought a torrent of blood spurting from his mouth; and he added, faintly, "But I've bate 'em, th' divvils, in their hopes of a soorprise!"

These triumphant words were the last that Dennis Kearney uttered on earth. As he spoke, a fresh outburst of blood came from his nostrils and mouth, a quiver went over him—and then he was dead. I do not believe that many men would have done what Dennis did: run a good quarter of a mile with an arrow through his lungs, and then die exulting because he had succeeded in warning the camp.

Rayburn had the situation instantly in hand. "Get the packs and saddles on quick!" he cried. "The Indians'll come around that hill and try to scoop us here in the open. They won't close in; they'll keep off, and just lie around for a week till we're played out, and then they'll step in and finish us; they'll do that, likely enough, anyway. But our one chance is to get to a place up the valley here, where they can tackle us only from in front. There's water up there, so we'll be all right, and we may be able to shoot enough of them to make the rest give it up, or they'll close in, and we'll have the comfort of getting the whole thing ended without any useless fooling over it."

All the while that he spoke he was working away, and so were we all, at saddling and packing; and, luckily, the animals, although the water and the food and the rest had put new strength into them, still were too tired to give us the trouble that animals give at such times when they are fresh. In a surprisingly short time we were ready to start; and yet not a sign had we had, save the warning that Dennis had brought us, that there was an Indian within a hundred miles of us. Indeed, but for his dead body on the ground beside our camp-fire, we might have imagined that our scare was only a bad dream. That it was a very bad reality was shown just as the last pack went on, when one of our Otomí Indians gave a howl as an arrow went through his leg, and I felt a sharp little nip on my forehead where an arrow just grazed it, and there was that queer, faint whirring sound in the air that only a flight of a good many arrows together will produce.

Rayburn took the body of poor Dennis before him on his own horse; he'd be damned if the Indians should get Dennis yet, he said; and away we went up the sandy bed of the *arroyo*, driving the mules before us, and the Otomí Indians pelting along on a dead-run. The Indian who had been hit coolly broke the arrow off short, and then pulled it out through the wound.

Suddenly we saw Young, who was riding a little ahead of the rest of us, half pull up his horse and look earnestly at a great shoulder of rock that jutted out from the mountain-side. "There's your King's symbol, and be damned to it!" he shouted; and added, "What's the good of a King's symbol when we're all goin' to lose our hair?"

He was under full head-way again in a moment. As we shot past the rock we all turned to look; and there, sure enough, was the long-sought-for sign.

CHAPTER VII

THE FIGHT IN THE CAÑON

As we fled along the valley, and in a few moments heard the sound of the Indians pursuing us, my mind was chiefly occupied with considerations of the quality which we denominate fear. I perceived that this purely occasional passion had a very direct bearing upon my own especial science of archæology. I reflected that had I been engaged in building a city at the moment when that irritating flight of arrows fell among us—the sting of one of which I still felt smarting upon my forehead—I should assuredly have ceased at once the building of that city, and should have moved rapidly away. And thus an excellently well-built city, that would have delighted archæologists of the future, would have been lost to the world. Putting the matter yet more closely: here I had just found the sign for which I and my companions had been toilsomely searching for a considerable time; the sign which unquestionably would lead us to the most interesting archæological discovery that ever had been made. And yet, instead of stopping to study this sign earnestly, that I might understand all the meaning of it, I was hastening away from it with all possible speed; and for no better reason than that certain barbarians, whose knowledge of archæology was not even rudimentary, were pursuing me that they might take my life—an imperfectly expressed concept, by-the-way; for life can be taken only in the limited sense of depriving another of it; it cannot be taken in the full sense of deprivation and acquisition combined. These several reflections so stirred my bile against the Indians in pursuit of us that I began to have a curiously blood-thirsty longing for our actual battling with them to begin; for I was possessed by a most unscientific desire to balance our account by killing several of them. And I confess that this desire was increased as I looked at the dead body of poor Dennis, lying limply across the fore-shoulders of Rayburn's horse.

It was with real satisfaction, therefore, that I obeyed Rayburn's order to halt, that we might make ready for the fight to begin. The valley up which we had been riding had narrowed by this time into a strait way shut in between high and nearly perpendicular walls; and the place that Rayburn had chosen for us to make our stand in was the mouth of a cañon setting off from the valley nearly at right angles. The walls of this cañon came almost together above, far overhanging their bases, so that assault from overhead was impossible; some fragments of fallen rock made a natural breastwork for us to fight behind; and a little stream of pure, sweet water flowed at our feet. Had this place been made for us expressly it could not better have suited our purposes; and finding it so opportunely put fresh heart into us. There was not, of course, a shadow of resemblance between the two, but, somehow, I fancied that the place where we stood resembled my old class-room at Ann Arbor; and I actually found myself repeating the opening sentence of the address that I delivered when I was formally inducted into the Chair of Topical Linguistics. I mention this fact not because it is of the slightest importance in this present narrative, but because I think that it well illustrates the tendency towards illogical association that is so curious a characteristic of the human mind.

I was not able to observe this phenomenon attentively, for Rayburn hustled us all about so sharply that I had no available time just then for abstract thought. The mules and the horses and El Sabio were driven into the cañon, and we were ranged behind the fragments of rock almost in a moment. Each man had his Winchester and revolvers in readiness, and a couple of cases of cartridges had been broken out from the packs and put where we all had easy access to them. While this work was going forward we could hear the Indians coming hotly up the valley, and we were barely ready for them when the foremost of their party came in sight.

"Wait a little," said Rayburn, quietly. "They don't know which turn we've taken, and they'll probably get into a bunch to do some talking, and then we can whack away right into the flock."

While we were thus making ready I could see that Fray Antonio was in great distress of mind. He was a very brave man, and I know that his strong desire was to fight with the rest of us. And yet, just as the Indians showed themselves, he deliberately turned his back upon them and walked away into the cañon's depths. His very lips were white, and there were beads of sweat upon his brow, and I saw that his fingers twitched convulsively. I know what he wanted to do, and I saw what he did. If ever a man showed the high bravery of moral courage, Fray Antonio showed it then. Even Young, in whom I did not look for appreciation of bravery of that sort, said afterwards that it was the pluckiest thing he ever saw.

As Rayburn had expected, the Indians halted—but keeping more under cover than he had counted upon—and held some sort of a council. But it did not seem, from what we could see of their gestures, to relate to the way that we might have taken so much as to the cañon in which we actually were concealed. They pointed towards the mouth of the cañon repeatedly, and it struck me that in their motions there was a curious indication of dread or awe. One old man was especially vehement in gestures of this unaccountable nature; and when at last the younger men in the council seemed to revolt against his orders, this man, and all the older men with him, retired down the valley whence they had come.

The young men, left to themselves, hesitated for a moment, and then with a cry—as though for their own encouragement—came charging towards us in a body. As we got a full view of them we perceived with much satisfaction that their only arms were bows and arrows and long spears, and that there were not more than twenty men in the lot. And then Rayburn gave the order to fire. I confess that my hand so trembled as I pulled the trigger of my rifle that I was not at all surprised to find that the man whom I had fired at—a very tall, powerful young fellow, who seemed to be in command— was not hit; but a man just behind him dropped, and I had a queer feeling in my throat, and certain odd sensations in my stomach, as I realized that I had shot him. Indeed, I was so engrossed with medita- tions upon the curious ease with which a man's life is let out of him, that I quite forgot for some seconds to continue firing. The others, luckily, conducted themselves in a more practical manner; and the little whirlwind of balls which sped from the Winchesters made it wonderful, not that so many of the Indians fell dead or wounded, as that any of them remained alive and unhurt. But eight of them did survive their charge in the face of the storm of bullets that we pelted at them; and these—headed by the tall fellow, who seemed bullet- proof—came rushing at us over our breastwork of rocks, shouting and flourishing their long spears.

I cannot say very accurately what happened during the next five minutes or so, for one of the Indians came directly at me, and before I could at all stop him—for I found that shooting at him with my revolver did him no harm at all; and this struck me as odd, for I had repeatedly hit the mark while practising in the corral—he had prodded his spear through the fleshy part of my left arm. It hurt severely. He had aimed his thrust, doubtless, at my heart, and he certainly would have penetrated that vital organ had I not at that moment slipped, and so disarranged his aim. He pulled the spear out of my arm, which action also gave me great pain, and his manner indicated that he was about to thrust it into some other part of me; which he surely could have done, for I was wholly at a loss as to what measures should be taken to assure my own safety. Indeed, I was very well convinced that my life was as good as ended, and a curious flash of thought went through me that I cannot coherently remember, but that was in the nature of a query as to whether or not in a future state the many scientific truths which as yet are but imperfectly understood will be wholly revealed to us.

However, the opportunity that I confidently expected would be given to me in a moment to obtain an answer to this interesting question did not then occur. Just as the Indian was lunging at me—I can see his ugly face now, as I close my eyes and let my thoughts turn backward to that critical moment—there was a flash of some bright object before me, and then the Indian's entire head seemed to shut up suddenly, something like an opera-glass, and he went down to the ground like a stone. As I turned, I saw that my deliverance had come from Pablo, and even in that very exciting moment I observed with astonishment that the weapon with which he had slain the Indian was a great jagged sword—if the *maccuahuitl* can be called a sword—such as the Aztecs used in ancient times. I could not then conveniently stop to question him whence he had obtained that very interesting weapon, for there was another Indian already close upon me; and I am pleased to say—for I do not wish the belief to go abroad that scientific men are worse than useless in practical emergencies— that, without assistance from Pablo or from anybody else, I managed to pick up my rifle, and with the heavy iron barrel of that weapon, used clubwise, I mashed the head of that Indian into a perfect pulp. I know positively that I mashed it into a pulp, for I tried afterwards to measure it, and found that for craniological purposes it was utterly valueless.

Even had I required Pablo's aid in this encounter he could not possibly have given it to me, for he was himself just then very hotly engaged. Indeed, but for assistance that come to him from an unexpected quarter his life assuredly would have been lost. He was in the act of hauling back to strike at the fellow facing him, and he did not at all know that he was in imminent danger of a thrust in the back from a wounded wretch who, having struggled upon his knees, was using what little life was left in him to deliver yet another blow. Just at this critical instant it was that Fray Antonio dashed into the thick of the fighting, and covered Pablo's body with his own against this assault in the rear; so that, as the Indian struck, the knife only cut through the monk's habit and slightly scratched his arm, instead of making a hole between Pablo's shoulder-blades that would have let the life out of him. Young, who was close beside Pablo, saw what was going on, and checked it before further harm was done by turning quickly and shooting off the top of the wounded Indian's head; and then Fray Antonio retired out of the fighting in which, without himself striking a blow, he had taken so gallant a part.

So far as I was concerned, the fight was at an end when I had so cleverly mashed the head of my second assailant. No more Indians came at me, and as I looked around I perceived that this was for the excellent reason that there were no more to come. Two were just advancing on Young; who had them covered with his revolver, and dropped them, one after the other, in less time than is required to tell about it. The only other survivor among the enemy—at least the only one able to keep his feet—was the tall young chief, and he and Rayburn were just finishing the last round of what probably was as fine a fight as ever was fought. They were well matched in size and in weight; and if the Indian was any stronger than Rayburn, I can only say that he must have been a most wonderfully strong man. They were fighting on even terms; for the Indian was armed only with a short club, that he held in his left hand—and this left-handed method made him all the more awkward to deal with—while Rayburn, having emptied his revolver, was using as a club its heavy barrel.

As I caught sight of them, the Indian was in the act of springing forward and delivering a tremendous blow; but Rayburn most skilfully parried this blow by throwing out his rifle, still retained in his left hand, in such a manner and with such force that the Indian's arm—at the same time striking and being struck with the iron barrel—was broken just above the wrist. He gave a yell of pain, as he well might; but he was a plucky fellow, and instead of dropping his club he only shifted it to his right hand. He never had a chance to strike again with it; for in that same instant Rayburn swung his revolver at arm's-length through the air and brought it down on his head with a sound so muffled and so hollow that I can liken it only to the staving-in of the head of a full cask. For a moment, while Rayburn drew back to strike again, the Indian's body swayed heavily; and then all his muscles relaxed, and he fell heavily and limply to the ground—while his brains spurted out from the ghastly trench made by that mighty blow from back to front across the entire top of his skull.

CHAPTER VIII

AFTER THE FIGHT

Rayburn stood panting for a moment over the Indian's body; and then, having satisfied himself by a look around among our fallen enemies that every one of them was either dead or dying, he stooped down beside the stream to drink from it, and then to bathe an ugly gash in his forehead made by a spear thrust that luckily had glanced aside.

Indeed, we all had wounds or bruises by which we were likely to remember our fight for a good many days to come. In addition to the cut on his forehead, Rayburn had an arm badly bruised by a crack from a club; Young had a cut in the calf of his leg that must have been made by one of the Indians after he had fallen wounded; Fray Antonio had the slight cut in his arm that he received in rescuing Pablo; a blow from a club on my shoulder had completely disabled my left arm, and my head was beginning to ache from the wound in my forehead where the arrow had nipped me; and Pablo, by a square knock-down blow on the head that tumbled him among the rocks, had a bad gash in his cheek and was bruised all over. And yet the very first thing that boy did when the fight was ended—being still dazed, no doubt, by the blow on his head—was to play a bit of "Rory O'More" on his mouth-organ in order to make sure that his beloved "instrumentito" had not been injured by his fall. The sound of this air gave my heart a wrench, as I thought of poor Dennis; whose gallant race with death assuredly had saved all of us from dying without a chance to strike a blow. And both of our Otomí Indians were dead too.

But while we had suffered thus severely we had the satisfaction of knowing that we had inflicted a most signal punishment upon our enemies. Of the whole company that had attacked us—eighteen in number, as we found by counting their bodies—only two remained alive when the fight ended; and these two speedily relieved us of all responsibility concerning them by dying of their wounds. As Young tersely expressed it, we had "given the whole outfit a through bill of lading to Kingdom Come!"

Notwithstanding the pain that I was in, the first thought that came to me after we had achieved peace (by the effective yet some-what radical process of killing all of our enemies) was concerning the strange weapon with which Pablo had been fighting; and by his prompt use of which in my defence my life had been saved. He had laid it upon a rock—while testing the integrity of his mouth-organ—and as I now carefully examined it I found that my glimpse of it as Pablo had mashed the Indian's head had not deceived me. It truly was a maccuahuitl, the primitive Aztec sword, but very unlike any description of that weapon that I had ever seen. The maccuahuitl, as described by the Spaniards at the time of the conquest and as shown by the Aztec pictures of it preserved in various museums, was a wooden blade from three and a half to four feet long and from four to five inches wide. Along its two edges, like great saw teeth, frag-ments of obsidian, about three inches long and two inches wide, were inserted; and as these were keenly sharp the weapon was a most fero-cious one. The sword that I held in my hand was identical in its essen-tial features with this primitive design; but it was shorter, narrower, and thinner. What was still more extraordinary about it was that, while it seemed to be made of brass, it had the bright glitter of gold and the temper and the elasticity of steel. Being tested by bending, it instantly sprung straight again; and notwithstanding the vigorous use that Pablo had been making of it on the bones of several Indians, the thin edges of the projecting teeth were only nicked a little—as the edge of a steel sword would have been nicked under like circum-stances—and not one of these teeth was bent out of place, as assur-edly would have been the case had the metal been ordinary brass.

Fray Antonio, by this time, had returned to us again—looking rather shamefaced because of the part that he had taken in the fight—and I eagerly showed him this strange weapon that had been so strangely found; for Pablo's account of it was simply that, just as his revolver was emptied upon the Indians charging towards us, when there was no time to reload, his eyes were caught by the glitter of the sword as it stuck in a cleft in a rock; whereupon he most gladly seized it—and instantly used it to good purpose upon the Indian was so close to ending me with his spear, and subsequently contrived with it to send two more Indians to their account.

Fray Antonio's knowledge of the matter having a wider prac-tical range than mine, for he knew well the contents of the several Mexican museums in which specimens of the primitive weapons are preserved, I thought it possible that he might be able to match this curious maccuahuitl with an account of another like it which he somewhere had seen. That there was no record in the books of this weapon made of metal I knew very well. But Fray Antonio's surprise over it was greater than my own; and he certainly found more in it to please him than I did; for this metal maccuahuitl, supposing it to belong to ancient times, settled in his favor a controversy that for some time past we had been amicably but earnestly carrying on. I had adopted the ingenious theory of my friend Bandelier that the serrated edge of the Aztec sword was accidental; resulting from the breaking away in use of portions of what at first was a continuous edge of obsidian. Fray Antonio, on the other hand, had held firmly to the ordinarily accepted opinion that the sword was such as I have described above (I must confess regretfully) the primitive weapon to have been.

My contention therefore was that the sword that Pablo had found was not an antique; and I fortified my position, as I considered impregnably, by the fact that while Aztecs, before the Spanish conquest, did make some slight use of copper and gold, they assuredly had no knowledge whatever of either brass or steel. And my natural irritation very well may be imagined, by any one familiar with controversies of this nature, when I add that Fray Antonio endeavored to cut the ground from under me by asserting that, inasmuch as the weapon obviously was not made of brass or steel, my argument was based upon false premises and consequently led to illogical conclusions. I am afraid that I showed a little temper on this occasion; for Fray Antonio manifested a persistence in his defence of what I regarded as his wholly untenable position that amounted to what I held to be downright pig-headedness. And so, for a considerable length of time, we stood there, among the bodies of the dead Indians, and first one of us and then the other handled the sword, and expressed with increasing warmth our views respecting it and each other; and we might have stood there much longer had not Young—with the best of intentions, no doubt, but in a way the certainly was not agreeable—taken upon himself to bring our controversy for the time being to an end.

"I don't exactly know what you and the Padre are jawing about at such a rate, Professor," he struck in; "but as well as I can catch on, it's about things which happened three or four hundred years ago. I don't want to interrupt you, of course; but I do want the Padre—he knows something about surgery, as I saw the other day when he took that cactus thorn out of Pablo—to do something to plug up this hole in my leg. It's bleeding a good deal, and it hurts like the very devil. And I guess Rayburn'd be glad to have that slit in his forehead tied up too."

To do Fray Antonio justice, he took this interruption in better part than I did; for I was deeply interested in the argument in which we were engaged, and wished to continue it. But when I explained what Young wanted, he turned to him at once, and very tenderly as well as very skilfully dressed his wound; and then bandaged the gash in Rayburn's forehead, and the cut in Pablo's cheek. Pablo decidedly objected to this bandaging, for it put a peremptory stop for a while to his playing on his mouth-organ. For me no surgery was required. Fray Antonio carefully felt my shoulder while he moved my arm—thereby hurting me most horribly—and as the result of his investigations he assured me that the bones were neither broken nor out of place.

Rayburn also examined the maccuahuitl with much interest. "Of course it is not brass," he said, "and of course it cannot possibly be phosphor-bronze. But, if such a thing were a metallurgical possibility, I should say that it was gold—treated in some manner that gives it as great a hardness as bronze receives when treated with phosphorus, but with some chemical change wrought in its constitution that gives it also the tempered quality of steel. Nothing but gold, you see," he added, "could lie around out-of-doors this way and not get tarnished by oxidization."

"What's the reason that it's not some queer thing belonging to the folks we're looking for?" Young asked; and his question expressed a thought that already had found a lodging in my own mind. For such good-luck as this would be I was quite willing to concede that Fray Antonio was right in his unpleasantly positive views in regard to the shape of the Aztec swords. And what Young said also put me sharply in mind of the graving on the rock of the King's symbol, that we had found only in the same moment to lose it again. To this matter I now adverted; and I said some very unpleasant things about the Indians who had prevented us from following the trail, that we had sought for so laboriously, when we did find it at last—and who still, for we doubted not that the main body was in wait for us lower down the valley, prevented us from returning to the spot where we had seen the sign and thence systematically continuing our search.

"If I was you, Professor," said Young as I ceased speaking, "I wouldn't be so everlastin'ly down on these poor devils of Indians for what they've done. They killed Dennis, an' that's a pretty bad business; an' they got away with our two *mozos*, too; an' they've pretty well battered th' rest of us. But I take it that we've about evened things up by killin' eighteen of 'em—or six of their crowd dead for each one dead in ours. I guess we can call that part of th' business about square. But what I'm gettin' at is, if it hadn't been for the Indians we'd never have come up this valley; an' so we'd never have struck th' King's symbol trail at all."

"But what good did it do us to find it, when we could not follow it?" I asked. "We cannot go back to examine the sign without risking our lives; and unless we do examine it we cannot know where the next one is, and so the trail is lost."

"I've just been waitin'," said Young, "t' see if I was th' only man in this party that God-a-mighty'd given a pair of eyes to. I guess I am. Suppose you just get up, Professor, an' turn around, an' take a look at that place where there's a brown mark on th' side of th' rock; an' suppose th' rest of you look there too. If that isn't th' King's symbol, just as plain as th' noses in all your faces, I'll eat every dead Indian in this cañon."

And Young spoke the truth. Just above the cleft whence Pablo had taken the sword, graven so deeply in the rock that after all the weathering of centuries it still remained distinct and clear, was identically the same figure that Fray Francisco in the far past time had represented in his letter, and that was repeated also on the far more ancient piece of gold. Above it was cut an arrow that pointed directly up the cañon.

It was a good thing that something came to cheer us just then; for what with the death of Dennis and of our two poor Indians, and our own hurts, and the melancholy feeling that must oppress men always—save those of cruel and hardened natures—when a fight is ended in which they have spilled freely human blood, we all were oppressed sensibly by a consuming sadness.

But here was cheer indeed. Not only had we surely found the trail at last, but we found it leading in precisely the direction that at that moment we desired to go. For us to return down the valley to the open country, we knew was full of most signal danger; for the Indians who so unaccountably had declined to take part in attacking us assuredly were lying in wait for us by the way. Our only chance to escape them was to strike into the mountains; and the sign that we now had gave promise that we should find some sort of a path along which we might go. Therefore it was with good heart that we set about getting as far into the depths of the cañon as possible before night should be wholly upon us; trusting, in regard to possible pursuit, somewhat to the superstition of the Indians which so unaccountably yet so obviously had been aroused, and also to the wholesome dread that they must have of us upon finding that every one of their companions had been slain. The bodies of our poor Otomís we placed in a deep fissure in the rock, and there heaped stones upon them, while Fray Antonio said over them the briefer office; but the body of Dennis we carried with us, that we might give him a more tender and reverent burial in gratitude for his brave struggle to save our lives when he knew that his own life was lost. As for the eighteen dead Indians—who had invited the death that so promptly had come to them—we did not bother ourselves about them at all. We left them to the coyotes.

CHAPTER IX

THE CAVE OF THE DEAD

Very dismal was our procession of faintly see figures moving cautiously through that wild solitude. At its head went Rayburn, leading his horse, on which was Dennis's dead body; all of us, being bruised and cut and bleeding, walked slowly and painfully; and behind us, ghastly forms torn by bullets and crushed by blows, lay the slain Indians in all manner of unnatural attitudes, made yet more hideous and fantastical by the gathering gloom of night. Indeed, night now was so close upon us that had not the cañon in which we were run east and west, we would have been for some time past in darkness. As it was, though shut off from the west by the great range of mountains, a faint light came down into its depths from the still bright eastern sky, where lingered ruddy reflections of the sunset: and so we could see to pick our way, along the edge of the little stream, among the rough masses of rock and trunks of trees which had fallen from above.

Our march ended sooner than we had counted on. Before we had accomplished more than half a mile of this rough travelling, there loomed before us a wall of rock which shut in the end of the cañon, and which rose as high and as sheer as did the cañon's sides. Our hearts sank within us, for we perceived that we were in a cul-de-sac; whence escape was possible only along the way by which we had come—and so to return, with the Indians still in wait for us, was to walk straight into the jaws of death. And, further, if our course in this direction was cut off, it was evident that the King's symbol graved upon the rock at the entrance of the cañon was a useless and misleading sign.

In the hope that we might find a sharp turn, not to be perceived until we were close upon it, we pressed on through the dusk until we came to the very end of the cañon, and the dark wall of rock that barred our way rose directly above our heads. And then we found, not a turn in the cañon, but a narrow opening (through which came forth the little stream) into the body of the mountain itself. Yet we hesitated about entering this black gap—for who could tell what depths, unseen in that dense darkness, we might not plunge into headlong?

Much dry pine wood, branches and whole trees, lay about us in the cañon; and of this apt material Rayburn presently constructed a great torch. Lighting this in the open cañon was not to be thought of, for while we felt tolerably certain that the main body of our enemies had not followed us, we could not be wholly certain that they were not close upon our heels and ready to open upon us with a volley of arrows and spears. Rayburn therefore struck a wax-match—with which excellent article of Mexican manufacture we were supplied plentifully—and with this to light his way, entered the narrow pass; and in his wake the rest of us followed. Almost in a moment the walls on each side of us spread out beyond the reach of the narrow circle of light, and we perceived that we were come into a cave. But before we could at all discern our surroundings the match was blown out by a sudden suck of wind setting in from the entrance, and we were in thick darkness. The air around us was so sweet and so fresh that we knew that the cave must be large, and with more than one opening—as, indeed, the suck of wind inward through the passage by which we entered clearly showed. While Rayburn struck another match, wherewith to light the torch, we all stood still in our places; and certain tremors went through our breasts because of the eeriness of our surroundings.

When the great torch blazed up, and threw everywhere save towards the high roof a flood of light, a real and rational fear took possession of us. The cave was nearly circular, and at its back, directly facing the entrance, was a roughly hewn mass of stone on which rested a huge stone figure—identical with the figures in the Mexican National Museum to which Le Plongeon, the discoverer of one of them, at Chichen-Itza, has given the name of Chac-Mool. But what filled us with dread was not this impassive stone image. Our alarm came from a much more natural cause, as we beheld, squatted on their haunches in long semicircular rows, facing the great stone idol, more than a hundred Indians. Truly, considering that our rifles were outside the cave and that we had with us only our revolvers, our momentary thrill of terror was highly natural.

Yet it was only momentary. The Indians, undisturbed by our presence and by the sudden blaze of light, remained unmoved in silent worship of their god; and Rayburn, the first of us to recover equanimity, set all our fears to flight as he exclaimed: "These are not the fighting kind. Every man Jack of 'em is as dead as Julius Cæsar. We've struck an Indian bone-yard."

Here, then, was the reason why a part of the force that had attacked us had drawn off when we made our stand at the mouth of the cañon that led to this home of the dead. Yet when, by the light of the torch, we examined our silent fellow-tenants of the cave, it did not seem that they had been placed there in recent times. Indeed, the more that Fray Antonio and I looked closely at their wrappings and noted the way in which their mummied forms had been ranged before this idol—that certainly belonged to a primitive time—the more were we inclined to believe that this weird sepulchre belonged to the very far back past. But for the moment it mattered not to us whence these dead forms came: the essential matter was that while we remained in the cave with them we were in absolute safety.

"Well," said Young, when we had reached this comforting conclusion, "since it's a sure thing that we're all right here, I move that we make ourselves comfortable. Let's bring in th' stock, an' get th' packs off; an' then we'll build a fire an' eat another supper. Fightin' Indians is hungry work, an' I feel as if I hadn't had anything to eat for a week"—which suggestions were so reasonable that we at once proceeded to act upon them.

It was hard work for us, wounded and sore and tired as we were, to unfasten the pack-cords; and still harder work to collect the wood for our fire. But we managed to accomplish it all at last; and most comforting and refreshing was our supper amid those extraordinary surroundings. There was even cheerfulness about our meal—and yet over in the shadows at the back of the cave, touched now and then by a brighter flash of firelight, lay before the heathen altar of old the body of our poor Dennis; and close beside us were the long rows of dead Indians. I sometimes have thought that it was strange that we then had any heart to eat at all, surrounded by so desolate a company. But there is that about killing one's fellow-creatures, and being in imminent peril of being killed one's self, I have found, that blunts for a while the souls of those who survive and makes them care-less of death's awful mystery. As the fire crackled and blazed, giving out a plentiful warmth that in that chill place was most grateful to our aching bodies, our spirits seemed to brighten with its bright-ness; and when the rich smell of strong coffee mingled with the smell of stewing meats told that Young's cooking was nearly ended, we sniffed hungrily and eagerly; and when we actually fell to upon our meal I remember that we even laughed over it.

Yet it is but just to Fray Antonio to say that his fine spirit did not fall to the level of grossness that ours were brought to by what, as it seems to me, was an instinctive gladness on the part of our fleshly bodies that, for a while longer, they would not return to the dust whereof they were made. Through our meal he sat gravely silent, yet with so sweet and so tender an expression upon his gentle face that in his silence there was no suggestion of reproof. And when our meal was ended, and we were for stretching out upon our blankets before the fire and smoking our pipes comfortably, he reminded us, with no touch of harshness in his voice, that a last duty was claimed of us by our dead companion.

And, truly, the funeral ceremonies over Dennis in that strange place of burial made the most curious ending of a man that ever I saw. In the fine dry sand wherewith the cave was bedded, directly in front of the altar on which was the heathen idol, we dug his grave— toilsomely and with pain, for all of our bodies were hurt and sore. While we labored, two great torches flared upon the altar, propped against the idol; and long, flickering rays of light shot out to us across the mummied bodies of the dead Indians—striking across their gleaming teeth, so that they seemed to smile at us—from the huge blaze of the fire.

From our stores Fray Antonio took out a little salt, and from the clear spring that bubbled up within the cave a cup of water, which elements he blessed and mingled as the rites of his Church prescribed; and with the water thus consecrated he sprinkled the body lying before the heathen altar, while his strong, sweet voice chanted the *De Profundis* so that all the cave rang with the rich melody of the holy strain, and our own breasts were thrilled by it. Gently we bore the body of poor Dennis from its resting-place before the altar to its last resting-place in the grave that we had dug there, while Fray Antonio said the *Miserere*; and as with our pack-ropes we lowered the body into the earth, the priest sang the *Benedictus*, with its promise of a better life to come; and then a prayer ended all, and we filled in the grave.

"I'm Congregational, myself," Young said, when our work was finished; "at least I was brought up that way; an' I'm down on th' Scarlet Woman from first t' last. But I go in for lettin' folks believe what they've got a mind to; an' when it cornea t' buryin' 'em it's only square t' give 'em th' sort of send-off that they'd really like. For a Catholic, I guess Dennis was a pretty good one; an' I must say I think it would 'a' done him good to see th' way we've given him a first-class funeral, just in th' shape he'd 'a' fixed things up for himself. But I guess what we've been at would have everlastin'ly shook up these dead fellows here, if they could have come t' life for about five minutes while it was goin' on!"

There was an element of grim humor in this suggestion of Young's that tickled my fancy; and it was, indeed, allowing for the quaintness of his phrasing of it, but an expression of my own thoughts. But my reflection was upon the curious incongruity of it all, and upon the way in which religious faiths supplant each other; even as the different races of men who formulate them and believe in them supplant each other upon the face of the earth. Together in this same cave were now the dead of two faiths and two races. Who could tell what dead of other faiths and races yet unborn would lie here also before the end of time should come?

When all was ended we were glad enough to lie down to give our battered bodies rest in sleep. We felt sure that no attack would be made upon us; yet we rolled some fragments of rock into the narrow entrance to the cave, arranging them in such a way that they would fall with a crash should any attempt be made to move them from outside. And, this precaution having been taken, we lay down upon our blankets thankfully, and never troubled ourselves to keep any watch at all.

It was brilliantly light when we awoke, for the rays of the just-risen sun were striking strongly into the cave through its entrance-way; and much light came also through a crevice higher up, and through a great hole in the vastly high roof. Viewed in this clearer light, there was a horrible ghastliness about the mummies ranged in their orderly rows, and presided over by the coarsely carved, coarsely conceived stone figure that in life they had worshipped as their god. On this image the sunshine fell full, and we perceived that its position evidently had been chosen carefully, so that the very first ray of light from the rising sun would strike upon it. No doubt, in ancient times, this cave had been a temple as well as a place of sepulchre.

We were well rested by our long and sound sleep; but the pain which was everywhere in our bodies, from our many bruises, and from our wounds, and from the aching stiffness of our muscles, made life for a time almost intolerable. Moreover, the languorous reaction following the undue exaltation that came of our battling and escape was upon us; so that our pain of body was accompanied by a most sombre and melancholy cast of mind. Yet, again, did the more balanced and delicate temperament of Fray Antonio shine out by contrast with our coarser make; for while he also suffered pains of the body, his mind was filled with a serene cheerfulness that found expression in kindly, comforting words, by which our flagging spirits were strengthened and upheld. There was in Fray Antonio's nature, surely, a fund of gentle lovingness the like of which I never knew in any other man.

And, in truth, our plight was such that we stood in much need of comforting. Not only were we sick with our many hurts, but we were also prisoners. By the full light of day we examined carefully the cave, and found no outlet to it; and we examined carefully, also, the walls of the cañon throughout its full length, and made sure that there was no path leading upward whereby a man could go. And escape down the valley was cut off, for the Indians—who knew, no doubt, the manner of place we were caught in—were on guard and watching for us; which fact came sharply to our knowledge with a half-dozen arrows that dropped among us as we went out a little way beyond the mouth of the cañon to see if the way was open to us. Had we been whole, we might have made a dash and fought our way through; but even this poor plan was not possible when our bodies were stiff and sore. Our one comforting thought was that, as we had an abundance of provisions and an ample supply of water, we could hold out for so long a time that the Indians at last would get tired of waiting for us. If they ventured to attack us in the cave, we knew that we could defend ourselves against any number of them successfully. If they simply abandoned the siege, then we would be free without fighting at all. But it was dismal work waiting in that dismal place for one or the other of these two ends to come.

And the fact that the King's symbol had proved a false guide also was a source of deep concern to us. By the full strength of daylight we again examined the graving at the entrance to the cañon, and there was no mistaking the way in which the arrow pointed. And, what was even more perplexing and disheartening, we found the graving repeated at the entrance to the cave, and the arrow pointing directly towards the statue of Chac-Mool. It was impossible that this cave, with mummies only for inhabitants, could be the walled city wherein the reserve force of men and treasure had been hid; and yet here, obviously, was the end of the trail. Of this we convinced ourselves by searching the cave exhaustively for another outlet—even sounding the walls in the hope that we might find a passage that had been artificially concealed. As Rayburn tersely put it, we were no better than so many rats in a trap with terriers waiting for us outside.

CHAPTER X

THE SWINGING STATUE

Four more days went by very wearily. Our wounds were healing—for we all were in good condition as the result of our vigorous life in the open air—but they still kept us in constant pain, and so tended to increase our melancholy. Out in the valley, beyond the mouth of the cañon, the Indians maintained their watchful guard. Rayburn tried the experiment of holding a hat and coat out on a pole, standing himself under cover of the rock, and in an instant a pair of arrows went through the dummy; and as one of these came from the right and the other from the left, it was evident that in both directions the valley was picketed.

We were safe enough for the time being, of course. Even should the Indians overcome their superstitious dread and enter the cañon—which was not probable, for they had not even ventured to remove their dead—they could not possibly make a successful attack upon us in the cave. Behind the breastwork that we had built in the narrow entrance, and armed with our repeating rifles and revolvers, we were absolutely secure.

"It's not a bad thing that we're safe," said Young, "an' that we've got plenty of grub an' water, an' even lots of firewood; if we've got t' be shut up here we might as well be comfortable. But what I want is a through ticket for home. This treasure business has gone back on us th' worst kind. That old Fray Francisco had his eye shut up by th' tall talk of th' fellow who pretended to be converted; and th' Cacique just promiscuously lied. That's about the size of it. An' for bein' fools enough to swallow their stuff, here we are, as Rayburn says, like rats in a cage."

There was so much probability in what Young said that I did not attempt to argue with him; yet was I convinced that in what Fray Francisco had written, and still more in what the dying Cacique had said to me, there was a substantial element of truth.

Finding that nobody replied to him, for all of us were sore at heart and so disposed to silence, Young turned to the statue of Chac-Mool and proceeded to abuse it vigorously, on the ground that it was an idolatrous product of the Aztec race that was at the root of all our troubles. For, as he truly said, had there been no Aztecs to begin with, our departure on a wild-goose chase after an Aztec treasure-house would have been an impossibility. His attention having been thus fixed upon the idol, his habit of investigation got the better of his ill-will towards it, and he mounted the altar to examine it more closely—continuing the while to address it in language that was eminently unparliamentary.

"A pretty-looking sort a specimen *you* are!" he said, in a tone of vast contempt. "But you're about what I'd expect folks like that friend of th' Professor's, th' Cacique, t' worship. It takes a low sort of a heathen, even in his blindness, t' bow down to a stone like you—with your twisted head, an' your stubby legs, an' your little fryin'-pan over your stomach. Why, where I come from they wouldn't have you even for a stone settee in a park. No, you're not fit even t' sit on—unless, maybe, it's on th' flat top of your crooked head;" and by way of testing this possibility, Young seated himself on the head of Chac-Mool.

And then a very extraordinary thing happened. The idol, and the great slab of stone on which it rested and of which it was a part, slowly moved; the head sinking, and the other end of the slab, on which the legs were carved, rising in the air! Young sprang up with a cry as he felt the stone sinking beneath him; and the figure, relieved of his weight, settled back into its former position with a slight jar. In a moment that the slab was in the air there had come from under it a gleam of light.

In the excitement wrought by this strange accident our hurts were forgotten; and we eagerly clambered upon the altar to investigate the matter further, while hope and wonder thrilled our hearts.

"Now, then, Young," said Rayburn, "try it again. It looks as though this idol wasn't all the blackguard things you've been calling it, by a long shot."

"No, I'll be hanged if I'll try it again," Young answered. "Try it yourself, if you want to. How do I know what's goin' t' happen with a stone thing that goes tippin' around that way? I don't mind sayin' that I'm a good deal jolted, an' don't feel like foolin' with it any more. Try it yourself, if you want to, I say."

"All right," Rayburn answered. "You and the Professor stand here where you can grab me if anything goes wrong. It looks to me as though there was a chance for us of some sort here, and I mean to see what it is."

Young and I stood on each side of Rayburn and held him by the arms as he seated himself on the idol's head. Borne down by his weight, the head slowly sank, the whole fore-end of the stone slab falling away into the rock, and the after-end correspondingly rising and disclosing a squared opening, through which came a strong burst of light. When the head was down to the level of the rock, and the slab stood up at an angle of nearly fifty degrees, the movement ceased. Looking into the opening we saw a flight of a dozen stone steps. On the bottom step the sun shone brightly, and in our faces blew a draught of fresh, sweet air. On the rock, beside the stair-way was carved the King's symbol, with the arrow pointing downward.

"Hurrah!" cried Young. "Here's a way out—an' it looks as if that old monk an' th' Cacique weren't such a pair of blasted liars after all!"

Rayburn jumped up to have a look with the rest of us; but before he could see anything the statue had fallen into place again and the opening was closed. "No matter, we know how to work it, now," he said. "We must prop it up somehow; that's all. I want to have a look at this thing. There's some mighty good engineering shown in the way the centre of gravity of that stone has been calculated; and there's a good mechanism in the way it's hung. Here she goes again. Just chock it with a bit of rock when I swing it open."

"Well, what I'm interested in," said Young, "is findin' out what sort of a place it'll get us into. It looks to me as if we might be goin' to strike the treasure right smack here."

Much the same notion was in all of our heads by this time, and we were full of eagerness—the statue having been swung again, and propped in place with a fragment of rock—as we went down the little stair. But what we found was only a continuation of the cañon—as though, by some curious freak of nature, the thin walls of rock enclosing the cave had been left thus in the very middle of it. Rayburn drew our attention to the fact that we were on the crest of a divide, for a spring that bubbled up here flowed away from us; and this also was a cheering sign that the cañon had an outlet. How far away the outlet might be we could not tell; for the cañon, half a mile or so from where we stood, bent sharply to the right. But being thus assured that a way of some sort out of our prison was open to us, we turned to examine the work of the skilled mechanics who in some far past time had set this swinging statue in its place. From below, the simple apparatus, that yet for its fitting required so high a grade of scientific knowledge, was plainly disclosed to us. Into the great slab of stone, presumably running through it from side to side, was set a round bar of metal—the same bright metal of which the sword was made—more than a foot in diameter; and this worked in two concave metal sockets in much the same manner that the sockets of a gun-carriage hold the trunnions of a gun. What struck Rayburn as especially remarkable was the trueness to a circle of both the sockets and the bar; both showing, as he declared, that they had been worked upon a lathe. And he was puzzled, as in the case of the sword, as to the composition of the metal that thus defied oxidization through long periods of time. "Gold is the only thing that fills the bill," he said; "but a bar of gold, even of that size, would bend double under such a strain. I'd give ten dollars for a chance to analyze it—for there's a bigger fortune in putting a metal like that on the market than there is in finding this treasure that we're hunting for: especially if it turns out that there isn't any treasure to find."

"Now, don't you go t' runnin' down that treasure," Young struck in. "Just now treasure stock is up. Me an' that idol have just boomed th' market. I'm sorry I called Jack Mullins, or whatever his name is, such a lot of cuss-word names. I take 'em all back. He isn't just th' sort of an idol that I'd pick out t' worship myself, at least not as a steady thing; but there are good points about him—especially th' way he tips up. I always did like an idol that tipped up. He's done th' square thing by us in gettin' us out all right from th' worst sort of a hole; an' I guess th' best thing we can do is t' yank our traps out of that cave an' get started again. Why, for all we know, th' treasure may be right around that corner."

There was no doubt as to the soundness of Young's suggestion in regard to resuming our march; but the very serious fact confronted us that we now must do our marching on foot. To get the horses and mules down through the narrow opening was simply impossible, and there was nothing for us but to leave them behind. Rayburn looked very grave over this phase of the matter, for leaving the mules meant also that we must leave the greater part of our ammunition and stores. That these things would be abundantly safe in the cave, for any length of time, was not to the purpose; the essential matter was that we would be deprived of them. It was hard, too, to think that our animals would fall into the hands of the Indians—for our only course with them must be to turn them loose in the cañon, whence they certainly would go out in search of pasture into the valley, and so be captured; but it was still harder to think that we must go ourselves on foot and with a scant outfit of supplies.

It was not very cheerfully, therefore, that we went back into the cave and began to sort out from our packs the articles which would be absolutely necessary to our preservation in the rough work among the mountains that probably was before us; and our shoulders already ached a little in anticipation of the heavy loads which they must bear.

It was while we were thus engaged that Pablo begged that I would step aside with him for a moment that he might speak to my ear alone. I saw that there were tears upon his cheeks, and as he spoke he scarcely could restrain his sobs.

"Señor," he said, "you know El Sabio?"

"Surely, Pablo."

"You know, señor, that he is a very small ass."

"It is true."

"And you know—you know, señor, how very tenderly we love each other. Since I came away from my father and my mother, in Guadalajara, and from my little brother and sister there, El Sabio is everything in the world to me, señor. I—I cannot leave him, señor. I should die if we were parted; and El Sabio would die also. And you say that you have perceived that he is a very small ass. Do not ask me to leave him, señor."

"But we cannot take him with us, Pablo. What would you have?"

"That is it, señor; truly, I think that we can take him with us. You see, he is so little; and it is quite wonderful through how small a place El Sabio can crawl. He can creep like a kitten, señor, and he can make himself into a very little bunch. And so I think that he can—if we help him, you know, señor—and speak to him so that he will not be alarmed, and will try to do his very best to make a small bunch of himself—I think that we can get him down through the hole, and so take him with us. But if we cannot, señor, then—you must forgive me, señor—I love him so very dearly, you know—then I will stay with him here. It would be better so than that El Sabio should think I no longer loved him. And he would think that, señor, were I to go with you and leave him here among these dreadful dead gentlemen alone."

It had not occurred to any of us that El Sabio might be condensed sufficiently to go through the narrow way; but if he truly were the collapsable donkey that Pablo declared him to be, we had a good deal to be thankful for. He was a sturdy little creature, and his small back could bear easily twice as much as any two of ours. With his assistance we certainly would be able to carry with us all of our ammunition and arms—of which defensive stuff we could not well afford to spare the smallest part.

And El Sabio, after Pablo had made a long explanation of the case to him, and had told him precisely what we expected him to do—to all of which he listened gravely and with an astonishing air of comprehending what was said to him—seemed to enter into the spirit of the situation, and to try his very best to meet its requirements. It is a puzzle to me to this day how El Sabio managed to shrink himself so that we got him through that narrow hole; but he certainly did manage it—and then went down the stone stair-way backward, as though he had been trained to be a trick donkey from his youth up. When the feat was accomplished, and he stood safely out in the cañon, the expressions of love, and of congratulation upon his cleverness, which Pablo lavished upon him were enough to have turned completely a less serious-minded donkey's head.

Such of our stores as we were compelled to leave behind us, including our saddles, and the pack-saddles, and all the heavier portion of our camp equipage, we heaped in one corner of the cave and piled rocks over; and then we turned our poor horses and the mules loose in the cañon, feeling certain that their instinct would lead them out to the valley in search of food. It went to our hearts to know that these good beasts of ours were doomed to hard service under Indian masters to the end of their days.

All being thus in readiness for our advance, we went down the stair-way beneath the swinging statue, and from beneath pulled out the piece of rock which propped up the great mass of stone. With a heavy jar it fell and closed the passage-way, and we prepared to start. Just then Fray Antonio remembered that he had left on a ledge in the cave—that we had used as a shelf for the storage of various small matters during our sojourn there—a little volume that he dearly loved: the *Meditations of Thomas à Kempis*. He was full of remorse for his forgetfulness, and did not ask that we should turn back to get his book for him; yet his distress over the loss of it was so evident that we had not the heart to go on.

"It will take only ten minutes to go back," said Rayburn, and as he spoke he ran up the stair-way and set his shoulders to sway up the stone. In a moment he called: "Just come here, Young, and help, will you? It don't work as easily from this side." But even with Young's help the stone did not move. Then the rest of us joined these two, and all five of us together pushed with all our strength—and the stone did not yield by so much as the breadth of a hair! And then rather a queer look came into Rayburn's face, and he said: "I think that I understand what is the matter. The point of leverage falls beyond the edge of the hole. From where we have a chance to push, we are working against the whole weight of the stone. We might as well try to lift the mountain itself!" And then he added, "I guess we'd better give this thing up and start."

Very curious feelings were in our breasts as we picked up our packs and set off along the cañon; for we knew that by that way only could we go, and that, no matter what was ahead of us, our retreat was cut off.

CHAPTER XI

THE SUBMERGED CITY

A sweet, warm wind blew in our faces as we set off along the cañon; the sun shone joyously upon us, and there was that fresh, tingling quality in the air that is peculiar to regions high above the level of the sea. In spite of the fact that the way behind us was irrevocably barred, and that no matter what dangers were ahead of us we had no option but to face them, our spirits were strong within us, and we went blithely on our way. Young, who was in advance, began to whistle "Yankee Doodle"; and presently, from the rear of our procession, where Pablo walked beside the heavily laden El Sabio, there broke forth a mouth-organ accompaniment to this spirited melody.

The bed of the cañon, through which a little stream ran, fell away before us along a slight down grade; which descent, since we found also a good foot-way beside the stream, made walking comparatively easy notwithstanding our heavy back-loads. Now and then our way would be barred by masses of rock fallen from above, and by whole trees blown down from their insecure roothold on the rocky cliffs; and twice we came to steep descents which would have given us trouble had we not brought along the ropes wherewith our packs had been bound. Shifting El Sabio down these places was our hardest task; but with the ropes, and the intelligent part that he took in the performance, we managed it successfully.

So we went on for half a dozen miles or more through the windings of the cañon, but keeping all the while a sharp lookout ahead—for in the mouth of this end of the cañon, supposing it to open as at the other end upon a grassy valley, we well enough might come upon an Indian camp. And that we had come upon such a camp we felt quite sure when, late in the afternoon, Rayburn signalled us from his advanced position—he having gone to the head of the line in Young's place—to stand still until he should reconnoitre a little. Being thus halted, we unslung our rifles and loosed our pistols in their holsters, so that we might be ready in case fighting suddenly should begin; and Rayburn went on around a turn in the cañon, and for a while we lost sight of him.

Presently he returned and signalled us to join him, but to move cautiously. When we came up with him he led us to the bend in the cañon, and there a broad view opened to us; for the cañon suddenly widened into a great valley, that was everywhere, so far as we could see, surrounded by walls of rock almost perpendicular and vastly high. In the bottom of the valley was a broad expanse of delectably green meadow-land, broken here and there by groves of trees; and in the valley's middle part, reaching from side to side of it, was a lovely lake, whereof the blue was flecked by white reflections of certain little idly drifting clouds: the sight of all which greenness and fair water and broad range of sky—after being for so long a season pent up in rocky fastnesses and wandering over brown, sun-baked plains—fairly brought tears into my eyes because of its fresh and open loveliness. And in the tender feeling that thus stirred my heart, as I could see in the quick glance that he gave me, Fray Antonio also keenly sympathized; for his nature was very open at all times to such gentle influences.

But Rayburn and Young, as was evident from their anxious looks, were thinking only of the dangers which this lovely valley might hold in store for us; for the shore of the lake nearest to us had many houses built upon it, and we could see faintly, for the width of the lake was nearly two miles, that there were other houses upon its farther shore. Standing hidden behind a rock, Rayburn examined the valley carefully through a field-glass for a long while.

"I must say this place beats me," he said at last, as he put the glass down from his eyes. "There's no doubt about there being a down down there; but I can't make out a sign of a single living thing. And what is still queerer, the houses seem to go right down into the lake. If you'll take the glass, Professor, you'll see that a few of them, on this side, stand all right on dry ground; and then, farther down the sloping bank, are a lot in the water; and beyond these there seem to be some roofs just showing above the level of the lake. And as far as I can make out, things are just the same over on the far shore. It looks as if the lake had risen after the town was built."

As I looked through the glass I saw that what Rayburn had said was true; and I observed with much interest that many of the houses were large, and that all seemed to be well built of stone. Their construction reminded me of the buildings which M. Charnay examined at Tula, and I was eager to get down to them and examine them closely. Young and Fray Antonio took the glass, in turn, and as none of us saw any signs of life in the valley, we decided to go on. And we were mightily stimulated in this resolve by finding, just at the end of the cañon, where the sharp descent began, a graving of the King's symbol on the rock, with the arrow pointing directly down the steep path.

"Here's a walled city, for sure," said Young; "and if this is where th' treasure-house is, we won't raise a row because th' folks have gone off an' left it. Just whoop up that burro of yours, Pablo, an' let's be gettin' along. It's a pity we had t' leave th' mules behind. If th' treasure's in silver, we can't get away with much of it with nothin' but El Sabio t' pack it on."

Pablo did not understand this speech, of course, but he recognized his own name and the name of El Sabio, and Young's gestures helped out the meaning of his words. Therefore Pablo grinned, and "whooped up" El Sabio; and we all set off briskly down the steep decline.

Presently we found our way much easier than we had been led to expect by its rough beginning. As we advanced along it there was ample evidence that the path had been graded and smoothed by the hand of man. In several places it was carried on a terrace supported by a well-laid retaining wall; a deep crevice was spanned by long slabs of stone, so placed as to form a bridge; and where it turned sharply around a high shoulder of rock, the face of the cliff had been quarried away. Yet that this all had been done in a very remote time was shown by the fragments of rock which had fallen into it here and there, and which were blackened by age. "The same fellow who set that statue in place probably was in charge here," was Rayburn's comment, "and he was a first-rate engineer. I wish I knew how he managed to swing those stone slabs over that crevice. There's no room there to set up a derrick, and it would puzzle me to set blocks like that without one."

And Rayburn's admiration for the professional skill of this engineer of a long past age was still further excited when the path came fairly into the valley, and thence was carried downward along the gentle slope towards the lake, by a perfectly even two-per-cent. grade, over a broad way paved smoothly with squared blocks of stone. And Fray Antonio and I were much interested in this work also, for we both perceived the identity of its structure with the paved way that is found on the east coast of Yucatan, and that is continued on the island of Cozumel.

By this paved avenue we entered the city—for, as we presently found, it was entitled to this more dignified name. The first houses that we came to were but small buildings enclosing a single room—such as are found, inhabited by working-people, on the outskirts of any Mexican city at the present day. They were silent and deserted; but they gave, at first sight, the impression of being but momentarily abandoned, for the belongings of their owners still remained in them as though the every-day affairs of life still went on within their walls. In the first that we entered we found an earthen pot still standing on a sort of fireplace, and beside the fireplace a little pile of charcoal. There was a fragment of bone in the pot, and beneath it were some scraps of charcoal which remained unconsumed. It was as though cooking had been going on here but an hour before. Rayburn even put his hand into the ashes to feel if they still were warm. But closer investigation gave us a juster notion of the long lapse of time that must have occurred since any fire had burned upon this hearth. In one corner of the room we found a pile of mats, but on touching these they crumbled into fragments in our hands; and the bone in the pot was so dry and so porous that it was light as cork.

As in this first house that we examined, so was it in all of them. All, at the first glance, seemed to have been but a moment before deserted; but all had signs about them which showed that they had been abandoned for a very long time. In one we found a loom—in construction very like that which the Navajo Indians use at the present day—on which hung, partly completed, a sheer filament that once had been some sort of heavy woollen cloth. In another, a cotton garment was lying carelessly upon a shelf, as though but a moment before cast aside; yet, as I tried to pick it up, it crumbled between my fingers into a fine powder.

Of humanity, the only sign that we found anywhere about this grim and desert place was the dried, shrivelled remnant of a woman that we came upon in an upper room of one of the larger houses farther on. She was lying upon a bed of mats, partly turned upon her side, and one arm was stretched out towards an earthen cup that stood just beyond her reach upon the floor. There was strong pathos in the action of the figure, for it told of the keen thirst of fever—of weakness so extreme that the inch or two between the hand and the cup was a gulf impassable—of a moaning struggle after the water so longed for—and then, at last, of death in that utter and desolate loneliness. And what added to the ghastliness of it all was that a thin ray of sunlight, coming through a crevice in the wall, struck upon the woman's teeth—whence the lips had dried away—and by its gleaming there made on her face a smile.

As we came close to the lake, we perceived, as Rayburn already had discerned by the aid of the glass, that houses, partially submerged, actually rose from the water, and that houses of which only the roofs were visible were farther on. That this whole valley was the crater of an extinct volcano was sufficiently evident; and we could only surmise that in later times some fresh cataclysm of nature had poured suddenly into it a vast body of water, and so had submerged the city that had been builded here. Whatever had brought about the catastrophe, it evidently had come with a most appalling suddenness. Everywhere the condition of the houses showed how hastily they had been abandoned; and the wild hurry of flight was shown still more clearly in the case of the woman—whose surroundings gave evidence that she had been a person of consequence—deserted in her age or infirmity and left lonely to die.

Young's face wore a melancholy expression as we stood upon the shore of the lake, and looked out across it towards the faintly seen western shore. "If this is th' place we're huntin' for," he said, "I guess our treasure stock is pretty badly watered, unless somebody's had th' sense t' keep th' treasure dry over on th' other side. We'd better move over there, I reckon, an' take a look for it, especially as we've got t' go that way anyhow in order t' get out. There ought t' be some sort of a path around th' lake, between th' edge of th' water and th' cliffs."

But when we came to examine into this matter we found that there was no path at all. On each side of the valley the walls of rock rose directly from the water, sharp and sheer.

"Well," said Rayburn, when we had finished our inspection, "we've got to get across somehow. I guess we'll have to sail in, the first thing to-morrow morning, and build a raft. These pine-trees down here by the water will cut easy and float well, and there's some comfort in that, anyway. But what I'm after right now is my supper."

Pablo already had started a fire, having first unpacked El Sabio, that he might refresh himself by rolling on the soft, green grass and by eating his fill of it, and Young presently had some ham fried and some coffee boiled. We had counted upon having fresh meat for supper that night, for there was everything in the look of the valley to promise that we would find game there; but, so far, not a four-footed thing nor a bird had we seen, nor even signs of fish in the lake.

In the morning we got out the axes and went to work at the building of the raft; and, notwithstanding what Rayburn had said in regard to the ease of cutting them, I must confess that for my part I found the cutting of pine-trees very wearying and painful. My hands were blistered by it, and the muscles of my back were made extremely sore by it for several days. Indeed, the construction of a raft big enough to float us all, and our heavy packs, and El Sabio, was a serious undertaking. We spent two days and a half over it, and I never in my life was more thankful for anything than I was when at last that wretched raft was done. As Young observed, as he regarded our finished work critically, there was no style about it—for it was only a lot of rough logs, of which the upper and lower layers ran fore and aft and the middle layer transversely, the whole bound together by our pack-ropes—but it was large enough for our purposes, and it was solid and strong.

In the late afternoon we carried our belongings on board of it, and Pablo succeeded by dint of much entreaty in inducing El Sabio to board it also, and we pushed off from shore. For driving the clumsy thing forward we had made four rough paddles, which well enough served our purposes, for there was no current whatever in the lake and the air was still.

As we went onward we discovered how considerable the city was that here lay submerged. Through the perfectly clear water we could see to a great depth, and beneath us in every direction were paved streets, lined with houses well built of stone. Near the centre of the valley the size of the houses greatly increased, and the fashion of their building was more stately; and fronting upon a great open square in the very centre of the city was a building of such extraordinary size that we took it to be the palace of a king; but here the water was so deep that we could make out but faintly the looming far below us of its mighty walls. Never have I been more pained than I then was; for in that place I found myself close to making discoveries of surpassing archæological value, and yet I was as completely cut off from them as though they had no existence.

Just beyond the palace, as we went onward, our raft almost

touched the roof of a noble building that stood upon the top of a vast pyramidal mound, the base of which we could see but dimly far down through the waters of the lake. This, evidently, had been the chief temple of the city; and as we passed over it and came to its eastern side, we had ghastly and certain proof of the terrible suddenness with which the city had been overwhelmed. On the broad terrace before the temple was the sacrificial stone, and upon this dark mass we saw distinctly the gleaming of human bones; and as we peered down into the water we perceived that all the terrace was strewn thickly with human bones also, showing that when the rush of water came many thousands of human beings had here perished miserably. For a little while, no doubt, all the surface of the water round about where we were had been dotted thickly with the bodies of the drowned which had floated upward; and then, one by one, they had sunk again to the place where death first found them—where their flesh wasted away from them until only their gleaming bones remained.

I pictured to myself the dreadful scene that once had passed, down there below us, where now was only the calm serenity of ancient death: the great crowd collected to witness the sacrifice, and then the sudden coming of the waters—possibly so quickly that the victim, held down by the neck-yoke upon the sacrificial stone, was drowned ere there was time to slay him. This great mound would be the last of all to be covered, and the wretched people gathered there must have seen their city disappear beneath the waters before death came to them. No doubt they thought themselves safe in that high place, made sacred by the presence of their gods. And when the water did reach them, what a writhing and struggling there must have been for a little while; what a crushing of the weak by the strong in mad efforts to gain even a moment's safety upon some higher standing-place! And then, at last, the water rose triumphant in its swelling majesty over all—and beneath its placid surface were hid the silenced terrors of all that commotion of mortal agony, whereof the outcome was the peaceful and eternal calm of death.

CHAPTER XII

IN THE VALLEY OF DEATH

As the raft approached the western shore of the lake we perceived beneath us no longer houses, but large walled enclosures which plainly had been gardens of pleasure—for gaunt trees, symmetrically planted in groves and beside stone-paved path-ways, yet stood in them; and seats of carved stone were placed in what once had been shaded nooks; and in many of the gardens were carved stone fountains of elegant design. Between the city and what once had been its charming suburb extended a broad paved way, like that which we had found upon the eastern shore; and this paved way was continued on the dry ground above the present level of the lake towards the cliffs westward. On the high western shore were a few houses, large and handsome, and having walled gardens around them, which evidently had belonged to persons of great wealth and consequence.

In these we found shadowy remnants of a past magnificence. On many of the walls were hangings, once rich and heavy, that now were mere films of ghostly stuff held together by the many gold threads which had been woven into their fabric. Pottery, wrought into beautiful shapes, yet ornamented with designs that told of but half-redeemed barbarism, was scattered about everywhere, and scarcely a piece was broken. Some very handsome weapons we found also— swords and spears and knives—of the same curious metal as the sword which Pablo so opportunely had laid hands upon in the cañon, but far more finely finished and more delicate in design. And of this same metal was made a great throne, as it seemed to us to be, that was in the largest room of the finest of all the houses; a house that we believed was once the pleasure palace of the king. The audience-chamber in which this throne stood was of finely wrought stone-work, whereof the whole surface was covered with low-reliefs of men and animals—scenes of battle, of council, and of the chase—surrounded by curious tracery of such orderly design that Fray Antonio agreed with me in the belief that it was some sort of hieroglyphic writing. But this matter is treated of so fully in my *Pre-Columbian Conditions on the Continent of North America* that I need not enter upon discussion of it here.

But in none of these houses, much to the disappointment of Rayburn and Young, did we find any scrap of the treasure for which they so earnestly longed. And, truly, if treasure remained in this wrecked city, it was less likely to be in these outlying country houses than in some strong building in the city's heart; and so beyond their reach in the depths of the lake. If this were indeed the walled city for which we were searching—as well it might be, for never was a city surrounded by grander walls than the mighty cliffs wherewith the valley was encompassed—our search was like to be a vain one so far as mere treasure was concerned; though I, for my part, felt myself well repaid for all that I had thus far suffered by the discovery of so much that was of archæological value. In this purer pleasure Fray Antonio shared; yet was he also dissatisfied—for he had come with us that he might preach Christianity to living souls: and here were only the bones of countless dead.

The paved way still led westward, and we followed it—for to the westward must be the valley's outlet. As it rose to a higher level the way widened; and on each side of it was a stone statue of the god Chac-Mool. As we came to these statues Young proceeded, in a most business-like way, and with no apparent appreciation of the queer figure that he cut, to sit down in turn on each of their heads. And he was mightily disappointed when he found that neither of them stirred. "They're not th' tippin' kind," he said, ruefully, as he got down from the head of the second one and looked at it with an expression of reproach.

But his countenance brightened, when we had gone a little farther, as he caught sight of another and much larger statue of the god that was set in a great niche cut in the cliff at the end of the paved way. To prepare here the god's abiding-place very arduous labor had been undertaken. For a space fully one hundred feet high and as many broad the whole face of the cliff had been quarried into; making a deep recess that was rounded above, and that from beneath was approached by a long flight of steps cut from the solid rock. In the centre of the recess, upon the terraced space above the stairs, was a huge squared mass of stone, on which the great stone figure of Chac-Mool rested. The opening faced directly eastward, and as we approached it the stone figure was seen but indistinctly in the duskiness of the recess, over which, and far beyond which into the valley, fell the shadow of the mighty cliff. From in front of this great altar all the valley was open to us; and hence, before the lake swallowed it, every part of the city must have been clearly visible in ancient times. As we mounted the steps and approached the idol I observed that Pablo hung back a little; as though in the depths of his nature some chord had been touched, some ancient instinct in his blood aroused, that filled his soul with awe.

Certainly there was no suggestion of awe in Young's demeanor towards the statue. With a monkey-like quickness, that I would not have given his stout legs and heavy body credit for, he climbed upon the altar and plumped himself down on the head of the figure almost in a moment. But again he was disappointed, for the idol did not stir. As we examined it closely we perceived that its fixedness was not unreasonable; for the figure, and the altar on which it rested, were one solid mass of rock that itself was a part of the cliff—left standing here when the niche around it was hollowed out. A very prodigious piece of stone-cutting all this was, and as I contemplated it I was filled with admiration of the skill of them who had achieved it. But Young came down from the idol moodily; and he said that the way these people had of playing tricks on travellers, by making Mullinses that didn't tip when they ought to tip, was quite of a piece with their putting their treasure where it couldn't be got at without a diving-bell.

Behind the altar the niche was cut into the cliff so far that the depths of it in the waning daylight were dusky with heavy shadows; indeed, so dense were these that Young came near to breaking his bones by falling into a little hole in the floor, that was the less easily seen because it was hidden behind a jutting mass of rock. But he caught the rock in time to save himself from falling, and eagerly struck a wax-match that he might see if here were a passage-way for us. Descending into the rock was a stair-way, the steps whereof were smoothed as though many feet had trodden them; and down these steps he promptly went, holding the lighted match before him—these Mexican wax-matches are as good as tapers—and having with him the full box of matches should further light be required. A minute later we heard his voice calling to us, but where it came from we could not tell—for he had descended into the rock below us, and the sound that we heard seemed to come from the air above. While we listened we saw the gleam of the light in the darkness below, and then he came up the stair laughing.

"Well, that's just th' boss trick," he said. "I guess th' old priests who used t' run this place would be everlastin'ly down on me if they knew that I'd tumbled to it. There's a hole right up into th' idol an' room inside of him for half a dozen men, an' there's a crack in his head that you can see out through while you're lettin' off prophecies an' that sort o' thing. Why, if you had a crowd t' work with who really believed in Jack Mullins, you could set 'em up for almost anything with a rig like that!"

But this curious discovery, in which Fray Antonio and I were deeply interested, did not forward our immediate purpose, which was to find a way out of the valley. We still cherished a faint hope, indeed, that we might find the King's symbol with the arrow pointing the way onward, and so be assured that the city buried in the depths of the lake was not the city of which we were in search. But in any event the need for getting out of the valley pressed upon us; and that we might accomplish our deliverance from this shut-in place, we examined closely the whole circuit of the cliffs at the western end. Not an inch of this great expanse of rock, for as far up the wall as our eyes could see clearly, escaped our attentive observation; yet nowhere was there, even by bold climbing, a place where the cliff might be scaled, still less an open path. And so, having walked slowly along the bottom of the cliffs to the edge of the lake on the north, and there turned upon our steps and come slowly back again to where we started from, and having made a like double journey of inspection to and from the edge of the lake to the south, we came at last to our first point of departure, and rested before the statue of Chac-Mool, disconsolate.

One discovery we had made in the course of our explorations which enabled us to understand how the fate that had overtaken the drowned city had fallen upon it. Close by the northern border of the valley we saw, high up above us, a vast rift more than a thousand feet wide in the face of the cliff; and below this the ground was torn into a deep wild channel, and everywhere huge fragments of rock were scattered over the ground. Here it was, then, that the water had poured in—bursting forth from a lake above—by which the city at one stroke had been overwhelmed. Some little notice, by the mighty roaring that must have accompanied so great a crash of rocks and so vast a rush of water, the dwellers in the city must have had; and the gleam of the pouring waters would have shown them the nature of the ruin that was upon them. There would have been time, before the water was waist-deep in the city streets, for them to make their way to the high mound on which their temple stood; and in the appalling horror of it all they might have clamored to their priests that a victim should be sacrificed to stay this terrible outburst of anger on the part of their gods. But it was more than likely that before the sacrifice could be completed they all—people, priests, and he who was to be sacrificed—perished together beneath the flood.

"Why," said Young, "th' Mill River disaster wasn't anything to it, an' that was pretty bad. I was runnin' th' way-freight on th' Old Colony road when that happened, an' I took a day off an' went up an' had a look at it. But this just lays that little horror out cold. It's as big as lettin' loose on Boston the whole of Massachusetts Bay."

That we should be prisoners in a place where death had wrought so swiftly such tremendous havoc was quite enough to fill our souls with a brooding melancholy. But in addition to the sombre thoughts which thus were forced upon us, bred of sorrow for the thousands who had here untimely perished, the gloomy dread of a more practical sort assailed us that we also in a little while would join the silent company of the thousands who had died here in a long past time. And the death that seemed to be in store for us was less merciful than that which had come to them. Theirs had been a short struggle, and then a gentle ending as the waters closed over them. But our ending was like to be a lingering one and miserable—by starvation.

With the loss of our mules and horses we had been compelled to leave behind us the greater portion of our stores; and for our protection against savages, and in the belief that in the mountains we should meet with an abundance of game, we had left almost all of our provisions, and made our lading mainly of ammunition and arms. But in this valley, so smiling and so beautiful, there was no live thing except ourselves. Not a beast, not a bird had we seen since we entered it; and in the lake, as we found presently, there were no fish; the only sign that animal life ever had existed here was that dried and withered remnant of a woman that we had found in the deserted house, and the bones which we had seen gleaming below us in the lake. This was, in truth, as we came thus to call it, the Valley of Death.

While we worked at building the raft we had not thought to be sparing in our eating—for building that raft was hungry work—and now that consideration of the matter was forced upon us, we found that we had with us food barely sufficient for three days. We could, of course, eat El Sabio—though such was our feeling towards that excellent animal that eating him would be almost like eating one of ourselves; and Pablo, we knew, would regard eating this dear friend of his as neither more nor less than sheer cannibalism. And even if we did eat El Sabio, the meat of his little body would but prolong our lives for a week, or possibly for two weeks more. And what then?

Had there been room in our souls for yet more sorrow, we could have had it in the thought that in all that we had set out to do we had completely failed. If this Valley of Death were indeed the place that we had been seeking, little good came to us from finding it. Of the souls which Fray Antonio had come forth to save, here there were none. Of archæological discovery, truly, I had something to make me glad; yet little compared to what was hidden beneath the waters; and even this little, since knowledge of what I had found soon must die with me, was of no avail. As for Rayburn and Young, the treasure which they sought might or might not be near at hand; but they certainly could no more come at it than, were it heaped up before them, they could carry it away. And most of all was my heart troubled by the fate that was like to overtake Pablo because of his love for me. Bitterly I blamed myself for permitting the boy to come with me; for I should have foreseen that a hundred chances might intervene to render impossible my intention to give him his free choice to go or to stay when the decisive turning-point in our adventure came. In point of fact, one of these chances had intervened; and the attack upon us that the Indians had made, and the closing of the passage in the rock behind us that rendered return impossible, had forced him to remain with us without voice of his own in the matter; and now would bring him, as it would bring the rest of us, to the most horrible death of which a man can die.

Night was falling as we ended our search along the cliffs for a way of escape, and found none, and so came again in front of the great idol—where our packs had been left heaped up, and where the Wise One, happily unmindful of the fate that might soon be in store for him, was energetically cropping the rich grass. We built a fire, for the air in that deep valley, mingling with the mists rising from the lake, was damp and chill; and beside the fire we made our evening meal. There was no good in talking about what was so apparent to all of us; but Young, who was our cook, showed his appreciation of the situation practically by serving only half rations and by making our coffee very thin and poor.

Silently we ate our short allowance of food; and thereafter we smoked our pipes with but little talk for seasoning, and that little of a melancholy sort. Of our own plight we did not speak at all, but in what we said there was constantly a reflection of the bitter sorrow with which all our hearts were charged. I remember that Young, who truly was as merry a man naturally as ever I knew, told us that night only of dreadful railroad accidents—of wrecks in which men lay crushed among the heaped-up cars, shrieking with the agony of their hurts; and then shrieking with dread, and with yet greater pain as the fire that seized upon the ruin around them came nearer and nearer until they fairly were roasted alive. And Rayburn told of a prospecting party besieged by Indians upon a mountain peak in Colorado; how, one by one, they slowly died in a raving horror of thirst until one man alone was left; and how this one man prolonged his life until rescue came by drinking the blood of his own body, and yet died in raging madness almost at the moment that he was saved.

For myself, I had nothing to add to these horrors; yet such was my frame of mind that I found a certain bitter gladness in listening to the telling of them, and in tracing between them and our own case the ghastly parallel. In our talk, which wont on in English, Fray Antonio took no part; but he could follow well enough the meaning of it in our tones. On his face was an expression of tender melancholy that seemed to me to tell of sorrow for us rather than of dread of what might be in store for himself; and that this truly was his mood was shown when the others paused, sated and appalled by the horrors which they had conjured up, and he spoke at last.

It was not a sermon that Fray Antonio gave us; but out of the abundant store of faith by which he himself was sustained he strove to comfort us with thoughts of better things than life can give. And with the promise of hope that he held out to us with the solemn authority that was vested in him by reason of the service to which he was vowed, he mingled a certain yearning for us, very moving, that came of the love and the tender gentleness that were in his own heart. And yet, though he knew that, excepting Pablo, we all were heretics according to his own creed, there was no word of doctrine in all of his discourse. Rather was what he said a simple setting forth of that primitive Christianity which has its beginning and its ending in a simple faith in an all-pervading, all-protecting love. And of this love, as it seemed to me, he himself was the human embodiment. Looking in his gentle face, which yet had such high courage, such noble resolution in it, I felt that in him the spirit of the saints and martyrs of long past ages lived again.

With our souls soothed and strengthened by what Fray Antonio had spoken to us, we lay down at last to sleep; yet was it impossible for us to drive out from our hearts that natural sadness which men must feel who know that they have failed in a strong effort to accomplish a project very dear to them, and who know also that they are standing upon the very threshold of a most tormenting death.

CHAPTER XIII

UP THE CHAC-MOOL STAIR

We awoke the next morning at the very moment that the sun rose above the mountain peaks to the eastward; and our waking was due in part to the sunshine striking upon our faces, but more to the prodigious braying, that echoed thunderously from the cliffs around us, with which El Sabio welcomed the advent of the god of day.

"It is a good sign, señor," said Pablo, "when El Sabio brays thus nobly at sunrise. He does not do it often, but when he does I know beyond a doubt that I am to have a lucky day."

"An' I must say," Young struck in, "that for a man who expects t' have t' eat his boots in th' course of a day or two I'm feelin' this mornin' most uncommonly chipper myself. For one thing, I mean t' have another look around that idol. I'm not at all sure that he's not th' tippin'-up kind. Maybe we didn't put enough weight on him yesterday; or he may do his tippin' up from th' other end. Anyhow, I'm goin' t' have another whack at him as soon as I've eat my breakfast; an' that's a performance that won't take long t' get through with, considerin' how thunderin' little there is t' eat."

Truly, the eating of our breakfast did not consume much time; and, so short did Young make our rations, I am not sure that we were not hungrier at the end of it than we were at its beginning. When we finished, the sun was still low in the east; and the bright rays struck full upon the statue of Chac-Mool, on the great stone altar, and into the depths of the niche that had been hollowed behind it in the face of the cliff. We observed that the idol was so placed that the very first rays of the sun, coming through a cleft between two great peaks to the eastward, shone brightly upon it, while yet all the rest of the valley save the cliff above the niche remained in shade.

With the strong sunlight deeply penetrating it, the recess behind the altar no longer was filled with the black shadows that had obscured it on the previous afternoon; and even the hole into which Young so nearly had fallen was plainly visible. Taking advantage of the better light, the lost-freight agent—who certainly had found a fitting berth in that department of railway service, for such a man for hunting for things, and for finding them, I never came across—made a more careful examination of the deeper portion of the recess, and presently he gave a shout that told of a discovery.

As we gathered around him he pointed in great excitement to a row of metal pegs, which were fixed in the rock one above the other, diagonally; and then to the point in the roof of the recess towards which these pegs tended. Even with the strong light that now aided us it was some time before I could make out among the black shadows of the roof a small opening; but the longer that I looked at it the more distinct it grew.

"We've struck th' trail once more," Young cried. "We've struck it sure. It don't look promisin', but here it is—for if this ain't th' King's symbol carved right by th' first of these pegs, then you're all at liberty t' kick me right smack over th' top of that idol for a damn fool! Hurrah!"

Pablo could not understand what Young was saying, but it was easy to perceive from his gestures the nature of the happy discovery that he had made. In a tone in which deference and triumph were curiously blended, Pablo said to me: "Did I not tell you, señor, that a good thing always happens when El Sabio brays at the rising sun?"

Before Pablo had ended this short but exultant deliverance, Young was half-way up to the roof of the cave, treading gingerly upon the metal bolts and testing each one before he trusted his weight to it. In a couple of minutes he reached the roof and disappeared through the hole; and almost instantly he called down to us: "We're solid—here's a regular staircase. Come along!"

We followed him promptly enough; while our hearts thrilled, and all our bodies trembled, with the gladness that possessed us as we found this way opening to us from the valley wherein we had thought that surely we must die. In a little chamber, cut in the rock above the opening into which the ladder of bolts led us, Young was waiting for us; and from this chamber a spiral stair-way ascended that was dimly lighted by crevices cut from it out to the face of the cliff. With Young leading us, up this we went; at first rapidly, but, later, slowly and wearily, for it seemed as though the stair would never end. Yet though our bodies were heavy our spirits were very light; for we know by the wearisome length of it that the stair must lead to the very top of the towering cliffs by which we had believed ourselves to be irrevocably shut in. And at last there was a gleaming of light above us; and this grew stronger and stronger until we came out with a shout of joy into the glad sunlight—and saw far below us the valley that we once more thought beautiful, now that it no longer held us fast.

In the depth below us we could discern El Sabio, looking no bigger then a rabbit; and he must have caught the sound of our shouting with those long ears of his, for there came up to us faintly from him an answering bray.

"It's pretty hard lines on that jackass," said Young, "leaving him behind down there. But he might be left in a worse place, after all."

I could perceive that Pablo was stirred by uneasy thoughts of the separation that now so clearly must take place between him and his dear friend; and he looked wistfully along the path across the mountain to the westward—cut and smoothed so that it was an easy path to go on—and evidently thought how simple a matter it would be for El Sabio to travel on with us if only once he were up the stair. But he did not speak, and I hoped that he was nerving himself to bear manfully this sore trial. For the rest of us, we had but one thought: to get our packs up the stair-way as quickly as possible—and at its quickest this work would be slowly and painfully done—and then once more go forward. Just as we turned to descend again an eagle came sailing slowly towards us—evidently without fear of us—and Rayburn was so fortunate as to bring him down with a pistol-shot. We tossed him over the edge of the cliff; and a famous breakfast we made on him when we returned into the valley again. I can't say that I would have much stomach for so dirty a bird now, but I certainly did think that eagle most delicious eating then.

The hearty meal that we made on him strengthened us mightily, and we went to work with a will at getting our traps up the stair. With our pack-ropes we hauled the various articles first into the little room at the stair-foot, and then toilsomely carried them to the heights above. Saving only that this work did not blister my hands, it was worse than the building of the raft had been; and all of us, using in climbing and in descending the stair certain muscles which normally are not brought often into play, found our legs so stiff and sore for the next day or two that walking gave us very lively pain.

It was as this heavy work went slowly forward that Pablo said to me, speaking in an insinuating and deprecating tone: "Up a stair such as this is, señior, the Wise One would bound like a deer."

I did not call in question Pablo's simile, for I knew that the boy's heart must be very sad. Laying my hand kindly upon his shoulder, I answered in a way to show that I was truly sorry for him: "The Wise One will lead a happy life, Pablo, in this beautiful valley—where nothing can do him harm, and where he will have an abundance of water and of rich fresh grass. Up the stair no doubt he could climb, for he knows wonderfully well how to use those dainty little feet of his; but even the Wise One could not climb up the ladder of metal bolts. Therefore must thou strengthen thy heart against the bitterness of this parting from him; for even if thou wouldst stay behind with him it is not possible—for thou canst not live, like the Wise One, on water and grass."

"But he is so little and so light an ass, señor," Pablo urged, "that surely, all of us pulling together, we could pull him up by the ropes, even as the other things have been pulled up; surely, surely, señor, that would be an easy thing for four men to do—and I also can pull at the ropes, señor, almost as well as any man."

It did not seem to me that even all of us pulling together could sway El Sabio up a hundred feet through the air; but Pablo was so pitiful in his entreaties, and seemed so resolutely bent upon remaining behind in the valley and dying there with his dear friend rather than go on without him, that I opened the matter to Rayburn and joined my plea to Pablo's that this curious effort should be made. And in addition to the sentimental reason for taking the ass with us, I pointed out to Rayburn—as, indeed, he understood without my telling him—how practically valuable El Sabio was to us in helping us to bear our heavy loads. Rayburn thought with me that the dead lift of so considerable a weight to such a height, without tackle of any sort to help us, was impossible. But Young, who had an inventive strain in his composition, was of the opinion that he could set up such rough tackle as would answer our purpose; upon understanding which, Pablo at once embraced El Sabio and danced for joy.

Young was, I think, the handiest man I ever knew. He had a natural genius for mechanics; and in the many years of his railroad life he had gained a knowledge of all manner of expedients by which the work of complicated machinery could be accomplished by very simple means. "When you have a freight smash-up right in the middle of the section," he said, "with nobody to help you inside of forty miles, and the express due to come bouncing down on you inside of two hours, you've just *got* to get things out of the way whether you've got anything to do it with or not. If I had the equipment of a first-class freight-cab here I'd yank that burro up inside of twenty minutes; and if I don't do it, anyway, inside of two hours I'll promise to eat him."

I did not translate the whole of this speech to Pablo, for talk even in fun about eating El Sabio was rather a delicate matter, considering how close a shave that worthy animal had had to being eaten in dead earnest; but I did tell him that the Señor Young felt sure that he could swing El Sabio up through the air to where the stair began. And with Pablo—who also could use his hands well—most willingly helping, Young contrived in a surprisingly short time to make a rough windlass, that was effective enough for the work to be done with it, and to pull it up bit by bit into the chamber in the rock and there fit it together over the hole. El Sabio, being brought into the recess behind the idol, regarded us all with a doubting expression that even Pablo's repeated assurances that we meant well by him could not change into a look of trustfulness. Pablo declared, however, that in his heart of hearts the Wise One knew that we all were his friends, and that even though we should hurt him a little he would understand that it was for his good. And the conduct of the ass during the exceedingly bad half-hour that he then went through seemed fully to bear out Pablo's words. Around his small body, with stays running forward around his neck and aft to his tail, we rigged looped ropes—which ropes were gathered together above his back and there made fast to the line that was pendent from the windlass above. From time to time, as this operation was going forward, El Sabio turned his head upon one shoulder or the other and gazed with a wistful expression at what we were doing to him; and the slow shake that he gave his head, whereby his great ears were set to wagging mournfully, as he finished each of these inspections, betrayed the grave wonder that was within him as to what it all could mean, together with a not unnatural apprehension of what might be its ultimate outcome.

By a good chance, the effect upon the Wise One of finding the solid earth drop suddenly from beneath his feet—when at last all was in readiness, and Young and Rayburn began to hoist away at the windlass—was to render him quite rigid with terror; and there was a most agonized look upon his face as he went sailing up through the air. Pablo, standing below with me, that we might steady the ass with a guy-rope during his ascent, addressed to him all manner of tender and comforting words; but for once the Wise One seemed to be insensible to his master's voice. Neither with his eyes nor his ears did he respond; and he well enough might have been taken for a dead ass going heavenward, but for the sharp twitchings of his tail. And when at last he was safely within the upper chamber, he fairly fell down upon the rocky floor of it in sheer exhaustion begot of fright. It was not until we had passed up a bucket of water to him, whereof he drank the very last drop, and had been soothed by Pablo's fondling of him and by Pablo's gentle words, that his broken spirit revived. And so limp and weak was he that it was a long while before we could in conscience urge him to ascend the stair. When at last he set himself to this undertaking, he was far from accomplishing it in the bounding and deer-like manner that Pablo had promised for him; but he certainly did at last get to the top—which was all that was required of him—and there drank gratefully the bucketful of water that Pablo had carried up that great height for his comforting when his toilsome climbing should end. And Pablo went down into the valley once more that night in order to bring back to his friend a hearty supper of rich grass.

By the time that all this hard work was accomplished the day was nearly at an end; and even had there been light for us to see our way by we were too tired to go on—for every bone and muscle in our bodies was weary and sore. Therefore we made our camp for the night on the flat expanse of rock where the stair ended; and we were thankful that enough of the eagle remained to us for our supper— and, indeed, we made our breakfast on him also, for he was a prodigiously large bird. Very different were our feelings as we wrapped ourselves in our blankets and settled ourselves to sleep on that open mountain-top—with the path clear before us, and with the cheering hope in our hearts that among the mountains we should find a plenty of wild creatures suitable for food—from the dull despairing languor that had possessed us as we sank to sleep the night before. And with our joy was also a reverent thankfulness—that was more strongly stimulated by certain words which Fray Antonio spoke ere we lay down to rest—that our deliverance was accomplished from that death-stricken valley wherein we ourselves so surely had expected that we must die.

CHAPTER XIV

THE HANGING CHAIN

By the winding way which we followed along the mountain-top (and that this was the way we wished to follow the King's symbol and the pointing arrow plainly showed), we came presently close beside the rift in the cliffs through which the waters of the upper lake had been discharged upon the city in the valley below and so had buried it. And here we made a very surprising discovery—which was no less than that the great rift in the rocks through which the water had been let loose was not, as we had supposed, the result of some fierce convulsion of nature, but very plainly was the fiercer work of man. Along the face of the opening whence the water had poured forth the rock was grooved, showing that drill-holes had been made, close together, from the edge of the cliff backward to the lake that once had filled all the valley now lying bare and empty before us; and with the field-glass we could see that there was a like channelling of the rock upon the farther side of the break. And all doubt in our minds in regard to this matter was removed by our finding a vastly long drill— made of the bright, hard metal that we now were familiar with, yet could not at all understand its composition—lying close beside the chasm upon the bare rock.

"There has been the devil's own work here!" said Rayburn, as he fully took in this extraordinary situation. "Whoever did this must have spent months over it, perhaps years, working with such tools as these. They evidently went at it systematically, with the deliberate intention of drowning the whole crowd down below. From an engineering stand-point I must say that it's a good piece of work. See how cleverly they've picked out this particular spot, where the wall of rock went down almost perpendicularly into the lake, and so got the full value of the thrust of the water when their cuts were finished. If I'm not mistaken, there was a third line of drill-holes sunk in the middle of the mass that they meant to cut loose. That's the way I should have done it: then there would have been a little giving in the centre that would have helped to loosen the sides. But what a lot of incarnate devils they must have been to go at such a job!"

Truly, there was something chilling to the blood in the thought of the slow labor of them who had toiled here, day after day and month after month, until their ghastly purpose was accomplished, and they had slain a whole city without striking a single honest blow. Such vengeance upon an enemy as here was taken never had its equal for cold, malignant cruelty since the world began. Down in the valley below we had seen gleaming beneath the calm surface of the lake the bones of the thousands who had perished when this diabolical work was completed, and the waters bounded forth, shining and sparkling in the sunlight, on their mission of death. And whoever let them loose must have stood just where we now were standing; and at sight of what came of their long labor there must have been such joy as no hell could adequately punish in their black hearts.

Our bodies shuddered as we turned and left the scene of this tremendous tragedy; that was the more appalling to us because of the profound mystery in which was buried everything related to it save the fact that it had been.

For a long distance our way went onward beside the bare, deep valley that had been the basin of the lake, and so the thought of the horror which had been wrought so devilishly with its innocent waters lingered gloomily in our minds. Involuntarily we associated the unknown people of a long past time who had perpetrated this hideous wholesale murder with the people for whom we now were searching, and an uncertain dread filled our souls as to what might be our own fate should we end by finding what we sought. From the tender mercies of a race in which stealthy craft and cold, malignant cruelty evidently were such conspicuous characteristics, little was to be expected. Therefore, it was in a sombre mood, and with but little talk among us, that we went forward upon our way.

The path that we followed showed the same care in the making of it that we had found in the path leading down from the cañon into the valley where the drowned city was. Throughout the length of it, by carrying it skilfully along the windings of the mountain-sides, an equable, easy grade was maintained; where it led across open spaces the loose stones had been cleared away and stood heaped along each side of it; where it skirted precipices the solid rock had been cut out in order to give a wider and a surer foothold; and here and there in its course crevices which traversed it were bridged with great slabs of stone. Rayburn was lost in admiration of the engineering skill that was shown in its construction, and declared that a very little extra work put on it would fit it for the laying of a line of rails.

The valley on our right, in which the lake had been, narrowed as we advanced; and as the path that we followed had a steadily rising grade (according to Rayburn's estimate, of a trifle more than three per cent.), the bottom of it fell away rapidly. As we reached what had been, as we found, the foot of the lake, we discovered fresh evidence of the enormous amount of labor that had been expended in order to make its waters an effective engine of destruction. Far in the depths beneath us, extending across the whole width of the valley—but here the valley had so narrowed that it was less a valley than a cañon—we saw a high and vastly broad stone wall. It was then that we perceived fully the whole of the devilish design, and realized the years that must have been given to its execution. By the building of the wall the level of the lake had been raised fully three hundred feet, and so a head of water had been obtained strong enough to thrust out the mass of rock that had been loosened by drilling through its centre and at its sides. It would have been possible, also, for the rock that was to be broken away to be greatly thinned by quarrying its open face while the water was rising slowly after the great dam was built. Clearly, the whole work had been planned with a calm, diabolical ingenuity that assured with absolute certainty the accomplishment of the horrible purpose that those who labored at it had in view. It seemed impossible, but for the proof that we here had of it, that human hearts could have in them enough of purely devilish cruelty to spend years in thus working out to perfection so hideous a vengeance; and to me it seemed all the more dreadful because of the time that had passed since this most evil deed was done. Centuries had vanished, and the slayers—living out the few years of their lifetime—had perished from off the earth as utterly as had the slain; yet here the whole proof of the great crime that had been wrought lived on in enduring stone that was like to last until the very end of the world should come. Thus had these sinners left behind them, raised by their own hands, a monument telling of their sin; which sin had not even the redeeming quality of passionateness, but was slow and subtle and cruelly cold.

We were glad to turn from sight of this place and press onward into the cañon, for such the valley now had become; and we found in the dark shadows which enveloped us in this deep cleft between the mountains a sombreness in keeping with the feelings in our hearts. So high above us towered the cliffs that at their top they seemed almost to meet, showing between them only a narrow ribbon of bright blue sky, and below us the chasm went down sheer for a thousand feet; a gloomy depth that our eyes could not have penetrated had there not gleamed at the bottom of it the foam and sparkle of a little stream. Here the path was hewn almost continuously out of the solid rock; and we could see that a like path was cut in the rock on the other side. That so prodigious a piece of work should be thus duplicated seemed to us a very astonishing waste of energy; for even Young did not have much faith in his own suggestion that two prehistoric railway companies had secured rights of way along the opposite sides of the cañon, and had begun the building there of rival lines.

But the matter was explained, presently, by our finding that this other path was but a doubling of the path that we were on. As we rounded a turn in the cañon we came suddenly to a broad natural ledge in the rock, over which hung a great projection of the cliff so that the sky above was hid from us. Here our path went off into the air, and began again on the other side of the vastly deep chasm, a good sixty feet away. "Rather long for a jump," was Rayburn's curt comment as we pulled up on the edge of the precipice and looked at each other blankly. Yet it was evident that those who had made with such great expense of toil and time these path-ways on the opposite sides of the cañon had crossed in some way from the one to the other at this point, and the only surmise that seemed to fit the facts of the case was that there had been stretched across the chasm a swinging bridge of *lianas*—such as still are to be found spanning streams in the hot lands of Mexico—and that in the course of ages this had rotted entirely away. But as this bridge, if ever there had been one here, was absolutely gone, we found ourselves in as shrewdly strait a place as men well could be in. To go ahead was as clearly impossible as was the hopelessness of turning back upon our path. At the most, we could only return to the valley out of which we had climbed with such thankfulness; and rather than go back to die of starvation in that place, so beautiful and so desolate, there was not one of us but would have chosen to end all quickly by springing into the gulf above which we stood.

But while we thus stood in dreary contemplation of the miserable prospect before us, Young, as his habit was, was spying about him sharply, and so spied out a way of deliverance for us. The announcement of his discovery was made in a very characteristic way.

"You set up to be some punkins of an engineer, now don't you?" he said, addressing Rayburn. "But did you ever happen to hear of a bridge that was hung up at one end an' that was operated by swingin' it backward an' forward like a pendulum?"

"No," Rayburn answered, promptly and decisively, "I never did."

"So I thought," Young went on. "Well, you've admitted that in sev'ral things th' man who was in charge of construction on this line could have given you points, an' this swingin' bridge notion is one of 'em. I can't say that I think much of it. It wouldn't do in railroads, for sure; but there is a good deal to be said in favor of it when it helps folks out of such a hole as we're in now—an' if it still is in workin' order, that is just what it's going to do. There it is. Do you catch on?"

We all looked in the direction in which Young pointed, for his gesture was so earnest that even Fray Antonio and Pablo caught the meaning of it, and so saw—pendent from a point far up on the over-hang of rock, and but indistinctly showing in the shadow—a great chain that at its lower end was caught in a metal hook set in the face of the cliff at the extreme back of the ledge on which we stood. For my part, I did not at once catch the meaning of Young's words even when I saw the chain, but Rayburn understood it all in a moment.

"By Jove!" he exclaimed, "that *is* a notion! You grab the end of it and just swing across to the other side!"

Young already had loosened the chain from the hook and was testing its strength by putting his weight on it. At the end of it was a crossbar big enough to get a good grip upon; and this, and the chain itself, were wrought of the bright, hard metal of which we had encountered so many specimens. The upper end was made fast high above us in the out-jut of rock, very nearly over the centre of the cañon; so that no great force was required to carry whoever grasped the crossbar, and so swung out boldly, clear across the chasm to the ledge on the other side. But I confess that the thought of such a passage made me feel a little dizzy and sick; and never did I long to be safely back in my class-room at Ann Arbor as I did just then!

"It seems t' be all right," said Young, "but I guess you may as well take a pull on it with me, Rayburn. There'd be no fun in havin' it fetch away when a man was about half across, an' we may as well make th' thing sure." And then, as the chain still held firm under the double strain, he added, "Well, here goes;" and, so speaking, took a running start and went swinging out over the abyss.

My heart was in my mouth as he leaped forth and shot out from and far below us; but in a moment he rose along the curve that he was traversing and was safely landed on the other side. "It's a boss invention. Workin' it is just as easy as rollin' off a log," he called across to us; and to show how easily the passage was made, he instantly swung himself back again.

Pablo had manifested signs of strong uneasiness while this talk and action were in progress, and in a very anxious tone he now inquired: "But how will it be with the Wise One, señor?"

"Why, gettin' *him* across will be as easy as open an' shut," Young answered, speaking in English to Rayburn and to me. "We'll just rig him in th' rope slings again, an' make him fast to th' chain, an' give him a good boost to start him, and over he'll go before he fairly knows he's started."

But when we came to apply this brisk statement of the case practically, we found it by no means easy of execution. El Sabio grew restive as we arranged the slings of rope about his body, evidently remembering, fearfully, the strange journey that he had made in the air when we had rigged him in a like manner in order to trice him up to where the stair began; and he grew yet more restive as we fastened the rope slings to the end of the chain. Rayburn had crossed to the other side—passing the chain back by weighting it with a rock—and stood ready to receive El Sabio when he was swung across. But partly owing to a want of skill in our management of him, yet more to his own unruliness—for just as we started him, with a strong push, he clapped down his fore-feet upon the edge of the cliff and so checked his swing outward—he did not swing within reach of Rayburn's hands. And so he came back towards us again, and then out once more towards Rayburn; and so swung slowly and yet more slowly until at last he hung motionless over the very middle of the gulf, with nothing between him and the rocks below but a thousand feet of air. And then El Sabio began to kick with a vigor that set to rattling every link in the chain!

Pablo was cast by this mischance into a veritable frenzy of fright; and we were most seriously frightened also—not only because the destruction of the poor ass was imminent, but because of the danger which menaced ourselves. Our party was divided, and should the chain give way, under stress of El Sabio's kicks and plunges, all possibility of our coming together again was at an end. Rayburn might leave us and go on; and so, perhaps, save his own life. But for the rest of us there would be no hope. Behind us was death by starvation. In front of us was this impassable gulf.

From Pablo, who was quite wild with dreadful anticipations of the parting of the chain and the loss to him forever of his friend, least was to be expected in the strait wherein we were; yet it was from Pablo that our rescue came. With a quick apprehension of the needs of the case, he rove a running-knot in the end of one of the pack-ropes, and with a dexterous cast of this improvised lasso set the loop of it about El Sabio's neck as that unfortunate animal for a moment ceased his strugglings and hung still. And then we all strained on the rope together, and in a minute had El Sabio safely with us again; but in such a state of terror that pity for him wrung our hearts.

But the limpness which the reaction from such deadly fear threw him into made handling him easy; and this time, when we launched him forth (taking the precaution, however, to fasten one end of a rope to the chain), he went sailing across the full width of the chasm, and Rayburn in a moment had him landed in safety. The instant that the chain was loosened Pablo hauled it back, and an instant later swung lightly across the cañon, and straightway fell to fondling the terrified creature and comforting him with all manner of tender words. And he so piteously besought us to give El Sabio one good drink that we passed the water-keg and the bucket across, and permitted the poor ass to drink half of our stock of water without debate of the sacrifice. Indeed, this refreshment was so necessary to him that without it I doubt if he could have gone on.

While El Sabio thus gathered courage and strength again, Young swung over to the other side, and we passed our stores across from ledge to ledge—having ropes made fast to the chain, and so steadying each load from the one side while we hauled from the other. This was easy work, and we quickly finished it. When it was ended I braced myself for the flying journey through the air across that gulf so deep that the bottom of it was lost in black shadows, through which the sparkling water faintly gleamed; and my heart so throbbed within me as I took the bar in my hands, with the knowledge that should I lose hold of it death waited for me below in those dark shadows, that my breath came irregularly and I heard a dismal ringing in my ears. Yet I had less to fear than either of the others who had crossed before me, for the ropes still were fast to the chain; and should I not swing far enough I would be helped to safety by my companions. But for shame, I should have made my body fast to the chain by a rope sling, and so have gone across as our stores had gone rather than as a man. But my pride forbade my surrender in this fashion to my fears; and it was a lucky thing for me that it did.

Holding the bar in my hands, I ran briskly across the ledge, and, with a strong kick on the edge of the cliff to give me additional impetus, I went spinning out into space. For an age, as it seemed to me, I sank rapidly; while that horrible feeling possessed me—the like of which people subject to sea-sickness feel as the ship drops away beneath them into the trough of the sea—of falling away from my own stomach. And then, just as my strength seemed to be failing, and my hold on the bar loosing, I perceived that I was rising again; and this put a little fresh heart in me, and I tightened my grip on the bar. Ten seconds, no doubt, was the full extent of the time that my passage consumed; but it seemed to me then, and it seems to me still as I think of it, a long ten years. And a thrill of terror goes through me as I think also of how near I then came to a horrible death; for at the very moment that I reached the farther side of the cañon there was a little tinkling sound in the air above me, and the bar that I held was twitched out of my hands, and then came a loud jingling of metal on rock, and as I turned quickly I saw a gleam of sunlight catch the great chain as it went twisting downward into the black gulf below.

CHAPTER XV

THE TEMPLE IN THE CLOUDS

Doubtless the violent strain to which the chain had been subjected by El Sabio's kicking and plunging had loosened the fastenings, centuries old, which held it to the rock; for the chain had not broken, but had come away entire. I sank down on the rock as weak with terror as the poor ass had been; and like him I drank greedily of water, and panted for a while, and at last found my courage coming back to me.

Yet my case was a happy one compared with that of Fray Antonio. Howsoever narrow my escape had been, the fact remained that I had come out from my encounter with Death safe and unharmed; but on Fray Antonio's shoulder we could but dread that Death already had laid his hand. And that he knew how close to him Death was standing we could see by a certain elate and confident air of courage in his bearing, and by the wonderful tenderness and sweetness of his smile. Truly, never did I know a man so ready at all times as this man was to lay down the life that God had given him; holding it but as a trust that might at any moment be called back to the source whence it came. Yet because it was a trust, meant to be put to useful purposes, Fray Antonio valued his life and cared for it. And at this time it was he himself who devised a plan by which it might be saved.

The ropes which were fastened to the chain, being held stoutly on the one side by Fray Antonio and on the other by Young, fortunately had broken as the great weight of the chain suddenly had come upon them, and had broken so close to the knots which held them that nearly the whole of their length remained. The plan that the monk now devised for coming across to us—and a bold heart was required even to think of this daring enterprise—was that with the two ropes fastened about his body at one end, and held by all of us at the other, he should swing down into the chasm and far under the promontory of rock on which we stood, and then that we should haul him up to us. The great difficulty in the way of executing this plan was in getting the line across between us; its great danger lay in the probability— notwithstanding the depth of the recess beneath us—that he would be dashed against the rocks with such force as to kill him outright.

But Young, who usually was ready for any emergency that might arise, roused out a ball of twine that was a part of our stores, and one end of this he made fast to a fragment of rock, and by a strong heave of it landed it safe on the other side; whereafter the rigging of the double rope across was an easy matter.

Very carefully, testing the knots as he made them, Fray Antonio fastened the double line about his body, beneath his shoulders, and so stood ready on the edge of the chasm; while we four stood holding the line, with all our muscles braced for the strain that would come upon it as he swung downward. For a moment he paused, with his face turned upward while his lips moved. Then he waved his hand, and smiled as he called across to us, "It is as God wills!" and so dropped away from the ledge, and like a flash went down beyond our range of sight.

We felt the jar on the ropes as his body struck against the face of the cliff far below us, and the reflex action as he swung out again, and thereafter the slower motion of the ropes as he swayed back and forth dangling over that black and awful chasm. And as the ropes settled into steadiness we drew him up towards us; yet dreaded, because of the dull weight of it, and because no assuring cry came up to us, that what we lifted was a corpse.

And, in truth, as we raised the body of Fray Antonio over the edge of the cliff it seemed as though this dread were realized; for a great bloody gash was upon his temple, and his limbs were limp and lifeless, and his face was deathly pale. At sight of which there came into my heart a bursting pain, as though some one had stabbed me there; and there were tears in Young's eyes; and Rayburn gave vent to his sorrow in a great curse that was half a groan. As for Pablo, whom no danger could daunt, and who would bear without flinching any hurt of his own, this dreadful sight so moved him that he fainted dead away.

Yet even in the moment that such deep sorrow seemed to be settling down upon us, Fray Antonio slightly moved his lips, and there came forth from them a low faint sigh—whereupon Young jumped up with a shout and relieved his mind by administering to Pablo a hearty kick, which he accompanied with the remark: "You infernal fool of a Greaser Indian, what do you mean by swoundin'? He ain't dead at all!"

As tenderly as I could for the trembling of my hands, I washed away the blood from about the cut and bathed Fray Antonio's pale face, while Rayburn gave him a sup of whiskey from his flask. And then, presently, his eyes opened and energy came into his body once more. In a little while he was on his feet again, and as well as ever, save for the smarting of his cut, and in his head a dizziness and a dull throbbing pain. Just what had happened he could not tell. He knew that he had struck against the rock with his feet, as he had planned to do; but he must have swung around, when the force of the impact had been thus partly broken, and struck his head against some sharp projection, and so have been cut and stunned. But it made no great difference how his hurt had come to him, since it had not proved to be a deadly one; therefore we forbore to question him further concerning it, and sought by quiet talk, that led softly into silence, to take his thoughts away from the peril that he had been in. Indeed, we all were glad to rest quietly where we were for the night, for our bodies were tired and our nerves were racked and strained.

We should have been most thankful for a big potful of coffee, but there was no wood with which we could make a fire. The best that we could do, and there was not much comfort in it, was to chew some coffee grains after we had made a supper upon one of our few remaining tins of meat; and then we rolled ourselves in our blankets and lay down upon the bare rock. And I must say that if anybody had asked me at that moment if archæology was a study that paid for the trouble that it cost, I should have said most unhesitatingly that it was not.

Even sleep, which I greatly needed, and for which I earnestly longed, did not come to me easily; for each time that I seemed to be dropping gently away into unconsciousness I would be roused by the feeling that I was holding fast to the chain again, and so was sliding down the long curve among the shadows, with the great walls of the cañon towering infinitely above me, and with the black depth below. And in my sleep I made again the dreadful passage, and heard the clinking of the chain as it parted, and the rattle of it as it struck the rocks, and felt the grasp of Rayburn as he caught me, just as the bar was twitched out of my hands—and so woke to find Young shaking me, and to hear him say: "There's no earthly sense in your kickin' around that way, Professor; an', anyhow, it's time t' get up. It's just a wonder how these Mexican mornin's put life into a man. Why, there's a freshness in th' air that's goin' t' waste in this cañon that's fit t' make a coffin stand right up on end an' dance a jig!"

Even Fray Antonio, but for the soreness of his hurt, felt strong and well; and we ate another tin of meat—which was much less than we wanted to eat—and so started along the path hewn out of the side of the cliff; and what with the brightness and joyfulness of the morning, we certainly were in much higher spirits than was at all reasonable in the case of men who had had such close companionship with Death so short a time before, and who still stood a very fair chance of dying dismally of starvation. The knowledge that, by the falling of the chain, our retreat had been again cut off did not at all trouble us. Even could we have crossed the cañon, and so have retraced our steps, we could have gone no farther than the valley of the lake; and we could as well die here as there. And we were stayed by the reasonable conviction that the path which we were travelling upon certainly would lead us out of the mountains at last—even if it did not lead us to the hidden city that we sought.

For five or six miles we doubled on our course of the day before, going back along the cañon and seeing the path that we had followed a little below us on the other side; then, by a very easy grade, our course began to ascend, and went on rising until the other path was so far below us that it ceased to be distinguishable. Thus we came to within a few hundred feet of the top of the cliffs, when a sudden turn to the left carried us into a narrow cleft in the rock. Here the path was very sharply inclined upward for a little way; and for the remainder of the distance to the top we ascended a long series of rudely cut steps, so steep that our legs fairly cracked under us as we neared the end of them.

But we forgot our weariness as we came out upon the summit at last, and a great view of clouds and mountain peaks burst upon us; the like of which I never have seen approached save by the view out over the Gunnison country from the crest of the Marshall Pass. But here we saw all around us what there is seen only in one direction; for we were on a vastly high, square crest—very like that called the Gigante, which the traveller by the Mexican Central Railroad sees to the left as he nears Silao—and clouds and mountain peaks rose up about us on every side.

But we did not long contemplate this heroic landscape, for a cloud, which almost enveloped us as we finished our ascent of the stair, was swept still farther away by the brisk wind then blowing; so that suddenly a vast building loomed largely through the flying vapor, and in a moment was clear and distinct before our eyes. To find upon this bare mountain-top, among cloud solitudes so profound as these, such overpowering evidence of the labor and strength of man, sent thrilling through our breasts a wonder that was akin to awe. It seemed unreal, impossible, that in such a place such work could be accomplished; and the very tangible reality of it made it seem to me one of those prodigies of man's creation which old stories tell of as having been wrought by a league with the devil and at the cost of a human soul.

Had there been any signs at all of human life about this solemn and majestic building, or upon the mountain-top whereon it stood, the chilling hold that it took upon our imaginations would have been less strong. What wrought upon us was the deadly silence, and the absolute stillness of everything save the drifting clouds. It seemed to us as though we had come out from the living world and our own time into a dead region belonging to a long dead past; and I remembered with a shudder that we had entered this region through that gloomy cavern, where hundreds of the ancient dead were clustered in silent worship about the great silent idol carved in everlasting stone. It seemed as though some evil spell hung over us, that doomed us forever to wander in wild solitudes—which were the more appalling because constantly uprose before us tangible evidence of the strong current of eager human life that had pulsed through them in former times. Young but put into his own rough language the thought that was in all our hearts when he declared, with a great oath, that for the sake of getting safe out of this lonely hole he'd contract to fight Indians three days in every week for the rest of his life, and be glad to do it for the comfort of having somebody around who was alive.

CHAPTER XVI

AT THE BARRED PASS

The whole top of the mountain, near a mile square, had been so levelled by nature that little remained to be done for its further smoothing by the hand of man. But the amount of work that had gone into the mere preparation for the building of the great temple was almost incredible. In the centre of the plateau a pyramidal mass of rock near a thousand feet square, of a piece with the mountain itself, had been so shaped and hewn that it rose in three great terraces to the square apex on which the temple stood. These terraces slanted upward, surrounding the pyramid by a continuously ascending way that had its beginning and its ending in the centre of the eastern front—so that, allowing for the diminishing size of the pyramid, the distance by this way from the bottom to the top of it was more than a mile and a half.

"It just took a slow-goin', lazy heathen Greaser t' think out a thing like this," Young observed as we went up the path. "Now, if th' Congregationalists that I was brought up among had put a church on a place like this—an' they wouldn't have been likely t' be fools enough t' do anything of th' sort—they'd 'a' had a set of steps runnin' smack from th' bottom t' th' top, an' folks would have got up in no time. It's just th' Greaser fashion all over t' spend a hundred years or so in makin' a path five miles long around a hill about as high as th' Boston State-house, so's they can get up it easy an' save their wind. But I wish they'd put in drinkin' fountains along th' road. I'm as thirsty as a salt cod—an' there's so precious little water left in th' keg that I'm afraid t' begin at it for fear of suckin' it all up."

"Drinking fountains?" Rayburn, who was a little in advance, called back to us. "Well, so they did. Come along and drink as much as you want to."

"Cut that, Rayburn," Young answered. "I'm too dead in earnest about my being thirsty to stand any foolin'."

"I'm not fooling"—we had caught up with him by this time—"look for yourself."

To which Young's only reply was to spring forward eagerly

and drink a long deep draught from a stone basin beside the path into which trickled a tiny stream from above. Finding water in this unlikely place was as great a surprise as it was a joy to us; for we all longed for it, yet dared not drink freely because our supply was nearly gone. It was touching to hear the long sigh of happiness that El Sabio gave when at last he lifted his dripping snout out of the basin; and then to see the look that he gave Pablo, as though to thank him for so blessedly plentiful a drink. In truth, the Wise One had not tasted a drop of water for nearly twenty-four hours—not since his perilous passage of the cañon—and his throat, and his poor little inside generally, must have been very dry.

When we came out on the top of the pyramid at last, which at that moment was wrapped in clouds almost as dense as London fog, we perceived the ingenious plan that had been adopted in order to secure water plentifully on this mountain-top. By careful scoring of the rock with many little channels, all leading to a cistern that seemed to be of great dimensions, the warm vapor of the clouds as it condensed into water on touching the chill stone surface was captured and safely stored away. And from the overflow of the cistern the fountain below was fed.

But we did not stop to examine very carefully into this matter, so eager were we to press on to the temple close before us. This stood upon a terraced platform, cut from the living rock, and was a perfectly plain structure—with walls slightly receding inward as they rose, and wholly destitute of ornamentation. For its majestic effect it depended upon its great size and upon its admirable proportions; and being built of the dark rock of which the mountain was formed, and having about it much of the sombre feeling that characterizes Egyptian architecture, it had an air of great solemnity and gloom.

In silence we ascended the short flight of steps that led to the broad, doorless entrance—the only opening through the massive walls—and so came into the vast shadowy hall that these great walls enclosed. From front to back of this hall extended many rows of stone pillars—like the single row found in the great chamber among the ruins of Mitla—and by these were upheld the huge slabs of stone of which the roof was made. Far away from where we stood, down at the end of a long vista of pillars, was a stone altar on which was carved in stone a colossal figure of the god Chac-Mool. Looking back through the open entrance, I saw a break in the mountain peaks to the eastward; and so perceived that the first rays of the rising sun must needs enter here and strike full upon the disk that was poised in the figure's hands. As Pablo caught sight of the great idol recumbent there, a momentary shudder went through him and he made certain motions with his hand before his eyes that were strange to me.

As we drew near to the altar we found that in front of it was a sacrificial stone, still darkly stained where blood had flowed upon it; and beneath the stone neck-yoke, still resting there, was a withered remnant of human vertebræ. There was something very ghastly in finding—preserved by the very stone that had held him down while life was let out of him—this mere scrap of the last human victim who had perished here. As in the desolate valley, so also on this desolate mountain-top, the only proof that human life ever had been here was found in proof of human death.

Save that our curiosity was gratified, and the blessing of the water which we found, our ascent of the great pyramid and our examination of the temple bore no fruit. Young, who still seemed to think that tilting up and disclosing secret passages was an attribute of all statues of the god Chac-Mool, was here again convinced that his generalization from a single case was not a sound one. In a serious way—that in itself would have been laughable but for the gloom of our surroundings—he climbed upon the altar and sat first on the head of the god, and then on his feet, and even tried the effect of seating himself upon the stone disk that the god upheld above his navel. But through all of these experiments the stone figure remained solidly immovable.

"I guess there was only one o' that tippin' kind," Young said, at last, "an' he sort o' flocked by himself. Let's get out of here, anyway. If this ever was the Aztec bank that we're lookin' for, there must have been a prehistoric run on it that cleaned it out. They must have done that sort o' thing in old times, eh, Professor? But it don't make much difference to us now what they did or what they didn't; an' we'd better fill up with water an' get out—that is, if there is any way of gettin' out except along the way we came. There's no good in goin' back that way. It would be better t' settle down here an' starve comfortably without wearin' out shoe-leather doin' it. But I don't mean t' do that until I've had a look all around th' top of this god-forsaken mountain, an' made sure that there's only one way down."

My own thoughts had been dwelling on the possibility that Young's words expressed; for at this definite point to which we had come, the path that we had come by very reasonably might end—so leaving us in this lonely region among the clouds to die slowly for lack of food. And there was a certain fitness in our having made our way so far among the dead only ourselves to die that added sombre fancies to our environment of sombre realities. Yet there was a heartiness in Young's resolutely expressed determination to search for a way out of our difficulties before at all yielding to them that insensibly cheered me. His words had a plucky ring to them; and bravery is as catching as is fear.

Our empty water-kegs were at the bottom of the pyramid, and when we reached the fountain on our downward way we waited there while Pablo went on with El Sabio and fetched them up to us. There was at least solid comfort in knowing, as we went on downward with the kegs all filled, that, whatever other death might come to us, at least we could not die of thirst. At the bottom of the pyramid we left Fray Antonio and Pablo, with El Sabio and the packs, and the three of us set out to explore the three sides of the mountain-top that were unknown to us in search of a downward path. A heavy mass of clouds had drifted over the mountain again, so thick that at a rod away all was white mist around us; and the light was growing faint, for the day had come nearly to an end. Indeed, had we been upon the lower levels of the earth night would have been already upon us.

Making my way along the edge of the precipice, where the plateau broke sheer off, was ticklish work; and half humorous, half melancholy thoughts went through my mind touching the absurdity of an ex-professor of Topical Linguistics in the University of Michigan being thus employed in path-hunting upon a lonely mountain-top in Mexico. Truly, adversity brings us strange bedfellows; but far stranger are the straits into which a man comes who takes up with the study of archæology at first-hand. But my path-hunting was without result, for nowhere along the edge of the plateau was there a break fit for the descent of any creature save such as had wings. At the end of near an hour the clouds once more lifted; and then I saw Rayburn coming towards me, but with a serious look upon his face that told that he also had been unsuccessful in his search.

"It has rather a bad look, Professor," he said, briefly, when I had told him that along all the face of the mountain that I had examined the rock went down sheer. He filled his pipe and lighted it, and we walked back to the base of the pyramid in silence, while he smoked.

Young had not returned; but presently we heard a shout that had so hopeful a sound in it as to start us both to our feet and forth to meet him.

"Have you found a way down?" Rayburn called, as he came nearer to us.

"You bet I have," he called back; "and, what's more, I've seen somethin' to eat."

"*Seen* something!" Rayburn answered, as he joined us. "Why the dickens didn't you *get* it?"

"Well, because it was better'n a mile away from me. It looked like a mountain sheep, as well as I could make out; but there it was for sure; an' thinkin' how good that critter will taste roasted has given me a regular twistin' pain all through my empty inside! But th' point is that down on that side o' th' mountain there's game; I saw birds, too, but I couldn't make out what they were; an', somehow, it looks different down there. It don't look like these d—n dead places we've been prowlin' through for more'n a coon's age. It looks as if God remembered it, an' it was *alive*! Why, th' very smell that came up had somethin' good about it; an' there was a different taste to th' air. I tell you, Rayburn, I didn't know what a lonely an' mis'rable an' lost chump sort of a way I was in until I looked over there into that place where th' whole business ain't run by dead folks. An' what's more, Professor, that's the trail for us; for, right where it starts down, there's th' King's symbol an' th' arrow, all reg'lar, blazed on th' rock."

"Is the trail good enough to make a start on now?" Rayburn asked; "we won't have more than half an hour more light, but I'd give a lot to get off this mountain before dark, and every foot down that we go we'll be that much warmer. We'd stand a pretty fair chance of freeing up here to-night without any fire."

"Th' trail's all right for a good half-mile, anyway," Young answered; "an' I guess it's good all th' way. It's pretty much th' same as th' one we come up by, an' that's good enough, where it don't jump cañons, t' go along in th' dark; but we must rustle if we mean t' do much by daylight."

We were back at the pyramid by this time, and we found Fray Antonio very willing to be off with us that we might try to get well down the mountain before night set in; for at that great elevation the quick beating of his heart added very sensibly to the throbbing pain of his wound. Therefore we lost no time in getting our packs upon our backs, and upon the back of El Sabio, and briskly started downward; and the keen cold that came into the air, as the sun sunk away behind the mountain peaks at last, warned us that it was safer to take the risks of a descent almost in darkness than to stay for the night upon that bleak mountain-top without a fire.

In twenty minutes we perceived a comforting change in the temperature; and at the end of an hour—during the last half of which we walked slowly and cautiously through the fast-thickening darkness—there was enough warmth in the air about us to make camping for the night endurable. But we still were at a great elevation, and the thin air was bitingly keen, and all the more so because of the scant meal that we had to comfort us and to put strength into us before we wrapped ourselves in our blankets for sleep.

"What's a mis'rable two pounds of corned-beef among five of us," Young exclaimed, in a tone of angry contempt, "when every man in th' lot is hungry enough t' eat th' whole of it, an' th' tin box it comes in, an' then go huntin' for a square meal? An' t' think o' that sheep I saw! I say, Rayburn, did you ever eat a roast fore-shoulder of mutton, with onions an' potatoes baked under it, an' a thick gra—"

"If you don't hold your jaw about things like that," Rayburn struck in, "I'll murder you!"—and there was such fierceness in his voice, and he truly was such a savage fellow when his anger was up, that Young was half frightened by his outburst, and so was silent. I must say that I wish that he had altogether held his tongue; for, somehow, the smell of mutton and onions and potatoes, all cooking together, was so strong in my nostrils, and this smell so set to yearning my very hollow inside, that it was a long while before I could sleep at all; and when I did sleep, it was to be pursued by dreams of painful hungriness which were but too surely founded in painful fact. Certainly, it was very indiscreet in Young, to say the least of it, to make a remark of that nature at that untoward time.

However, that was the last day that we suffered for want of food. I was awakened in the very early morning by the sound of a rifle-shot, and sprang to my feet, brandishing my revolver, with a confused belief in my sleepy mind that we were attacked by Indians again; and, truly, my first feeling was one of pleasure at the thought of meeting, even in deadly combat, with men who were alive.

"It's all right, Professor," Rayburn said. "We're not fighting anybody. But I've killed a mountain sheep, and if we only can get him we'll have a solid breakfast, even if we have to eat him raw. He was over on that point of rock, and he's tumbled down clear into the valley, and the sooner we get down there and hunt for him the better."

In the bright light of the early morning we could see below us a glad little valley, in which trees and grass grew, and in the centre of which was a tiny lake. But what gave as most joy was seeing birds flying over the face of the water, and half a dozen mountain sheep scampering away at the sound of Rayburn's shot. Truly, the sight of these live creatures was the most cheery that ever came to my eyes; and as I beheld them, and realized that at last we had emerged from the dreary, death-stricken region in which as it seemed to me we had spent years, a great wave of happiness rolled in upon and filled my heart. As it was with me, so was it with the others: who gave sighs of gladness as thus they found themselves no longer wanderers among the chill shades of ancient death, but once more moving in the warm living world.

The path, cut out along the mountain-side, went downward by a sharper grade than that by which we had ascended; and we descended it joyfully at a swinging trot, with a new life in us that made us break out into lively talk and laughter that set the echoes to ringing. And presently, in a very jerky fashion because of his rapid motion, Pablo piped away on his mouth-organ with "Yankee Doodle"—and this was the first time that he had had the heart to play upon his beloved "instrumentito" since our passage of the lake beneath which lay the city of the dead.

In an hour we came fairly down into that bright and lovely valley, where was the sweet sound of birds calling to each other, and the glad sight of these live creatures flying through the air. As for the sheep that Rayburn had killed, he was knocked pretty well into a jelly by his half-mile or so of tumble down the mountain-side. But we were not disposed to be over-fastidious, and we quickly had his ribs roasting over a brisk fire: that yet was not so brisk as was our hunger, for we began to eat before the meat was much more than warmed through. When our ravening appetite was appeased a little, Young got out the coffee-pot and set to making coffee. And then, with meat well cooked and coffee in abundance, we made such a meal as can be made only by half-starved men who suddenly have come forth from the dark shadows of threatening death into the glad sunshine of safety. Of what further perils might be in store for us we neither cared nor thought. Our one strong feeling was the purely animal joy bred of deliverance from gloom and danger, and the packing of our bellies with hearty food.

When, at last, our huge meal was ended, we settled back upon our blankets, and fell to smoking. Presently Rayburn gave a prodigious yawn and laid aside his pipe. "I think I'll take a nap," he said. I saw that Young already was nodding and that Pablo had sunk down into slumber; while El Sabio, who had come even closer to starving than we had come, most thankfully rummaged among the rich grass. My eyes were heavy, and I stretched myself out on my blankets, with the warm sunshine comforting my stiffened body, and presently sunk softly into delicious sleep.

I partly woke a few minutes later, as Fray Antonio rose, thinking that we all were lost in slumber, and walked a little apart from us. He alone had made a meal in reasonable moderation, and I saw now that he had gone aside to pray. For a moment the thought stirred in me that I would join him in what I knew was his thanksgiving for our deliverance; but sleep had too strong a hold upon me, and my body slowly fell hack upon the blankets and my eyes slowly closed, carrying into my slumber the sight on which they last had rested: the monk kneeling upon the grass beside a great gray rock, with clasped hands and face turned upward, pouring his soul out in grateful prayer.

It was well on in the afternoon when we all woke again; and Young's first remark was that it must be about supper-time. Rayburn fell in with this notion promptly, and so did I myself—rather to my astonishment, for it seemed unreasonable that after such a stuffing I should desire to eat so soon again. But we did make a supper almost as hearty as our breakfast had been, and in a little while wrapped ourselves in our blankets, with our feet towards the heaped-up fire, and went off once more to sleep, and slept through until sunrise of the following day. In truth, the mental strain, bred of our gloomy surroundings and of the dread of starvation that had possessed us, had taxed our physical strength more severely than our mountain climbing and our lack of nourishment. The great amount of strong food that we ate, and our long slumber, showed nature's demand upon us that our waste of tissue should be made good.

When we woke again on the second morning, we all were fresh and strong and eager to press onward. There was little left of the sheep to carry with us; but Rayburn shot half a dozen birds, some species of duck, as we skirted the lake in our passage across the valley, so there was no fear that we should lack for food. At its western end the valley narrowed into a cañon. There was no choice of paths, for this was the sole outlet, and we were assured that we were on the right path by finding the King's symbol and the pointing arrow carved upon the rook. The cañon descended very rapidly, and by noon we were so far below the level of the Mexican plateau that the air had a tropical warmth in it; and so warm was the night—for all the afternoon we continued to descend—that we had no need for blankets when we settled ourselves for sleep.

Rayburn was of the opinion that we were close upon the Tierra Caliente, the hot lands of the coast; and when we resumed our march in the morning he went on in advance of the rest of us, that he might maintain a cautious outlook. If he were right in his conjecture as to our whereabouts, we might at any moment come upon hostile Indians. It was towards noon that he came softly back to us and bade us lay down our packs and advance silently with him, carrying only our arms. "There's something queer ahead; and I thought that I heard voices," he explained. "But there must be no shooting unless we are shot at. Some of these Indians are friendly, and we don't want to start a row with them if they are willing not to row with us."

The cañon was very narrow at this point, and high above us its walls drew so closely together that the shadows about us were deep. As we rounded a bend in it, the rock closed above our heads in a great arch, so that we were in a sort of natural tunnel; at the far end of which was a bright spot showing that a wide and sunny open space was beyond. But over this opening were bars which cut sharply against the light, as though a gigantic spider had spun there a massive web; and as we drew nearer to this curious barrier we saw beyond it a broad and glorious valley, rich with all manner of luxuriant tropical growth and flooded everywhere with the warm light of the sun.

We approached the strange barrier cautiously, and our wonder at it was increased as we found that it was made of the bright metal of which we had found so many specimens; and still more we wondered as we found that the bars were fastened on the side from which we approached, so that we could remove them easily, while from the side of the valley they presented an impassable barrier. In strong excite-ment we drew out the metal pins which dropped into slots cut in the rock and so held the bars fast, and in a few minutes we had cleared the way for our advance. Just as we were making ready to pass through the opening we heard the sound of voices; and as we quickly drew back into the shadows two men sprang up suddenly before us, and cried in wonder as they saw that the lower bars across the opening were gone. Yet the expression upon their faces was not that of anger; rather did they seem to be stirred by a strong feeling of joy with which was also awe. Both men were accoutred in the fashion which the pictured records show was usual with the Aztec warriors, and one of them—as was indicated by his head-dress and by the metal corselet that he wore—was a chief; and they challenged us sharply, yet with gladness in their tones, in the Aztec tongue.

So sudden and so ringing was this challenge, and so startling was the uprising of the men before us, that as we sprang back into the shadow we instinctively stood ready with our arms. But Fray Antonio, not having any intent to join in the fight, was cooler than the rest of us, and instantly perceived that fighting was not necessary. Therefore he it was who first spoke to these strangers; and his first word to them was, "Friends!"

Then the watchmen, for such they seemed to be, spoke eagerly together for a moment, and pressed to the opening to look upon us; yet seeing us but dimly because of the dark shadows which surrounded us. Pablo was closest to them, and I marvelled to see how like them he was in look and in air. Him they first caught sight of, and as they saw him they both turned from the opening, and, as though calling to some one at a distance, gave both together a great glad shout. Instantly, at some little distance, the cry was repeated; and so again farther on and yet farther, with ever more voices joining in it; so that it swelled and strengthened into a great roar of rejoicing that seemed to sweep over the whole of the valley before us, and to fill it everywhere with tumultuous sounds of joy.

As though the duty that they were charged with had been thus accomplished, the men turned again to us, and he of the higher rank, speaking the Aztec language, yet with turns and changes in that tongue which were strange to me, eagerly called to us:

"Come forth to us! Come forth to us!" he cried. "Now is the prophecy of old fulfilled and the watch rewarded that our people have maintained from generation to generation through twenty cycles here at the grated way! Come forth to us, our brothers—who bring the promised message from our lord and king!"

I turned to Fray Antonio as these words were spoken, and I saw in his face that which made me confident in my own glad conviction that here at last was the secret place for which so long, and through such perils, we had sought. Here indeed had we found the hidden people of whom the dying Cacique had spoken and of whom the monk's letter had told; the strong contingent of the ancient Aztec tribe that ages since the wise King Chaltzantzin had saved apart, that when their strength was needed they might come forth to ward their weaker brethren against conquest by a foreign foe. And the great happiness begotten of this glad discovery filled all my body with a throbbing joy.

Yet as we went out through the opening that we had made between the bars, and the watchers saw us fairly in the sunlight, they sprang back as though in alarm. Rayburn met this demonstration promptly by making the peace-sign—raising aloft the right arm—that is common to all North American Indians; and after a moment of hesitation the chief answered to this in kind. So there was peace between us as we advanced; but it seemed to me that their regard of us now had in it more of wonder and less of awe.

CHAPTER XVII

OF OUR COMING INTO THE VALLEY OF AZTLAN

So unexpectedly had we come upon these strangers, and so marvellous was the finding thus of the hidden tribe for which we had sought so long, that I could not but dread, as we advanced towards the Aztec warriors, lest I should wake suddenly and find that it all was a dream. And they, also, as it seemed to me, looked upon us doubtingly, and with somewhat of dread in their regard, as though uncertain whether we were beings from another world, or men of flesh and blood like themselves.

Not until we were close upon them did further words—after that first challenge and answer—pass between us; and then the elder of the two, still making the peace-sign with his raised right hand, and speaking with a trembling in his voice, as though deep emotion moved him, called to us: "Have our brothers need of our strength? Bring ye the token that summons us to their aid?"

I should have been glad just then for opportunity to consult with my companions as to what answer I should make to these questions, for I perceived that our position was a very critical one, and that even our lives might depend upon the wisdom of my reply. For a moment I waited in the hope that Fray Antonio would make answer; but as he remained silent, there was nothing for it but that I should take the hazard upon myself. Therefore, bringing forth the ancient piece of gold from the snake-skin bag—for so I had carried it constantly, even as the Cacique had done before me, and others before him, for more than three hundred years—I held it towards the man who had spoken, and said, firmly: "Here is the token of summons left behind him by Chaltzantzin; but we come not to call you forth to battle, but to bring tidings that the fate which that wise king and prophet foresaw for his people, long since was fulfilled. In the time appointed, the stranger foemen overcame and enslaved your brethren, bringing to pass that which Chaltzantzin foretold; and the message that then was sent to call you forth to their aid reached you not, because even the wisdom of Chaltzantzin was powerless against the will of the gods. Yet the gods desired not to destroy your brethren, but to punish them; and their punishment now is at an end. Once more are they free, and once more is their ruler a wise and valiant man of their own race. Therefore, the news which we bring you is not sorrowful, but glad."

While I was thus speaking, the ringing cries which at the first alarm had sounded over all the valley grew louder and stronger; but as yet we saw only the two men who at the first had confronted us— for we were in a deep recess in the mountain, whence the ground dropped away in front, so that the immediate foreground was hid from us, and we saw only some distant meadows, and then a broad lake, and over this more meadows and a sweep of heavy timber, and back of all great mountains rising against the clear blue sky.

But as my speech ended, and before those to whom it was addressed at all had digested the wonder of it, and so hesitated in their reply, a half-dozen men and a woman or two came in sight in the narrow way before us, panting after their rapid ascent of the acclivity; and the calls of others pressing up the slope behind them sounded loudly, and in a very little while a crowd of a hundred or more pressed about us, all gazing at us and questioning us with a most eager surprise. For the most part these seemed to be laborers from the near-by fields; for many of them carried agricultural implements, and their bare legs and arms were splashed with mud and were grimy of the soil. As for the look of them, save that the flowing garments of cotton cloth which the women wore were embroidered in a fanciful fashion, I could not have distinguished these people from the tallest and strongest of the Indians dwelling in the hot lands of the coast about Vera Cruz. The men, who wore only a cloth twisted about their loins, were as magnificent fellows as I ever saw. Every one of them was tall and straight, with broad shoulders and narrow hips, and the muscles of their arms and legs stood out like cords. From Pablo, who was an unusually tall and well-formed lad, they differed only in the color of their skins— which were decidedly darker than his, as was to be expected in the case of men dwelling in this tropical region at the level of the sea.

Towards Pablo these people manifested a familiar curiosity quite unlike their reverential manner towards the rest of us, who so obviously were not of their own race. And Pablo was as much perplexed by their questions as they were by his answers; for never was a conversation carried on so hopelessly at cross-purposes. Our boy, being spoken to by folk who obviously were as entirely Mexicans as he was himself, and in a tongue that practically was that which he had been born to—for the Indians dwelling in the Guadalajara suburb of Mexicalcingo, being the direct descendants of a pure Aztec stock, speak the Nahua language very correctly—could not at all realize that he was at last among the ancient race for which we had searched so long. It was his belief that we had come out, in accordance with Rayburn's forecast, into the coast country, and that the people around him were the ordinary dwellers in the hot lands. And the Aztecs, knowing him to be one of themselves, no doubt believed that he knew of the purpose for which they had been left to dwell apart, and so plied him with questions concerning their brethren from whom through long ages they had been separated.

As their talk went on, getting the more involved with every question and reply, a tendency towards ill-temper began to develop itself on each side; for Pablo considered that these people, who professed to be ignorant of so important a city as Guadalajara, were making game of him; and they were not less disposed to believe that he either was answering them falsely or that he was a fool. Fortunately, before any harm came of these misunderstandings, an interruption brought a temporary end to their talk.

There was a stir among the crowd, and then an opening was made in it, through which came an elderly man wearing military trappings similar to, but much handsomer than those worn by the two warriors whom we had first encountered; and it was obvious, from the air of deference with which these saluted him, that he was their superior officer. In spite of the dignity of his demeanor it was evident that he was greatly excited by our advent, and his voice quivered and broke a little as he asked us who we were and whence we came. As I repeated what I had already told the guard, and showed the gold token, the expression upon his face was that of extreme perplexity. That the gold token gave us a strong claim upon his respect, almost upon his reverence, was apparent in his manner as I showed it to him; but the conditions under which it was presented obviously rendered him very uncertain as to what action was proper for him to take.

When I had finished my statement, and had returned the token to its place in the snake-skin bag (for the wisdom of carefully retaining this potent talisman in our possession was evident), the officer turned to the two warriors, and they conversed for a while in low tones apart from us. Of their talk I could catch only a few words, but several times I heard repeated the name Itzacoatl, and frequent reference was made to the Twenty Lords. I gathered, too, that the name of the officer was Tizoc, and that the name of the elder of the two warriors, a swarthy man, was Ixtlilton. In the mean time, out of respect to the officer, the crowd had drawn away from us—being now swelled to very considerable numbers—but those composing it gazed at us in wonder, and among them was a steady murmur of low talk, like the buzzing of a hive of bees.

When his conference with the warriors was ended, Tizoc approached us, and with him came a younger man, who carried a roll of paper in his hand. The face of the officer still wore a troubled, doubting expression, and these feelings were expressed also in the tones of his voice as he spoke to us. "For the coming of the token from our lord Chaltzantzin we who dwell in this Valley of Aztlan have waited through many ages," he said; "but the promise was given that the token should come to us from our brethren in the time of their need, and should be brought by those of our own race. But you tell us that the time of need long since is past, and ye who bring the token are of a race that is strange to us; and even this one among you who seems to be of our brethren speaks strangely of strange things. Had ye come in the way that long past was promised, there would have been no room for questioning your right of entry here nor your authority over us; and I, who am the Warden of the Pass—being in right succession from him whom our lord Chaltzantzin appointed to this high office—would have been the first to do you reverence and honor. But in this strange case that has arisen I hold it to be my duty to send news of your coming to the Priest Captain, Itzacoatl, that he and his Council of the Twenty Lords may decide what now is right to do. In this I mean no disrespect and no unkindness; and while we await the Priest Captain's orders I shall have the pleasure to offer you that rest and refreshment of which you stand in need."

To this firm but courteous speech I was in the act of replying in fit terms of equal courtesy—for all that Tizoc had said was so reasonable that no exception could be taken to it—when an outburst on Young's part interrupted me.

"Hold on there, young fellow!" he cried. "I'll be shot if I'm goin' t' stand bein' made a fool of that way! If you can't make a better likeness of me than that, you'd better shut up shop an' go out of th' business."

I turned quickly, and saw Young standing beside Tizoc's attendant, and looking half angrily and half laughingly at the sheet of paper that he held in his hand. Fearful that some harm might come from Young's maladroitness, I joined them quickly; and only a strong sense of the gravity of our situation restrained me from laughing outright as I behold the cause of his wrath. For the secretary, as I now perceived him to be, had made sketches in color of each member of our party; and while they all did violence to our vanity, that of Young—with a bald head out of all proportion to the size of his body, and with most aggressively red hair—was so outrageous a caricature that there really was some justice in his resentment of it.

But this was not a time when resentment could be safely manifested, and I hurriedly explained to Young that these pictures, no doubt, were to be transmitted as a part of the report that Tizoc was about to make to the King concerning us, and that he must find no fault with them.

"He's goin' t' send that thing t' th' King an' say it's me, is he? No, he's not—not by a jugful! See here, Professor! here's a photograph that I had taken last spring in Boston. I meant t' give it to a girl before I came away, but she went back on me an' I didn't. It's not much of a photograph, but it don't look like a squash trimmed with red clover. If they want to send anything, let 'em send that." And before I could stop him, Young had taken the photograph out of his pocket-book and had handed it to the secretary, with the remark, "Just say t' him, Professor, that he is t' give that t' th' King, an' tell him t' tell th' King that Mr. Seth Young, of Boston, sends it with his compliments."

After all, no harm came of this absurd performance, but rather good; for the secretary exhibited the photograph to Tizoc, and both of them, and the two warriors also, were lost in wonder at its marvellous likeness to the original, and evidently held us in increasingly great respect because we were the possessors of such an extraordinary work of art. Young was a good deal chagrined, however, because the picture of him that the secretary had drawn was forwarded as a part of Tizoc's despatches. He said that since he had set up a good likeness of himself, it wasn't the square thing to send the King a bad one.

When the secretary, bearing the despatches, had departed, Tizoc requested us to accompany him to the near-by guard-house, where we could refresh ourselves by bathing, and where food and drink would be provided for us. This order, for such it was, we obeyed gladly; for we were both weary and hungry, and the prospect of what

Young described as a good wash and a square meal after it, was very pleasing to us. A detachment of men from the guard-house, accoutred in the same handsome fashion as Ixtlilton and his companion, had arrived while the secretary's portrait-work was in progress; and I observed that all of these guardsmen (excepting only Ixtlilton, whose skin was dark,) were much lighter in color and more gracious in bearing than the men in the crowd around us. So marked, indeed, was this difference that they seemed scarcely to belong to the same race.

As we moved away through the opening that the crowd made for us, with a platoon of guardsmen in advance, and another in our rear, Pablo touched my arm and was about to speak to me; but before his mouth could open there sounded suddenly from the hollow way in the mountain behind us a mighty bray. "Ah, the little angel!" Pablo cried. "Hearken to him, señor, calling to me." And so moved was Pablo by this evidence of El Sabio's affection that only my firm grasp upon his arm restrained him from attempting a dash through the guards to where the creature was penned in by the metal bars.

Truly, there is no sound more terrifying to those who are strangers to it than the braying of an ass; therefore, I was not at all surprised that a very considerable part of the crowd incontinently took to its heels; and I needed no better evidence of the bravery of the guardsmen who composed our escort than the steadiness with which they faced about in readiness to meet whatever danger might come forth from the gap in the mountain in the wake of this great roaring. Yet what they saw there was only the mild face of the Wise One extended towards us through the opening in the bars.

To Tizoc, who was standing beside me, and who had not displayed even the slightest tremor of alarm as the appalling noise had broken upon us, I explained that the roaring creature was not harmful, but gentle and biddable; and I begged that other of the bars might be removed, so that it might come forth and join us. That he acceded instantly to my request gave me a good opinion of his own faithfulness and honesty; for a man of a suspicious and crafty nature assuredly would have believed that my request was but a trap laid for his destruction; and thereupon the bars were removed. And the truth of my words was made manifest, as El Sabio came instantly to Pablo and received his caresses with every sign of gentleness and affection. But even Tizoc did not disguise his wonder upon beholding this strange beast, for the largest four-footed creature in all that valley, as he told me, was a little animal of the deer species, that was not much bigger than a hare. And when I bade Pablo mount upon El Sabio's back, the look of surprise in Tizoc's face changed suddenly to an expression of troubled doubt, in which was also alarm. Under his breath I heard him mutter, "Can it be that the prophecy will be fulfilled?" But whatever the cause of his inward disturbance was, he spoke not of it, but turned once more forward, and gave the order to march.

The crowd, seeing that no harm was like to come to them, pressed forward once more, and gazed with open-mouthed wonder—and also, as it seemed to me, with awe—at the prodigious spectacle which Pablo, gravely riding upon the ass's back, presented to them. And so, with the guards before and behind us, we marched onward into the Valley of Aztlan.

CHAPTER XVIII

THE STRIKING OF A MATCH

As we emerged from the nook in the mountain-side the whole of the valley lay open before us, and never was a more lovely spot beheld by the eyes of man. A half-dozen leagues in front of us rose the great mountain wall which shut in its farther side, and about as far away to the right and to the left these walls swept around in vast curves and joined the cliffs through which we had come by the hollow way that tunnelled beneath them. A noble lake extended nearly the whole length of the valley, and covered near a third of its width, and so seemed less like a lake than like a calm and majestic river. From the water-side the land rose in broad terraces, broken by belts of timber and by many groups of smaller trees, which, because of the regularity of their growth, I took to be fruit plantations. All the open country seemed to be one vast garden, most carefully tended, and everywhere cut up by little canals, whence water for irrigation was drawn. Scattered everywhere about the valley were single houses embowered in trees, and from where we stood we could see also four or five little towns, which also were plentifully shaded. And on the lake many boats were passing, of which several were of a considerable size, and were fitted with curiously shaped sails. And all this exquisite tropical beauty of ample water and luxuriant foliage shone richly beneath the bright splendor of a deep blue tropical sky.

Yet that which most strongly attracted our attention was not this charming display of the manifold excellencies of God's handiwork, but rather a wonderful manifestation of the handiwork of man. Over against us, on the far side of the lake, slantingwise from where we stood, rose a mass of buildings of such vastness and such majestic design that at the first glance we took it to be one of the square-topped mountains which are found not uncommonly in this portion of the world, and around the bases of which are sloping heaps of the fragments of rock which have broken away through countless ages from their weather-worn sides. Yet in a moment we perceived that what we saw was a walled city built upon a great promontory, that jutted out from the mountain-side; and in the same breath Fray

Antonio and I called out together, "It is the city of Culhuacan!"

As we uttered this name Tizoc turned towards us quickly, and with a startled, troubled look upon his face. "They are not of our race," he said, as though speaking his thoughts aloud; "yet the sacred name, that among us only a few know, is known to them!" and the troubled look upon his face deepened as we went onward.

The way by which we descended was a narrow road carried zigzag down the cliff—for the pass by which we had entered the valley was fully six hundred feet above the level of the lake—and at short intervals along its course this road was defended by walls of very solid masonry, pierced with openings so narrow that only one man at a time could pass through them. That the walls were for defence was shown by the piles of metal bars on the inner side of each opening—the side towards the mountain—so arranged that in a moment they could be slipped into sockets in the stone-work, thus closing effectually the way.

Perceiving that we regarded with surprise this curious system of fortification, Tizoc explained: "These are the barriers set up against the Tlahuicos, who, heeding not the order given of old by our lord Chaltzantzin, have striven many times to break forth from the valley—for among these men there are many of perverse natures and evil minds."

In *tlahuico* I recognized a Nahua word that means "men turned towards the earth," but what its meaning might be in the sense in which Tizoc employed it I did not know. I should have asked for further explanation—for the manner of this man was so frank and so friendly that it invited a cordial familiarity—but as I was about to speak we passed through the narrow opening in a wall of unusual height and strength, and so came into a charming garden, in the midst of which stood a large house well built of stone. For the making of this garden a natural nook on the side of the mountain had been enlarged by filling in along its outer edge against a great retaining-wall, built up from a depth of a hundred feet from the slope below; and on the farther side of the plateau thus created, where the path down into the valley went on again, were heavy defensive walls. Near this exit, also, was a long low building that I took to be a guard-house.

The crowd that had followed behind us from the height above went on across the plateau, and out through the gate beside the guard-house—its members casting many curious looks at us as they departed—and the guardsmen who had formed our escort, at an order from Tizoc, went on to their quarters. But Tizoc led us across the garden to the large house that stood in the midst of it, and there, with a formal courtesy, bade us enter. This was his home, he said, and we were his welcome guests.

The house was so like the houses ordinarily found in Mexico that we had no feeling of strangeness in entering it. It was built of stone neatly laid in cement; was but a single story in height, and enclosed a large central court, in the midst of which a fountain sparkled, surrounded by small trees and shrubs and beds of flowers. All of the rooms opened upon this central court, and in the outer wall the only opening was the narrow way by which we had entered—for the prompt closing of which there lay in readiness a pile of metal bars. The flat roof, also of stone, was reached by a stone stair-way from the court, and had about it a heavy stone parapet that was pierced with narrow slits through which javelins and arrows could be discharged. But these arrangements for defence did not by any means produce a gloomy effect, as they would had we encountered them in a country-house in our own part of the world—for similar defence arrangements are found in every hacienda in Mexico at the present day, and even I, though my stay in the country had been so short, already had become accustomed to them.

A buzzing chatter of talk, in which women's voices predominated, ceased suddenly as we entered the court; and from the swaying and twitching of the curtains hanging in the front of the openings leading into several of the rooms, we inferred that we were undergoing a keen inspection. In response to a call from Tizoc, some men-servants came out from one of the rooms and received his order to prepare food for us; and he then led us to a large room in a corner of the court that was arranged very delightfully as a bath. Here was a great stone tank, twenty feet or so square, and with a slanting bottom, so that the depth of it ranged from two feet to nearly five, in which was fresh running water; and over the portion of the room that the tank occupied there was no roof but the bright blue sky. On the stone floor were beautifully woven mats, and towels of cotton cloth hung upon pegs driven into the walls, and in earthen bowls were fresh pieces of a saponaceous root that I have seen the like of in use among the Indians of New Mexico. It seemed to strike Tizoc as odd that we preferred to make use of the bath successively rather than all together; but he was too polite a man to interpose any objections to our eccentricities. Pablo only—coming last of all of us—had a companion in his bathing in the person of El Sabio; and the sleekness of that excellent animal, when Pablo had brushed carefully his long coat when his bath was ended, was a wonder to behold.

Being thus refreshed, we heartily welcomed the excellent meal that was served to us in the cool shade of the veranda by which the court-yard was surrounded. Our eating was somewhat in the Roman fashion, for the table was a broad slab of stone, raised but a little from the ground, and around it we reclined upon mats, with cushions woven of rushes to lean upon. The food was excellent—a small animal of the deer species, but no larger than a hare, roasted whole; birds very like quails, delicately broiled; little cakes made of maize, which were rather like the hoe-cakes of our Southern negroes than *tortillas*; some sort of sweet marmalade; and a great abundance of oranges, mangoes, bananas, and other fruits common to the hot lands of Mexico; all of which fruits were much more delicate in flavor than Mexican fruits usually are; the result, as we found later, of the great care bestowed upon their culture. Only water was served with the meal, but at the end of it a small jar of some sort of potent liquor was brought, very cool, and with an excellent spicy taste, that Tizoc warned us must be taken but sparingly; and truly he was right, as I found from the warm and mellow feeling of benevolent friendliness that but half a cup of it infused into me. Tizoc himself did not follow very rigidly the advice that he had given us; and to this fact, probably, was due the exceeding frankness with which he subsequently spoke with us concerning grave matters, of which he surely would have been reticent had he been in a less genial mood.

"Just ask th' Colonel if he minds my smokin' a pipe, won't you, Professor?" Young said, when our meal was ended; and as I myself wanted to smoke, and as I was sure that Rayburn did also, I made the request general. Tizoc, to my surprise—for I believed smoking to be common to all the indigenous races—evidently did not at all understand my meaning; but perceiving that I asked to have some favor granted, he courteously gave the permission that I desired. As we filled our pipes he watched us curiously; but when we drew out our matches and struck fire by what seemed to him but the turn of our hands, he started to his feet and manifested a strange excitement, in which there seemed to be less of alarm than of awe. His voice shook, and his whole person trembled, as he asked, "Are ye the children of Chac-Mool, the God of Fire, and therefore the chosen servants of Huitzilopochtli the Terrible, that ye thus can do what among us is done only by our Priest Captain Itzacoatl?"

Both Fray Antonio and I heard with delight this utterance, that in a moment settled the long-disputed question as to whether or not Chac-Mool was an idol, and settled it, also, in favor of the ingenious hypothesis presented by the learned Señor Chavero. The moment was not a favorable one, however, for pursuing the matter in its archæological bearings, for all of our tact and skill just then were required to restore Tizoc to calmness. As well as this was possible in the language common to us—we suddenly realized how difficult it was to express in the Nahua tongue more than rudimentary concepts of the ideas that we sought to convey—we explained to him how matches were made; and illustrated our words by showing him how fire was induced by friction, even as the rubbing of two pieces of wood together produced fire also. This explanation was less exact than ingenious; but it was one that he could understand, and it had the effect of allaying his alarm sufficiently to permit him to resume his seat, when he at once drank off a whole bowlful of the strong, spicy liquor at a draught. Added to what he already had inside of him, this draught set his tongue to wagging in the free way that I have already referred to, and he grew bold enough to take a match in his hand. But even in his cups he manifested a certain reverence in his handling of it; and presently, from a little bag that was hung about his neck, he produced the burnt remnant of a match that he compared with it critically. "They are the same?" he asked, as he extended the whole match and the fragment together towards us that we might examine them.

"They are the same," Fray Antonio answered. "Whence comes the one that you guard so carefully?"

"From the Priest Captain—from Itzacoatl. With such things does he miraculously set burning the fire of sacrifice; but he does not speak of them lightly, as you do; he tells us that they are the handiwork of the Fire God, Chac-Mool; and when the fire of sacrifice is kindled he gives what remains of them as high rewards to those who have served well the State by brave acts or honorable deeds. This which I cherish was my reward for crushing a revolt among the Tlahuicos."

Fray Antonio and I exchanged curious glances, for the conviction was forced upon us both that the Priest Captain of whom Tizoc spoke must either have invented friction matches, or that he must have some secret channel of communication with the outside world. In either case it was evident that he must be a man of unusual shrewdness; and it also was evident that his feeling towards us—since we also could perform a miracle that he obviously made use of as a means of manifesting his divine right to rule—must be that of strong hostility.

To Rayburn and Young, who had observed wonderingly Tizoc's extraordinary conduct, I rapidly translated what he had said; and explained how serious our situation appeared in the light of this new development.

"Well, it certainly *is* cold weather for this Priest Captain fellow," Young commented, "if we've got hold of his boss miracle; and I guess you're about right, Professor—he'll want t' take it out of our hides. Just poke up th' Colonel t' telling all he knows about this old dodger. Th' Colonel's got his tongue pretty well greased just now with his own prime old Bourbon—pass me that jar, Rayburn, I don't mind if I have another whack at it myself—and we may get something out of him that will be useful. Try it on, Professor, any way. Here's luck, gentlemen."

That Young's tongue also was a little greased, as he put it, by this very agreeable beverage was quite evident; but his wits were sharpened rather than dulled by the drink, and his present suggestion evidently was a very good one. As for Tizoc, his disposition towards us obviously was most soft and friendly; and as his mind slowly absorbed the fact that, somehow or another, the Priest Captain had made a fool of him with a miracle that was not really a miracle at all, his choler rose in a manner most favorable to our purposes. Yet this very feeling of resentful anger—showing a growing irreverence of one to whom all the traditions of his people gave reverence second only to that due to the gods themselves—was startling evidence of the menace that our presence was to the theocratic ruler's temporal and spiritual power. Therefore it was with a keen curiosity that we listened—and Tizoc needed, to induce him to talk freely, but little of the poking-up that Young had suggested—to what was told us concerning the strange people among whom we had come by ways so perilous, and of their chieftain, the Priest Captain Itzacoatl— with whom, as no spirit of prophecy was needed to tell us, we were destined soon to engage in a conflict that must be fought out to the very death.

CHAPTER XIX

THE SEEDS OF REVOLT

For the sake of brevity I shall summarize here the statement that Tizoc made to us, and for the sake of clearness I shall add to it some facts of minor importance which came to our knowledge later—thus at once exhibiting the whole of the troublous condition of affairs that stirred dangerously the people dwelling in the Valley of Aztlan at the time of our coming among them.

At this period the political situation, as I may term it, was exceedingly critical. Three powerful factions were in existence; and peace was preserved only by the generally diffused belief that open revolt, on the part of either one, would be crushed instantly by a temporary coalition of the other two. The beginning of this unpleasantly volcanic condition of affairs dated back six cycles—that is to say, a little more than three hundred years—and was the direct result of a violation of the law set forth by the wise King Chaltzantzin when the colony was founded, by which it was ordained that all among the Aztlanecas who, on coming to maturity, were weaklings or cripples, should be put to death.

Being once suggested, the repeal or the modification of this law found many advocates. Naturally, the change was urged most strongly by all those whose sons and daughters were sickly or malformed, and so were doomed to die in the very blossom of their years. It was urged by the nobles because the more astute among them perceived the possibility of so manipulating it that it would result in the creation of a distinctively servile class; and the priests urged it because they also perceived a way by which it might be made to provide more victims for sacrifice to the gods. And so it came to pass, through the influence of these diverse elements operating together towards a common end, that the law which Chaltzantzin had promulgated was set aside, and a law was made that embodied the provisions demanded by the nobles and the priests, whereby should be created a new social class; which class, because of the infirmities of those composing it, received the name of Tlahuicos—"men turned towards the earth." Thereafter, the sickly and the crippled were not slain upon reaching maturity, but then passed out from the class into which they were born and became servitors. And when the first cycle was ended after the making of this new law, and thenceforward every year, one in every ten among the Tlahuicos was taken by lot to be sacrificed to the gods—for the priests craftily had gained the barbarous concession that they demanded by placing the first fulfilment of it at a time so far in the future that all concerned in the granting of it would be dead in the course of nature before it became operative. Yet to the end that those of noble birth might be saved from the ignominy of servitude, it was provided that children which by reason of natural infirmity were doomed to become slaves, might be saved from that fate upon coming to maturity by being then surrendered by their parents to the priests for sacrifice. Other grace there was none. Excepting between death and slavery, there was no choice for the weak or the malformed.

As time passed on, the Tlahuicos, marrying among themselves, had greatly increased in numbers; and so far from remaining a weakling race, the had become, by reason of their frugal mode of living and of the wholesome, hearty labor in which they constantly were engaged, exceptionally hale and strong; the weak and crippled among them being mainly those who each year, because of such infirmities, were added to their number from the higher ranks of the community. And thus was collected together material as dangerous as it was inflammable; for the fresh additions to the Tlahuicos kept constantly alive in the whole body a spirit of moody discontent, that time and again, at the season when the lots were cast by which one in every ten was doomed to death, was fanned into armed mutiny. These revolts ever had as their single object escape from the valley; which fact made evident enough the need for the elaborate system of defensive works by which the outlet of the valley was barred.

From the Tlahuicos were drawn the house-servants of the rich; and by those of this wretched class who were stout of body all the heavy labor of the community was carried on—the tilling of the fields, the quarrying of stone, the building of houses and bridges and roads, the felling of timber, the carriage of all burdens, and the working of the great gold-mine, concerning which I shall hereafter have more to tell. And all of these people were held in absolute bondage, either as the serfs of individual owners or as the property of the State; for each year the new accessions to the class were sold publicly at an auction to whoever would bid the most for them; and those which none would buy, being too infirm to be useful as laborers, the State laid claim to—but only that they might be kept alive until such time as they should be needed by the priests for sacrifice.

Yet out of this custom of sale, that on the face of it was harsh and barbarous, some slight mitigation of the cruelty of the system had come; for the practice had grown up of permitting parents to buy back their own children—nominally thereafter holding them as slaves— and so to save them at a single stroke from both death and servitude. One strong cause of the hatred of the Priest Captain Itzacoatl, Tizoc said (and we wondered then at the trembling in his voice, and at the evidently deep emotion that overcame him as he spoke), was that he had but lately forbidden the continuance of this practice, by which only the letter of the law was obeyed.

Until the promulgation by the Priest Captain of this decree, the priesthood, the military aristocracy, and the mass of the army had constituted, politically, one single class. The civil government was vested in a body styled the Council of the Twenty Lords, the members of which originally had been chosen by Chaltzantzin, and from him had received authority, in perpetuity, to fill the vacancies which death would cause among them by selecting the wisest of each new generation to be Councillors. While the composition of this body was distinctively aristocratic—for its members were either military nobles or priests of a high grade—there was in it also an element of democracy; for both the priesthood and the army were recruited from all classes of society (saving only the servile class), and among the Twenty Lords there were always men who had risen from obscurity to distinction solely by their own merit. Over this body the Priest Captain presided; yet was his will superior to that of the Council, for he was the visible representative of the gods, and so centred in his own person their high authority and dreadful power.

Until the time of Itzacoatl, each successive priest captain, in the long line that here had ruled, had exercised so discreetly his theocratic rights, and in all ways had shown such wisdom in his government, that no conflict had arisen between the temporal and the spiritual powers. And thus wisely had Itzacoatl governed in the early years of his reign. But as age stole upon him—and he now was a very old man—his rule had grown more and more tyrannical. He had drawn about him certain priests for intimate advisers, and these constantly led him to run counter to the will of the Twenty Lords, not only in matters about which divergent opinions reasonably might be held, but in matters wherein the will of the whole people was at one with the advice that the Council gave. Thus, gradually, two parties were built up within the State: that of the priests, which strongly seconded the disposition that Itzacoatl manifested to make the spiritual power absolutely supreme, and that of the nobles and people of the higher class, which sought to maintain the Council's ancient rights in matters temporal. In regard to these two factions, the affiliations of the army were so nicely balanced that neither side ventured to resort to open violence—for each dreaded that the other would turn the scale against it by invoking the aid of the servile class. Thus it was that the despised Tlahuicos actually held the balance of power. Yet of this fact, Tizoc declared—but I noticed that just here there was a curious hesitancy about his speech, as though he knew more than he was willing to disclose—the Tlahuicos were but dimly conscious; while they did know certainly that in the present state of affairs any attempt on their part to rise in mutiny would be met, as it had been met many times in the past, by all the forces of both factions of their superiors overwhelmingly united against them.

But the bond that was stronger than all others in holding together this community, in which, beneath the surface, were working such potent elements of disintegration, was the loyal resolve pervading it to execute the mission to which its members were destined when they were set apart from the remainder of their race a thousand years before. Excepting only among the Tlahuicos—who, in the nature of things, could have no share in it—there had ever been among all classes a fervent longing for the summons that should call them forth to aid their brethren in the battling with a foreign foe that Chaltzantzin had prophesied. And by reason of this loyalty to a lofty purpose the open rupture that assuredly otherwise would have come had been thus far restrained. Honor forbade, Tizoc declared, that by falling to warring among themselves they should put in jeopardy their power to respond instantly to the summons that might at any instant come.

It was therefore with a profound and solemn interest—for the grave import of it was plain to him—that Tizoc, having ended his own statement, questioned us as to the full meaning of the words which we had spoken when first we entered the valley: that the prophecy of Chaltzantzin long since had been fulfilled, and that now, having in its appointed time miscarried, the summons would never come.

With awe, and in sorrowful silence, he listened as Fray Antonio and I told him how exactly the prophecy had been verified by the coming of the Spaniards, and by their conquest and enslavement of the Mexicans; yet was he cheered again as our narrative continued, and he learned of the brave fight for freedom that his brethren had made, and of the happy success that had crowned it in the end. Of the period between the achievement of independence and recent years we said but little—it is not a period of which those whose feeling towards the Mexicans is friendly have much desire to talk—contenting ourselves with emphasizing the fact that the race so long oppressed, having risen successfully against its oppressors, remained independent under a ruler of its own blood.

To that part of our narrative in which we told how we had gained knowledge of the hidden city of Colhuacan, and possession of the token of summons, Tizoc gave but little heed. It was evident that his mind was engrossed with consideration of the more important matters of which we had told him, and of the direct bearing that they had upon the troubled condition of affairs in which his own people were involved. Seeing which, we left him to his own thoughts while we talked of these same matters among ourselves.

Rayburn, in his quick, clear-headed way, grasped the situation promptly and accurately. "About the size of it is," he said, "that we've knocked the false work right from under everything that these folks have been building for the whole thousand years that they have been living here; and what they've built isn't strong enough to stand alone. As Young says, it's a cold day for the Priest Captain because we have got hold of his boss miracle; but it's still colder weather for him because the news that we have brought makes it all right for the crowd that wants to fight him to go right ahead and do it; and I guess they will do it, too, as soon as they get the fact fairly into their heads that there no longer is a chance of their being called off in the middle of their row. Unless I am very much mistaken, we shall see some pretty lively times in this valley inside of the next thirty days."

"And unless *I'm* mistaken," Young struck in, "th' Colonel here will be about th' first man t' take off his coat—that is, th' thing that I suppose he thinks is a coat—an' sail in. I don't know just what he's got against th' Priest Captain, except that he seems t' be a sort of pill on gen'ral principles, but I'm sure that he's down on him from th' word go. From what th' Colonel says, I judge that his crowd has a pretty good chance of comin' out on top—for th' other crowd seems t' be made up for th' most part of parsons; an' parsons, as a rule, haven't much fight in 'em. What we'd better do it t' tie t' th' Colonel, an' when we've helped him an' his friends t' wallop th' other fellows they'll be so much obliged to us that they'll let us bag all th' treasure we want an' clear out. An' that reminds me, Professor—we haven't heard anything about any treasure so far. Just ask th' Colonel if there really is one. If there isn't, I vote for pullin' out before th' row begins. It's as true of a fight as it is of a railroad—that runnin' it just for th' operatin' expenses don't pay."

Tizoc answered my question on this head somewhat absently, for he evidently was debating within himself some very serious matter; but his answer was of a sort that Young found entirely satisfactory. In the heart of the city, he said, was the Treasure-house that Chaltzantzin had builded there; and within it the treasure remained that Chaltzantzin had stored away. What it consisted of, nor the value of it, he could not tell. The Treasure-house was also the Great Temple; and of the treasure only the Priest Captain had accurate knowledge. In the Treasure-house, Tizoc added, was stored the tribute that the people paid annually, and the metal that was taken from the great mine. This metal was the most precious of all their possessions, he said, for from it their arms were made, and also their tools for tilling the earth, and for working wood and stone. It had not always been of such value, for it naturally was too soft to serve these useful purposes; but at a remote period, until which time their implements had been made of stone, a wise man among them had discovered a way by which it could be hardened, and from that time onward the people dwelling in the valley had prospered greatly, because they thus were enabled to practise all manner of useful arts.

"And what is this metal like?" I asked, with much interest, for my archæological instinct instantly was aroused by hearing summed in these few words a matter of such momentous importance as the transition of a people to the age of metal from the age of stone.

"It is like this," Tizoc answered, simply, disengaging as he spoke a heavy bracelet from his arm, "only this remains in its natural state of softness. To be of great value it first must be made hard."

I had no doubt in my own mind as to what this metal was, but I knew that Rayburn, who was an excellent metallurgist, could pronounce upon it authoritatively.

"Is this gold?" I asked, handing him the bracelet.

"Certainly it is," he answered, in a moment—"and it seems to be entirely without alloy."

"Then your guess about the bright, hard metal that has been such a puzzle to us," I continued, "was the right one; it is hardened gold:" and I repeated to him what Tizoc had told me.

Rayburn was deeply interested. "Scientifically, this is a big thing, Professor," he said. "These fellows can give points to our metallurgists. But for our purposes, of course, what they've caught on to here has no practical value. Gold has got to come down a good deal, or phosphor-bronze has got to go up a good deal, before it will pay us to turn gold dollars into axle-bearings and cogs and pinions. But it's mighty interesting, all the same. Fusing with silicium would give a gold-silicide that might fill the bill for hardness; but I can't even make a guess as to how they do the tempering. Ask the Colonel what the whole process is, Professor. It will make a capital paper to read before the Institute of Mining Engineers at their next meeting."

As I turned to Tizoc to ask this question, I perceived that his regard was fixed upon something on the other side of the court-yard, and in his look most tender love was blended with a deep melancholy. Following the direction of his gaze, I saw that its object was a beautiful boy, a lad of twelve or fourteen years old, who was half hidden behind some flowering shrubs, and from this cover was peering at us curiously.

"It is my Maza—my little son," Tizoc said, as he turned and saw the direction in which I looked. And then he called to the boy to come to him. For a moment Maza hesitated, but when the call was repeated he came out from behind the screen of flowers and so towards us across the court-yard; and as he advanced I perceived that he was lame. In his face was the look of wistfulness which cripples so often have, and there was a rare sweetness and intelligence in the expression of his large brown eyes. In a moment I understood why it was that Tizoc resented so bitterly the abrogation by the Priest Captain of the custom that had permitted parents to buy back their crippled children, and so to save them from slavery; and a selfish feeling of gladness came into my heart as this light dawned upon me—for I knew that when we faced the danger that threatened us (a most real danger, for our coming into the valley was nothing less than a deadly blow at Itzacoatl's supremacy) we surely would find in Tizoc an ally and a friend.

CHAPTER XX

THE PRIEST CAPTAIN'S SUMMONS

There was so much meaning in my look as I turned towards Tizoc that I had no need to speak; he knew that I had comprehended the situation, and so answered my look in words.

"Do you wonder that I rejoice over your coming, and over the news which you bring? The will of the gods no longer is that we shall do the work for which our lord Chaltzantzin destined us; therefore are we free to set aside the custom that he decreed by which our weak ones are condemned to death, and with it the custom, yet more cruel, of our own devising, by which they are saved from death only that they may be made slaves. To my boy neither slavery nor death shall come. Through you the gods have spoken, and he is saved. And now also is fulfilled the prophecy that of ancient times was spoken, that with the coming into the Valley of Aztlan of a four-footed beast, bearing upon its back a man, the power of the Priest Captain should end."

Much more, doubtless, Tizoc would have said to us, for an exalted emotion stirred him; but at that moment there was the sound of hurrying feet in the outer enclosure, and then Tizoc's secretary came through the narrow entrance into the court-yard, followed closely by a detachment of the guards. The secretary spoke hurriedly to his master, apart from us, and from his excited manner in speaking, and from the anxious look upon his master's face as he listened, we inferred that some very stirring matter was involved in the communication that he brought.

For a few moments Tizoc stood in silence, his head bowed, as though engaged in earnest thought. Then he turned to us and spoke. "The Priest Captain has sent his order that you shall be brought before him," he said, "and that you must go hence without delay." And then he added, taking me aside and speaking in a low voice: "There is great commotion already in the city, for the soldiers have noised abroad the news which you bring. The Council of the Twenty Lords has been called together, and I am told that a messenger from the Council is on his way hither. That my order to take you to the city in such haste, and directly to the Priest Captain, is so stringent, I cannot but think is caused by his desire to get you hence before the messenger from the Council shall arrive. His purpose towards you surely is an evil one; but fear not—you bring a message of freedom and deliverance that has only to be published to raise around you a host of friends. And now we must go."

In a few moments we had quitted Tizoc's house, passed out through the fortified gate-way in the heavy wall by which the little plateau on the mountain side was defended; and so, by a broad road that descended sharply, went downward towards the border of the lake. Our order of march was the same as that adopted in bringing us from the Barred Pass: before us and behind us were detachments of the guards, and Tizoc walked with us. In accordance with his desire, that he expressed to me in a cautious whisper, Pablo rode upon El Sabio's back. There was no need for him to explain his motive in making this suggestion. It was his purpose, evidently, to exhibit the fulfilment of the prophecy as conspicuously as possible, and so to prepare the ground for the sowing of the seeds of revolt.

I had an opportunity now to tell Rayburn and Young of what Tizoc had been speaking at the moment when the summons from the Priest Captain came; and also of the strong personal reason that he had for protecting us, even to the extent of forwarding the outbreak of revolution, in his desire to save from death or slavery the son whom he so well loved.

"I'm not at all surprised to hear that what we've told 'em is going to start a revolution," Rayburn said. "That's just the way I sized the matter up, you know, as soon as I got down to the first facts. If they'd had a decent sort of a fellow at the head of things, they might have worked along so as to take a fresh start without fighting over it. But this Priest Captain chap isn't that kind. He goes in for Boss management and machine politics, I should judge from what the Colonel says, as straight as if he was a New York alderman or the chairman of a State campaign committee in Ohio. No doubt he's got a pretty big crowd back of him; but that kind of a crowd don't amount to much in a fight, when there's any sort of a show for the other side to win. It sort of gets out of the way, and stands around with water on both shoulders, and then, when one side begins to get pretty well on top—it don't matter which—it says that that's the side it's been fighting with all along, and begins to kick the fellows that are down.

Where our chance comes in is in having the respectable element, the solid men who pay taxes and have an interest in decent government, to tie to. They may not pay taxes here, but that's the kind I mean. And that kind, when it takes to fighting, fights hard. Then there must be a lot of fathers with crippled children, like the Colonel here, who are down on the Priest Captain the worst kind, and will be only too glad of a chance to go for him; and they can be counted on to stand in with us, and to fight harder than anybody. I'll admit, Professor, that we're in a pretty tight place; but it might be a good deal tighter, and I do honestly believe that we'll get out of it."

"And so do I," said Young, "'specially now that I know that that burro of Pablo's is part of a prophecy. I always did think that there was style about El Sabio, any way, an' now I know what it comes from. When I was a boy, th' one thing that used t' keep me quiet in church was hearin' our minister read that story about Balaam and *his* burro; but I never thought then that I'd actually ketch up with a live ass that was in the prophesyin' line of business for itself—or had prophecies made about it, which is pretty much the same thing. T' be sure, this prophecy don't come down t' dots quite as much as I'd like it to; but I s'pose that that's th' way with 'em always—eh, Professor? Th' prophets sort o' leave things at loose ends on purpose; so's they can run 'wild' on a clear track, without any bother about schedule time or connections."

"Well, our burro lays over Balaam's," Rayburn struck in. "In that case it took the combined arguments of an ass and an angel to convince Balaam that he was off about his location, and was running his lines all wrong; but, unless we count in Pablo, El Sabio is playing a lone hand; and I'm sure that the Colonel's not fooling us about this prophecy business, either. It's rubbish, of course; but that don't matter, so long as the people here swallow it for the genuine thing. Just look at that old fellow there. He's tumbled to it, and he's regularly knocked out."

We were close to the shore of the lake by this time, and as Rayburn spoke we were passing a small house, in front of which was gathered a group of Indians. In the midst of the group was a very old man, who with out-stretched arm was pointing towards Pablo and El Sabio, and who at the same time was talking to his companions in grave and earnest tones. There was a look of awe upon his age-worn face, and as we fairly came abreast of him he dropped upon his knees and raised his arms above his head, as though in supplication to some higher power. The action, truly, was a most impressive one; and even more strongly than we were affected by it did it affect those who were clustered around him. In a moment all in the group had fallen upon their knees and had raised their arms upward; and then a low moaning, that presently grew louder and more thrilling, broke forth among them as they gave vent to the feeling of awful dread that was in their hearts.

"That's business, that is," Young said, in tones of great satisfaction. "Those fellows do believe in th' prophecy, for a fact; and if th' folks once get it fairly into their heads that th' time has come for their rascally Priest Captain t' have an upset, that's a good long start for our side towards upsettin' him. It was just everlastin'ly level-headed in th' Colonel t' make Pablo ride El Sabio, and so regularly cram th' thing down these critters' throats. I don't know how much of th' prophecy he believes himself, but he's workin' it for all it's worth, any way. There don't seem t' be any flies worth speakin' of on th' Colonel—eh, Professor? And I guess that anybody who wants t' get up earlier 'n th' mornin' than he does'll have to make a start overnight."

By this time the road that we followed had come down to the lake-level, and presently we reached the end of it, which was a well-built pier that extended out from the shelving shore into deep water. Here a boat was in waiting for us—a barge of near forty feet in length, with twenty men to row it, and carrying also a mast, stepped well forward, so rigged as to spread a sail that was a compromise between a lug and a lateen. There was some little talk between the officer in charge of the barge and Tizoc, and then the latter motioned us to go on board. The barge-master gave the order to the guard to follow us, as though the command of the party now had devolved upon him; and it seemed to us, from the close group that the guard made around us in the boat, and from the anxious looks which the barge-master cast upon us, that very strict orders must have been given concerning keeping us closely in ward. Under these circumstances, it caused us some little wonder that we were permitted to retain our arms, until the thought occurred to me that these people, having no knowledge of such things, did not at all realize that our rifles and revolvers were arms at all. To test which theory I drew one of my pistols—not violently, but as though this were something that I was doing for my own convenience—and so held it in my hands that the muzzle was pointed directly at the heart of the soldier who sat beside me; yet beyond the interest that its odd shape, and the strange metal that it was made of aroused in him, it was evident that the man regarded my action entirely without concern. I drew the attention of Rayburn and Young to what I was doing, and to how evident it was that fire-arms were unknown to this people; and in their ignorance we found much cause for satisfaction.

"If they don't know enough to corral our guns," Young said, "we've got a pretty good-sized piece of dead-wood on 'em. Th' way things are goin', we may have a rumpus a'most any time, I s'pose; and if it does come to a rumpus, they'll be a badly struck lot when we open on 'em. Robinson Crusoe cleaned out a whole outfit of Indians with just an old flint-lock musket; and I should say that we'd simply paralyze this crowd when we all get goin' at once with our revolvers an' Winchesters. Isn't that your idea of it, Rayburn?"

But Rayburn did not answer, for while Young was speaking he had taken out his field-glass and was examining the city, to within three or four miles of which we now were come. "Well, that *is* a walled city, and no mistake!" he said, as he lowered the glass from his eyes. "Take a look, Professor. These people may be easy to fool when it comes to prophecies, but when it comes to engineering and archi-tecture they're sound all the way through. Just look at the straight-ness of that wall running up the hill, and how exact the alignment is of the two parts above and below that ledge of rocks. They had to get that alignment, you know, by taking fore-sights and back-sights from the top of the ledge; and I must say that for people who haven't got far enough along in civilization to wear trousers, it's an uncommonly pretty piece of work."

As I looked through the glass I was less impressed by this technical detail, involving the overcoming of engineering difficulties which I did not very thoroughly understand, than I was by the majestic effect produced by the city as a whole, in conjunction with the site on which it was reared. At this point the lake came close up to the vastly high cliffs by which the valley everywhere was girt in, and here jutted out from the cliff a great promontory of rock, whereof the highest part was fully two hundred feet above the lake-level. For the accommoda-tion of the houses which everywhere were built upon it, the sloping face of this promontory had been cut into broad terraces, of which the facings were massive walls of stone; and the whole was enclosed by a wall of great height and enormous thickness that swept out in an immense semicircle from the face of the cliff, and thus shut in the terraced promontory and also a considerable area of level land at the base of it between the lowest terrace and the margin of the lake.

On the highest terrace, crowning and dominating the whole, was a majestic building that seemed to be half temple and half fort—a square structure, resting solidly against the face of the cliff, and thence projecting a long way outward to where its façade was flanked by two low, heavy, square towers. Architecturally, this building, unlike any other of which I had knowledge in Mexico, saving only the temple that we had found upon the lonely mountain-top, was pervaded by a distinctly Egyptian sentiment. Its walls sloped inward from their bases, and no trivial nor fretful lines weakened the effect of their massive dignity; for the whole of the decoration upon them was a broad panelling that was gained by a combination of heavy pilasters and a heavy cornice; and with the exception of a central entrance, the front was unbroken by openings of any kind. Possessing these characteristics, the building had about it an air of solemnity that bordered closely upon gloom; and the obvious solidity of its construction was such that it seemed destined to last on through all coming ages in defiance of the assaults of time. There was no need for me to question Tizoc; for I knew that what I beheld before me, crowning with sombre grandeur this strange city, girded with such prodigious walls, was the Treasure-house that Chaltzantzin, the Aztec King, had builded in the dim dawning of a most ancient past.

Young took his turn in looking through the glass, and as he handed it to Fray Antonio he said: "If at any time in th' course o' th' past few weeks, Professor, you've got th' notion from any o' my talk that I thought that dead friend o' yours, th' old monk, was a liar, I want t' take it all back; and I want t' take back all that I've said about that other dead friend o' yours, th' Cacique, havin' set up a job on us. It's clear enough now that both o' your friends played an entirely square game. They said that there was a walled city, an' there it is; they said that there was a big Treasure-house, an' there *that* is. They were perfect gentlemen, Professor, and I want t' set myself right on th' record by sayin' so. If one of 'em hadn't been dead for more than three months, and if th' other one hadn't been dead for more than three hundred years, and if they both were here, I'd knuckle under and ask 'em t' take my hat."

CHAPTER XXI

THE WALLED CITY OF CULHUACAN

Our use in turn of the field-glass was a mysterious performance that aroused keenly the barge-master's curiosity. I heard him ask Tizoc for an explanation of it; and Tizoc, who also was much interested, referred his question to me. Had I been dealing with Tizoc alone I should have tried to make the matter clear to him; but in the case of the barge-master, whose feeling towards us, I was convinced, was anything but friendly, I thought it wiser to be less frank. Therefore, covering the action with a negligent motion of my hand, I screwed the glasses close together, so that in looking through them there was to be seen only a mass of indistinct objects looming up in a blurred cloud of light, and so handed them to him. Naturally, neither he nor Tizoc arrived at any very satisfactory conclusion in regard to the real use of them; and from their talk it was evident that they conceived the ceremony in which we had engaged in turn so earnestly to be in the nature of a prayer to our gods. Fray Antonio was both shocked and pained by their taking this view of the matter, and was for making a true explanation to them; but at my urgent request he held his peace. Yet it was evident that he brooded over the matter in his mind, and so was led to earnest thoughts of the mission that had brought him hither into the Valley of Aztlan. Therefore was I not surprised—though I certainly was alarmed by the thought of what might be its consequences—when presently, in low and gentle tones, he began to speak to those about him of the free and glorious Christian faith, which in all ways was more excellent than the cruel idolatry in which they were bound. Naturally, he was not permitted long to speak in this strain, for the barge-master speedily ordered him in most peremptory tones to keep silence; which order doubtless would have been still more quickly given had not the officer been fairly surprised by Fray Antonio's temerity into momentary forgetfulness of the dangerous outcome of this gentle talk. And Fray Antonio, knowing the value of the word in season that is dropped to fructify in soil ready for it, did not attempt argument with the barge-master—by which the thoughts of those who listened would have been diverted from the hopeful promise of a better faith that he had offered to them—but obeyed the order meekly and so held his peace. That what he had spoken had taken hold upon the hearts of some at least among his hearers I was well assured by their grave look of thoughtfulness, and especially did Tizoc seem to be deeply moved; but—as I supposed for fear of the barge-master—there was no open comment upon what had passed.

By this time, the barge being all the while urged rapidly forward by the steady strokes of the twenty oarsmen, the city rose so broadly and so openly before us that we could see the whole of it distinctly with our naked eyes. And what at this nearer view seemed most impressive about it was its gloominess; that was due not less to the prison-like effect of its heavily built houses and its massive walls than to the dull blackness of the stone whereof these same were made. Nowhere was there sparkle, or glitter, or bright color, or brightness of any sort to be seen; and it seemed to me, as I gazed upon this sombre stronghold, that dwelling always within it well enough might wear a man's heart out with a consuming melancholy begotten of its cold and cheerless tones.

That it was indeed a stronghold was the more apparent to us the nearer that we came to it. The plan of it was that of a great fan, spread open upon the hillside, and extending also across the broad sweep of level land between the base of the promontory and the lake. The promontory had been so cut and shaped that its gentle slope had been transformed into six broad semicircular terraces, above the highest of which was a semicircular plateau of very considerable size, on which stood the Treasure-house, that also was the great temple. Along the face of each terrace, and around the face also of the plateau, a heavy defensive wall rose to a height of twenty feet or more; and from the base of the crowning plateau, thence accessible by a single broad flight of stairs—being led through openings in the rampart walls of the terraces, and down each terrace face by means of stair-ways—twelve streets descended, of which the central six ended at the water-side and the remainder against the great outer wall. It was this outer line of strong defence that gave the city—which otherwise would have corresponded curiously closely with the fortified city of Quetzaltepec, described by the Mexican chronicler Tezozomoc—its most distinctive characteristic. Such a vastly thick wall, for the great length of it, as this was I never have seen in any other place; and so solid was the building of it that it would have been proof against any ordinary train of siege artillery. For defence against a foe whose only missile weapons would be javelins and slings and bows, this great wall made the city absolutely impregnable. And that the protection that it gave might be still more complete—and also, as Tizoc explained to us, that in the case of siege the water supply might be assured, together with a supply of fish for food—the wall was carried out into the lake so far as to enclose a basin of more than four acres in extent; within which, should an enemy gain access to the valley, all the boats upon the lake could be brought together and held in safety. And finally, the one entrance to the city was by way of a tunnel-like canal cut in the wall thus rising from the water; the outer end of which canal was closed in ordinary times by a heavy grating, while in war time the inner end also could be closed by means of great metal bars.

It was towards this entrance that the barge that carried us was heading. Presently we reached it, and the grating was raised for our admission by means of chains which were operated from the top of the wall. So low and so narrow was the passage that our heads were within a few inches of the huge slabs of stone of which its roof was formed; and the rowers had need to unstep the mast and then to lay their oars inboard, while they brought the barge through by pushing with their hands against the roof and sides. The canal was fully forty feet long, and thus the enormous thickness of the wall was made apparent to us. It truly was, as I observed to Rayburn, a work that well might be attributed to the Cyclops.

"I never met a live Cyclop, Professor," Rayburn answered, "and I don't believe that these fellows ever did either; but it bothers me to know how they managed to do work like this without a steam-derrick. If we get out of here with whole skins and our hair on our heads, I hope it won't be until I've had a chance to talk to some of their engineers, and so get down to the facts."

A moment later we emerged from the tunnel through the wall, and so entered the enclosed basin that extended along the whole of the city's front. Within the basin were lying many canoes, and also boats of a larger sort that carried oars and that were rigged with a sort of lug-sail; but these all kept away from us, even as all the boats which we had seen during our passage of the lake had given us a wide berth. That our barge—one of those employed exclusively in the Priest Captain's service—was thus shunned was due, as I found later, to the wholesome dread in which the special servitors of the temple and of its head universally were held; for these very frequently abused the authority acquired through their semi-sacerdotal functions by using it as a cloak to cover acts of purely personal oppression, while at all times they were feared as the executors of their master's wrath. There was, indeed (though I did not mention this fact to Fray Antonio), a curiously close resemblance between the officials of this class and the familiars of the Inquisition, both in the duties which they performed and in the fear and hatred which they everywhere inspired.

But even dread of entanglement with the Priest Captain's servants could not restrain the curiosity of the crowd that pressed towards us on the broad pier upon which we disembarked. It was evident that this crowd was not made up of the common folk of the city, and also that it was moved by a purpose far higher than that of a mere idle longing to see something that was strange. From their dress, and still more from the beauty of their ornaments and the elegance of the arms which many of them carried, it was obvious that for the most part these men were citizens of the highest rank; and this fact was still further attested by the dignity of their demeanor and by the reverent age to which the majority of them had attained. So far from manifesting any vulgar excitement, the crowd maintained an absolute silence; and with this an exterior air of calm that was the more impressive because the eager, almost awe-struck expression upon every face showed how strong was the emotion that thus strongly was restrained. But when El Sabio, after much coaxing, crossed the gang-plank between the boat and the pier, and so came to where he could be seen of all plainly, there was a curious low sound in the air as though all at once every man in the crowd had heaved a sigh; and the sound swelled into a loud murmur as Pablo, in obedience to a quick order that I gave him in Spanish, briskly mounted upon the ass's back. In this murmur only one word was intelligible, and that I caught again and again: the prophecy!

But Pablo was no more than fairly seated upon El Sabio's back than the officer in command of our guard took him roughly by the shoulders and snatched him thence to the ground again; which act led Tizoc and me to a quick exchange of startled glances, for it showed very plainly that the Priest Captain—to whom the messenger telling of our coming into the valley had been sent before any of these people had seen Pablo mounted upon El Sabio's back—had anticipated this sign of the fulfilment of the prophecy and had given orders to prevent it. Luckily, the celerity with which Pablo had executed my quick order to mount had saved the day for us; and even more than saved it, for as we passed through the crowd, on our way from the water-side into the city, I caught here and there fragments of comment upon what had just passed which showed that not only was the sign told of in the prophecy recognized, but that the effort on the part of the officer to neutralize it was understood.

But before our going into the city there was a stirring conflict of authority concerning us between the temporal and the spiritual powers. We were no more than fairly landed, indeed, when an officer addressed the barge-master, who continued in charge of our party, and gave him a formal order to bring the strangers directly before the Council of the Twenty Lords. And to this the barge-master replied that he already was under orders to bring the prisoners, immediately upon their landing, before the Priest Captain—and there was something both curious and ominous, it struck me, in the marked manner in which the term "strangers" was employed by one of these men and the term "prisoners" by the other.

At this juncture we had further proof of the foresight of the Priest Captain, and of the determined stand that he was prepared to make rather than to suffer the miscarriage of big plans. While the barge-master and the messenger from the Council still were engaged in hot talk as to which of the two conflicting orders should be recognised, there was the sound of tramping feet and of arms clanking; and then a body of fully one hundred soldiers came quickly from behind a house that was near by the water-side and swept down on a double-quick to where we were standing at the end of the pier. The crowd, jostled aside to make way for the passage of the soldiers, evidently regarded them with astonishment; and this astonishment rapidly changed to anger as the purpose that brought them thither was made plain. In a moment they had closed in around us, separating us from the Council's messenger and from Tizoc; the barge-master placed himself at the head of them, and in sharp, quick tones gave the order to march; and the whole force, with ourselves in the centre of it, went off the pier at a round pace, and thence along a street that led towards the city's heart. Evidently acting under orders, the men broke their platoons and closed in around us; and I was well convinced that this unsoldierly marching was adopted to the end that El Sabio might not be seen.

Fray Antonio agreed with me that the Priest Captain was carrying matters with a dangerously high hand in thus opposing the will of the Council with armed force. This act of his, if Tizoc had correctly represented to us the excited condition of popular feeling, was quite sufficient in itself to stir into violent activity the slumbering fires of mutiny. But whether the revolt that we now believed must surely come would come in time to be of service to ourselves, we could not but look upon as a very open question.

"If this old scoundrel is as sharp as he seems to be," Rayburn said, "and if he keeps things up in the way he's begun, it's about all day with us. His play should be to get rid of us as quick as he can manage it; and I should judge, from the cards that he's put down, that that's precisely the way he means to manage the game. It's not much comfort to us to know that after he's cleaned us out somebody else will rake his pile."

As we talked, we went on rapidly through the city; and even the danger that we were in, and the excitement that attended this sudden shifting of our fortunes, could not prevent me from studying with a lively curiosity the many evidences of an advanced civilization that I beheld. The plan of the city, as I had discerned while we were approaching it, was that of a wide-open fan. From the Treasure-house, on the height in the centre, twelve broad streets radiated outward, of which three on the northern side and three on the southern ended against the great enclosing wall, and six came down through openings in the walls along the several terraces directly to the water-front. All of these streets were well paved with large smooth blocks of stone, and were led up the faces of the terraces by wide and easy stairs. The transverse streets were true semicircles, starting from and ending at the face of the cliff, and were carried along the outer edges of the terraces, just inside their facing walls. Rayburn was even more astonished than I was by the exactness with which these great semicircles were laid off; for he apprehended, as I did not, the difficulty attendant upon running a line in a true and regular curve. But I am not prepared to say that this work could not have been accomplished by mere rule of thumb. My friend Bandelier, in the course of his admirable analysis of the ruins at Mitla, has made clear to me how easy it is to attribute to scientific knowledge work that is the result only of manual skill. As I have pointed out in my discussion of this matter in my *Pre-Columbian Conditions on the Continent of North America,* the plateau at the top of this range of terraces easily might have been laid off in a true semicircle by the simple means of a pointed stick at the end of a long rope; and from the true line thus established the line of the terrace below it could have been had—and so on down to the lowest terrace of all.

There could be no doubt, however, that engineering skill of a high order—howsoever crude might have been the actual method of its application—was exhibited both in the preparation of the site, and then in the city's building. On the site alone an almost incredible amount of labor had been expended; for the rocky promontory—that primitively, as the result showed, had been broken and irregular—had been so cut away in some places, and so filled in in others, and the whole of it had been so carefully trimmed and smoothed, that in the end it became a huge mass of rock-work, in the regularity of which there was not perceptible the smallest flaw. And in this preliminary work, as well as in the building of the houses afterwards, fragments of stone were used of such enormous size that the moving of them, Rayburn declared, would be wellnigh impossible even with the most powerful engineering appliances of our own time. Nor was the use of these huge pieces of stone confined to the foundations of the houses. Some of them were high above the ground; indeed, the very largest that we observed—the weight of which Rayburn estimated at not less than twenty tons—was a single block that made the entire top course of a high wall.

All of the stone-work was well smoothed and squared; and while the exteriors of the houses were entirely plain, we could see through the open door-ways that the interiors of many of them were enriched with carvings. All were destitute of windows opening upon the street; and their dull, black walls, and the dull black of the stones with which the streets were paved, gave a dark and melancholy air to the city that oppressed us even more heavily when thus seen closely than it had when we beheld it from afar off. Yet the interior court-yards, so far as we could tell from the glimpses that we had of them through open door-ways, were bright with sunshine and gay with flowers; thus showing that the gloom of these dwellings did not extend beyond their outer walls. I observed with much interest that the provision for closing the entrances from the street was not swinging doors of wood, but either metal bars, such as we had seen in Tizoc's house, or else a metal grating, that was arranged like a portcullis to slide up and down in a groove; and I attributed the absence of wooden doors less to a desire for stronger barriers than to the comparative recentness of the acquisition of the knowledge of wood-working tools. Here, I thought, was a curious instance of development along the lines of greatest resistance; for in itself the invention and the making of a swinging door of wood was a much easier matter than was the invention and the making of these finely wrought sliding doors of hardened gold.

As for Young, the sight of all this gold-work quite took his breath away. "It regularly jolts me, Professor," he said, "t' see th' genuine stuff, that's good t' make gold dollars out of, slung around this way. A front door of solid gold is a huckleberry above Jay Gould's biggest persimmon; an' as t' Solomon, these fellows just lay Solomon out cold—regularly down th' old man an' sit on him. Why, for just that one front door of th' big house ahead of us I'd sell out all my shares in this treasure-hunt, an' be glad t' do it. But I guess I'd have to hire Samson—who was in that line of business—t' carry it off for me. It must weigh a solid ton!"

By this time we had mounted all of the terraces, and the house towards which Young pointed as he spoke was built directly beneath the crowning plateau on which the great temple stood. It was the largest and by far the most elegant house that we yet had seen, and the sliding grating of gold that closed the entrance was unusually heavy, and very beautifully wrought. Sentinels were stationed here, wearing the same uniform as that of the soldiers who formed our guard; and this further indication of the importance of the building gave us the impression that it was the dwelling of some great dignitary. Close by the portal we were halted, while the commander of our guard spoke through the grating to some one inside. A moment later the grating was slowly raised, and we were marched through the narrow entrance, and so along a short passage-way into a long, narrow chamber that obviously was a guard-room; for spears and javelins were ranged in orderly fashion upon racks, and swords and shields and bows and quivers of arrows were hung upon the walls. Here we were halted again; and while we stood silent together, wondering what might be in store for us in this place, we heard the heavy grating behind us close with a dull clang.

CHAPTER XXII

THE OUTBREAK OF REVOLUTION

So dismal was this sound, and so many were the dismal possibilities that it suggested, that as I heard it a cold chill went down into my heart; and I was glad enough that we at once were led forth from the guard-room, and that in consideration of matters of immediate moment my mind was diverted from dwelling drearily upon a future that seemed full of gloom.

For all the brilliant blaze of sunlight that brightened the large court-yard into which we were conducted, there was about it curious coldness and cheerlessness. As in the case of all the other houses which we had observed, the stone-work of the walls and of the pavement was a dull black; but here there were no flowers, nor bright-colored hangings over the inner doors, nor brightness of any sort or kind. The carving of the stone was extraordinarily rich, to be sure; but the bass-reliefs which covered the walls were wholly of a gloomy sort—being for the most part representations of the slaughter of men in sacrifice, and the tearing of hearts out—so that the eight of them made me shiver, notwithstanding the warmth of the sun. From the centre of the court-yard abroad stair-way ascended to the plateau above on which the temple stood; and this direct way of communicating with it led me to the conclusion that the building was a dependency of the temple, and that very likely the higher members of the priesthood were housed here.

However, little time was given for looking around us, for our guard hurried us—El Sabio following close at Pablo's heels—across the court-yard to a door-way at its farther side, before which hung in heavy folds a curtain of some sort of thick black cloth. Across this entrance the guard was drawn up in orderly ranks behind us; and then the barge-master, who had preserved absolute silence towards us since our march through the city began, held aside the curtain and silently motioned to us to enter.

From the bright sunshine we passed at a step into a chamber so shadowy that we involuntarily stopped on the threshold, in order that our eyes might become accustomed to the semi-darkness before we advanced. The only light that entered it came through two narrow slits in the thick wall above the portal that we had just passed; and the glimmer diffused by the thin rays thus admitted was in great part absorbed by the black draperies with which everywhere the room was hung. As our eyes adjusted themselves to these gloomy conditions we perceived that we were in a hall of great size; and presently we were able to distinguish objects clearly enough to see that at the far end of it was a raised dais, having a sort of throne upon it; but not until, being urged forward by the officer, we had traversed more than half the length of the hall did we discern upon the throne the shadowy figure of a man.

Being come close to the dais, the officer halted us by a gesture; but no word was spoken, and for several minutes we stood in the semi-darkness of that strange place in absolute silence. For myself, I must confess that I was somewhat awed by my surroundings, and by the impassive silence and stillness that the dimly seen figure upon the throne maintained, and I am sure that Fray Antonio's imaginative nature was similarly impressed; as for Pablo, I distinctly heard his teeth chattering in the dark. But neither Rayburn nor Young, as the latter would have expressed it, awed easily, and it was Rayburn who presently spoke.

"This fellow in the big chair would be a good hand at private theatricals. He's got a first-rate notion of stage effect. Hadn't I better stick a pin in him and wake him up?"

"There's no good in stickin' pins into *him*," said Young, in a tone of great contempt. "What's the matter with him is, he's not real at all—he's stuffed!"

There was something so absurdly incongruous in these comments that they acted instantly upon my overstrained nerves, and I burst into a laugh, in which the other two immediately joined. Evidently, this was not at all the effect that this carefully arranged reception was intended to have upon us; for the seated figure started suddenly and uttered an angry exclamation, and at the same time gave a quick order to the officer.

"I take it all back," said Young; "he ain't stuffed. I guess he was only asleep."

As Young spoke there was a slight rustle of draperies, and in a moment the curtains which had veiled four great windows in the four sides of the hall were pulled aside, and the darkness vanished in a sudden blaze of light. While we shaded our eyes for some seconds, Rayburn said, with great decision: "This settles it. He must have been in the show business all his life."

But the man whom we now saw clearly did not look like a showman. He was a very old man, lean and shrivelled; his brown skin so wrinkled that his face looked like some sort of curiously withered nut. Yet there was a wonderful sinewiness about him, and a most extraordinary brightness in his eyes. His face was of the strong, heavy type that is found in the figures carved on the ruins in Yucatan; a much stronger type than I have observed anywhere among the Mexican Indians of the present day. His dress was a long, flowing robe of white cotton cloth, caught over his left shoulder with a broad gold clasp, and richly embroidered with shining green feathers; and shining green feathers were bound into his hair and rose above his head in a tall plume. His sandal-moccasins (for the covering of his feet was between these two) repeated the sacred combination of colors, green and white; and on his breast, falling from his neck, were several richly wrought gold chains. Even apart from his stately surroundings, his dress—and especially the shining green feathers which were so conspicuous a part of it—would have informed me that this man was a priest of very exalted rank; and the conditions of our presentation to him assured me that he was none other than the Priest Captain, Itzacoatl. And I may add that if ever a high dignitary of a heathen religion was in a rage, Itzacoatl was in a rage at that particular moment. Young's comment lacked reverence, but it was to the point: "Well, he *has* got his back up, for sure!"

With an alertness that was astonishing in one of his years, Itzacoatl rose quietly from the throne; and as he pointed to us with a commanding gesture, he asked, sharply, why we had been allowed to retain our arms, and ordered them to be taken away from us; which order troubled us greatly, and also occasioned us a very lively surprise. As for the barge-master, he evidently was vastly puzzled by it; for, according to his notions, we were not armed. He did not venture to reply, but his uncertainty was to the duty that was expected of him was apparent in his hopeless look of entire bewilderment. It seemed to me that for a moment the Priest Captain was slightly confused, as though he recognized the incongruity between his own knowledge in this matter and his officer's ignorance; and in explaining his order he took occasion to refer to the superior knowledge with which he was endowed by the gods. Fray Antonio and I glanced at each other doubtingly as he spoke, for this explanation struck us as being decidedly forced. The gods of the ancient Mexicans pre-eminently were war gods; but they certainly were not likely to have any very extended knowledge of Winchester rifles and self-cocking revolvers.

However, when the officer comprehended what was required of him, he was prompt enough in his actions. Without any ceremony at all he laid hands on Young's rifle, that was hanging by its strap on his shoulder, and endeavored to take it away from him. This was a line of action that the Lost-freight Agent by no means was inclined to submit to. Without any assistance he unslung the rifle, cocked it as he jumped back half a dozen steps, and then raised it to his shoulder, with his finger on the trigger and the muzzle fairly levelled at the officer's heart. "Shall I down him?" he asked.

"Don't shoot!" Rayburn cried, quickly; and in obedience to this order Young slowly dropped the rifle from his shoulder, yet held it ready for action in his hands. The perfect calmness of the officer through this exciting episode afforded the most convincing proof that fire-arms were wholly unknown to him. And the conduct of the Priest Captain afforded equally convincing proof that he not only understood the nature of fire-arms, but that he was very much afraid of them; for, at the moment that Young made his offensive demonstration, he very precipitately sheltered himself by crouching behind the throne.

"Don't shoot!" Rayburn repeated. "We may have a chance to pull through if we don't rile these follows; but if we go killing any of them now it's all day with us, for sure. We'd better let 'em have our guns; but there's something mighty odd in their having found out all of a sudden what a gun is."

Very reluctantly Young surrendered his rifle to the officer, who looked at it contemptuously, as though he considered it but a poor sort of weapon in case real fighting was to be done. In turn, the rest of us gave up our rifles also; and we were mightily pleased because the officer did not attempt to take our revolvers away from us. But in this our satisfaction was short-lived, for the Priest Captain quickly ordered the officer to relieve us of them, and of our cartridge-belts as well; nor was it until we had been thus entirely disarmed that he arose from his undignified position and resumed his seat upon the throne.

While the disagreeable process of disarming us was going on I spoke to Fray Antonio of the curious possibilities suggested by the knowledge of fire-arms which the Priest Captain, alone among all the Aztlanecas, so obviously possessed; and he, in reply, bade me remember what Tizoc had told us of the use that Itzacoatl made of wax-matches in lighting the sacred fire. "Can it possibly be, then, that he is in communication with the outside world?" I exclaimed.

As I uttered these words I glanced at Itzacoatl, and the expression on his face was that of one who listens intently, and who is greatly enraged by what he hears. At the same moment Rayburn cried: "That man understands Spanish. He is listening to you."

Doubtless, some sort of an explanation would have followed this strange discovery, for that we had made it was very obvious, but at that moment a man—seemingly, from his dress, a priest of high rank—came into the hall hurriedly, and very earnestly delivered a communication to Itzacoatl in low, excited tones. That the substance of this communication was highly disagreeable to him was shown by his manner of receiving it; and for a moment he slightly hesitated, as though very grave consequences might attend upon the decision that he then made. But it was for a moment only that he stood in doubt. Then he called the barge-master to him, and gave some order in a low voice; and then, accompanied by the priest, went out rapidly from the hall.

Evidently in obedience to the order that he had received, the barge-master bade us follow him, and so led us into the court-yard again. Young proposed, since we had only this one man to deal with, that we should make short work of him, and so get back our arms—which remained where he had placed them in a pile beside the throne. But Rayburn's more prudent counsel overcame this tempting proposition. As he pointed out, the promptness with which the curtains had been pulled back showed that attendants of some sort were close at hand; and, in addition to these, we knew that the guard of soldiers was just outside of the entrance to the hall. It was certain, therefore, that we could not regain our arms without immediately using them in very active fighting; and no matter how well we fought, under these conditions we must certainly be defeated in the end. All of which was so just and so reasonable that Young could not in anywise gainsay its propriety; but he was in a very ill humor at being restrained from the pleasure of having it out with them, as he grumblingly declared; and as we passed out into the court-yard he relieved his mind by swearing most vigorously.

For my part, even the peril that we were in did not suffice to distract my mind from curious consideration of the strange state of affairs that existed among the folk dwelling in this hidden valley if our surmise in regard to the Priest Captain's knowledge of the outer matches, his acquaintance with fire-arms, and his knowledge of the Spanish tongue. The implication was unavoidable that this extraordinary man actually had a more or less complete knowledge of the powers and appliances of the nineteenth century, and that he was using his nineteenth century knowledge to maintain his supremacy over a people whose civilization was about on a par with that of European communities of a thousand years ago. From the standpoint of the ethnologist, a more interesting situation than the one time developed could not possibly be devised. What I most longed for was the establishment of such friendly relations with Itzacoatl that I could carry out a systematized series of scientific investigations among the Aztlanecas before the impending crash of discovery came; and my keenest regret at that moment was caused by the conviction that the incapacity of Itzacoatl to understand the value of scientific inquiry into such curious ethnologic facts would result in his mere vulgar killing of me, whereby a precious store of knowledge would be withheld from the world at large.

As we came out into the court-yard we heard the sound of voices, which seemed to be raised in angry altercation, coming from the direction of the main entrance, with which there was also a slight clinking sound as of arms being got in readiness; and, much farther away, the sound seemingly coming from distant quarter of the city, the tapping of a drum. When we first had crossed the court-yard it had been entirely deserted; but now many priests and soldiers were standing in groups about it, and more were coming down the stair from the temple; and all of these men had a look of eager alertness, as though some decisive event were imminent in which they expected to have a part. But we had only a moment in which to observe all this, for we were hurried away towards the corner of the building that was most remote from the street, and here, before I well could understand what was being done with me, I was thrust so suddenly and so violently through a narrow door-way that I fell heavily upon the floor. Before I could regain my feet Young had tumbled down on top of me, and then the others tumbled on top of us both—they having been in the same rude fashion injected into the apartment; and while we thus were lying in a heap together—my own body, being undermost, having the breath wellnigh squeezed out of it—we heard the rattle of metal upon stone as the door-way was quickly closed with heavy bars.

We struggled to our feet in wellnigh total darkness—for outside the bars a curtain had been dropped that shut off almost wholly the light of day—and I am confident that no one room ever contained two angrier people than Rayburn and Young were then; for their very strength and hardihood made them the more ragingly resent being thus tumbled about as though they were bales or boxes rather than men. Rayburn's language was not open to the charge of weakness; but the words in which Young gave vent to his feelings were so startlingly vigorous that even a Wyoming cow-boy would have been surprised by them; yet I must confess that at the moment—so greatly was my own anger aroused—I thought his observations exceedingly appropriate to the occasion that called them forth, and I even was disposed to envy him the command of a technical vocabulary that enabled him to express so adequately his righteous wrath. However, I was for once well pleased that Fray Antonio did not understand English.

But our anger quickly was swallowed up in anxious grief as we discovered, when our eyes had become somewhat accustomed to the very faint light, that only we four were in the room together; and a great dread fell upon us because of the imminent peril to Pablo which this separation of him from the rest of us implied. Assuredly there was strong reason why he should be an especial object of Itzacoatl's fear and hatred. He and El Sabio together were the visible sign which told that the prophecy touching the Priest Captain's downfall was about to be fulfilled; and, more than this, Pablo's simple statement of the condition of affairs among the modern Mexicans—showing that the crisis in their fate that Chaltzantzin had foretold, and for which he had so well prepared, long since had come and gone—would be far more convincing to the masses of the Aztlanecas than would be any exhibition of these same facts that we could make to them; for we were aliens among them, while Pablo was of their own race and class. That we all were like to be done to death by this barbarous theocrat we did not for a moment doubt; but it was plain enough that every motive of self-interest must prompt him to put Pablo and the poor ass most summarily out of the way. And as the logic of these facts irresistibly presented itself in my mind a keen and heavy sorrow overcame me, for I could not shirk the conviction that, whoever might strike the blow that killed him, I myself was the cause of this poor boy's death. Fray Antonio could not see my face in that shadowy prison, yet his fine nature divined the pain that I suffered and the cause of it, and he sought to comfort me with his sympathy. He did not speak, but he came close beside me and tenderly laid his hand upon my shoulder; and his loving touch, telling of his sorrow for me and with me, did bring a little cheer into my heavy heart.

Meanwhile the commotion outside increased greatly, and even through the thick folds of the curtain we could hear plainly the clanking of arms, and the heavy tread of men, and sharply given words of command. We pressed close to the bars and tried to push, the curtain aside that we might see out into the court-yard; but the bars were so near together that our hands would not pass between them, and we therefore could gather only from the sounds which we heard what was going on outside. But the sounds were unmistakable. There could be no doubt whatever that a vigorous assault upon the building was in progress, and those within it vigorously were defending it; and we knew that the cause of the fighting certainly must be ourselves. Already, it would seem, the prophecy of the Priest Captain's downfall was assuming a tangible reality; for this rising in arms against him could mean nothing less than that his high-handed refusal to permit us to be carried before the Council of the Twenty Lords had fairly brought matters to a crisis, and that the long-threatened revolution actually had been begun.

CHAPTER XXIII

A RESCUE

That the two parties should be thus battling for possession of us gave us a gleam of hope for the saving of our lives. While we remained prisoners, in the ward of the Priest Captain, we knew that our death was inevitable; inasmuch as the witness which we bore against him, if suffered to be published, must of necessity bring his authority to an end. But should we pass into the ward of the Council, there was every reason why we should be cherished and protected; because, in their behalf, we would be witnesses to the justice of their rebellion against Itzcoatl's rule. Nor would this feeling of amity towards us be confined to the leaders of the revolt; for we had perceived the substantial nature of the reasons which Tizoc had given us in support of his assurance that the hope of deliverance from oppression which our coming brought would raise up around us a host of friends. Therefore we knew that upon the issue of the battling that we heard the sounds of so loudly, and yet that might as well have been a thousand miles away for all that we could see of it, our fate must depend.

And knowing this, it was a hard trial of our nerves and tempers to be forced to remain there idle in the dark, without the chance to strike in our own behalf a single blow. Young strode backward and forward in such a fashion, and the mutterings beneath his breath were so like growls, that the likening of him to a wild beast in a cage, while trite, is strictly accurate. Rayburn, not less resolute, but more self-contained, pressed close against the bars and never stirred, save that now and then he cracked his thumbs and fingers together with such vigor that the sound was like a pistol-shot. And even I, who am not naturally of a blood-thirsty disposition, found the need of walking briskly about our prison in order to quiet a little my strong longing to be outside with a weapon in my hands wherewith I could crack some skulls open. Indeed, among us all, only Fray Antonio maintained an outward show of calm.

Thus far, all the sounds which we had heard had come to us from the direction of the front of the house, whence we inferred that the fight was being waged, greatly to the disadvantage of the assailants, through the grating by which the entrance was closed. But suddenly there was an outcry of alarm close by us in the court-yard, and then the sound of hurrying feet there, and then a roar of shouting mingled with the fierce clash of arms—so that we knew that the assailants, either by beating in the grating or by scaling the roof, had got inside. They and the defenders were engaged, hand to hand, almost within arm's-length of us. We could hear loudly the yells with which every stroke was accompanied, and the clang of metal striking upon metal, and the dull, crushing sound of the blows which went home truly and carved through flesh and bone—and we could see no more of it all than if we were dreaming, and these sounds of savage warfare were but the imaginings of our brains! One man, being, as we supposed, pursued by another from the central part of the court-yard—where, as it seemed, the fight raged most hotly—made a stand just outside the curtain that overhung the bars whereby we were pent in; and we could hear him panting as he struck and parried there, and then the splitting of his flesh and the crash of his bones as a tremendous blow overcame his guard, and the soft, deep groan that he gave as his life left him. His body fell against the curtain and dragged it a little; and presently, as I stood there by the bars, I found that my feet were in a pool of blood.

It was only a moment or two after this that the sounds of conflict very sensibly diminished, and we heard a rush made, and the confused tread of feet upon the stairs that led upward to the temple, and then came so jubilant a shouting that we knew that to one side or the other had come victory.

"If th' Priest Captain's outfit's on top," Young said, grimly, "I guess we've about got t' th' end of a division; an' there's not much chance of our changin' engines an' keepin' on with th' run." To which figurative suggestion Rayburn gave an immediate grunt of assent.

But at that very instant there was a lull in the tumult outside, and we heard a voice that I recognized as Tizoc's loudly calling to us; and to his hail, that carried such joyful meaning with it, I joyfully and loudly answered. To Rayburn and Young, of course, the call was unintelligible, nor did they recognize the voice of him who called; and they therefore were disposed to think, when I fell to shouting, that my brain was addled. However, they changed their views a minute or two later—the dead body resting against the curtain having been thrown aside, and the curtain itself torn down—when they saw Tizoc's friendly face outside the bars, and then saw the bars rapidly removed.

"Colonel," said Young, very seriously, as we stepped forth thankfully once more into the sunshine, "you may not know what a brick is, but you are one. Shake!" and very much to Tizoc's astonishment, though he perceived that the act was meant to express great friendliness, Young most vigorously shook his hand. Under more favorable circumstances Tizoc, no doubt, would have asked for an explanation of this curious ceremony, but just then his whole mind was given to making good his retreat and so securing us against recapture. There was not a moment to lose, he said; throughout the city the priests everywhere were rallying forces to Itzacoatl's support, and at any instant we might be attacked. As he spoke he drew us away with him towards the street, where the main body of his men still remained— for only a small part of them had joined in scaling the roof, and so taking the enemy by surprise in the rear.

"But what of Pablo, our young companion?" I asked, stopping short as I spoke.

"My men are looking for him; they will find him in a moment; he surely is safe; he may be already outside. Come."

The possibility that Pablo truly might be outside of the building was the only argument that could have induced us to leave it without him; and that possibility was so reasonable a one that we made no more delay. Indeed, we fully realized the necessity for promptness. From all parts of the city came a humming, angry sound, which assured us that everywhere the people were aroused; and Tizoc bade us arm ourselves with what weapons we could use most effectively among those which were scattered about the pavement of the court-yard, as we surely would have need of weapons soon. A sword was the only instrument of warfare of which I had knowledge—which knowledge was acquired during my German student days—and I took, therefore, one of the heavy maccuahuitls; and the others also, excepting Fray Antonio, similarly armed themselves, each with a sword that they found lying beside the dead hand that never would wield it more. It was as we obeyed Tizoc's order that we saw how fierce and how bloody the fight had been; for the court-yard was red with blood, like a slaughter-house, and over the stones everywhere dead bodies were lying, all cut and gashed with ghastly wounds. Excepting a few of Tizoc's men, who had bound up their hurts, and who staggered along with us, not a wounded man remained alive; whence we inferred that the fight had been waged on strictly barbarous principles, and that no quarter had been given. And of this we had proof; for as we passed through the guard-room we found there a moaning wretch, belonging to the Priest Captain's party, in whose chest was a great hole made by a spear-thrust—and at a sign from Tizoc one of our men stepped aside, and with a blow of his heavy sword coolly mashed in the wounded man's skull, and so finished him.

The metal grating that closed the entrance had been raised by Tizoc's people from the inside, and we passed out beneath it to where the main body of his men was drawn up in readiness to march. But of Pablo and El Sabio there was no sign. Tizoc was not less distressed by the loss of the lad than we were, for he had counted upon the moral effect which the exhibition of Pablo and El Sabio most certainly would produce to aid powerfully in fomenting the spirit of revolt. When, therefore, we refused to go forward until further search had been made, he did not oppose us; but he told us plainly that further looking for him in that place was useless, for already every room in the building had been examined without the finding of a trace of him. There could be no doubt, he said, that when we had been made prisoners Pablo, and El Sabio with him, had been taken up the stair to the temple for greater security; in which place, if they were not both by this time dead, they still remained. Whereupon Young was for making an attack upon the temple instantly, and in this project Rayburn and I warmly seconded him; and even Fray Antonio said that this was a case in which he felt justified in using carnal weapons, since the fighting would be to rescue from among infidels a Christian soul.

But Tizoc hurriedly explained to us the hopelessness, at that time, of such an assault. The success that had attended his bold rescue of us had been due to the suddenness of it; for the majority of the people in the city, including the large force of soldiery there, assuredly was on the Priest Captain's side. It was outside the city that the strength of the revolution must be gathered; and his orders were, when his rescue of us should be accomplished, to carry us safely out beyond the walls with all possible speed. Such of the Council of the Twenty Lords as had decided to take the chances of revolt—being all the members of that body save the five priests that had belonged to it—already had gone down to the water-side, together with the small force that they had gathered, that they might seize the water-gate and hold it until we should join them. Even now it was certain that in going down through the city we should have to fight our way, and each moment that we delayed our retreat increased our danger. Capturing the temple now was a sheer impossibility. Our only hope of saving Pablo's life lay in our getting away promptly, and so beginning the preparations that would lead to ultimate victory.

All the while that Tizoc spoke he was edging us away towards the outer face of the terrace, where steps led downward; and when the men who had been searching the building once more for Pablo returned without him, he resolutely gave the order to march. To the arguments that he had advanced we were compelled to yield; but our hearts were heavy with sorrow for the boy whom we were leaving behind us, and little hope was in our breasts that we ever again should see him alive.

The truth of Tizoc's words about the great danger that we ourselves were in became apparent as we crossed the terrace next below that on which our march began. Where the street passed through the rampart by a narrow portal, and so by a flight of stone steps descended to the next level, soldiers were clustered together with the evident intention of disputing the way with us. Their number was so much less than ours that we made short work of them; killing a few, and driving the remainder down the steps before us. But those who escaped ran on ahead of us to where the next rampart was, and there joined themselves to a much larger body that lay in wait for us. Here our work was less easy; for the force that confronted us was nearly our equal, and some resolute fighting was required before we could drive it before us and so pass on. Some of our men were killed there, and more of the enemy; and I got a trifling hurt in my arm from the point of a javelin, that, luckily, did little more than graze the skin. I do not think that I killed anybody there, but I remember very plainly the look of pain and of anger on the face of that fellow who poked his javelin at me when I gashed his arm, and broke the bone of it, with a blow from my sword. I was glad, at the moment, that I had succeeded in giving him a worse hurt than he had given me; and then the absurdity occurred to me of my thus fighting with a total stranger, against whom I had no personal ill-will; and I could not but feel sorrow for him as I thought of the long time that he must suffer severe pain and great inconvenience because I had chanced to strike him that blow. However, from the way in which they went cutting and slashing about them, it was evident that neither Rayburn nor Young were troubled with any compunctions of this nature. They were only too glad, apparently, to get a chance to whack away at any of the Priest Captain's representatives; and they made such use of their opportunity that the Aztlanecas fighting with us cried out in admiration of their prowess and their strength. Fray Antonio was more sorely tried than any of us during this passage, for I knew that his flesh greatly longed to take part in the fighting, and that only the strong spirit which was within him subdued the flesh and so held his hands.

With a final rush we succeeded in forcing the enemy through the narrow opening in the rampart, and so down the steps beyond; but as we pursued them across the next terrace, keeping close at their heels so that they might not have time to form again, many of our wounded fell out from the ranks and dropped by the way—and we had left behind us a dozen or more of our dead on the ground where the fight had been.

Our tactics of rapid pursuit of the force that we had defeated served us well at the next rampart; for the men whom we pursued and we ourselves came to it almost in one body, and thus threw into such confusion the fresh force that was waiting for us that, without any long fighting about it, we drove right through them and went on downward; and in the same dashing fashion we carried the rampart beyond. However, when those men whom we had pushed aside from our path so easily got over their surprise at being so lightly handled, they formed in our rear and came hurrying after us; the result of which was that as we approached the last of the ramparts that we had to pass through, where was gathered the largest body of men that we had yet encountered, we found ourselves fairly wedged in between two bodies of the enemy and outnumbered four to one. Here, too, the passage through the rampart had been closed by the metal bars that were in readiness for that purpose. Setting these in place was no real barrier to our passage, for, being intended to close the portal against assailants from below, the fastenings which held them were on the side nearest to us. But to remove them it was necessary that we should fight our way through the crowd—with no possibility of driving the enemy before us, as we had done upon the upper terraces, since here the way was closed. What we did was literally to cut a path through the throng; and over the men who fell dead or wounded beneath our blows we made our advance. There was a curious creeping, uneasy sensation in the region of my stomach as I trod thus on the bodies of wounded men who were not dead yet, and felt them moving, and heard their groaning; and I was conscious of a feeling of relief when a body that I trod upon did not squirm beneath my foot, and so by its stillness assured me that I was standing only on dead flesh that had no feeling in it.

Very slowly did we go forward, for while the living barrier that we had to deal with was not at the outset more than twenty feet, or thereabouts, in thickness, hacking it down took us a tediously long time. While still we faced a dozen or more very desperate fighters, who held us off most resolutely from the metal bars which closed the way, a pang of dread and sorrow went through me as I perceived that Fray Antonio, who a moment before had been close beside me, had disappeared. That he might the better restrain his longing to take part in the fighting he had remained in the centre of our men; and it was hard to understand how, in that position, harm could have come to him, for missiles had no share in the work that was going forward, which was a fiery struggle hand to hand.

As I looked for him in the throng—so far as I could do this and at the same time keep up my guard against the man whom at that moment I was fighting with—I saw some signs of uneasy movement among the enemy in advance of us, and several of them evidently made an effort to reach down as though to get at something that was on the ground; which effort was wholly futile, for they were wedged so tightly together by our pressure upon them that reaching downward was impossible. By a lucky blow, I just then finished the man with whom I was contending, and so had a moment's breathing spell; and at that instant I saw one of the enemy, whose back was ranged against the bars, rise up in the air as though a strong spring had been loosed beneath him, and then fall sidewise upon the heads and shoulders of his fellows. And then, in the place thus made vacant, the cowled head of Fray Antonio instantly appeared—whereby I guessed, what afterwards I knew certainly, that he had crawled along the ground through the press until he reached the place that he aimed at, and then had risen up beneath one of the enemy with such sudden violence that he fairly had sent the man spinning upward into the air. What his purpose was I saw in a moment, for no sooner did he stand upright than he had his hands upon the metal bars, and then I heard the clinking together of stone and metal as he lifted them bodily away.

CHAPTER XXIV

THE AFFAIR AT THE WATER-GATE

Rayburn gave a great roar of gladness as the clinking sound made him turn and he saw what was going forward; and Young and I joined him in lusty Anglo-Saxon cheering, while our allies, in the savage fashion natural to them, vented their joy in shrill yells. In the midst of which cheering and yelling we pushed forward so hotly that the enemy, disconcerted by this sudden shifting of fortune in our favor, and the men directly in front of us being most seriously incommoded by their comrade lying sprawled out and kicking upon their heads and shoulders, seemed suddenly to lose heart so completely that we had no difficulty in cutting them down. Even had they not been too closely wedged in to turn upon Fray Antonio, our strong dashing upon them would have compelled them to leave him unharmed in order to defend themselves; and so it was that, by the time we had cut a path to the portal, the monk had released the whole tier of bars from their fastenings, and the way was free.

As we sprang down the steps—with Fray Antonio, once more in the guise of a non-combatant, safe in the midst of our company—we heard a great outcry from below, and saw a considerable body of men marching up towards us steadily from the water-side; but the alarm that sight of them gave us was only momentary, for their shouts, and the shouts of our men in answer, showed us that these were friends come to our support. However we had no great need of them, for those of the enemy whom we left alive behind us seemed suddenly to have grown sick of fighting, and made no attempt to follow after us down the stairs. Yet the coming of this supporting force, to be just in the matter, no doubt was the saving of us; for more than half of the men who had been with us when we started on our march down through the city had been slain by the way, and nearly all in our company were more or less disabled by wounds. Tizoc and Young and Rayburn had come through it all without as much as a scratch, and because of their extraordinary strength these three were almost as fresh as when the fighting began; but the rest of us were sorely weary, and our breathing was so heavy and so tremulous that each breath was like a long-drawn sob. Truly, then, we were glad to fall in in advance of the supporting column and so make our way, with a strong rear-guard for our protection, across the bit of level land that lay between us and the lake.

At the water-side boats were in readiness for us, and here we found also the members of the Council who had ordered, and who were the recognized leaders of, the revolt. There was still more fighting ahead of us, for the necessity of sending back the relief party had prevented the seizing of the water-gate; and this was a matter that had to be attended to quickly, for we could see bodies of men coming down several of the streets in pursuit of us, and unless we escaped outside the wall before they overtook us there was a strong and dismal probability that our whole plan would fail. Therefore, we tumbled aboard the boats with all possible rapidity, and while the pursuing parties still were far in our rear we shoved off from the shore.

Two minutes' quick rowing sufficed to carry our flotilla of boats across the basin, and so brought us to the long pier that extended landward from beside the water-gate, and from which an open stairway ascended to the top of the wall. On the pier there was no one at all to oppose our landing; and the force on the wall was not likely to be a large one, for the outbreak had come so suddenly that there had been no time to increase the small detail maintained in this position in times of peace. Only a few of our men, therefore—thirty or forty, perhaps—were ordered out of the boats to the attack, of which the leader was Tizoc, and with which Rayburn and Young went as volunteers. I also would have joined the party; but Rayburn, knowing that I was slightly wounded, begged me to stay where I was; and Young, as he ran up the stairs, called back to me: "You just see that they keep steam up, Professor. We'll attend t' takin' off th' brakes."

What went on above us, on top of the wall, we could not see; but the work done there was done quickly. There was a little shouting, a sound of arms clashing, and then four or five men—as though this were the easiest way of getting rid of them—were thrown over the parapet, and fell near us in the water. To these short shrift was given. As they came to the surface, our fellows instantly finished them with a spear-thrust or two. Then we heard the sound of a windlass creaking, and the clanking of chains; and as we looked through the opening in the wall we saw the grating that closed its farther end rise slowly until the way before us was free. Two of our boats already were in the passage, so that no time might be lost; and as these passed out into the lake, the others followed after them rapidly. One boat remained to bring off the attacking party, and we wondered a little because its coming was a good while delayed. But we wondered still more when it joined us at last, and we found that Tizoc and Young and Rayburn were not in it; indeed, at that moment I saw the three of them standing together on top of the wall. In answer to the shout that I gave, Rayburn leaned over the wall and motioned to me to keep silence; and so I knew that they had not been left behind through treachery, but were staying there because they had some plan against the enemy that they thus could execute. And for knowledge of what their plan was we did not have to wait long.

As we lay on our oars, off the outer end of the water-gate, we could see through it into the basin that lay before the city, and in a very few minutes the pursuing boats of the enemy came into view. As they neared us, we saw standing in the bow of the leading boat the same officer who had commanded the guard that had brought us as prisoners before the Priest Captain; the man of whom I have spoken, for what his real title was I do not know, as the barge-master.

He was calling to his men savagely to row faster; for our boats were so scattered that he only could see the one in which we happened to be, and he doubtless imagined that the others had gone forward, and that this one waited to carry off some of our men who yet remained on the wall. He evidently hoped to be able to cut us off from the rest of our party, and his eagerness had so communicated itself to his oarsmen that his boat led the others by nearly a hundred yards. So far as this one boat was concerned, we felt no alarm, for the moment that it came out through the wall our whole force was ready to dash upon it; yet we wondered why Tizoc permitted even a single boat to come out to the attack, when, by dropping the grating, they all could be penned in so effectually as to give us the advantage of a long start.

As the boat neared the water-gate the barge-master went back from his place in the bow to the middle part of it, and there crouched down; and some soldiers who were standing crouched down also; and almost as the bow entered the low, narrow passage the oars were unshipped and taken aboard. So cleverly was the unshipping of the oars managed, and so good was the steering, that the boat shot into the passage under full speed, and so came nearly through it before losing head-way. And we who were nearest to it got our arms in readiness—

for we were convinced that in another minute the barge-master would lay us aboard. But this was not destined to be, nor were the men in that boat destined ever to do any more fighting in this world.

All this while Rayburn had stood close by the parapet, bending over it and intently watching the outside of the water-gate; above which the heavy metal grating had been hauled up, in the metal grooves that it ran in, almost to the top of the wall. At the moment that the bow of the boat showed outside the opening he raised his hand, as though signalling to Young and Tizoc behind him; and in that same instant we heard the shrieking of the windlass and the quick clanking of the unwinding chains, and saw the metal grating rushing down the face of the wall. With all the force generated by the fall from so great height of so ponderous a body, the grating came crashing into the boat just amidships, fairly dividing its heavy timbers and forcing the fragments of it, together with all the men that it carried, down into the water's depths. But the barge-master died by a quicker death than drowning. He still was crouched in the middle of the boat, and the sharp angle of the lower bar of the grating struck him just on the nape of his neck so keenly that his head was cut off and seemed of itself to spring forward and away from him; while the broad flat bar, coming down upon his bowed shoulders, crushed his body into a mere quivering mass of flesh.

A great yell of delight went up from our boats as this brilliant stroke so brilliantly was delivered; and an answering cry of triumph—that was one-third a yell and two-thirds a cheer—came back from Tizoc and the others on top of the wall. However, they had no time to waste in shouting over their success, for the remaining boats of the enemy had come by this time to the pier inside the wall, and it seemed highly probable that in a minute or two more our three men would be prisoners. But for all their danger they coolly finished the work that they had in hand. As they explained to me afterwards, Rayburn stood at the head of the stair to hold the enemy in check should they come before the work was finished—and very strong as well as very brave men must the man have been who would have ventured to attack him as he occupied that position of overpowering advantage—while the other two cast off from the windlass the chains by which the water-gate was operated, and dropped them over the wall into the lake; and as the gate itself was jammed and wedged fast by the fragments of the boat, this throwing down of the chains made the raising of it a serious undertaking that well might require a day or more to accomplish.

As the chains fell with a splash, and we comprehended the thoroughness of the work that these three were doing, our people burst forth into yells again; and a perfect roar went up from them when, the gate being closed and the apparatus for raising it being entirely disabled, Rayburn sprang from the outer edge of the parapet into the lake, and Tizoc and Young instantly followed him. In truth, a more gallant feat of arms had not been essayed, nor carried to a more triumphant conclusion, since the Roman gate was held by Horatius; and in my admiration of it I shouted until the muscles of my throat were strained and aching. Our boat already was near the wall—having pulled in that the soldiers aboard of it might spear such of the enemy as came up to the surface alive—and we had the three out of the water and safe among us in very short order; and then we pulled away towards the other boats with all possible speed—for the wall now was manned by the enemy, and they were beginning to make things unpleasantly hot for us with the heavy stones which they heaved over the parapet, that our boat might be sunk by them, and by a rapid discharge of darts. Luckily, none of the stones struck us, and because of the rapid way that we were making, only two of our men were struck with the darts. So, on the whole, we came out of this encounter very well; for these two men killed in our boat were all that we lost, while of the enemy at least forty were drowned or speared. However, we owed our light escape mainly to the fact that the enemy, having armed hurriedly, and expecting only to fight with us at close quarters, had with them neither bows nor slings—but for which fortunate fact it scarcely is possible that a single man in our boat would have come off alive.

Dripping wet though they were, I fairly hugged Rayburn and Young when they were safe aboard with us, as did also Fray Antonio, whose daring spirit was mightily aroused by witnessing their splendid bravery. And in giving them hearty words of praise for what they had done—which yet fell far short of their deserts—I naturally likened them to the Roman hero. Indeed, I may say that the parallel that I there drew was an apt one, and in some of its turns was not devoid of grace.

"I can't say, Professor," Young answered, when I had finished, "that I ever heard o' th' party you refer to, but if this Horace—what did you say his last name was?—pinched his fingers in th' drawbridge chains as damnably as I pinched mine in th' chains of that infernal grating, I'll bet a hat he was sorry that he hadn't run away!" And I truly believe that Young thought more about his pinched fingers than he did about the resolute bravery that he had shown in finishing his work upon the wall in the very face of the advancing enemy.

Being once out of range of the darts, we pulled towards the other boats leisurely; for now we were entirely safe against pursuit, and were free to go upon the lake in whatsoever direction we pleased. That some positive line of action had been determined upon was evident, for the flotilla already was in motion as we came up in the rear of it—the boat containing the members of the Council leading—and the order was passed back to us that we should follow with the rest. From the direction in which we were heading, Tizoc inferred that we were bound for the only other considerable town in the valley, that which had grown up around the shafts leading to the great mine whence the Aztlanecas drew their supply of gold. There was a very grave look upon his face as he told us of our probable destination; and presently added that the population of this town—save the few freemen who were in charge of the workings, and the large guard of soldiers that always was maintained there—was made up wholly of Tlahuicos who had been selected from their fellows to be miners because of their exceptional hardiness and strength.

It was among these men, he went on to tell us speaking in a low, guarded voice, that the most dangerous of the revolts of the Tlahuicos invariably had their origin; for the miners were fierce, half-savage creatures, naturally turbulent and rebellious, and were stirred constantly to resentful anger because of the life of crushing toil that they were condemned to lead. So dangerous were they that the only effective means of keeping them in subjection was to hold the major part of them continually prisoners underground in the mine, with a guard stationed at the mouth of each shaft under orders to kill instantly any man who attempted to come forth from the mine without authority. In order that their labor, a thing of positive value, might not be lost through their dying of being thus imprisoned in the bowels of the earth, they were divided into ten great companies, each one of which, in regular order, was employed in the surface work under the constant supervision of a strong guard. Yet even these stern measures were not wholly effective in preventing mutiny. Many times great revolts had broken out here that had set all the valley in an uproar, and that had been crashed only after pitched battles had been fought between the rebels and the entire military force of the state. The town was a veritable volcano, Tizoc declared; and because of the dread of it that universally obtained, by reason of the frequent outbursts there of lawless violence, it had received the name of Huitzilan: the Town of War.

And there could be no doubt, he added—while the tones of his voice and the look upon his face showed how great he believed to be the risk involved in this line of policy—that in now directing our course towards the mining town the deliberate purpose of the Council was to incite these semi-savage, wholly desperate miners to join forces with us in our rising against the Priest Captain's power.

CHAPTER XXV

THE GOLD-MINERS OF HUITZILAN

As we rounded a mountain spur that extended a long way out into the lake, a deep bay opened to us; which bay ran close in to the cliffs whereby the valley was surrounded, and was at no great distance from the Barred Pass, through which we had made our entry. At the foot of the bay, built partly upon the level land near the water-side, and partly upon the steep ascent beyond, was the town of Huitzilan— whereof the most curious feature that at first was noticeable was a tall chimney, whence thick black smoke was pouring forth, that rose above a stone building of great solidity and of a very considerable size.

On archæological grounds, the sight of this chimney greatly astonished me; and Rayburn, who was a very well-read man in all matters connected with his profession, was greatly astonished by it also; for the chimney obviously was a part of extensive reduction-works, and we both knew that such complete appliances for the smelting of metal, as seemed from this sign to exist here, were supposed to be the product of a high state of civilization in comparatively modern times. As for Young, he declared that the chimney gave him a regular jolt of homesickness; for, excepting that it was built of stone instead of brick, it might have been, for the look of it, transplanted hither directly from the region of the Back Bay. "I s'pose we'll be hearin' th' noon whistle next," he said, mournfully; and presently he added: "Do you know, Professor, I b'lieve I'm beginnin' t' see daylight in all this tall talk you say th' Colonel has been givin' us about th' 'rebellions,' as he calls 'em, that go on here. He don't mean t' close our eyes up, th' Colonel don't, for he's a first-class gentleman; but, bein' born an' bred a heathen, he don't know any better. What he's tryin' t' tell us about, an' can't, because he don't know th' English for it, is *strikes*. That's what's th' matter. Miners are bound t' go on strikes. It's their nature, an' they can't help it. That chimbly gives th' whole thing away. You just tell th' Colonel that we've got down t' th' hard-pan an' really know what he's been drivin' at. An' t' think of there bein' strikes in Mexico! I didn't b'lieve that a Greaser had backbone enough, or ambition enough, t' strike at anything!"

However, as I had no great amount of faith in Young's theory, I did not attempt to translate to Tizoc what he had said to me; nor was there any opportunity for further talk at that time. Already the foremost boats of the flotilla had made a landing at a well-built pier that extended from the shore into deep water; and a minute or two later our boat also pulled in to the pier, and we disembarked. The general view of the town that I then had showed me that it was closely built over an area rather more than half a mile square; that the houses for the most part were mere hovels, of which the largest could not contain more than two small rooms; and that the few houses of a better sort were within the strong stone wall by which the reduction-works also were enclosed. At the pier where we landed a boat was in process of lading with bars of gold for transport to the Treasure-house in the city; and I thought that I never had seen anywhere more savage-looking fellows than the almost naked laborers by whom the work of lading was carried on. Physically these men were magnificent creatures—tall and well-shaped and vigorous, and the ease with which they handled the great bars of gold showed how enormous must be their strength. But so full of venomous hate were the sullen looks which they cast upon us, and so savage was the effect of their coarse, dishevelled hair falling down over and partly veiling their great glittering eyes, whence these angry glances were shot forth at us like poisoned darts, that I was thankful to see that, all told, there were not more than a dozen of them, and that three times as many heavily armed soldiers served as their guard. And looking at these creatures, who were truly less like men than dangerous wild beasts, I could not wonder at the grave concern which Tizoc had manifested at thought of the risk which we ran in taking them for allies. "It's as easy t' start 'em," Young said, when he came to an understanding of the situation, "as 'tis t' start a freight-train down a three per cent. grade. But what I want to know is, when we want 'em t' stop, how in th' h—ll are we ever goin' t' set th' brakes?"

Yet, dangerous to ourselves though the use of it must be, our hopes of success rested mainly upon our ability to control and to employ effectively this savage material. Fortunately, it was not the whole of our reliance; and it was our intention to leaven this dangerous lump with the very considerable number of trained and trustworthy soldiers that we had available as the substantial nucleus of our fighting force, and also with the larger body of both slaves and freemen—not regularly drilled soldiers, to be sure, yet many of them trained in the ways of war—that we counted upon to join us from among the people at large.

This outline of the plan of action that the Council had determined upon was exhibited to us by Tizoc during our passage down the lake; and I was glad to find that Rayburn—for whose judgment I had much respect in such matters—was disposed to think well of it.

"If I expected to stay here, Professor, after the row was over," he said, "I mightn't be quite as well satisfied with this plan of theirs for running things. The war part of the programme is all right. They won't have any difficulty in getting their Tlahuicos to fight anything in the way of an army that the Priest Captain shows up with. Fighting is just what will please them more than anything else. Where the trouble is going to come in is when the fighting is over and they go in for reconstruction. It's one thing to make fighters out of this sort of stuff, but it's quite another thing to make respectable citizens out of it. That's where the hitch will be. But as we don't intend to settle down in this valley—unless we find that there's no way out of it—we needn't bother about that part of the performance at all. That's their funeral, not ours. So, for my part, the sooner they get their army in shape, and get the fighting part settled, the better I'll be satisfied."

To do the members of the Council justice, they seemed to be even more eager than Rayburn was to forward the work that they had in hand. From the pier they went directly to the enclosure in the centre of the town, within which was the building ordinarily occupied by the commandant of the post and by the officials of the civil government; and in this place, Tizoc informed us, they intended immediately to organize the new government, and then to proceed with all possible despatch to make arrangements for placing an army in the field.

In Tizoc's company, but more leisurely, we also went on to the Citadel—as we found the enclosure about the smelting-works was called—where comfortable quarters had been provided for us in the same building wherein the Council was housed. Here we waited, in somewhat strained idleness, while the Council carried on, in a chamber not far removed from us, its exciting work of destroying a government that had endured for more than a thousand years; and we were mightily surprised, knowing how prodigious was the change that then was being wrought in ancient institutions, by observing how quietly it all went on. The murmur of talk that came to us, unchecked by any intervening doors, had no sound of excitement or of anger or of violent emotion of any sort; and I could not but hold in admiration the calm, self-contained natures of these men who thus equably and rationally could deal with such vastly weighty affairs.

While this great matter—which could end only in wild commotion and fierce battling—went forward in this quiet way, Tizoc opened to us much that was of curious interest touching the near-by gold-mine and they who mined the gold. Of the existence of the mine, he said, the Aztlanecas had remained ignorant for many generations after their coming into the valley; and for many more generations but little gold had been taken from it, because the metal was of no value to his people save for the making of ornaments. But when the process had been discovered by which this metal could be hardened, and so made serviceable for all manner of useful purposes—and this the more because, by the manufacture that then ensued of tools wherewith the rock could be easily worked, mining in a large way became possible—the development of the mine upon a great scale had been begun, and had been continued upon a constantly increasing scale from that time onward. All the earth beneath where we then were, he said, was honey-combed with passages which followed the several veins; and of these there seemed to be no end at all, for ever as each vein was exhausted another not less rich was found—and thus is seemed as though all the substructure of that great mountain range were one huge mass of gold.

What the measures of weight were with which he estimated the annual output of the mine, I could not clearly understand, but the matter was made approximately plain to us by his statement that the daily product of the mine never was less than one of the great bars of gold that we had seen upon the pier in process of carriage to the Treasure-house; and that sometimes, when veins of extraordinary richness were encountered, even so much as four of these bars had been smelted from the ore that the mine yielded in a single day.

"Those bars don't weigh an ounce less than two hundred pounds apiece," Rayburn said, when I had translated to him what Tizoc had told me. "That makes the output of the mine not less than three tons a month, and, in a rough way, a ton of gold is worth just about half a million of dollars. If the Colonel isn't mixed in his figures, and if you've translated him straight, Professor, these fellows are taking out somewheres in the neighborhood of twenty millions a year."

Young gave a long whistle. "Great Scott!" he exclaimed, "that just is an all-fired big pile of money t' be wasted on a lot of barelegged heathen critters like these, who don't know th' Ten Commandments by sight, an' who've never even heard of a cocktail! D' you know what I'm goin' t' do, Rayburn, when I realize on this investment? I'm goin' t' buy th' Old Colony Railroad, just for th' sake of bein' able t' bounce th' Superintendent. He bounced me after that freight smash-up—and it wasn't my fault that th' operator got mixed an' gave me th' wrong orders—and I'll give him a taste o' th' same kind. Won't it just paralyze him when he gets his orders t' quit, signed 'Seth Young, President,' an' finds out it's th' same old Seth Young who used t' run Thirty-two on th' Fall River division?"

"Hadn't you better let him down easy by telegraphing him right now to begin to look out for a new place?" Rayburn asked. "We'll wait for you here, while you step over to the Western Union office"— which cool comment upon Young's enthusiastic discounting of a bright future brought the gloomy present so clearly before his mind that his castle-building ended suddenly, and he lapsed into silence.

But great though our wonder was at the prodigious quantity of precious metal that this mine yielded in each year, and amazed though we were by thought of the vast store of treasure that the valley now must hold, I, for my part, felt a far deeper interest in what Tizoc went on to tell us concerning the men by whose toil the treasure had been accumulated. And, truly, so bitter and so dreary was the life of the Tlahuicos who were forced to labor here unceasingly, and through so long a period had they been thus cruelly dealt with, that it seemed to me there must rest upon all the Valley of Aztlan a heavy curse that only some signal act of expiation could remove. And the coincidence struck me as most curious that here among the Aztecs, wrought by themselves upon the men of their own race, should be found identically the same cruelties which the Spaniards practised upon the Indians whom they enslaved as miners in New Mexico: whereof came that fierce outburst of revolt two hundred years ago, when the Pueblos ravaged with sword and flame the whole valley of the Rio Grande from Taos to the Pass of the North.

There was small ground for wonder that the Tlahuicos, thus crushed by over-heavy labor, and dealt with as though they were not men, but fierce and dangerous brutes, should cherish at all times in their breasts a sullen fire of mutiny; nor that on every occasion at all favorable to their purposes there should spring forth from the glowing embers of their hatred a vivid and consuming flame. Only by the strength and the vigilance of the guard that constantly was maintained over them was their tendency to rebellion held in check; and even the guards could not prevent frequent outbreaks—which ended only in the cruel slaughter of all concerned in them—so passionately eager was the longing of these desperate creatures for revenge.

Only once, a vastly long while past, Tizoc said, had success attended an effort on the part of the Tlahuicos to release themselves from their cruel slavery, and that they then eluded the vigilance of their masters was due to their employment of strategy against force. The whole matter, he continued, was now but a half-remembered tradition, yet the main details of it were clear. In that far-back time a vein of extraordinary richness had been followed for a very long distance in the direction of the Barred Pass; and, as the event proved, the gallery was carried beyond the bars, passing far beneath them, and so went onward, steadily rising, until an outlet was had into the cañon. That the secret of this outlet might be kept among the men who had opened it, these slew the guard that watched over them and thrust his body out into the cañon, thus most effectually placing it beyond the reach of the search that would be made for it; and the opening that they had made they closed carefully, and continued a little way onward into the rock the gallery in which they were working: so that the superintendent of the mine might see clearly (what, indeed, was the truth) that the vein of ore had been followed to its end.

Tizoc knew not how long a time passed before the Tlahuicos made use of the way of escape thus opened to them; but their flight could not have been taken hastily, because it included a very great number of them, and included also carrying with them large quantities of arms for warfare, and of useful household stores. He could say certainly no more than that when all their well-laid plan was ready to be executed, they rose against the soldiers which guarded them with such suddenness and brave violence that they succeeded in seizing and in holding the Citadel; which gave no chance for grave uneasiness, for the officers of the force thus for a moment driven off thought that because of their retiring within so narrow a place they speedily must surrender for dread of being starved there; and it was held to be but a sign of their still greater simplicity—since thus would there be more hungry mouths to fill—that they carried their women and children with them into the stronghold where they lay besieged.

But so strange was the desolate silence that hung over the place into which so great a multitude had retired, that the besiegers presently were moved by it to a wonder wherein was a strong feeling of awe; and still greater was the marvel that they had to ponder upon when, at last, meeting with no opposition, they broke in the grating that barred the entrance to the Citadel, and found within the enclosure not one single living soul! And so cleverly had the fugitives closed the way behind them that a long while passed before it was known certainly what had become of this living host that, as it seemed, in a moment had vanished from off the face of the earth. More than half a lifetime went by without the shedding of light upon this mystery; and it seemed as though a ghost had risen when one day a very aged man came forth from that long-abandoned passage in the mine and surrendered himself to the first of the guards whom he encountered—and then told that he was a priest whom the fleeing rebels had carried captive with them, and whom they had held a prisoner through all these many years. And he told also how the rebels had made their home in a certain fair valley that was shut in and hidden among the mountains; and how that they had built a great city—resting fearless in the conviction that they were safe from harm. By the heavy toil that had been needful to open anew the way into the mine from the cañon, the little remnant of strength in this old man's body had been exhausted; and presently, having told his story, he died.

Then it was that the Priest Captain and the Council who ruled in that ancient time, having assured themselves by the sending out of spies that all which the old man had told them was true, planned to bring upon the rebels a very terrible vengeance; which was to drown them all in their city by letting loose upon them the waters of a mighty lake. And this plan, though its accomplishment was not arrived at until two full cycles had passed away, so mighty was the labor that it involved, at last was executed: and in one single day every living creature in all that valley was overwhelmed by the flood let loose into it; and where so great a mass of teeming life had been there remained thereafter only the desolate silence and stillness of universal death.

It was with long-drawn breaths that Fray Antonio and I listened to Tizoc's telling of this tradition, which in many ways was far more real to us than it possibly could be to him; for we but lately had passed through that death-stricken valley—and ourselves had been like to die there—and every feature of the scene, that he could but vaguely describe to us, we had clearly in our minds. And thus we came to know the full meaning of the great catastrophe whereof we had seen the outworking, both in the destruction wrought by it and the way of its accomplishment, but of which we had divined no more concerning its cause than that in some way it must have resulted from a slowly worked-out vengeance prompted by a most malignant hate.

CHAPTER XXVI

THE GATHERING FOR WAR

Although the whole of the discussion of their plan of revolt was carried on by the Council with so calm a gravity, there was enough of energy and of quick movement when their deliberations came to an end; and we augured well of the result because they thus had delayed their action until their plan for making it effective had been fully matured. The whole of that first day in Huitzilan, and much of the following night also, was given to arranging clearly what must be done in order to set up a temporary government and to get an army together; and how well this preliminary work was accomplished was shown by the precision and celerity with which the plans then made were executed during the immediately ensuing days.

During this period we had ample time to look around us; and, being now upon a most friendly footing with the strange people among whom we thus strangely found ourselves, we were heartily aided—so far as this was possible because of the exigencies of that stirring time—in investigating the manner of their lives. The material then was obtained for my chapter on the "House Life and Domestic Customs of the Aztecs"; and the knowledge which Rayburn gathered (also embodied in his own paper, that attracted so much attention when read before the American Institute of Mining Engineers) he has permitted me to use in my chapter on "Mining and Metalworking among the Aztecs"; which two chapters are among the most note worthy *Pre-Columbian Conditions on the Continent of North America*. Rayburn, indeed, was lost in wonder as he came to understand how far scientific investigation had been carried among this isolated people, and how well they had learned to apply their scientific knowledge to their practical affairs. In many matters, to be sure, they fell far behind the remainder of the civilized world; but a large part of the useful knowledge that has been gained by study under civilized conditions elsewhere we found here also as the fruit of independent discovery. In many cases the discovery was identical in every respect with our own. Thus, their process (the adding of hydrochloric acid to a neutral solution of auric-chloride) for producing from gold a rich purple stain, that was employed in the coloring of hard-wood and bone, was precisely that which Boyle mentioned in 1663; and, as nearly as I could determine the date, it was about that very time that they, also, first effected this combination. In the matter of hardening gold, and thereafter giving it all the qualities of tempered steel, they had made a step that was distinctly in advance of anything which our metallurgists had accomplished; and I am strongly inclined to the belief that—at least among the priests—knowledge had been gained of a process quite unlike that known to us for producing a gold fulmi-nate. I was not so fortunate as to gain more knowledge of this matter than could be learned from hearsay, but from several sources I heard of the splitting asunder of a certain great rock by the Priest Captain—which wonder was accompanied by a thunderous noise and a gleam of flame and a bursting forth of smoke—whereby he was considered to have proved that the aid of the gods was at his command. But to my mind, and also to Rayburn's, the proof was, rather, that he had at his command—in some way that as yet our chemists have not fathomed—the aid of a gold fulminate that could be controlled in use as readily as we control gunpowder. That this agent, whatever it might be, was not easily available, was indicated by the fact that the Priest Captain never had given more than this single exhibition of the wonders which he could accomplish with it; and that it then had served his purpose well was shown by the obvious awe with which all who told me of it spoke of the dreadful havoc that thus visibly was wrought by what they termed the thunder of the gods.

Indeed, a very serious difficulty that the leaders of the revolution had to overcome was the unwillingness on the part of the people at large to defy the power of their spiritual chief; which feeling among the upper classes was mainly because disobedience to the Priest Captain was, in effect, heresy; while among the lower classes there was joined to a like horror of heresy a very lively dread of the punish-ment, both temporal and spiritual, that the Priest Captain could bring upon them because of his intimate relations with the supernatural beings by which the forces of the world were controlled.

Yet out of this condition of affairs arose an opportunity that Fray Antonio was not slow to make the most of. Our coming into the valley with news of the outside world that directly controverted the Priest Captain's claim to infallibility gave a great shock to the religious faith of the community, and so induced a willingness to listen to the preaching of a new and purer creed. And on the part of those of the Council who were organizing the revolution—among whom religion seemed to be regarded less as a vital fact than as a matter of political expediency—there was a strong disposition to encourage the spread of doctrines which obviously, by weakening the Priest Captain's hold upon the people, would increase their own strength. Therefore, Fray Antonio found himself free to preach to this heathen multitude the glorious Christian faith; and that he was granted this most rare and signal opportunity, the like of which was not given even to the blessed Saint Francis himself, so filled and exalted his soul with a radiantly joyful thankfulness that he was as one transformed. And his holy enthusiasm, that thus made every fibre of his being vibrate with a grateful gladness, gave him also so eloquent a command of beseeching language that it was a living wonder to perceive how his inspired words penetrated into the minds, darkened by superstitious doctrines, of those to whom he spoke, and so sunk into their hearts and brought the restful happiness of the faith Christian to those who had known only the restless terror of idolatry throughout all their lives. Like a pure flame, the doctrine that he preached ran through that host of the heathen, burning out from among them the impure creed whereby their souls had been held in a most cruel and desolate bondage, and giving in the place thereof the tender comfort of a saving Christian grace.

Yet the very fervor of Fray Antonio's preaching, and the strong hold that the gentle doctrine which he set forth took upon the hearts of the multitude, tended also to stir up against him a lively enmity among those who, refusing to hearken to him, remained steadfast in the ancient faith. Many such there were among us at that time in Huitzilan; but because of the firm grasp that Fray Antonio had upon so many hearts, and also because of the countenance which the Council gave him, these did not venture to assail either him or his doctrine openly; yet, as I noted at times the evil glances which they shot forth at him—which surely would have killed him could he thus have been slain—I was filled with dread that hate so malignant as here was shown must surely find expression in a direct attempt upon his life. Fortunately, there no longer were any priests among us. Of these there had been a considerable number in Huitzilan upon our first coming there, but silently, one by one, they had disappeared—going, as we well knew, to join themselves to the force which the Priest

Captain was gathering against the time when the issue between us would be settled by the arbitration of arms. And those who went from our camp to his must have carried with them news of the peril that menaced the ancient faith through the new faith that Fray Antonio preached so zealously in such burning words; for of his knowledge of what Fray Antonio was doing, and of his dread of what might therefrom result, we presently had proof in a way that filled our hearts with a very dismal fear.

All the while that this curious, and to me most interesting, conflict between a primitive and a highly developed religion went on, the more practical work went on also of establishing a new government and of organizing an army whereby it might be maintained. So far as the setting up of a government was concerned, the matter was comparatively easy; for the majority of the Council had come out with us from Culhuacan, and these had but to adapt to the requirements of the new situation the governmental machinery that already was established and at their command. And they were surprised pleasurably by finding how readily this transformation was effected; for among the higher classes—from which classes the officials of the government exclusively were drawn—the feeling of hatred against the Priest Captain, begotten of his many acts of cruelty and oppression, was so strong that the opportunity now offered to turn against him was seized upon most gladly. In every town throughout the valley the emissaries of the Council were warmly welcomed; and presently the new government was established everywhere save in the capital city and in certain villages upon the lake border lying close beneath its walls.

The work of organizing an army, however, was a more difficult matter; for very serious obstacles, both moral and material, had to be overcome before we of the revolutionary faction could place an effective fighting force in the field. Of what I may term regular troops, that is to say, thoroughly drilled and disciplined soldiers, we could count upon but few; for, practically, the whole body of the army had remained faithful to the Priest Captain and was with him in Culhuacan. For the most part, also, the regular troops scattered through the garrisons of the various towns had betaken themselves immediately to Culhuacan upon the acknowledgment by the civil officers of these towns of the authority of the new government; and at the same time had departed with them nearly all the priests, and such few persons of the upper classes as desired the maintenance of the ancient order of things. The result of which general movement at least gave us the advantage of carrying on unmolested our own work of concentrating and organizing; and, so far, was a positive service to us.

As the nucleus of our army we had the corps that Tizoc commanded, the highly organized body of troops charged with the important duty of guarding the Barred Pass; and we had also the few hundreds of men who had come out with us from Culhuacan. From these sources we were able to draw officers to command the irregular force, largely made up of Tlahuicos, that the Council rapidly got together; while for the organizing of the main body of our troops, the savages who worked in the mine, the bold stroke was made of mingling them with the men who, until then, had been their most relentless enemies—the soldiers who had served as their guards. That it was possible to put in operation this daring plan was due, I think, in great part to the fact that both guards and miners were led to accept the extraordinary fellowship that it created by a genuine shock of surprise; and before they had at all recovered from their astonishment their interests became identical, through their common need of defending themselves against a common enemy. And, further, I am well convinced that the Tlahuicos had been in part prepared, before our coming into the valley, to join in the revolt that under any circumstances could not have been much longer delayed. In regard to this matter, Tizoc persistently evaded my questions; but I remembered very distinctly his curious hesitancy when he had told me of the effective part that the servile class could be made to take in the event of a rebellion; and I perceived many evidences of a secret understanding between him and certain of the miners during the time that the gathering for war was going on in Huitzilan. Therefore, I inferred that the seeds of revolt which germinated so readily had been long since sown.

Of all the disabilities under which we then labored, the most serious was the lack of an adequate supply of arms. The great arsenal of the Aztlanecas was in Culhuacan; and thus nearly the whole of the supply of munitions of war in the valley was in the Priest Captain's hands. Fortunately, the shipment of hardened gold that we had intercepted—by landing at the pier whence in a few hours it would have been despatched to the Treasure-house—gave us a good supply of raw material out of which spear-heads, and the heads of darts, and swords could be made; and night and day the forges blazed in Huitzilan while the manufacture of these weapons went on. Of bows and arrows it was not possible to make many in that short time, but of slings there was no difficulty in making enough to supply our entire force—and among these people, who are wonderfully skilful in the use of it, the sling is a most deadly implement of war. We lacked time, also, to make any large number of shields, and our deficiency in this respect was regarded by Tizoc, and by all the military officers who were with us, as a most serious matter; for not only would our men without shields be the more easily slain in battle, but their fighting value would be lessened by their consciousness that they were without this piece of furniture that all savage races hold to be so necessary in war.

However, of defensive armor we had a good supply, for it chanced that in the Citadel there was a great store of cotton cloth, suitable for making long kirtles of many thicknesses of cloth quilted together; which kirtles were arrow proof, and well protected a man from his neck downward almost to his knees. Young was disposed to think but lightly of this curious armor, but when Tizoc, to convince him of its utility, demonstrated its power to resist a well-pointed arrow shot at very short range he was forced to confess its entire applicability to the purpose for which it was designed.

"Tell th' Colonel that I give in, an' think it a first-rate notion, Professor," he said. "But if you can get it into his head, an' I'm afraid you can't, just tell him that when this barelegged army of ours gets fitted out with those little night-shirts they'll look for all th' world like a lot o' fellows who've scrambled out of a hotel that's caught fire in th' middle o' th' night. All that'll be wanted t' make th' thing perfect'll be a couple o' steam fire-engines, an' a crowd with all their clothes on, an' a line of policemen. I guess it's goin' t' be one o' th' funniest lookin' armies that was ever seen outside of a lunatic asylum. What I'd like to do, Professor, instead o' tryin' t' do any fightin' with it, is just t' take th' whole outfit back t' th' States an' make a show of it. I'd get Benito Nichols t' go in with me—he's a first-class man, Benito is, an' he's a boss hand as a show manager—an' we'd call it 'Th' Aztec Warrior Army an' Circus Combination,' an' we'd just rake in th' dollars quicker'n we could count 'em. That makes me think o' that show we were talkin' about makin' with Pablo an' his burro." Young's voice changed as he spoke, and there was a huskiness in it as he added: "I s'pose by this time there ain't much left for show-makin' purposes of either of 'em. No, I guess I'll stay around an' take a hand in any fightin' that's goin' on; for I'd pretty near be willin' t' be killed right away after it myself for th' chance t' square things with that old devil for killin' our boy. He was a good boy, Professor, an'—How this devilish dust does get into my eyes an' make 'em water." With which highly irrelevant remark—for there was no dust blowing just then—Young suddenly ceased speaking and walked away.

This was the only time that we spoke of Pablo while we lay at Huitzilan, for talk about the boy only increased the bitter sorrow for him that was in all our hearts. As for my own heart, it was well-nigh broken as I thought that but for me his gentle life would still be flowing on smoothly—as I had found it flowing when, in an evil hour, I joined his fortunes with mine, and so had brought him to so untimely and to so cruel a death. And I, too, longed for the fighting to begin that I might avenge him; for the accomplishment of which vengeance I was not merely in part, but altogether ready to yield up my own life.

Indeed, excepting only Fray Antonio, who saw in warfare only the wickedness and the cruelty of it, we all were most eager for our inaction to end, and for the battling to begin that would give us opportunity to let the life out of some of those by whom Pablo had been slain. It was with delight, therefore, that we noted the rapidity with which the preparations for the impending campaign were carried forward, and saw how each day the disorderly host that had been gathered at Huitzilan was changing from a confused mass of good fighting material into a body fairly well adapted to the needs of war. It was, in truth, astonishing to us—for we could not well comprehend how essentially warlike were the instincts of this people, and how quick, therefore, they must be in military matters—to observe the promptness that was shown in getting our army in readiness for the field. And with our astonishment came also a comforting conviction that the force that could be so quickly, and, as it seemed, so effectively organized, must surely hold well together, and fight well together, when the hour for fighting came.

CHAPTER XXVII

AN OFFER OF TERMS

During the time that our various preparations thus went forward we had no direct news from the stronghold of the enemy; yet many vague rumors reached us of the army that was being set in order there to take the field against us. On the other hand, the constant departure from among us of those who were loyal to the ancient government kept the Priest Captain well informed of all that was in progress in our camp. No effort was made by the Council to prevent these departures, for all of our plans were working so well, and our forces were increasing so prodigiously, that it was to our advantage that the enemy should have news of our rapidly augmenting strength; and especially was it hoped that the news thus carried to the city might incline many there who wavered in their allegiance to take open part with us—or, at the least, to refuse to take part against us—and that in this way there might be stirred up a very dangerous spirit of mutiny within the enemy's lines.

The plan of campaign that the Council had adopted struck me as being an exceedingly prudent one. This was that we should not attempt an attack upon the city—for, indeed, to assail such fortifications without artillery would have been utterly hopeless—but should wait until the enemy came out to assail us, and then meet him on our own chosen ground. In every way this plan was in our favor. It most obviously was to our advantage to delay as long as possible the battle that was inevitable, and that, when it did come, must decide the fate of the rebellion finally. Every day that this was deferred was a substantial gain to us, in that the organization of our army was thereby rendered the more complete, and also in that the effective hold of the new government upon the people throughout the valley was thereby strengthened. On the side of the enemy, delay would produce no corresponding gain, rather would it tend to weaken the hold of the Priest Captain upon those who remained faithful to him; and, being shut up with his whole army and a multitude of non-combatants within those great stone walls, a very terrible foe, against which stone walls are no defence, presently would attack him in the shape of hunger. Therefore we had only to wait—maintaining the while a vigilant patrol of guard-boats on the lake, so that no fresh supplies might reach the garrison in the city—in the sure conviction that our foe would of his own accord come forth to give us battle, and that we then would have the advantage of standing wholly on the defensive until some happy turn of chance should so favor us that we would risk nothing in making an assault.

It was a very fortunate thing for us that matters stood in this way; for wellnigh the whole of the trained army of the Aztlanecas was with the Priest Captain, and against this well-disciplined body of men our own hastily assembled and imperfectly organized army would have made but a poor showing had we met on equal terms. Even under the existing circumstances, so favorable in many ways to our success, Tizoc and the other military officers who were with us did not at all disguise their anxiety as to what might be the outcome of the battle so soon to be fought; and especially did they dread some well-planned stealthy movement of the enemy, by which our camp might be suddenly set upon and fairly carried before our own untrained forces could be rallied from the bewilderment and confusion into which they would be thrown by the shock of such surprise.

Rayburn, who had seen a good deal of Indian fighting in his time, fully shared in this feeling of anxiety. "Indian fights, you see," he said, "are not like any other kind of fights. The side that wins has got to do it with a whoop and a hurrah. Indians haven't got any staying power in them. They can't hold out against anybody who stands up against them squarely, and won't be scared by a howling rush into running away. That's the reason why our little bit of an army at home is strong enough to police our whole Indian frontier. A single troop of our boys—if the fighting's square, and they haven't been corralled in an ambush—can stand off a whole tribe; and they can do it because they just get their backs together and won't give in. What bothers me about the fight that we're going to have is that the regulars are on the other side. Of course, being Indians too, regulars like these don't amount to much; but they are bound to be a long chalk better than this rowdy crowd of ours. We've got a pretty fair chance to win, because we're in a strong position, and because our people mean to wait until the other fellows come at 'em; but I tell you what it is, if ever they manage to get inside here, or if ever we go outside after them—that is, while they're fresh and full of fight—it's bound to be all day with us. These miners, and the rest of this Tlahuico outfit, will fight like wild-cats as long as they're on top, but every bit of fight will go right out of them the minute they find that they're beginning to get underneath. That's the Indian way. I'm trying hard to believe that our crowd will whip the other crowd; but I must say, Professor, that I'm not betting on it."

"Well, I'm bettin' on it, and bettin' on it high," said Young. "I don't pretend t' know as much about this sort o' thing as Rayburn does; but I do think I know a live devil when I see one—an' these miners are about as lively an' about as devilly as anything that ever broke loose from hell. They're just as full o' th' wickedest sort o' fight as they can stick in their ugly skins, an' they're just sick for a chance t' let it get out of 'em. All we've got t' do is t' worry th' other crowd for a while by lettin' 'em monkey around tryin' t' bag us; an' then, when they've been pretty well shot off, an' are gettin' tired, just make a rush for 'em an' scoop 'em in. Regulars or no regulars, these miners'll go through 'em like a limited express; an' the' first thing th' Priest Captain knows we'll have walloped him right smack out o' th' baggy things he wears on his feet an' thinks are boots. That's th' size of it, Rayburn. That's what's goin' t' happen right here—an' don't you forget it! An' then, if there's any way out o' this d—n valley, we'll load up with dollars an' pull out for home."

For my own part, I was not disposed to be either so doubtful as Rayburn or so sanguine as Young. In what each of them said there was much truth, and my inference from such of the facts in the case as were within my knowledge and my comprehension was that the chances for and against our success were very evenly divided. Had I listened only to the promptings of my hopes, I should have entertained no doubt whatever touching the certainty of our victory; for I was at that time so elated by the knowledge that I had acquired, and that each day was increased by the acquisition of new and most precious facts, whereby a flood of light was let in upon what hitherto had been hopelessly dark places in Aztec archæology, that I was disposed to believe as firmly as ever did the first Napoleon in the assured ascendency of my lucky star. However, I did not wholly permit my wits to be run away with by the joy begotten of my truly wonderful discoveries; and I strove even to contemplate calmly the possibility that I might myself be slain in the battle that was so close upon us; and that thus the exceedingly valuable information which I had acquired would be lost to the world, and to myself would be lost the honorable fame due me for having gathered it. Yet I regret to state—for until that time I had entertained unreservedly the belief that I truly was a philosopher—my attempt at calm contemplation of this dismal and far from improbable combination of evil circumstances had no other effect upon me than to throw me into a most violent rage. It seemed to me so stupidly unreasonable that some mere common brute of an Indian, by the crude process of splitting my skull open, might deprive me, and through me the scientific world, of the priceless knowledge that with much effort I had stored within my brain.

But all thought of my own fortunes, and of this possible sudden cutting of my life-strings, presently was thrust aside by the inroad of another matter that was of far more serious moment to me, inasmuch as there was involved in it a menace against the life of one of my companions; and, indeed, this matter was one which startled our whole camp, for it was nothing less than a formal offer on the part of the Priest Captain to condone the rebellion, and to compromise with the rebels, on certain far from exacting terms.

The envoy sent to treat with us came in a manner befitting his dignity and the importance of his mission, having a considerable retinue with him in his barge, and being himself a grave and dignified man well advanced in years. Two of our guard-boats accompanied his barge across the lake, and he alone was permitted to land in Huitzilan. Being led before the Council, he delivered himself briefly of his message, and added to it neither argument nor comment of his own. The Priest Captain, he said, desiring to avoid the shedding of blood among brethren, was willing to forgive the wrong already committed, and was willing even to concede in part the demands made by the rebels, in consideration of the acceptance by those now in arms against him of certain very easy terms. For his part, he would yield in so far as to restore the custom of permitting parents to buy back their own children, and so to save them from being sacrificed or from becoming slaves; and he would withdraw also his claim to the exercise of certain rights (which need not here be specified) in civil matters, to which a counter-claim was set up by the Council. In return for these concessions, he demanded that the army raised by the rebels should be immediately disbanded; that order should be restored in Huitzilan by returning the miners to their work, and the Tlahuicos generally to their masters throughout the valley; and that the arms which had been manufactured should be turned over to the keeper of the arsenal in Culhuacan. The final demand made by the Priest Captain related to ourselves; and the Council was given to understand that upon its punctual and exact fulfilment the whole of the negotiation must depend. Young and Rayburn and I, the envoy said, must be thrust out through the Barred Pass, whence we came, and there left to shift for ourselves; Fray Antonio must be without delay surrendered—that the dreadful sin that he had committed by preaching vile doctrines, subversive of the true faith, might be punished in so signal a manner that the gods whom he had outraged would be appeased.

Both Fray Antonio and I were present in the Council chamber when the envoy delivered his message; and when this final demand was made—hearing which made me grow sick and faint, so keen was the pang of sorrow that it caused me—I turned towards him quickly, expecting that he also would feel the hurt of the blow which through him, because of my great love for him, had stricken me so grievously. But so far from being at all cast down by the knowledge thus rudely conveyed that a very cruel death menaced him, there was upon his face a look of such joyful elation, of such rejoicing triumph, that it seemed as though the very greatest happiness that life could hold for him had been thrust suddenly within his grasp.

Within the Council, and outside of it also, when the terms which the envoy offered were spread abroad, there was at once aroused a very hot antagonism between contending factions in regard to the wisdom of placing trust in the Priest Captain's promises, and to the justice of yielding to his demands. So far as the Council was concerned, its members having no especial regard for our welfare now that we had served their purpose, the slaying of Fray Antonio, and the expulsion from the valley of the rest of us, were trifling matters which well enough might be conceded if thereby peace might be secured. The matter of importance that this body had to consider was how far the Priest Captain could be trusted to fulfil promises made to rebels in arms, when these same rebels voluntarily had submitted to disarmament and were at his mercy; and on this essential point the whole debate that followed turned. The faction that favored disarmament insisted that such yielding was not surrender, inasmuch as the Priest Captain had conceded all that the rebels had asked; while those of the faction that favored war rested their case on the ground that the promises of concession were made only to be broken, and that this sudden willingness on the part of the Priest Captain to grant what he had heretofore so persistently refused was proof that he recognized the hopelessness of his position, and so was seeking to retain by craft the power that he no longer could hold by force. These latter, therefore, urged that his false promises should not be heeded; and that the matter at issue should be settled surely and finally by carrying to a triumphant conclusion the war, for the waging of which all needful preparations had been made.

The debate upon this matter continued throughout the whole day without any conclusion being arrived at, and we listened to it—Fray Antonio and I translating to the others—with a very earnest interest, inasmuch as the outcome of it all might be the instant slaying of one of us, and for the rest of us an imprisonment in wild fastnesses among bleak mountains for what was like to be the whole remainder of our lives. When night came, and the Council, being still unresolved, broke off its session until the day following, we came back to our quarters and there talked over the situation, and not cheerfully, among ourselves.

"Even if these fellows understood algebra," said Rayburn, "I don't see how they could get an answer to the problem that they're trying to work. All the x's that ever were made are not enough to represent an unknown quantity like the Priest Captain; and it simply is not in the conditions of the case that they possibly can know what allowance to make for the factor of error. For the last three hours, as far as I can make out, they've just been talking in a circle, and going over and over the same ground. The size of the business is that half of them believe the Priest Captain is telling the truth, and the other half believe that he is lying. This is a matter of conviction; it is not a thing that they can argue about. As far as I can see, there is nothing to prevent them from keeping on talking without getting anywhere for the next twenty years."

"Well, all I can say," said Young, "is that if they'll put me in th' cab, an' let me run their train for 'em, I'll get it up this grade in no time; an' what's more, I'll just take it down th' other side o' th' divide a-kitin'! What's th' matter with th' Priest Captain, an' only half of 'em have th' sense t' see 't, is that he's just solidly lyin'. He's been lyin' to 'em from away back, I reckon; an' he's lyin' to 'em now; an' he'll keep on lyin' to 'em right smack along till he gets t' th' end of his run. If they're fools enough t' believe him they're bound t' get left th' worst kind. They've got him in a hole now, an' he knows it—an' that's more'n they do, t' judge from th' way they're goin' on. I did have some respect for that Council. So far, they've managed things first-rate. They've run in advance o' their schedule right along, an' they've kep' up a rattlin' head o' steam with mighty damn bad coal. But if they really mean t' draw their fires, just when they ought t' put on th' forced draught an' let her go for all she's worth, I must say I haven't any more use for 'em. Seein' 'em shilly-shallyin' around like they're doin' now, when they ought t' be takin' their coats off an' sailin' in, just makes me sick!"

Fray Antonio—whose habit of quiet was such that he rarely sought to take part in the talks that we had in English among ourselves— somewhat surprised me by asking me to translate to him what Young and Rayburn had been saying; and when he had heard it all he was silent for a while, and evidently was engaged in earnest thought. At last, speaking very gravely, he asked us if we greatly feared being thrust out from the valley in case the Council decided to accept the Priest Captain's terms; and without giving us a chance to answer, he bade us remember that we had not at all explored the last valley that we had passed through before we entered the cañon that ended at the Barred Pass, and that from it there well might be some outlet through which we could return to the civilized world; and even were we forced to end our days in it, he continued, speaking quickly and urgently, a much worse fate might come to us; for the valley was a bright and beautiful one, as we had seen, and had in it an abundant supply of food. Would living there, he asked, be any worse for us than living where we then were—where we were equally shut in? And even supposing that the war ended in victory for us, and that our allies gave us entire freedom of action, what more could we do than end our days in the Valley of Aztlan, or else go back to that other valley and search for an outlet thence whereby we could get into an open way among the mountains, and so once more to our homes? And then, still denying us opportunity to answer, he went on to speak of the pain and misery and despairing sorrow that the threatened war would bring; and then, more gently, of the duty that pressed upon us of averting this calamity, that was also a crime, even though to do so we must sacrifice hopes and wishes very dear to our hearts.

"What th' dickens is th' Padre drivin' at, anyway?" Young

exclaimed; "I don't ketch on at all."

"No more do I," said Rayburn. "It's a first-rate sermon that he's giving us, but I don't see where he means the moral of it to fetch up."

For myself, so closely were Fray Antonio and I bound together by bonds of sympathy, I saw but too plainly what he meant should be the outcome of his discourse; and I was not surprised, therefore—though hearing thus plainly expressed in words what I had been dreading, sent a dull, cold pain into the very depths of my heart—when he unfolded to us the whole of the plan that he had been forming within his mind. What he said was said very simply, and with a loving sorrow for the pain that might come to us through shaping our actions in accordance with his strong desire; and this desire was: that, of our own free-will, we should retire from the valley by the way that we came thither, and so leave the Council free to accept unhesitatingly the Priest Captain's terms.

"And what of yourself?" I asked; for I felt within me a strong conviction that for himself he had in view a very different fate.

He hesitated for a moment before answering me, and his color changed a little; and then an unwonted ruddiness gave animation to his face, and a light of glad and strong resolve shone in his eyes as he replied, in a voice that was very low, and at the same time very clear and firm: "I shall go to the Priest Captain, in Culhuacan!"

"And so go to your death," I said, speaking brokenly, for the pain that his words caused me went through me like a knife-thrust.

"Say, rather," Fray Antonio answered, "that I go to win the life, glorious and eternal, into which neither death nor sin nor sorrow evermore can come!"

CHAPTER XXVIII

THE SURRENDER OF A LIFE

Knowing as I did Fray Antonio's resolute nature, and under-standing far more clearly than it was possible for the others to under-stand the heroic impulses which stirred within him, I took no part in the attempt that they then made to oppose the purpose which he had declared. But when they somewhat shifted their position— perceiving how hopeless was their effort to shake by argument his firm resolve—and sought to win him to their way of thinking by consenting to leave the valley if only he would accompany them, then I most earnestly joined my entreaties to theirs. But no more by entreaty than by argument was Fray Antonio to be moved.

And, in truth, there was a logical consistency in what he urged in answer to us that, much though we might resent it, we yet were compelled to respect. He had come with us, he said, for the single purpose of preaching the saving grace of Christianity to heathen souls which otherwise would perish utterly in their idolatry. And this was not a matter wherein he had any right of election, but was a solemn duty that the vows by which he was bound compelled him to fulfil. He was not free, therefore, as we were free, to consider side issues relating to his personal well-being or to mere expediency; his sole endeavor must be to accomplish by the most efficient means the duty wherewith he was charged. It was evident, he urged, that should there be war in the valley the chance for the further spread of Christian doctrine would he scant; for the seed that he had sown, and that already was well rooted in many hearts, would die quickly and be utterly lost in the foul growth of evil passions which would spring up rankly amid this bloody strife. But if the war could be averted, not only would these people be spared the misery that war must bring upon them, and the crime also of slaying each other, but their hearts would remain open to the gentle doctrine that he had taught; and his willingness—should such sacrifice be necessary—to yield his life that peace might be preserved, would force upon them strongly the conviction, tending thus to their own strengthening, of his faithful trust in the creed which he avowed. And it well might happen, he said, that such grace would be given him that even within the very stronghold of the heathen faith he might win souls to the purer faith which it was his glorious privilege to preach and still remain unharmed; in proof of which possibility he cited the case of the blessed St. Januarius, whom the lions refused to devour. But whatever might be the outcome of thus yielding himself into the Priest Captain's hands, his duty was so clear, he declared firmly, that no evasion of it was possible. And what he purposed doing, he said, finally, was but what countless of his brethren had done in the course of the six centuries since the founding in Assisi of the Order to which they and he belonged—and precisely was it what was done by the glorious proto-martyr of Mexico, San Felipe de Jesus, who boldly carried the Christian faith among the heathen, and so died for that faith upon the cross in Japan.

Rayburn was far from willing to yield to this line of argument; yet he understood it, as I did also, and perceived that it was the only logical outcome of the only premises which Fray Antonio would recognize. Young, on the other hand, did not in the least understand it, and Fray Antonio's reasoning simply threw him into a rage.

"It's all damn nonsense," he said, "for th' Padre t' talk about his duty towards a set o' critters like th' Priest Captain's crowd. What's th' life o' that whole outfit worth compared t' one life like his? He might just as well sit down an' chop his own head off as go in among those fellows; an' he knows it, too. I never heard o' th' man he's talkin' about who didn't get eat up by th' lions—somebody in th' show business, I s'pose—but if he thinks there'll he anything worth speakin' of left of him two hours after he gets back into that city, he's makin' a pretty d—n big mistake. Oh, I say, Professor, we've *got* t' stop this. Th' Padre's off his head, that's all there is to it; an' we've got t' look after him till he braces up an' gets sensible again. I'll do anything reasonable that he wants, but I'll be damned if I'm goin' t' stand by doin' nothin' while he cuts his own throat!"

Young was quite ready, I am sure, to resort to the radical measure of clapping Fray Antonio into a strait-jacket; and had the opportunity arisen for bringing their difference of opinion to a practical issue I am confident that we should have witnessed an exceedingly curious conflict, in which heroic self-devotion would have struggled with a rough but very honest love. And that Fray Antonio anticipated such a conflict was shown by his taking effective measures to render it impossible. During the remainder of that day he steadfastly refused to discuss the matter further; not harshly, but by shifting away into other channels our earnest talk. Only at night, before we lay down to sleep, of his own motion he turned once more to the matter; and when he briefly had exhibited to us again the motives which urged him forward upon a way so perilous, he begged that we would not think ill of his insisting upon traversing our wishes, but that once more we would clasp hands with him in sign of our forgiveness and continued love.

So tender was the mood that came upon us with his gentle words that none of us well could answer him; and this he understood as in turn we took his hand and strove to utter that which was in our hearts, and only could say huskily a word or two, of which the meaning was conveyed for the most part by the sorrow and the longing that were in our tones. Young's natural instincts were wholly opposed to any display of the softer emotions, and for shame of the weakness that in this case he could not help but show, his face and neck flushed red, and he declared that he had the toothache. And then, as a vent for his overwrought feelings—of all things in the world—he fell to cursing the Superintendent of the Old Colony Railroad: on the ground that but for this functionary, who most unjustifiably had discharged him, he never would have come to Mexico at all!

For my own part, I was well convinced that Fray Antonio meant then to say good-bye to us; and for a long while, as I lay awake that night, my thoughts went backward over the time that we had been companions together, and so dwelt upon the faithfulness of his friendship, and upon his gallant bearing in all times of peril, and upon the pure and perfect holiness which characterized his every act and word. Into the future I dared not let my thoughts wander, for I could foresee no outcome to the purpose which he had planned so resolutely but a dreary sorrow that would rest heavily upon me through all the remainder of my days. And at last, worn out by my own grief, I fell into a troubled sleep.

The faint gray light of early morning shone dimly in the room as Rayburn awakened me by shaking my arm; and the first words which he spoke to me were, "The Padre is not here!"

As I roused myself fully, and sat up and looked into his face, I saw by the look that he gave me how fully he shared the dread that was in my heart. Young still was sleeping, and we waited to rouse him until we should make sure that what we feared must be the truth really was true. Together we went out quietly into the court-yard and so to the main entrance of the building, where a guard was stationed. But this man was asleep; and when I wakened him, and questioned him as to whether the monk had gone forth, he could give me no answer. Therefore we went on to the gate of the Citadel—which gate, being a vastly heavy grating, raised and lowered by chains, was not usually closed even at night—in the hope that there we might gain some certain knowledge. And here also we found all of the half-dozen men on guard slumbering, saving only one man, who seemed to have been aroused by the sound of our footsteps, and who raised himself on one elbow and looked at us with a sleepy curiosity.

Even the urgency of the quest that we were upon did not suffice to distract our attention from the peril that we all were in because of the slumbering of these sentries. "If this is a specimen of the way all the watches are kept," Rayburn said, angrily, "we stand a pretty good chance of being murdered in our beds. It all comes of trying to make soldiers out of savages. These Tlahuicos will fight well enough, I never doubted that, but to put such men on guard is simple idiocy. They have been slaves all their lives, and they haven't the least notion in the world of personal responsibility. It's a lucky thing that we have found out their methods, for I shall give the Colonel a talking to about putting on guard some of his own men who can be trusted. It's clear that these fellows cannot tell us anything. We'd better keep on down to the landing; if the Padre has gone"—there was a sudden break in Rayburn's voice as he said these words—"it's pretty certain that he has gone by water, and we may come across somebody down there who happened to be awake and saw him start."

There were slight signs of wakefulness beginning to show themselves as we went down towards the water-side; a few doors already were open; here and there thin threads of smoke curled upward through the still air; around a fountain a half-dozen women were clustered, drawing water in great earthen pots, and chattering together softly in half-drowsy talk. At the pier, however, we found some people who really were wide-awake: fishermen just returned with a boat-load of fish that they had caught in the lake. And these, when I questioned them, in a moment resolved all of our troubled doubts into a sad certainty. Only an hour before, as they lay out on the lake, a canoe had passed them paddled by a single Indian, and in the canoe they had plainly recognized Fray Antonio. It was impossible that they should be mistaken, they declared, for the habit which the monk wore made him very plainly recognizable; and they had observed him with a particular care, for they had been greatly surprised by perceiving that the canoe was heading directly for "the great city"—by which name all save the priests were accustomed to speak of Culhuacan.

Neither Rayburn nor I spoke, as we walked back together through the town to the Citadel. Our hearts were altogether too full for words. Even I, who had been in part prepared for Fray Antonio's departure by the tenor of his speech with us the night before, had not anticipated his going from us so suddenly to what surely must be his death; and to Rayburn his departure came with the startling force of a heavy and unexpected blow. Young was awake when we returned, and was in much anxiety concerning us; for our custom at all times was to hold closely together, and he knew that something out of the common must have happened to make us break through this very necessary rule; and his fears were further aroused when he perceived the sad gravity of our faces, and that Fray Antonio was not in our company. Yet, though thus prepared to learn that evil of some sort had over-taken us, he was not at all prepared to learn how great that evil was. When, therefore, we told him of what we had discovered, which gave absolute assurance that Fray Antonio had carried out his purpose of surrendering himself into the Priest Captain's hands, Young stared at us for a moment in a dazed sort of way, as though by no means grasping the meaning which our words conveyed. And then the whole meaning of them seemed to come to him suddenly, and he burst forth into such a raving volley of curses that it seemed as though he were fairly maddened by his ungoverned rage.

I envied Young, as I am sure Rayburn did also, the relief that must come to him with this rough but frank and natural expression of his bitter grief. For ourselves, we stood sad and silent, yet with our hearts almost breaking within us, as we thought how small was the chance that ever in this world should we see the face of Fray Antonio again.

CHAPTER XXIX

THE ASSAULT IN THE NIGHT

Neither the Council, in its irresolute parleyings, nor Fray Antonio, in his resolute action, had at all considered certain factors which they themselves had interjected into the problem that they then were dealing with from such widely different stand-points and in such widely different ways. The Council, at a stroke, had transformed the Tlahuicos into soldiers, and had given the promise that in reward for their faithfulness and valor these slaves thenceforward should be freemen. Fray Antonio had preached to all those assembled at Huitzilan a creed that had taken strong hold upon many hearts, and that especially had won the hearts of those of the long-oppressed servile class—to whom its doctrine of equality seemed to hold out an absolute assurance that their life of slavery was at an end.

When, therefore, the terms which the Priest Captain offered were spread abroad through the town, and through the camp close beside the town in which the army lay—being there in readiness instantly to occupy the Citadel should the enemy appear—a very lively anger was aroused because such terms should even be listened to. For what the Priest Captain demanded was that the apostle of the new religion should be relinquished to him to be slain as a sacrifice to the Aztec gods, and that once more the Tlahuicos should be thrust back into slavery; while what he conceded—in that it affected only the higher classes—made the lot of the Tlahuicos but the more unjustly cruel and hard to bear.

And those who resented the delay on the part of the Council in sending back the Priest Captain's envoy with a sharp denial, presently went on from hot words to violent deeds; being directly led from mutinous talk to mutinous action by the knowledge that the Council had so far accepted the offered terms as to send Fray Antonio to the great city to be slain—for not one among them could be led for a moment to believe, so impossible from their stand-point did such an act appear, that the monk truly had gone thither of his own free-will.

Practically, the whole army was involved in the movement that then took place; for even its officers, while not of the servile class, dreaded the punishment that their revolt might bring upon them, and so preferred to take the chances of the war rather than to yield themselves to be dealt with as the Priest Captain might dispose. Therefore it was, on the day that Fray Antonio departed from us, that all the soldiers together marched in from their camp and massed themselves compactly about the Council Chamber within the Citadel, and then with loud cries demanded that the envoy should be sent back to the great city with an absolute refusal of the offered terms. Thus was there created a rebellion within a rebellion; and one that the Council was powerless to put down, for the reason that practically the whole of the force which it had created to serve against the enemy was now risen against its own authority with a most masterful strength.

In the case that thus was presented there was no opportunity to temporize. The fierce, wild creatures of whom soldiers suddenly had been made stood there before the Council Chamber, shouting and waving their spears angrily and clashing together their arms. And so they continued, without one moment of quiet, until their will was obeyed. Through the savage and tumultuous throng the envoy was led forth—his looks showing plainly his very natural expectation that his life would be let out of him amid that ferocious company—and so down to the water-side; and thence was sent back again to Culhuacan with the firm assurance—which message of defiance the soldiers themselves dictated—that the terms offered by the Priest Captain would be accepted only when all the Tlahuicos then risen together in arms against him had been slain!

"Bully for th' Tlahuicos!" cried Young, as I translated to him these ringing words. "Just tell 'em, Professor, that I've volunteered for three years or th' war, an' that they can count on me t' keep up a full head o' steam as long as there's any fightin' t' be done. Accordin' t' my notions, now that th' Padre's over there in th' city—t' say nothin' o' what we owe 'em on Pablo's account—th' row can't begin one minute too soon. These Tlahuicos are th' boys for me! Didn't I tell you that nobody could stop 'em when they once got fairly started? They're a tough lot; but they're just everlastin' rustlers—an' their style suits me right now all th' way down t' th' ground floor!"

The sharp excitement attendant upon this vigorous action gave place, as the day wore on, to a dull heavy pain as our thoughts dwelt upon the fate that Fray Antonio had gone forth to meet, and upon our present powerlessness to defend him in any way against it. Although

the envoy had been sent back, and war was now resolutely determined upon, the situation remained unchanged in so far as concerned
the necessity of our waiting for the Priest Captain to take the initia-
tive. To attack that great walled city was so hopeless a task that even
the Tlahuicos—flushed though they were by their victory over the
Council—did not venture to propose it; for they knew, as we all did,
that our only chance of carrying the enemy's stronghold lay in first
defeating its garrison in a battle in the open field. Yet this dull inaction of waiting was a scarce of grave danger to us, in that it tended to
wear out the spirits of our men and to make them still more careless
of their guard. What Rayburn and I had seen that morning had shown
how little trust could be placed in them, in so far as the soldierly
attribute of watchfulness was concerned; and Tizoc, with whom we
conferred in regard to this important matter, had little to say that
we found comforting. Being himself a thorough soldier, he perceived
the danger to which the unsoldierly lack of vigilance on the part of
the Tlahuicos exposed our camp; but the situation was such that he
was powerless to take effective measures for our protection. The few
regular troops in our little army were not enough to do sentry duty
everywhere, and the best that could be done would be to dispose them
at the points most open to attack—"And then trust to luck," Rayburn
put in, rather bitterly, "that the enemy will be polite enough to try
to surprise only the part of the camp where the sentries are awake!"

Partly that we might see for ourselves how our pickets were
disposed, but more that by action of any sort we might divert our
thoughts from the sorrow that was gnawing at our hearts, we walked
out together in the late afternoon to the rocky heights of the promontory that on the western side of the town extended far into the lake.
From a military stand-point this position was of great importance
to us, inasmuch as bowmen or slingmen gaining access to it could
command a considerable part of the town, and even could annoy very
seriously the garrison of the Citadel; and it also was of value to us as
a place of lookout whence an attacking party coming by way of the
lake from the city could be perceived while yet it was a long way off.

We were surprised, therefore, when we had come well out upon
the promontory, that no sentinel challenged us; but our surprise
vanished a moment or two later as we perceived one of our men
curled up comfortably against a sunny rook and apparently sound
asleep. However, as we got close to the man it was clear to us that his

sleep was one that he never would waken from, for a pool of blood stained the rock beside him, and an arrow was shot fairly through his heart. We made but a short stop beside this fellow—who plainly had been shot in his sleep, and so deserved the fate that had overtaken him—and then went forward anxiously that we might see how the other sentinels stationed hereabouts had fared. The result of our quest was as bad as it could be; for in one place or another among the rocks we found all five of the men who had been posted upon the promontory, and all of them were dead. Three more of them certainly had been shot while asleep or wholly off their guard, as was shown by the easy attitudes in which we found them sitting or lying among the rocks. The fifth had not been instantly killed; as we inferred from finding a broken arrow sticking in his left arm, and some signs of a struggle about where he lay, and a great split in his skull, as from a sword stroke, that finally had let the life out of him. It struck us as strange that this man had not aroused the camp with his shouts; but his post was at the extreme end of the promontory, so that he must have called very loudly in order to be heard; and it was possible that in the suddenness of his danger he never thought to call at all. However, the important matter, so far as we were concerned, was that these five sentinels had been slain close beside the town and in broad daylight, and that but for the chance of our coming out upon the promontory the most important of our outposts would have remained unguarded until the night relief should have come on. It was Rayburn's theory that the plan of the enemy was to place his own men on the vacant posts—trusting to the reasonable certainty that in the dusk of evening one naked Indian would look much like another—and so despatch the relief, one by one, as the guard was changed.

Of those of the enemy who had accomplished this piece of work so skilfully we could see no sign—unless it were a boat that we dimly saw a long way off on the lake, and that presently wholly disappeared in a bank of haze; and despite the hot sunshine basking upon us a chill went through me at thought of the stealthy daring and truly devilish cunning of the men who thus could do their evil work in the full light of day, and close to the encampment of an army, and yet could get safely away without leaving a trace of their presence save the dead bodies of their foes.

Having made sure by carefully searching among the rocks

throughout the length of the promontory that none of the enemy was hidden there, we hastened back to the town to tell what we had come upon, and to provide for mounting fresh sentinels in the place of those who had been relieved by death. We had expected that the news which we brought would stir up a great commotion; and we were not a little troubled, therefore, knowing how serious the matter was in its exhibition of the carelessness of our guards, by finding that only Tizoc and a few other tried soldiers were more than lightly discomposed by what we had to tell. The general feeling seemed to be—inasmuch as our lucky discovery had dispelled the danger—that there was no need to worry about a calamity which had not occurred; and what after all was the most essential consideration—the constant danger that threatened us by reason of the criminal laxity of the watch maintained by our pickets—practically was lost sight of. Apparently neither the Council nor the higher officers of the army had the power to remedy this dangerous condition of affairs. At no time had any very strong authority been exercised over the Tlahuicos—for all the orders which until now had been given to them had been directed only towards urging them along a way that they were glad enough to follow of their own accord—and since their assertion of their will that morning, what little control had restrained their waywardness seemed to have been wholly lost.

However, as there was a chance in it of fighting, and as fighting was what they longed for earnestly, our unruly soldiers were willing enough that a strong detachment should be placed in ambush on the promontory, to the end that the force which the enemy probably would land there that night might be summarily dealt with. And the better to carry out our plan of a counter-surprise the dead sentinels were left where we found them. Tizoc was given the command of the ambushed force, and he willingly granted our request that we might accompany him; which request was prompted by the desire that we fully shared with the Tlahuicos to get at close quarters with the enemy, and also by the conviction that in Tizoc's company— though in his company we were like to have hot fighting and plenty of it—we would have better chances of safety than anywhere else in all our camp.

For this expedition we put on for the first time our armor of quilted cotton cloth; and the look of these garments certainly did justify Young's comments upon them. "It's a pity we can't get photographed now," he said, "so's t' send our likenesses in this rig home t' our folks. You'd just jolt the Cap Cod folks, Rayburn, with that pair o' telegraph poles you call your legs stickin' out from under th' tails o' that thing that looks like a cross between a badly made frock-coat and an undersized night-shirt. And I guess your college boys'd be jolted, too, Professor, if they could get a squint at you. And I s'pose that if some o' th' hands on th' Old Colony happened t' ketch up with me dressed this way they'd think I'd gone crazy. But I haven't got anything t' say against these little night-shirts except about their looks. When you get right down t' th' hard-pan with 'em, they're a first-rate thing."

For three American citizens, belonging to the nineteenth century, we certainly presented a strange appearance, and appeared also in very strange company, as we marched out from the town late that afternoon with Tizoc and his men. Each of us carried half a dozen darts, and strapped around our waists, outside our cotton-cloth armor, we each wore a maccahuitl—the heavy sword with a jagged double edge that we knew from experience was an excellent weapon when wielded by a strong hand. Indeed, Young and I carried the darts rather to satisfy Tizoc than because we expected to make any very effective use of them, and all of our reliance both for assault and defence was upon what we could do with our swords at close quarters. Rayburn, however, had been practising dart-throwing very diligently, and as he naturally was an extraordinarily dextrous man he had made rapid progress in this savage art. The soldiers in our company, naked creatures, lithe and sinewy, were armed for the most part with spears and slings; and the officers wore each a sword and carried each a handful of darts. As we all stepped out briskly together I could not but think how amazed would be the President of the University of Michigan, and my fellow-members of the Faculty of that institution of learning, should they happen to encounter me in that barbarous company, and arrayed in that most barbarous garb!

It was a little before sunset when we reached the place that Tizoc had selected for our ambush upon the promontory; and an hour later, just as the shadows of evening were beginning to fall, one of our lookout men reported that a large boat—of which the oars must be muffled, for no sound came from it—was pulling around a point just beyond where we lay. There was a little stir among our men when this news was received, and a shifting and arranging of weapons, so that all might be in readiness when the moment for opening the ambush came; but we had a picked force with us, each man of which fully understood how necessary was silence to the success of our plans, and the quick thrill of movement was so guarded that it scarcely ruffled the deep stillness of the night.

But the moments lengthened out into minutes, and the minutes slowly slipped by until a full hour had passed, and the thick darkness of tropical night was upon us, and still there was no sign of a foe. Tizoc grew uneasy, for it was evident that we were in error in our conception of the enemy's plan. Had he intend-to mount his own men as sentinels in place of our men whom he had slain, and then get save possession of the promontory by killing the relief as it came on, we should have been long since engaged with him; but here the night was wearing on, and, excepting only the boat that our scouts had seen, there had been nothing to show that the attack which we had expected so confidently was anything more than a creation of our own fears. Yet our only course was to remain where we were until morning; for some accident might have delayed the attack, and the necessity of holding the promontory was so urgent that we could not take the risk of withdrawing our force.

It was weary work sitting there in the darkness, after all the weariness of so exciting a day, and as the hours dragged on I found myself now and then sinking into a doze, for which I reproached myself; yet also excused myself by the reflection that I did not at all profess to have either the training or the instincts of a soldier, but had been brought up, as a man of peace and as a scholar, in accordance with the sound principle that night rationally is the time set apart for sleep. It was from a most agreeable nap—in which I was dreaming pleasantly of my old life in Ann Arbor—that I was roused suddenly by Rayburn's quick grip upon my shoulder, and by his sharp whisper, "What's that?"

In an instant I was thoroughly awake, and as I bent forward and listened intently I heard very distinctly a faint cry of alarm, that seemed to come from a long way off. Tizoc, I perceived—for he had risen to his feet—also was most eagerly listening; and I heard a slight sound of movement and of arms clinking as our men roused themselves, showing that they also had heard that warning cry.

But in a moment there was no need to strain our ears to catch the sounds which came to us. The cry that a single throat had uttered was taken up by a thousand; and so grew into a dull, distant roar, that pierced the black and sullen stillness of the night. And with this came also the higher notes of savage yells, and then we heard the clash of arms—which evidence that fighting was going on, no less than the direction whence, as we now perceived clearly, the sounds came, assured us that while we had maintained our watchful guard on the promontory the enemy had surprised our camp.

Rayburn sprang up with a growl like that of a savage beast. "By God!" he cried, "they meant us to do just what we've done, and we've walked into their trap like so many damn fools!"

CHAPTER XXX

THE FALL OF THE CITADEL

Tizoc, I was glad to see, had his men well under his command, as was shown by the orderly manner in which they waited, despite their eager impatience to be off, until he gave the command to march. And hard marching we found it, as we floundered about that rough, rocky place, tripping and stumbling, and now and then hearing a crash in the darkness as one of our men went down. But, somehow or other, we certainly managed to get over the ground very rapidly; and all the while the sounds of the fight that was raging hotly struck with a constantly increasing clearness upon our ears.

The whole width of the town lay between our camp and the foot of the rugged path that led down from the promontory; but when we were fairly in the streets, and no longer had rough rocks to stumble over in the darkness, we went forward at a very slashing pace. And we were further helped now by the fact that day was breaking, so that we could see clearly where we were going; and we had also within us that feeling of cheer and encouragement that ever is given to man by the return of the sun. In but a few minutes more, in that tropical region, a flood of daylight would be about us; and Tizoc's hope was that when the horror of darkness, ever appalling to barbarians, should be lifted, and when our coming should afford a firm centre to rally around, our army might regain the courage and steadiness which it had lost in the terror and bewilderment of a night surprise.

But he quickly found that this hope was doomed to disappointment. Only a little beyond the gate of the Citadel we came upon a flying body of Tlahuicos—though no pursuers were in sight beyond them—and these were so completely demoralized that they took our company for a detachment of the enemy, and with wild cries fled away from us down a side street and so disappeared. "What do you think of your friends now?" Rayburn asked Young, grimly. But Young's only answer was to curse the vanished Tlahuicos for cowards.

A moment later the whole street in front of us was filled with a howling mob of our men, and these came surging towards us with the evident intention of seeking safety in the Citadel. Tizoc saw at a glance the hopelessness of trying to rally a rout like this until the terrified creatures, fleeing like sheep from a pack of wolves, had been given rest for a while in some safe place where their courage might return to them. Being once within the Citadel they would be for a time wholly out of danger; for even should the enemy try to set scaling-ladders in place, and so break in upon us there, it would be an easy matter for a few determined men to hold the walls until some sort of order had been restored among our broken forces. Tizoc therefore promptly wheeled our little force aside into an open space, and so made a way for the struggling crowd to sweep past us. We noted, as the stream of terror-stricken men flowed by, that their officers were not with them; from which Tizoc drew the hopeful augury that the officers, being all trained soldiers, had drawn together into a rear-guard that sought to cover this wild retreat. And presently we found that Tizoc was right in his inference, for soon the crowd began very perceptibly to grow thinner, and the sound of loud cries and the rattle and clashing of arms rang out above the tumult, and then there came around a turn in the street, a little beyond where we had halted, a compact body of men who were falling back slowly, and who were laying about them most valiantly with their swords. Our party gave a yell, by way of putting fresh heart into these gallant fellows, and Tizoc quickly disposed our company in such a manner that the retreating force fell back through our midst; and then we promptly closed in, and so took the fighting to ourselves.

I cannot tell very clearly how our retreat to the Citadel was managed, nor even of my own part in it; for fighting is but rough, wild work, which defies all attempts at scientific accuracy in describing it—and for the reason, I fancy, that it engenders a wholly unscientific frame of mind. Reduced to its lowest terms, fighting is mere barbarity; a most illogical method of settling some disputed question by brute force instead of by the refined reasoning processes of the intelligent human mind; and by the anger that it inevitably begets, the habit of accurate observation, out of which alone can come accurate description, is hopelessly confused. Therefore I can say only that foot by foot we yielded the ground to the enemy that pressed upon us; that wild shouts rang out—in which I myself joined, though why I should have shouted I am sure I do not know—together with the sharp rattle of clashing swords; and that through the roar of this outburst of fierce sounds there ran an undertone of groans and sobs from the poor wretches who had fallen wounded to the ground. The one thing that I remember clearly is a set-to with swords that I had with a big fellow, just as we had come close to the Citadel, that ended in a way (that would have surprised him mightily had he lived long enough to comprehend it) by my finishing him by means of a stop-thrust followed by a beautiful draw-cut that was a famous stroke with my old sabre-master at Leipsic. And I well remember thinking, at the moment that I made this stroke—and so saved my life by it, for the fellow was pressing me very closely—how happy it would have made the old Rittmeister could he have seen me deliver it.

As we made a rush for the gate of the Citadel, that we might get inside this place of safety and drop the grating before the enemy could follow us, we were surprised by finding many of our own men lying dead about the entrance; and what was far worse for us, we found that unskilled hands had been at work with the machinery whereby the gate was lowered and by their bungling had managed to start it downward in such a way that it had jammed in the grooves. What actually had happened there, as we knew afterwards, was that the first of the cowardly wretches who had entered the Citadel had tried to drop the gate in the faces of their companions and so secure their own safety; whence a fight among themselves had sprung up, in course of which many of them very deservedly were slain, and, most unhappily for us, their frantic efforts to lower the gate had resulted in thus disabling it.

We had a moment of breathing space before the enemy came up with us, and in this time Rayburn and Young and I had a grip of each other's hands, in which, without any words over it, we said good-bye to each other; for we neither of us for one moment doubted that our last hour had come. Tizoc stood a little distance from us, as steady and as gallant in his bearing as ever I saw a man; but that he also counted surely upon dying there was shown by the glance of grave friendliness that he gave us, and by his making the gesture that among his people is significant of farewell. Then we ranged ourselves across the gate-way, holding our swords in hand firmly, and Rayburn, who had caught up a javelin, stood with it poised above his shoulder in readiness to discharge it as the enemy came on. The sight of his splendid figure towering defiantly in that heroic attitude set my mind to running upon the Homeric legend of the glorious battling of the Greeks before the gates of Troy, and of Hector uplifting the rock; and

I was very angry with Young, whose disposition to seize upon the whimsical side of everything was the most irrepressible that ever I came across, when he exclaimed: "I'll bet you five dollars, Rayburn, that when you throw that clothes-prop you don't hit th' man you fire at!"

But Rayburn did hit his man, straight in the heart too, a moment later, as the enemy with a wild yell charged us; and then, with his back set well against the wall, he fell to work most gallantly with his sword.

From the very beginning of it we knew that our fighting was utterly hopeless; for all of our company together did not number fifty men, and we were confronting there a whole army. Up the street, as far as we could see, the troops of the enemy were solidly massed; and for every man whom we struck down twenty were ready to spring forward, fresh and vigorous, to exhaust still further the strength that rapidly was leaving us. That we fought on was due not to our valor but to our desperation; and also—at least such was my own feeling—to a swelling rage that made us long to kill as many as possible of these savages before we ourselves died beneath their blows. Death, we knew, was the best thing that could happen to us; for it would save us from the worse fate, that surely would come to us should we be captured, of being turned over to the priests, that they might torture us before their heathen altars, and in the end tear our still quivering hearts out. And that the wish of our enemies—according to the Aztec custom—was rather to capture us than to kill us was shown by the way in which they fought; for all their effort was to disable us, and so to take us alive; nor did they seem to have any great care, if only this purpose could be accomplished, how many of themselves were slain.

Sometimes in my dreams the wild commotion of that most desperate combat comes back to me. I see again before me the crowd of half-naked men, curving in a semicircle measured by the length of my sword, their faces distorted by the passionate anger that stirred their souls; and I see one fierce face after another lose out of it the look of life, yet not the look of hate, as my sword crunches into the vitals of the body to which it belongs; and I hear the wild din around me, and the yells of rage and of pain, and my feet tread in slippery pools of blood, and my body aches with weariness, and sharp thrills of agony dart through the strained muscles of my right arm—yet still I fight on, and on. And, truly, all this seems more real to me now in my sleep than it did to me then in its reality; for a dull weight of most desolate hopelessness settled down upon me as I fought out to the end that most hopeless battle—so that my spirit shared in the numbness of my body, and I cut and parried and gave men their death-blows with the stolid energy of a mere death-dealing machine.

It had been from the first no more than a question of minutes how long this unequal fight would last; and when I heard a great yell from the enemy, and perceived a flood of soldiers swirling inward through the gate-way just beyond the fellows whom I was dealing with, I knew that Tizoc's men had been beaten down or slain, and that the end was very near at hand. As I glanced across the shoulders of the man whom I just then put forever on the list of the non-combatants, I saw what seemed to be an eddy in the midst of the crowd that was rushing into the Citadel; and in the thick of the tightly knotted group that thus choked the narrow way I saw Tizoc still laying about him with his sword. He was a very ghastly object, for a cut on his head had loosened a piece of his scalp, that hung down over his forehead and waved and trembled there like a draggled plume; his face was bathed in blood from this horrid wound, and his armor of cotton cloth was soaked with the blood that had run down upon it from the cut in his head, and also from a wound in his neck. In the moment that I had free sight of him he made as fine a sword-stroke as ever I saw, where-with he fairly severed from its body the head of one of his assailants; and at the very same instant, while that head still was spinning in the air, a man directly behind him forced back the pressing crowd by main strength and so gained a free space in which to swing his sword. I shouted to Tizoc to warn him of the danger, and he half turned to ward against it; but before he could turn wholly around the blow had fallen, splitting his whole head open from the crown to the very chin. And in the midst of the fierce yell of triumph that went up as this cowardly stroke was delivered there passed from earth the soul of as brave and as true a man as earth has ever known.

A dizziness came over me as I saw Tizoc fall, and saw in the same moment the wild rush forward of the enemy over his dead body into the Citadel; and so I suppose that what with this dizziness and my great weariness I must have dropped my guard. I faintly remember hearing a shout of warning from Young, who was close beside me, which shout mingled with the shrieks of those inside the Citadel whom the enemy everywhere were cutting down, and the great roar of victory that went up from all the army, both within and without the Citadel, rising tempestuously in mighty waves of sound: and then a crash like that of a thunder-bolt burst directly upon my head, and a sickening pain shot through me, and I seemed to be falling through untold depths into vast gloomy chasms (so that I thought I was dropping once more into the hollow darkness of the cañon), and there was a very dreadful surging and roaring and ringing in my ears; and then all this horror of evil sounds grew fainter, and I felt myself slipping quickly into the awful stillness and blackness that I surely thought must be the entrance-way to death. And with this thought a numb sort of gladness came over me, for in death there was promise of restfulness and peace.

CHAPTER XXXI

DEFEAT

After all, the life that I thought was lost, and had but little sorrow for the losing of it, slowly came back to me again. For a good while before I recovered consciousness fully, I understood a little of what was going on around me by sounds which, no doubt, were loud and ringing, yet which seemed to me to come faintly from a long way off. They plainly were the sounds of fighting—of weapons rattling together, of shouts and yells and death-cries—but I did not associate them with our present battling, but thought that we still were in the cañon, and were still fighting those wild Indians by whom poor Dennis was slain. And I knew that I had been hurt badly; for in my head was a throbbing pain so keen that it seemed like to split my skull open, and my stomach was stirred by most distressing qualms, and my weakness was such that I could not ease the sore muscles of my body by moving by so much as a hair's-breadth from the cramped position in which I lay.

It seemed to me a vastly long while that I remained in this dreary condition of half-consciousness, with no certain knowledge of anything save the pain that I suffered; and then I felt some one touch me, and a hand laid upon my heart; and this touch so far roused me that I heaved a long sigh and slowly opened my eyes. For a moment I did not know the face that I saw bending over me; nor was this wonderful, for in place of its usual ruddiness was a death-like pallor, that was the more marked by contrast with the blood that trickled down over it from a great gash across the brow whereby the bone was laid bare. But there was no mistaking the voice that called out: "He's alive, Rayburn!" and added, "I don't see what right he's got t' be alive, either, after a crack like that. I guess studyin' antiquities must everlastin'ly harden an' thicken a man's skull!"

"Studying engineering doesn't harden a man's leg, anyway," I heard Rayburn answer. "That cut pretty near took mine off. But now that we've stopped the bleeding I guess I'm all right. I think I can work over to you on my hands and knees and help you with the Professor. Now that I know he's alive I seem to be a lot more alive myself."

"Just you stay where you are," Young called back, sharply. "If you move you'll start that bandage an' I'll have t' tie you up all over again. I'll attend t' th' Professor." And then Young bent over me, and, with a tenderness that I never would have thought his rough hands capable of, set himself to bandaging my wounded head. But the best thing that he did for me was to give me a draught of water from a gourd that had been slung about the neck of one of the soldiers lying dead there; which draught, with the comfort that the cool wet bandage about my head gave me, brought back to me so much of my strength that I was able presently to sit up and look around.

Truly, a more ghastly sight than that which my eyes then rested upon I never saw. The gate-way of the Citadel was a very shambles. Piles of dead men lay all around me; and the prodigious number of the enemy lying slain there testified with a mute eloquence to the desperate fashion in which our handful of men had fought. Over the rough pavement, down the slope towards the lake, there flowed a stream of bright red blood that in places shone a brilliant vermilion where it was touched by the glintings of the sun. Among the dead I did not see Tizoc's body, and for this I was glad. Half a dozen of the enemy stood by us as a guard; but these suffered us to minister to each other, evidently feeling that no great amount of caution was necessary in dealing with three badly wounded men. Indeed, these guards, in their way, manifested a kindly feeling for us; for when they perceived that our gourd of water was empty one of them picked up another full gourd from amid the dead and handed it to us. From inside the Citadel there still came a tumult of fierce sounds which gave proof that though the battle—if it could be called a battle— was ended the work of killing still was going on; but these sounds sensibly diminished while we lay there waiting to know what fate would come to us, and we concluded, therefore, that there remained no more rebels to be slain.

Rayburn was seated upon the ground at no great distance from me, his back propped against the wall. As he saw that I was looking towards him, and had again my wits about me, he greeted me with a very melancholy smile. "It's been a pretty cold day for us, Professor," he said, "and there's no great comfort in knowing that it's partly our own fault that these fellows have laid us out. I didn't give them credit for such good tactics; and even with the bad watch that we kept I don't see how they managed to get their men round on the other side of our camp. Well, it must please them to know how straight we walked into the trap that they set for us, like the pack of fools that we were."

"You won't ketch me joinin' in any more Indian revolutions, anyway," Young put in. "I did think I could bet on those Tlahuicos, an' they've just gone back on us th' worst kind. Do you feel strong enough, Professor, to tie th' ends o' this rag?" He had been binding up the cut in his forehead, and now he got down on his hands and knees in front of me, and bent his head down within easy reach of my hands; and my strength had so far returned to me that without being very tired after it I was able to make the ends of the bandage fast. The blow on his head had glanced from the skull, luckily; but it had been heavy enough to stun him for some minutes after he received it—and his falling as though dead had been the means, no doubt, of saving his life, even as in the same manner my life had been saved. Rayburn's wound was a worse one than either Young's or mine, for a great gash in his thigh had wellnigh cut his leg off, and until, with Young's help, he had improvised a tourniquet, from a bowstring and a broken fragment of a javelin, he had been in great danger of bleeding to death.

For more than an hour we were suffered to lie in the gate-way; while the work went on of slaying the wretched Tlahuicos, and then of marshalling the more important personages who had been reserved alive as prisoners, and, finally, of restoring order in the victorious ranks. At the end of this time an officer with a squad of men came to where we were lying, and roughly ordered us to rise, to the end that we also might be placed among the prisoners. Young and I had so far recovered our strength that we managed to scramble on our feet with no great difficulty; though in my case this exertion, which made the blood flow more briskly in my veins, suddenly increased so greatly the pain in my head as to bring upon me for a little while a dizziness that compelled me to lean against the wall for support. In Rayburn's case standing was quite out of the question; and I shortly told the officer in what manner he was wounded, and that to make him rise and walk assuredly would start the bandage on his leg, and so lead to his quickly bleeding to death. Thereupon the officer gave an order to some of his men to fetch a stretcher such as their own wounded were carried in; yet at the same time he said to me: "This companion of yours is a brave man; and but for my orders, I would loosen the bandage with my own hands, and so let him die without further pain;" which speech, notwithstanding the obviously kind intention of it, I did not translate to Rayburn at that time.

While we waited for the stretcher to be brought, the soldiers fastened about Young's neck and about mine heavy wooden collars, which set well out over our shoulders and were not unlike great ruffs. I confess that for my own part my professional interest in this curious piece of gear entirely overcame my repugnance to wearing it, for I instantly recognized it as the cuauh-cozatl, with which, as the ancient records tell us, the Aztecs were accustomed to secure their prisoners of war. But Young, who could not be expected to share in my delight at seeing actually alive, and ourselves made party to it, a custom that was supposed to have been extinguished to more than three centuries, grew exceedingly indignant at having thus placed about his neck what he coarsely described as "an overgrown damn goose-yoke." Nor was I at all successful in my attempt to soothe him by telling him that the discomfort to which we were subjected was a very trifling matter in comparison with the gain to the science of archeology that flowed from this positive identification of an exceedingly interesting historical fact.

"Oh, come off, Professor," he growled. "What th' devil do I care for historical facts, or for historical lies either?—an' they're all about th' same thing. What I want t' do is t' punch th' head o' th' fellow who put this thing on me, an' I can't. They'll be hangin' me up by my heels an' stickin' a corn-cob in my mouth next, I s'pose, an' makin' a regular stuck-pig out o' me; an' then likely enough you'll try t' make me believe that *that* proves something or other that nobody but you thinks ever happened, an' so want me t' feel pleased about it. Antiquities be damned! I've had as much of' em as I want, an' more too!"

While the collars were being placed about our necks, and while Rayburn was being lifted upon the stretcher which the soldiers had brought, we heard from within the Citadel the sound of drums tapping, and then the measured tread of soldiers marching; and as we looked through the gate-way we saw that the troops had been formed in regular order and were moving towards us. At the head of the column were the prisoners—numbering three or four hundred, and all wearing wooden collars about their necks—covered on both flanks by a strong line of guards. They were ranged in order of their dignity, the unlucky members of the Council coming first, and after them the other officers of that short-lived government; then the military officers, and in the rear a few private soldiers. The fact that no Tlahuicos were among the prisoners led me to conclude that such of these as had not been slain had been held under guard until they might be returned to their owners or set again to toiling hopelessly in the mine.

The importance that in the estimation of our captors attached to ourselves was shown by their placing us at the very head of the column, in advance even of the members of the Council; and this was a compliment that we willingly enough would have declined, for such honorable consideration, according to the customs of this people, meant surely that we were reserved for a very exemplary fate. But we were in no position to raise objections of any sort just then, and we therefore fell into the place assigned to us and tried as well as we could to show a bold front as we went downward towards the lake.

Only a few terrified women and children, who fled away as we advanced, were in sight as we passed through the streets of the town; and from many of the hovels came the moans of poor wounded wretches who had crawled to their miserable homes to die in them; and from others came the lamentations of women over their dead; and in nooks and corners, whither with their last strength they had dragged themselves, we saw men lying dead in pools of their own blood. But down by the water-side there were live men in plenty, soldiers and oarsmen, and the pier was crowded with them; while out beyond the pier the whole bay was swarming with the boats in which the enemy's forces had stolen down upon us in the darkness from Culhuacan; making their landing, as we now learned, just beyond the town in a bay that ran up close to where our army was encamped. And this scene of bustling activity in the bright sunshine made a joyous and brilliant picture; that was all the brighter because of its setting in that sunlit bay, opening out between beaches of golden-yellow sand upon the broad expanse of restful water which fell away in gleaming splendor into a bank of soft gray haze.

But the picture was still more stirring that we saw as we looked landward, when the barge that we were put aboard of pulled out from the pier and our rowers lay on their oars, and so waited while the work of embarkation went on. Right in front of us was the broad central street of the town; and the whole length of this, from the pier to the Citadel, was filled with a solidly massed body of soldiers that came down the steep descent slowly, and halting often, to the boats which were in waiting to bear them away. Barbarians though they were, these soldiers made a gallant showing. In front of each regiment was borne its feather standard, and in the midst of each company was its rallying flag of brightly painted cotton cloth. The higher officers wore wooden casques, carved and painted in the semblance of the heads of ferocious beasts; the cotton-cloth armor of all the officers was decked with a great variety of strange devices, wrought in very lively hues, and similarly strong hues were used in the decoration of the universally-carried light round shields. And all this brilliant color, the more vivid because of its background of bare brown skins, was flecked with a thousand glittering points of light where the sunshine sparkled on swords and on spear-heads of hardened gold.

"Its not much wonder that those fellows got away with us," Rayburn said, as he watched the orderly manner in which the disciplined ranks moved out upon the pier and stepped briskly into the boats at the word of command. "They're as fine a lot of fighters as I ever saw anywhere. Just look how steadily they stand at a halt, and how sharply they obey orders, and how well set up they are! I must say I don't see what the Colonel could have been thinking about when he said that we had a fighting chance against an army like that. Well, he's paid for his mistake about as much as a man can pay for anything. It breaks me all up to think that the Colonel is dead. He was good all the way through. And I wonder what will become of that little lame boy of his now? They'll make a Tlahuico of him, I suppose. By Jove! what a mess we've made of this whole business from first to last!"

My heart was too heavy for me to answer Rayburn save by a nod; for while he spoke the thought came home to me very bitterly that upon me rested the responsibility of the black misfortune in which he and Young were involved; and with this came also a great burst of sorrow as I thought how still more closely at my door lay Pablo's death—for Rayburn and Young at least had come into my plans with a reasonable understanding of the danger to which they exposed themselves; but Pablo, having no such knowledge, had followed me unquestioningly because of his loving trust that I would hold him safe from harm. My sorrow concerning Fray Antonio was keen enough, Heaven knows; but in his case I had the solace of knowing surely that he had come to his death not because of my urging, but in pursuance of his own strong desire. There was a little comfort in the thought that even one of these four lost lives could not be charged to my account; and yet this reflection seemed only to make my sorrow heavier as I thought of the woful weight of my responsibility for the other three.

For nearly two hours we lay there in the bay while the embarkation of the prisoners and the troops went on—our boat moving farther out from the pier from time to time as the double line of boats behind it lengthened. In that sheltered place there was little wind blowing, and the blazing heat of the sun beating down upon my wounded head gave me so sharp a pain that I gladly would have died to be rid of it; and I could see, from the drawn look of their faces, that Young and Rayburn were suffering not less keenly. We were thankful enough, therefore, when at last the embarkation was completed—more than half of the army remaining in Huitzilan to restore order there—and we pulled out from the bay into the open waters of the lake and were comforted by the light breeze, which yet brought with it a delicious refreshment, that was blowing there.

All the bright beauty of that lovely lake was around us, having for its background the green meadows and the darker green of the forests hanging above them on the upward slopes, and beyond all the towering height of the cliffs, which shaded in their colorings from delicate gray to dark brown, and were touched here and there by patches of black shadow where some great cleft opened; and yet all that we then thought of was that across those blue waters, which gleamed golden in the sunlight, we were going swiftly to a cruel death, and that the cliffs, whereof the beauty was hateful to us, irrevocably shut us in. Which gloomy feelings pressed upon us throughout that dismal passage, while all our oarsmen pulled stoutly together, and we went gliding onward over the sunlit waters towards the evil fate that we knew was waiting for us within the dark walls whereby was encircled the city of Culhuacan.

CHAPTER XXXII

EL SABIO'S DEFIANCE

While yet we were a long way off from the city, we heard faintly the yells of triumph with which the watchers above the water-gate gave notice to those within the walls of the return of the victorious army; and from all the boats of our flotilla there went up a shrill chorus of answering yells. Our barge was the first to pass through the water-gate, out from which we had come so gallantly so short a time before, and thence went onward across the basin to the very pier that we had started from with such high hopes to gather the forces for the rebellion that had come to so sorry an end.

All the water-side was black with the crowd that had gathered to watch our landing; but, considering that these people were there to welcome a victorious army, it seemed to me that they were strangely still and dull. There was, to be sure, no lack of yelling, but it came for the most part from a company of priests clustered on the pier where we landed, and from the soldiers and oarsmen in the boats—not from the townsfolk at large. And when we were marched upward through the city—following the same street that we had fought our way along when last we traversed it—I saw in the crowd so many sullen and dejected faces that it seemed to me there still was in that city a good deal of material for the making of another mutiny.

This time we were not taken to the house in which we had met the Priest Captain, and whence we had been delivered from imprisonment by Tizoc's gallant rescue of us; but, passing a little beyond this house, we were led up a broad stair-way to the plateau which crowned the city, and on which stood the great Treasure-house that also was the temple in which the Aztlanecas housed their most venerated gods. And I confess that my delight at seeing closely this building, that until then I had beheld only from afar off, for a time completely overcame the dread and sorrow that had oppressed me; and the very strongest desire that stirred within me just then was for a tape-measure and a pair of compasses and a steel square, together with the opportunity to fall to work with these several instruments upon those mighty walls. Indeed, I almost had forgotten that I was a prisoner, and was like to die soon a very dreadful death, when a groan that poor Rayburn gave—wrung from him by the pain that he suffered in being carried up the stairs—recalled me suddenly to a realizing sense of our situation, and so pressed home upon me the sad conviction that the science of archæology would gain nothing of all that I might see or learn during the little while that I should remain alive.

The outer facing of the plateau, like that of the terraces below it, was a prodigiously heavy wall of squared stones set in cement; and for a coping this wall had great stones carved in the similitude of serpents' heads, with mouths wide open, that instantly recalled to my mind the like enclosure that the Spaniards found surrounding the principal temple in the city of Tenochtitlan—and I had a sudden strong longing that my friend Bandelier might be with me at that moment to see how precisely his very ingenious speculations concerning the snake-wall about the great Teocalli were here confirmed.

Through a portal formed of two huge blocks of stone carved to represent two serpents coiled upon themselves, the heads meeting above in a sort of arch (not a true arch, for each of these serpents was a monolith, and was supported wholly on its own base), we entered the large enclosure before the temple. I was surprised to find—for of such a thing among the ancient Aztecs there is no record—that in the centre of the enclosure the rock had been hewn away in such a fashion as to create a vast amphitheatre; and that this was the place where sacrifice was offered by the priests was shown by the blood-stained altar in the centre of it, to which fragments of flesh also adhered, whence was wafted up to us a dreadful stench that instantly racked us with queasy qualms. Save directly in front of the entrance to the temple, where was a great stone balcony with a smaller balcony below it, all the sides of the amphitheatre were cut in steps, which made, also, benches where the multitude could sit at their ease and behold the bloody work going on in the pit below them; and so enormous was this rock-hewn cavity that fully forty thousand people could at once be seated there. Under the balcony there was visible the entrance to a dark tunnel-like passage, that evidently communicated with the temple, and a smaller passage, not large enough for a man to pass through, slanted downward to where it opened on the terrace below; which last was to drain the blood away, and also to free the amphitheatre from water in the season of rains.

We held our noses as we skirted this shocking place, and we were glad enough when we got beyond it and came to the entrance to the temple—a very noble portal, severely simple, and because of its simplicity the more majestic, in which, as in the whole of the façade, was manifest the grave and sombre Egyptian feeling that I had before observed. Through this we passed into the shadowy interior, lighted by only a few narrow slits cut in the enormously thick walls, where the lofty roof was upheld by a wilderness of columns which opened before us seemingly endless vistas where an eternal twilight reigned. Of interior decoration there was nothing save a broad and simple panelling upon the walls, and the great pillars were mere round monoliths without either bases or capitals.

As we entered this, to them, most sacred place a hush fell upon our escort, and even I felt something of that reverent awe that is inspired by any building which has been sanctified by the worship of multitudes within it through countless years. But that Young did not at all share this feeling with me was made manifest by his observing, after taking a long look around him: "Well, this wouldn't answer for a Congregational church, anyway. There ain't a pew in th' whole place, an' here in broad daylight you couldn't see a hymn-book if you tried. I wonder what they'd say, Professor, to a bid for puttin' in a dynamo for 'em an' lightin' this dark old hole with electricity? An' it 'u'd take off a lot o' this chill an' dampness if they'd have a steam-heater put in at th' same time. It's enough t' give all hands rheumatism th' way cold creeps strike up your legs." But at this point Young's observations were cut short peremptorily by the hand that one of the guards laid across his mouth; which hint that it was desirable for him to keep silence was quite unmistakable.

This decided repression of Young's chattering, no doubt, was the more vigorous because we now were approaching the farther end of the temple, where loomed before us amid the shadows a great idol, set upon an altar-like throne. This figure, fully ten feet high, was a strange medley of grotesque and hideous carvings that yet in its entirety was like a man; and so cruel and so ferocious was the general air of it that it well might inspire a very lively terror in simple souls. The most striking feature of the figure was a dismal skull, that was outheld from the region of the waist by two great hands placed there arbitrarily and without any relation to the figure's arms; and for a crest—repeating the motive of the gate-way—it had two serpents' heads, the bodies pertaining to which were twisted and involved about the whole mass. For eyes this evil thing had large and gleaming green stones—being, in truth, emeralds, though I did not at that time recognize them as such—and golden serpents, very beautifully wrought, were twisted about it, and a collar of golden hearts was hung around its neck over a sort of apron of shining green feathers; and feathers of a like sort rose above the heads of the serpents in a thick plume; and over every part of the figure were scattered glittering objects—emeralds, and disks of gold, and scraps of mother-o'-pearl, and fragments of obsidian—whence shone through the heavy shadows faint, shimmering points of light. In one of its out-stretched hands the figure held a bow, and in the other a bunch of arrows; but even without these unmistakable attributes I should have known from the skull and from the serpents' heads that this fierce and hideous idol represented the god Huitzilopochtli: the first divinity, and throughout the whole time that their bloody religion endured, the principal divinity, that the ancient Mexicans adored. Young did not venture to speak aloud again, but he turned to me with a long sigh and whispered, earnestly, "That certainly is, Professor, the very damnedest thing I ever saw!"

As I knew, it was in keeping with the Aztec customs that prisoners taken in war thus should be brought first of all before the god Huitzilopochtli, that they and their captors together might do him reverence; therefore, I was not surprised when a priest came forth from behind the altar and bade us prostrate ourselves in adoration of the idol. As this order was given, all the Aztlanecas with us bowed themselves to the floor; but Young, who did not understand the order, and I, who felt my gorge rising at the thought of thus humbling myself, remained erect. However, we did not continue through many seconds in that position; for a couple of soldiers instantly laid hands upon each of us, and by shoving our shoulders sharply forward, and at the same moment kicking our legs from under us, they summarily laid us face downward at full length upon the floor. As for Rayburn, they seemed to be satisfied with his recumbent position upon the stretcher; at any rate, they suffered him to remain as he was.

While I lay prone, quivering with rage at the double indignity of being thus roughly handled, and of being compelled even in form to worship a disgusting idol, I heard an odd little pattering upon the stone floor, and then something cold and clammy was thrust against my hand, and at the same instant I heard close beside me a curious snuffling noise; and while a glad doubt, that I scarce ventured to give way to, was rising within me, the clammy thing was taken away from my hand, and there straightway rang out through the gloomy silence of the temple a thunderous braying that seemed fairly to shake the walls. There was no mistaking the voice of the friend who with this triumphant blast welcomed me; and as I heard it there came into my heart a sudden glow of hope that Pablo, and that even Fray Antonio also, might still be alive. And this hope was destined to be immediately and most joyfully realized, for as we rose to our feet again I saw the lad standing, with El Sabio beside him, not a dozen feet away from me; and a little beyond them was the monk, his face all lighted up with a bright look of happiness and love. And seeing these three once more standing alive and well before me was the most amazing and also the very gladdest sight that ever met my eyes.

It was a sore trial to me that I could not immediately hold converse with Pablo and with Fray Antonio, and so come to know through what adventures they had passed, and by what miracles their lives had been saved; but the ceremony in which our captors were engaged was but half completed, and the better to assure our orderly conduct during its continuance we were kept asunder in the procession that then was formed—the object of which procession, as my knowledge of the Aztec customs led me rightly to infer, was that the ceremonial of triumph might be ended by leading us thrice around the sacrificial stone. And in truth I dreaded less the fate which this leading us about the altar of sacrifice implied was in store for us than I did the close association, made necessary by the ceremony, with the direful stench which that vile altar exhaled.

At the edge of the amphitheatre, where already the evil odor was almost overpowering, the soldiers who had charge of us relinquished us—as it seemed to me, most thankfully—to a company of the temple priests; whereof the chief was a round, fat little man, whose shortness of legs very obviously was accompanied by a corresponding shortness of wind. He was, in truth, a most hopelessly undignified little personage; yet he did his best to assume a look of dignity as he waddled down the steps in advance of us, and he manfully endeavored to conceal the difficulties encountered by his short fat legs in the course of this descent. And I was glad enough that we had his absurd performances to distract our minds a little from the dismalness of our surroundings, and especially from the queasiness that again beset our stomachs as our noses were assailed more and more violently by that most evil smell. The priests, I observed, had cotton stuffed in their nostrils; but for us there was nothing for it but to hold our noses tightly with our hands.

El Sabio, who had a most generous and broadly open nose, and who was not blest with hands to hold it fast with, grew restive as the first whiff struck him; which resulted less, I suppose, from the intrinsic vileness of the smell than from the fact that he, in common with all peace-loving animals, had aroused in him an instinctive terror by the odor of blood. Pablo's voice, and Pablo's touch, possibly might have soothed and quieted him; but the efforts which the priests who were leading him made to restrain him only served the more to terrify him, and so to increase his violence. And the priests, who now for a considerable time had seen him daily, and had known him only as the most gentle and biddable of creatures, were mightily astonished, and evidently were terrified, by this sudden outbreak of a fierce temper that most reasonably took them entirely by surprise. Partly by pulling at the rope that they had about his neck, and partly by such pushes as they dared to give him while he was momentarily at rest, they succeeded in forcing him down the steps; and so at last into the large circular space at the bottom of the amphitheatre, in the midst of which stood the stone of sacrifice and where the smell of blood was overpoweringly strong. But by the time that this victory was won El Sabio had ceased to be a quiet orderly donkey, accustomed to conform to the usages of human society, and had become a veritable crazy creature, inflamed by the madness of fear and rage.

By some miracle—a very happy miracle for those whom the poor ass most naturally regarded as his tormentors—El Sabio's nimble heels had until this moment lashed the air harmlessly; but just as the last step downward was accomplished he let out both of his hind-legs together, and with such precision that both of his hoofs struck a remarkably tall priest who had taken a very active part in persecuting him. The blow was landed fairly on the tall priest's stomach, and instantly the two long halves of that priest shut together like a jack-knife, and he fell to the ground with a gasp that told how thoroughly the wind was knocked out of him. Doubtless this outburst of violence served but to increase El Sabio's terror, for he straightway gave so strong a plunge that he fairly broke away from the men who were holding him; and then he bent all his energies to working such destruction as never was worked by one single ass since the very beginning of the world!

Fortunately for our own safety—for El Sabio was in no condition to discriminate between friends and foes—we still were at some distance from the bottom of the amphitheatre when this outbreak occurred; the greater part of the priests having preceded us, and El Sabio having been led in the van of the prisoners. It was wholly upon the priests, therefore, that his mad rage was expended, and the way that he "got in his work," as Young expressed it, on these enemies of his and ours was a joyful wonder to behold. Being closely penned in—for the way whence they had entered the amphitheatre was barred by the crowd of which we were a part, and the entrance to the subterranean passage leading to the temple was closed—the priests had no chance to escape from the furious creature save by clambering up the smooth wall, fully eight feet high, by which was enclosed the circular space that immediately surrounded the altar. Even an agile man, going at it quietly, would have found a little difficulty in executing this gymnastic feat, that required for its accomplishment sheer lifting of the body until a leg could be thrown over the top of the wall; and as these priests, for the most part, had grown fat and sluggish in their sacred calling, they were wellnigh incapacitated from performing it. Furthermore, El Sabio manifested what had the appearance of being a most diabolical ingenuity—yet that, no doubt, was no more than chance—in delivering flying kicks against the legs of these dangling creatures; wherefrom such keen pain resulted that they instantly let loose their hold, and came tumbling to the ground.

So far as we were concerned—our sympathies being wholly on the side of the ass—this astonishing spectacle remained a broad farce until the very end; but it presently became to the men engaged in it a very serious tragedy. As he made his wild charges, El Sabio galloped backward and forward again and again over the bodies of his prostrate enemies; in the course of which gallopings his sharp little hoofs cut their naked flesh savagely, and now and then, when he happened to land a kick fairly against a man's body, we could see, from the sinking in of the fellow's ribs and the gush of blood that burst from his nostrils, that the ass had delivered a death-blow.

As for the noise that attended this most extraordinary performance, words can but faintly describe it. From the men directly engaged with El Sabio came yells of fear and shouts for assistance and cries of anger, beneath all of which was a dull undertone of groans; the crowd around us and higher up behind us gave vent to a shrill roar of shouts and yells that seemed to be partly in the nature of advice, and partly the result of that instinct which prompts all barbarians to yell whenever anybody else yells, on general principles. Pablo interpolated a most despairing note in the way of beseeching cries of "B-u-r-r-r-o! B-u-r-r-r-o!" whereby he sought to allay El Sabio's frenzy, and so to save him from the direful fate that well might be expected to overtake him in recompense of his direful deeds; and Young fairly tossed his battered Derby hat up into the air as he shouted: "Go it, El Sabio! Give it to 'em, my boy! Ten t' one against th' fat priest! Three cheers for th' jackass! Hip-hip-hurrah!" In short, it seemed as though Bedlam had broken loose among us, and as though all of us together were going mad.

What with dodging behind his fellows, and keeping clear of El Sabio's frantic charges by the display of an agility that I would not have given him credit for, the little fat priest managed to preserve his small round body unharmed until all of his companions had either escaped over the wall or had been, as Young put it, knocked out by El Sabio's heels. Once or twice he had made a dash for the passage-way in which we were standing, but the lower end of this was choked with the dozen or more badly wounded wretches who had crawled thither in their efforts to escape; and these the priests in front of us, being but cowardly creatures, had made no effort to succor or to lift away, for the reason that so long as this barrier remained they themselves were safe from El Sabio's fury.

Having, therefore, no longer any one to hide behind, the fat little priest evidently realized that his only hope of salvation lay in making an effort, truly heroic in one of his height and girth and woful shortness of wind, to clamber up the face of the wall; and to this wellnigh impossible task he most resolutely set himself. It was only by jumping that he was able to get a grip over the top of the wall; yet when this grip was gained he could get no farther on his way to deliverance, and so he hung dangling there, his face to the wall, jerking his short fat legs about spasmodically, and wasting in most piercing yells what little there was in him of wind.

It did really seem as though El Sabio's action in these premises was dictated by reason, for when he saw the priest in this wholly unprotected position he deliberately took his stand at precisely the point behind the little man where all of his kicking power could be most effectively used. There was a momentary hush as El Sabio thus placed himself, for every one perceived how very open was the priest to assault; and at the same time it was apparent that while El Sabio's kicks assuredly would be exceedingly painful, they were not likely to inflict upon the priest, while he remained in that attitude, a deadly wound. In an instant the two small heels flashed through the air, and there was heard a dull, soft sound—such as might come from the striking of an over-ripe melon with a heavy club—and with this burst forth a most piercing shriek of pain. Yet the little priest, knowing that his life depended upon it, most gallantly retained his hold. Again El Sabio kicked, and again a piercing shriek sounded; and one hand loosened for a moment and then clutched fast again. But when El Sabio kicked for the third time human nature was too weak to resist further against brute violence. With a yell that fairly cracked our ears the priest let go his hold and fell downward and backward; and at that same instant El Sabio delivered a final kick that struck fairly on the head of the falling man and battered in his skull.

As for El Sabio, it seemed as though he himself were like to die in the very moment of his victory; for with a sort of groan that, coming from a brute beast, was most pitiful to listen to, the poor terrified creature, utterly exhausted by his fright and his outlay of energy in furious violence, sank down panting by the side of the man whom he had slain.

CHAPTER XXXIII

IN THE AZTEC TREASURE-HOUSE

Even with El Sabio reduced to this condition of complete quiescence, the Aztlanecas, soldiers as well as priests, still were terribly afraid of him; being firmly convinced, as was not at all unnatural, that for the time being there was embodied in him a devil of a most dangerous sort. Therefore they were but too glad to yield to Pablo's burning eagerness to get to the poor ass; and when he called for aid to carry the exhausted creature out from the amphitheatre, and so away from among the dead and wounded and from the dreadful smell of blood, Young and I promptly were pushed forward and ordered to perform this piece of work that even the bravest of them shrunk from undertaking.

However, there was no real peril in it, for El Sabio was so weak that he could not even stand, and still less was he strong enough to kick anybody. Lifting him in this dull, limp state, and carrying him up the steep steps, was heavy work for us, wounded and weary as we were; but with Pablo's help we managed it, and so got him up from the depths of the amphitheatre to its windward side—where a fresh sweet breeze that was blowing, and some water that a soldier brought when Pablo called for it, in a little while put new life into him. Why the ass was not made to pay the penalty of his sins, by being there and then killed, at first was a good deal of a puzzle to me; but presently, from the talk that went on about us while Pablo ministered to him, and while the wounded lying around the altar were being cared for, and the dead borne away, I gathered that no one dared to kill him for fear of being himself possessed by the devil that needs must enter another body upon being thus set free. And as this seemed to be a view of the case that was worth encouraging, I very gravely told one of the priests that I myself had seen a man all in an instant go raving mad upon slaying one of these creatures and so letting the devil loose from him. As this story was circulated among the crowd I was glad to perceive that the dread of El Sabio obviously greatly increased.

As a result of the untoward outbreak that had occurred, no attempt was made to complete the ceremonial of triumph. Indeed, the victory now lay so decidedly with El Sabio that there was but little to triumph over. Therefore we presently were herded together by a party of soldiers—who took good care that Pablo should lead the ass, and that Young and I should walk directly behind him as a protection against any further uplifting of his heels—and so we all were marched once more into the temple. This time we did not stop in front of the great idol, but went on beyond it towards a portal in the rear of the building that opened on an inner court; on the farther side of which court, as we knew from the description of the place that Tizoc had given us, was the Treasure-house, in which was stored not only the treasure placed there in long past ages by King Chaltzantzin, but also the treasure belonging to the State and to the temple that had been accumulated in later times.

At the entrance to the court-yard, where the way was closed by a metal grating over which a heavy curtain hung, the soldiers formally relinquished us into the charge of a company of priests; and then the curtain was drawn aside and the grating was raised, and we passed out into the bright sunlight—and saw close before us the place which for so long a time had so largely filled our thoughts. It was a building of no great size, being but a single story high, and was dwarfed by the vastly stupendous cliffs which so far overtopped it that they seemed to extend upward to the very sky; but it was most massively constructed, and the actual available space within it was far greater than was indicated by the relatively small dimensions of its exterior walls. When we entered the building, through a narrow opening protected by a metal grating, the chamber into which we came was of so considerable a size that a part of it, we perceived, must extend actually into the cliff; and that the work of quarrying out the living rock had been carried still farther was shown by an opening at its rear end that evidently gave access to some hollow depth beyond.

It was towards this inner recess that our guards led us. Here another grating was raised that we might pass, and we went onward through a narrow passage cut in the rock, along the sides of which were many openings giving access to small cell-like rooms. Nor was this place, as we had expected to find it, wholly dark; for narrow slits had been cut through the rock out to the face of the cliff, through which came so much light that we could see about us very well. And but for that blessed light, faint though it was, I doubt not that we should have gone mad there; and even with the light to cheer and to comfort us I felt a black despair settling down upon me at the thought of being thus imprisoned within the very bowels of the mountain, with no possibility of other release than being taken thence to die.

At the extreme end of the passage the rock had been hollowed away smoothly and carefully so as to form a chamber nearly thirty feet square and at least twenty feet high, whereof all the walls were covered with plates of gold which overlapped each other in the manner of fishes' scales; and advantage had been taken of some wide crevice or deep depression in the cliff above to open in the roof of this chamber a small aperture, whence a pale light entered in long fine rays which gleamed through the shadows, and gleamed again more faintly in reflections from the golden walls. In this oratory—for such it evidently was—stood a statue, smaller than that in the temple yet still more magnificently arrayed, of the god Huitzilopochtli; before which odious image we were thrown upon our faces by our guards. When this ceremony was ended we were led forth once more into the passage, and so into two of the little cells which had been meagrely prepared for us by tossing into each of them a bundle of mats; and there our guards left us to shift for ourselves—shutting the grating behind them with a sharp ringing of metal on stone that echoed dismally through the rock-hewn chambers wherein we were held fast.

For a while we stood in melancholy silence about the stretcher on which poor Rayburn lay; and very pale and worn he looked after his great loss of blood and heavy fatigue and the pain and excitement of the last few hours. Pablo had taken up his quarters with El Sabio in a cell on the opposite side of the passage—for within the limits of our prison we were left to arrange ourselves as we pleased—and we could hear him talking to the ass in a fashion that at any other time we should have laughed at; for by turns he upbraided him for his rash acts, and complimented him upon his bravery, and expressed dread of the punishment that might be visited upon him, and told him of his very tender love—all of which, so far as we could judge, El Sabio took in equally good part.

"There ain't no good in standin' 'round here doin' nothin'," Young said, at last. "This don't look like much of a place t' break out of, but we may as well see how things are, anyway. Th' Padre'd better take a squint at Rayburn's busted leg an' set th' bandages straight; an' while he's attendin' t' that, me an' you, Professor, can do a little prospectin'. This is th' Treasure-house, for sure, an' it'll be some satisfaction t' see what it amounts to. I'll bet a hat there ain't anything worth havin' in th' whole place, after all."

I was glad enough to have any occupation that would change even a little the sad current of my thoughts, and I therefore very willingly acted on Young's suggestion—after first making sure that Fray Antonio had no need of help in his work of dressing Rayburn's wound—and together we set about this curious exploration; that had in it a strong charm for me, notwithstanding my heavy sorrow, because of the possibility that it opened of finding curious traces of a new community so far advanced in civilization as was that which the King Chaltzantzin had brought with him into this valley a thousand years ago. Here, unquestionably, was the oldest deposit of the belongings of any of the primitive dwellers upon the American continent; and I trembled a little with excitement at the thought of what archæological treasures I here might find—and then I heaved suddenly a long sigh as I remembered how useless in my present case would be even the most brilliant of discoveries.

As for Young's bet of a hat that there was no treasure here worth having, he would have lost it, had it been accepted, at the very first of the rooms which we examined; for the whole of this room, a cube of about ten feet, was packed full of bars of hardened gold from the mine at Huitzilan. And so was the next room, and the next, until we had found five rooms thus filled. But all the remaining rooms were entirely empty, and of the treasure set aside in long past ages by King Chaltzantzin there was no sign. Yet here, truly, was stored wealth the like of which the richest monarch in the world could not match for greatness; and as Young beheld before him such enormous riches his face grew ruddy, an eager light came into his eyes, the muscles of his throat worked convulsively, and his breathing was labored and short—until I demolished all his fine fancies at a blow by saying: "Much good this treasure is to us, when there isn't a ghost of a chance that either of us ever will get out of this valley alive!" As I uttered these bitter words his look of animation left him, and for some moments he was silent; and when at last he spoke, it was in a tone of calm though melancholy conviction, and with a most dispassionate air.

"I shall be obliged t' you, Professor, really obliged t' you," he said, "if you'll just kick me for a blasted fool. Ever since that night in Morelia when you told me an' Rayburn about this treasure I've regularly had it on my brain. Through all these months I've been thinkin' about it when I was awake an' dreamin' about it when I was asleep. An' it's true for a fact, Professor, that never until this blessed minute, when we've really struck it, has th' notion come into my fool head that when we did ketch up with it the folks it rightly b'longed to might want t' keep it for theirselves! Yes, just kick me, please. Just kick me for a forlorn, mis'rable, blasted fool!"

I was not disposed to laugh at Young's words; rather was I disposed to weep over them. For they brought freshly and strongly to my mind the fact that I was responsible for alluring him, by the hope of acquiring great riches quickly, into this accursed valley, where in a little while he would be most barbarously done to death. And I knew too that I was responsible for the like fate that must overtake Rayburn, and that in regard to Pablo my guilt was greatest of all. It was a comfort to me, truly, that not one of these ever by look or word reproached me for thus so wofully misleading them; and yet, in a certain way, their very forbearance but added to my pain.

Therefore was I a little gladdened, when we returned again to the others, to find that Fray Antonio was speaking to Rayburn, with a grave, calm hopefulness, of those spiritual realities which are higher and better than material realities, and without steadfast trust in which, most of us, in the course of this sorrowful thing that we call life, assuredly would go mad in sheer despair. And listening to this comforting discourse, which was not checked by our return, did much to strengthen me to bear my heavy load of vain regret. Presently Fray Antonio shifted his ground—for he had the wisdom to speak but shortly on these grave topics, yet using always pregnant words which sank down into men's hearts and germinated there— and told us of what had befallen him since he had stolen away from us that night in Huitzilan.

In truth, he had but little to tell, for his adventures had been of a very simple kind. Upon his arrival in the canoe at the water-gate he had been at once recognized and admitted, and had been carried directly to the building in which, on our first coming into the city, we all had been confined. And there he had been imprisoned until he was led up to the temple to take part in the triumph that El Sabio's violence so seriously had marred, and so once more was in our company. Of the Priest Captain he had seen nothing at all; nor had any answer come back to him from that dignitary to his urgent plea that, inasmuch as he had thus surrendered himself, his companions—that is, ourselves—should be suffered to leave the valley in peace; which silence on the part of the Priest Captain was not surprising, however, in view of the brave defiance in words sent by the Tlahuicos, who afterwards were such cowards in deeds.

In fact, during the brief time of his imprisonment Fray Antonio had not spoken to a soul save the man who brought him drink and food. Yet his talk with this man, scant though it had been, had filled him with the hope that, could he only hold free converse with the people at large, even as he had done at Huitzilan, the purpose that he had in mind in coming into the valley would be fulfilled. Although a priest of the temple, his jailer had listened with a most earnest and hearty attention to the expounding of Christian doctrine that was opened to him, and had shown a very cheering willingness to recognize the shortcomings of his own idolatrous belief as compared with the principles of this purer and nobler faith. And he had told Fray Antonio that many of his companions in the service of the temple, having heard somewhat of the new creed from those who had tome up from Huitzilan, were eager to know more concerning it; so that it would seem, Fray Antonio declared, as though there were a harvest there ready to be reaped to Christianity by his hand. The case was such, he thought, that could he but speak publicly to the multitude, and especially could there but be vouchsafed from Heaven some sign by which the verity of his words might be established, he yet would win to the glorious Christian faith this whole community, that, through no fault of its own, until that time had remained lost in heathen sin.

Rayburn and I exchanged glances as Fray Antonio spoke of aid being given him in his work by a sign from Heaven, for to our notions the time of miracles was a long while past. But Fray Antonio, as we knew (for once or twice we three had spoken together of this matter), did not at all hold with us in believing that miracle-working had come to an end; and indeed his faith was entirely logical; for, as he himself put it, those who believed that miracles ever had been wrought for the advancement of Christianity could not reasonably draw a line at any year since the Christian Church was founded, and say that in that year miracles ceased to be. In this matter, as in many others, the resemblance between Fray Antonio and the founder of his Order, Saint Francis of Assisi, was very strong.

Pablo's experience as a prisoner had been of a far more trying sort;

for the priests had sought earnestly, he said, by most stringent means, to pervert him from Christianity to their own faith. When we had been so rudely separated that day, after our interview with the Priest Captain, he, and El Sabio with him, had been hurried up the stairs to the temple, and thence to the Treasure-house; and there, though not in the part of it in which we then were, he had been ever since confined. Strong measures certainly had been taken to make a heathen of him. He had been starved for a while, and he had been deprived of water, and he had been cruelly scourged, and very harrowing presentments had been made to him of the death that he must die should he much longer refuse to yield. That the lad had remained firm in his faith, he told us, sobbing a little at memory of his hardships, was because of the sorrow that he knew his yielding would bring upon Fray Antonio and upon me; which certainly was not the reason that Fray Antonio most would have approved, but it did not in the least detract from the steady courage that he had shown in holding out firmly under pressure that would have made many a man succumb. In all the time that so many cruelties had been practised upon him, only one man had shown him kindness—an old man, who seemed to be in charge of the archives that the Treasure-house contained, who twice had risked his own life by secretly giving him water and food. But he never had been separated from El Sabio, Pablo said joyfully, in conclusion, nor had his mouth-organ been taken away from him; and these blessings had done much to lessen the misery that he was compelled to bear.

When, in our turn, Rayburn and Young and I had told of the far more stirring adventures that we had passed through, and of our high hopes seemingly so well founded that had suffered so dismal a downfall, we all of us wisely refrained from speculating at all upon the future; instead of which profitless and painful topic we strove to speak cheerfully of indifferent matters; and this we did not only that we might the better keep our hearts up, but that we might not excite Rayburn, who already was in a dangerously feverish condition by reason of his wound. But, though we spoke not of it, we none of us doubted what our fate would be; nor did we imagine that the death that surely awaited us would be long delayed.

It was a source of wonder to us, therefore, that day after day went by without bringing the end that we so confidently expected. From the man who brought us our food we could learn nothing; but this was not from ill-will on his part, but because he himself knew nothing of the Priest Captain's plans. This man, though a priest, was not unkindly disposed towards us, and he even listened to the words which Fray Antonio addressed to him touching Christian doctrine; but while he listened—being made of a sterner stuff than the priest who previously had been Fray Antonio's jailer—he gave no sign of assent. The only other person whom we had a chance to speak with, and this but rarely, was the old man who had shown kindness to Pablo, the guardian of the archives—who, by right of his official position, had free access to that portion of the Treasure-house from which the second grating cut us off. At the grating he and I had some very interesting conversations together upon archæological matters; but Fray Antonio took but little interest in him when he found how slight was the impression made upon him by the most serious of doctrinal talk. In truth, this old fellow—wherefore my own heart warmed to him—was wholly given to the study of antiquities; and so full was his mind of this delightful subject that there was no room left in it for thoughts about religions of any sort. He was entirely catholic in this matter, for his unconcern respecting Christianity was neither more marked nor less marked than was his unconcern toward his own avowed faith.

Many curious things this old man told me touching the history of his people; and he showed me, also, the manner in which their annals were kept—an obvious evolution from the picture-writing of the Aztecs that had advanced to a stage closely resembling the cross between ideaographs and an alphabet that the Coreans use—all of which I have dealt with exhaustively in my larger work. And he told me also, with a wonder that did not seem uncalled for, that several times in each year the Priest Captain retired to the very place in which we then were imprisoned, and remained there sometimes for as much as a whole month cut off from his people, without food or drink, while he communed with the gods.

But what seemed strange to me, and also bitterly disheartening, was that this old man, notwithstanding the office that he held and his hungry love for ancient things, could tell me nothing of the treasure that King Chaltzantzin had stored away. He knew of this treasure, he said, only as a vague tradition; and although, at one time or another, he had explored every chamber in the Treasure-house, he never had found of this ancient deposit the smallest trace; for which excellent reason he had concluded that if ever there had been such a treasure it long since had been dispersed. No doubt—considering how useless to me, beyond the mere gratification of my own curiosity, would have been its discovery—my regret at this abrupt ending of my hopes was most unreasonable; but I confess that, so far as I myself was concerned, the very keenest pang of sorrow that I suffered through all that sorrowful time was when I thus learned that the archæological search that I had entered upon so hopefully, and that I had so laboriously prosecuted, had been but a fool's errand from first to last.

CHAPTER XXXIV

A MARTYRDOM

Heavily and wearily the days dragged on as we lay in that dismal prison hewn from the mountain's heart; and as they slowly vanished there stole upon us a new sorrow, that was deeper and more searching than the doubting dread by which we were beset touching the cruel ending of our lives.

Rayburn's wound—a very savage cut in the thigh, made by the jagged edge of a maccahuitl—from the first had been a dangerous one; and the danger had been aggravated by inflammation that had followed that long, hot journey across the lake, and by the rough handling that his bearers had given him, and by the excitement that had attended El Sabio's fiery outburst beside the sacrificial stone. Even Fray Antonio's skill in surgery, without which he assuredly would have quickly died, only barely sufficed to keep him alive while the fever was upon him; and when at last the fever left him, the little strength remaining to him grew less with every passing day. It was pathetic to see this man, who until then had been the very embodiment of rugged vigor, so worn with suffering that without Fray Antonio's tender assistance he scarce could move; and still more pathetic was it to hear him moaning in his pain, and uttering heart-sick longings for sunlight and fresh air, for need of which, Fray Antonio affirmed, he was dying there quite as much as because of his wound. Indeed, the chill chamber in the rock where he was lying was no fit place even for a well man at that time to dwell in; for the season of rains had come, and all the nights were cold and damp, while through the afternoons and in the night-time, during which portions of the day the rain fell in torrents, the whole mountain was shaken by the tremendous peals of thunder which roared and crashed about its crest.

It was after one of poor Rayburn's pitiable outbreaks of weak moaning that Young led me away into the oratory, with the evident intention of delivering himself of some matter that pressed heavily upon his mind.

"See here, Professor, I just *can't* stand this any longer," he said, when we were alone. "I'm goin' t' send word t' th' Priest Captain t' ask him if finishin' me off in short order won't make him willin' t' let Rayburn out o' this damp hole into some place where he can be comfortable, an' where in th' mornin's he can get some sun an' air. Rayburn won't mind bein' squarely killed after he's healthy again. He ain't th' kind t' be afraid of anything when he's feelin' all right. But it's just infernal cruelty t' kill him this way—it wouldn't be fair to a dog. So I'm goin' t' try what I can do. It's nothin' much t' do, any way—only runnin' a little ahead o' th' schedule, that's all."

Oddly enough, something of a like purpose had been for some time past slowly forming in my own mind—though what I intended to do would have, I hoped, still better consequences; for my notion was to urge that for the pleasure that could be had from killing me, my companions should be given such freedom as was to be found in that rock-bound region beyond the Barred Pass. Therefore, when Young thus brought up the matter openly between us, I told him of my own intention; and with some emphasis I advised him that inasmuch as I first had thought of it, to me belonged the right to carry this project into execution; and especially was this right mine, I urged, because but for me neither he nor any of the rest of us—saving only, possibly, Fray Antonio—ever would have come into that valley at all. Thereupon we fell to wrangling somewhat hotly; for Young was a most pig-headed man when his mind was set upon anything, and his notions of argument even at the best of times were of the loosest kind.

How our talk might have ended I cannot tell, for each of us most resolutely was determined to have his own way; but it actually did end because of an interruption by which we presently learned that a will finer and stronger than either of ours had been acting, while we had been only thinking, in a fashion that cut the ground completely from under us both. And all that followed within the next hour or two came upon us with so startling a suddenness that it seemed less like reality than like a terrible dream.

The first intimation that we had that anything was upon us out of the common run of our drearily dull prison life was hearing a creaking noise that we knew must be caused by the raising of the grating that shut us in; and as we hurried out from the oratory into the long passage-way we saw a company of soldiers coming towards us, at the head of which was a priest. Fray Antonio and Pablo, startled as we had been by the sound caused by the opening of the grating and the tramp of feet, also had come out into the passage; but while Pablo evidently was wondering, even as we were wondering, what might be the purpose that these men had come to execute, the look upon the monk's face was of expectation rather than of surprise. And without waiting for the others to speak, he asked, eagerly: "Is it to be?"

"It is to be," the priest answered; and it seemed to me that there was sorrow in the look that went with his words, and sorrow also in the tone of his voice; and that this man truly was sorrowful because of the message that he brought I doubt not, for he was the priest who had been jailer to Fray Antonio, and whose mind had seemed so open to receive the doctrine that Fray Antonio taught.

But there was only joy in the bearing of the monk as his question thus was answered; and there was a ringing gladness in his voice as he replied—being most careful first to draw us away from the room in which Rayburn was lying—to our looks of wondering inquiry. "The Priest Captain has granted my request," he said, and added quickly: "Do not sorrow for me, my friends. Dying for the Faith is the most glorious ending that life can have; and happier still is he to whom, with this rare privilege, is given also that of dying that those whom he loves may yet be saved alive. The Priest Captain has promised that when I have paid this little debt of life you whom I love so greatly shall go free—"

"Don't you believe him! He's a blasted liar from the word go!" Young struck in, clean forgetting, in the passionate sorrow that was rising in his breast, that what Fray Antonio so plainly had in mind to do he himself had been most strongly bent upon doing but a moment before. But Young spoke in English, and without heeding him Fray Antonio went on: "You two, and the boy, surely will live; and perhaps life may be given also to our friend. He is in God's hands. And then, until—"

But further speech was not permitted to him. Two soldiers stepped forward and grasped his arms, yet first suffering him for a moment to clasp hands with us, and so led him towards the open grating; and behind him Young and I and Pablo were conducted in a like fashion by the guards. As we passed the room in which Rayburn lay we heard him moaning faintly; and so weak was he that it seemed to me a very likely thing for us to find him dead there upon our return—if, indeed, we ever returned at all.

As we passed out into the inner court of the temple, where the sum shone joyously—for the day still was young, and the rain-clouds had but begun to gather about the mountain peaks—we heard a murmur in the air like the distant sound of bees buzzing; and as we entered the rear portal of the temple this sound grew louder, yet still was soft and blurred. In the temple, Fray Antonio was separated from us, being led towards the inner entrance of that subterranean passage which opened into the pit of the amphitheatre; and as we went onward to the great portal in the temple's front we cast towards him sorrowful looks, in which all the bitter pain that was in our hearts was concentrated, but had in answer from him, as he walked with elate bearing between his guards, only looks of most joyful hope in which was also a very tender love.

The noise that at first had seemed to us like bees buzzing grew louder as we advanced, until, when we came out upon the open space before the temple, it swelled into a mighty roar. And there the cause of it was plain to us; for before us lay the great amphitheatre crowded with a seething multitude, and all the thousands gathered there were uttering savage cries of delight at thought of the savage spectacle that now in a few moments would gladden their fierce hearts. In the midst of this tumult we were hurried into a sort of balcony, heavily built of stone, that hung upon the slope of the amphitheatre; just behind and above which was a much larger balcony of richly wrought stone-work that was covered by a canopy of colored stuffs, and that had in its midst a sort of throne. And at sight of us a great shout went up, that in a moment died away into a hush of silence as the Priest Captain, with a company of priests about him, entered the balcony behind us and took his seat upon the throne.

But in another instant the shouting burst forth again as Fray Antonio came out from the passage that opened beneath us, and in a moment was lifted bodily by his guards and placed upon the Stone of Sacrifice in plain view of all. I wondered as I saw that only soldiers accompanied him, and that there was no sign of the coming of the priests by whom the sacrifice would be made. But my wonder ceased, and the burning pain that then consumed me was a little lessened, as there came forth from the underground passage, guarded by four soldiers, a very tall, strong Indian, whose muscles stood out in great knots upon his lithe body and legs and arms, and immediately following him six others no less powerful—for then I knew that Fray Antonio was not to die the cruel and bloody death of a sacrificial victim, but was to have, in accordance with the Aztec custom, such chance of life as was to be found in fighting these seven men in turn and receiving his freedom when he had slain them all. Yet as I looked at the slim figure of the monk, and then at these burly giants ready to be pitted against him, I knew that but one result could issue from that unequal combat; and a sudden dizziness came upon me, and for a moment all around me was dark. Nor was this momentary darkness wholly imaginary; for just then—with a low growl of distant thunder—a fragment broke away from the great mass of black cloud that hung upon the crest of the cliff above us and drifted sluggishly across the face of the sun.

When my dizziness had passed, and I could again see clearly, the warrior was standing upon the Stone of Sacrifice—naked save for his breech-clout, and armed with a round shield and a maccahuitl of hardened gold. The monk still wore his flowing habit, whence the hood had fallen back, so that his head was bare; in one hand he held his crucifix, and with the other he was motioning away the sword and shield that a soldier held out to him: at sight of which refusal on his part to be armed there was a shrill outcry among the multitude that the fight would not be fair; and to this sharp noise of strident voices there was added a solemn undertone that came in a low roll of thunder from the overhanging cloud.

As though to still the clamor, the monk waved his hand; and when at this sign the outcries ceased, he asked—yet addressing not the Priest Captain but the whole mass of people gathered there— if certain words which he desired to utter would be heard. And in answer to him there went up a shout of assent, in which was drowned completely (save that we, being close beneath him, heard it) the Priest Captain's order that the fight should begin. And it struck me that the Priest Captain showed his appreciation of the critical situation with which he then was dealing, and his dread of the forces which an ill-timed word in opposition to the will of the multitude might let loose against him, by refraining from repeating his order when silence came again, and all the thousands gathered there leaned forward eagerly to hearken to what Fray Antonio would say.

And what he did say was the most moving and the most exalted deliverance that ever came forth from mortal man. To that great multitude he preached there shortly, but with an eloquence that I doubt not was born directly of heavenly inspiration, a sermon so searching, so full of God's great love and tenderness, and so full also of the majesty of His law and of the long-suffering of His mercy and loving-kindness, that every word of it falling from his lips seemed to burn into the depths of all those heathen hearts. My own heart was thrilled and shaken as it never had been stirred before, and the boy Pablo wept as he listened; and even Young, to whom the spoken words had no meaning, grew pale, and sweat gathered upon his forehead as his soul was moved within him by the infinitely beseeching tenderness of Fray Antonio's voice: for most wonderfully did his voice rise and fall in its cadenced sweetness and entreaty, and there was a strangely vibrant quality in his tones that matched the tenor of his words, and so held all that vast multitude spellbound.

As he spoke on, a hush fell upon them who listened; and then through the throng a tremor seemed to run, but less a sound of actual speech than a subtle manifestation that in a moment a great outburst of assent would come, and I felt within me that the work which Fray Antonio had dared death to accomplish already was triumphantly concluded; and so waited, breathless, to hear this heathen host proclaim its glad allegiance to the Christian God.

But the Priest Captain also perceived how imminent was the danger that menaced the ancient faith, and dared to take the one chance left for saving it, and that a desperate one, by breaking in upon Fray Antonio's discourse with a ringing order that the fight should be no longer delayed; whereat a deep growl of dissent ran through the crowd, that was echoed in a still deeper roar of thunder in the dark sky. In truth, the gathering of the storm in the heavens above seemed to be wholly in keeping with the storm that with an equal celerity was gathering on the earth below. There was a heavy languor, a dense stillness in the air, and the cloud above us had drifted out from the face of the cliff so far that it now hung over all the city like a vast black canopy. From this sombre mass, that buried all beneath it in gloomy shadows, flashes of lightning shot forth that each moment increased in fiery intensity, and the rolling roar of thunder each moment grew louder and sharper in its dark depths. Even as the Priest Captain spoke there came a yet more vivid flash, and almost with it a crashing peal.

At the word of command, so vehemently given, the warrior faced about upon Fray Antonio, and held high aloft his sword; but the monk, firmly standing there, while in his eyes shone so glorious a light that it seemed as though the wrath of outraged Heaven blazed forth from them, opposed to this earthly weapon only his out-stretched crucifix, and thus confronted the death that menaced him with so splendid a bravery that for an instant his huge antagonist was held still by a wonder that was born half of admiration and half of awe; and in the breathless hush of that supreme moment Fray Antonio cried out, in tones so clear and so ringing that his words were heard by all the thousands gathered there:

"I call for help upon the living and the only God!"

And even as these words still sounded in our ears there shot forth from the cloud above us a swift red flash of blinding light, and with this came a crash of thunder so mighty that the cliffs above strained and quivered, and great fragments of rock came hurtling down from them, and a shivering trembling surged through the whole mountain, so that we felt it swaying beneath our feet.

And as we gazed in awe, through the gloom that from all parts of the heavens was gathering towards the height whereon we were, we saw before us God's wrath made manifest; for the warrior, still holding raised the metal sword that had tempted death to him, trembled, reeled a little, swayed gently forward, and then, with, a sudden jerk, swayed backward again, and so fell lifeless—his bare right arm, and all the length of his naked body to his very heel marked by a livid streak of bloody purple that showed where the thunder-bolt had passed. For a moment the monk also seemed stunned; and then, kneeling beside that lightning-blasted corpse, and holding his hands out-stretched towards heaven, whence his deliverance had come, he cried in a clear strong voice, of which the solemn tones rang vibrant through that awful silence: "The Christian God liveth and reigneth! Believe on Him whose love and whose mercy are not less tender than is terrible His transcendent power!"

There was no mistaking the thrill of movement that ran through the multitude as these words were spoken. I drew a long breath of thankfulness, for I felt that Fray Antonio was saved, and that in another instant my ears would be nigh burst by the thunderous roar of all those thousands—won to him by his own most moving eloquence, and by sight of the miracle whereby his deliverance had been wrought—that he should be set free.

And in this instant—in the very moment that this sigh escaped me, while yet the pause lasted before that great shout came—the Priest Captain sprang from, his seat above us into the balcony where we prisoners stood guarded, on downward into the arena below, and thence upon the Stone of Sacrifice—all with a demoniac agility most horrible to look upon in one of his withered age—and there, with a fierce thrust of a spear that he had caught from a soldier's hand in passing, he pierced Fray Antonio between the shoulders straight through the heart; and the monk, still grasping in his hands his crucifix, fell face downward upon the Stone of Sacrifice, and lay there dead!

Then Itzacoatl, standing with one foot upon the monk's dead body, and grasping still the spear that he had planted in that noble heart, cried out, triumphantly, "Behold the victory and the vengeance of our Aztec gods!"

And the multitude, swayed backward from the very threshold of the Christian faith, shouted together in one mighty voice, "Victory and vengeance for our gods!"

CHAPTER XXXV

THE TREASURE-CHAMBER

Close in the wake of that great thunder-crash there burst upon us so mighty a flood of rain that it seemed as though the lightning had riven solid walls asunder within the thick black mass of overhanging vapour, and so had let loose upon us the waters of a lake. In a moment the whole pit of the amphitheatre was awash, knee-deep, and before those who were standing there could flounder to the steps leading upward they were buried to their waists—and this although the water was pouring out through the vent provided for it with such violence that we could hear the rush and gurgle of it above the dashing and roaring of the falling rain. And all the dark mass of cloud above us was aflame continuously with blinding flashes of red lightning, while a continuous crash of splitting peals of thunder rang through the shattered air.

Doubtless this storm was our salvation. That the Priest Captain's intention, even from the first, had been to kill us also, and so make his victory complete, I do not for a moment doubt; but he was too shrewd to waste upon a few terrified spectators an exhibition that would carry with it a salutary demonstration of his power; and with the bursting of the flood upon us, the crowd that filled the amphitheatre had begun a tumultuous flight to the temple; going thither partly for shelter, and partly being awe-struck by what had passed before them and by the tremendous fury of the storm, that they might find safety in the abiding-place of their gods.

Therefore, the order was given hurriedly that we should be taken back to our prison; in obedience to which command our guards led us through the temple—where they had difficulty in forcing a way for us through the dense throng that had gathered within its walls—and thence to the Treasure-house beyond; and they were in such haste to be quit of us, that they also might seek safety in the temple, that they scarce waited to close the grating behind us before they sped away.

So overwhelming was the grief that had fallen upon us that for some moments we stood as though stunned where the guards had left us; and, for myself, my one regret was that the chance of the storm, by saving me yet a little while longer alive, had lost to me the happiness of dying in the same hour with the friend whom I had so strongly loved. I think that this thought was in Young's heart also, as he stood there silent beside me, the blood so drawn away from his face that a dull yellow pallor overspread his bronzed skin, while his breath came short and hard. As for the boy Pablo, his whole being was shattered. He sank down on the rock at our feet, and seemed to be moaning his very life out in long quivering sobs.

But presently, as our minds grew steadier, the thought of Rayburn came to us; and the strain upon our heart-strings was relaxed a little by remembering that our lives still were worth holding fast to in order that we might minister to his needs. Yet when we came again into the room where he lay, it seemed at first as though he also was lost to us; for even in that faint light we saw that his face was a deadly white, and when we spoke to him he neither spoke nor moved. But, happily, our dread that he had died in that gloomy solitude was not realized; for as I laid my hand upon his bare breast I felt his heart feebly beating, and at the touch of my hand he sighed a little, and then slowly opened his eyes.

"He's only swounded," Young cried, joyfully. "It's th' smotherin' shut-upness o' this forlorn hole he's lyin' in. There's a little more air out in th' big room. Just grab t'other end o' th' stretcher, Professor, an' we'll yank him out there—nobody's likely t' come in t' stop us while this storm lasts. An'—an' we must be careful how we talk, Professor, y' know," he added, in a lower tone, as we raised the stretcher. "It won't do for him t' know about—about *it* now." There was a break in Young's voice as he spoke, and I could feel by the momentary quiver of the stretcher that a shiver went through him as he thought of that "it," about which we must for a time hold our peace.

Young bore the forward end of the stretcher, and as we came into the oratory I felt him start as he exclaimed, "What th' devil's broke loose here?"

The darkness of the storm outside shrouded the oratory in a dusky twilight; but even through the shadows which lay thick about us we could see that there had been within this chamber some outbreak of extraordinary and tremendous violence; for the image of the god Huitzilopochtli had been cast down and broken into fragments, and just behind where it had stood there was a dark rift in the gold-plating of the walls, where several plates had been wrenched bodily away.

A strong odor of sulphur hung heavily in the air, and, as I perceived it, the whole matter was plain to me. But Young sniffed at this odor suspiciously when we had brought the stretcher gently to rest upon the floor, and in a startled voice exclaimed, "Th' devil has been bustin' around in here for sure, an' he's left his regular home-made stink for a give-away!" and as he spoke there was manifest a decided bristling of his fringe of hair.

I could not help smiling at this quaint proof of the shattered condition of Young's nerves—for, under ordinary circumstances, he was the very last man in the world to place faith in things supernatural—but I answered him promptly: "Then the devil did a stroke of honest business at the same time, for all this is the work of the same thunder-bolt, or of a part of it, that killed that Indian. Didn't you hear the rocks flying from the cliff where it struck?"

"That's just what I was goin' t' say myself," Young replied, a little awkwardly. "An' that's what's the matter with Rayburn, an' made him swound away. How d' you find yourself now, old man?" he went on—rather glad to change the subject, I fancied—as Rayburn, at sound of his own name, moved a little.

"I feel queer," Rayburn answered. "Sort of numb and dizzy. Where's the Padre?"

"An' it's not much blame to you that you do feel queer," Young replied, hurriedly. "This last thing you've taken it into your fool head t' do is bein' busted all t' bits by a stroke o' lightnin'. Most folks would 'a' been satisfied with havin' their legs pretty much sliced off by Injuns—but reasonableness ain't your strongest hold, Rayburn; an' I guess it never was."

Rayburn smile faintly as Young spoke, but instead of attempting to answer him—being still numbed by the heavy shock that he had received—he settled his head back upon the rolled-up coat that served him for a pillow, and languidly closed his eyes. Whereupon Young, seeing that there was nothing further that we could do for his comfort, betook himself—as his bent at all times was when any strange matter presented itself, and in this case with the half-crazed eagerness with which those upon whom a great sorrow has fallen seek instinctively to engage their minds with any trifling matter that will change the current of their thoughts—to investigating carefully the work of destruction that the thunder-bolt had wrought: examining the fragments of the idol, and the loosened plates of gold and the place on the wall whence these last had been wrenched away; which examination was the easier because the storm-cloud was leaving us—though the almost continuous loud rolling of the thunder still stunned our ears—and a stronger light came in through the opening in the roof.

I seated myself beside Rayburn and paid no attention to what Young was doing; for my brooding sorrow was like a slow fire consuming me—as the tragedy that I had but just witnessed, and the infinite pathos that there was in seeing Rayburn thus miserably dying, overwhelmed me with a desolate despair. Even when Young called to me, in a tone so eager and so penetrating that at any other time I should have been startled into quick action by his words, I did not rouse myself to answer him; though, in a dull way, I knew that he would not thus have spoken unless some matter of great moment had aroused the full energy of his mind.

"Professor! I say, Professor!" he repeated: "Get right up and come here. Don't sit there like a chuckle-headed chump. Get up, I tell you. Here's some sort of a show for us. Here's what looks like a way out o' this God-forsaken hole!"

As I heard these words I did get up, and in a hurry, and so joined Young where he was kneeling on the floor close beside the rear wall of the oratory, directly behind where the idol had stood until the thunder-bolt had dashed it down. It was at this point, apparently, that the lightning had entered the chamber; for here several of the plates of gold with which the walls were covered—overlapping each other like fish-scales—had been loosened, while three of them had been wrenched entirely from their fastenings and had fallen down. As I joined him, Young excitedly pointed to the opening thus made, through which was visible not a solid wall of rock but a dark cavity, and from which was blowing a soft current of cool air.

"It's a way out! It's a way out! I tell you," he cried. "This suck o' wind proves it. If we only can get some more o' these blasted plates loose we'll light out o' this and euchre the Priest Captain an' his whole d——n outfit yet! Ketch hold here, Professor, an' put your muscle into it for all you're worth. Grab right here; now!" And Young and I together pulled at the same plate with all our might and main. But for all the impression that we made upon it we might as well have tried to pull down the mountain; the plate did not stir. Young gave a hearty curse (and I confess that hearing him swearing in that natural way again was a real comfort to me), and then we took another pull; and all this while, so much does the thought of saving his life put cheer into a man, my heart was bounding within me and the hot coursing of my blood seemed like to burst my veins. Young's fervor was not less than mine, and we wrenched and tugged together, and never stopped to mark our cut and bleeding hands.

"We've *got* t' do it!" Young exclaimed, as we paused at last, without having loosened the plate in the least degree. "There's some way o' workin' this thing, I know. It must be some sort of a door, an' if we only can get th' hang of it we'll be all right. Have you got your wind again, Professor? Let's try 'f we can't sort o' prize this plate out; it's a little loose. Just get your fingers under it an' we'll sort o' pull it up an' out at th' same time. So! Now sling your muscle into it. Heft!"

We were stooping a little, and so had a strong purchase, and with all our united strength we heaved away together. There was a rattling of metal, a yielding of the plate so easy that our tremendous effort was out of all proportion to it; my fingers seemed suddenly to be nipped in a red-hot vice; Young uttered a yell of pain, and then we both were sprawling on our backs on the floor, while in front of us was a broad opening in the wall where a wide section of the panelling had risen upward (the plates sliding up under each other), and so had made an open way.

"H—ll! how that did hurt!" Young mumbled, with his nipped fingers in his mouth; and I must say that the vigor of his language was not uncalled for, as I well understood by the pain that I myself was suffering. I never remember pinching my fingers so badly as I did then in the whole course of my life.

However, we did not suffer our hurts, which were not really serious, to delay us in exploring this hidden place that so suddenly and with such unnecessary violence had opened to us. Pushing upward the ingeniously contrived door from the bottom, we easily raised it until an opening was discovered the full height of a man; and through this we went into a narrow passage in the rock that in a moment turned and so brought us into a room that was nearly as large as the oratory that we had just left, and that, as we presently found, actually communicated with the oratory by means of two narrow slits high up in the wall; which apertures here were plainly visible, but on the other side were so cleverly disguised by an ingenious arrange-ment of the overlapping plates as to be entirely concealed. Like the oratory, too, this room had an opening in its roof through which air entered, and so much light that we could see about us plainly. And the very first glance that I cast around me in this strange place assured me that, by sheer accident, we had found our way at last to the secret chamber wherein King Chaltzantzin's treasure had lain hidden for a thousand years.

Rude shelves had been cut in the rock on all four sides of the room, and on these were ranged earthen pots of curious shapes, ornamented with strange devices that my newly acquired knowledge enabled me to recognize—to express the matter in the terms of our system of heraldry—as the arms of a king quartered with the arms of certain princely houses or tribes. On these shelves, also, were many quaintly wrought vessels and some small square boxes, all of which were of gold—together with a score or so of small idols moulded in clay or roughly carved in stone, in which last the workmanship was so far inferior to that of the earthen-ware pots and golden vessels as to show at a glance that they were the product of a much earlier and ruder age; but belonging to the same age as the gold-work, or to a period even later, was a very beautiful Calendar Stone most delicately carved in obsidian, that was identical, save in the matter of size, with the great Calendar Stone that now is preserved in Mexico in the National Museum. This was placed at one end of the room upon a carved pedestal; and at the opposite end of the room, the end farthest removed from the entrance, was a great stone image of the god Chac Mool. Lying upon the Calendar Stone was what at first I took to be a cross-bow made of gold; but more careful examination convinced me, especially in view of the place where I had found it, that this certainly was an arbalest—called also a Jacob's staff and a cross-staff—such as in no very ancient times, until the invention of the quadrant, was used by Europeans in taking the meridional altitude of the sun and stars.

At the moment that I made this last most curious and exceedingly interesting discovery, Young, who had been investigating on his own account, gave a yell of delight, and bounded towards me flourishing his own brace of revolvers in his hands. "They're all here!" he cried. "All our guns are here, an' th' ca'tridges too! Now we *have* got the bulge on these devils for sure!"

As he spoke I also was thrilled with joy at the thought of the vengeance which this recovery of our arms might enable us to take upon Fray Antonio's murderers; but my joy was only momentary, for

I could not but reflect that, after all, these Aztlanecas had but acted in accordance with their lights—excepting only the Priest Captain, for whom the most cruel death would be all too merciful—and that our slaying them would not be vengeance, but mere brutal revenge. Having which thoughts in mind, I answered, "At least we can shoot ourselves with them, and so be safe from death by sacrifice."

"Not much we won't shoot ourselves," Young replied, with great energy; "an' nobody's goin' t' come monkeyin' 'round us with sacrifices, either. Why, man alive, we ain't goin' t' stay here—not by a jugful! We're goin' t' light right out o' this an' be smack off for home."

"How?" I asked, blankly, and with real alarm; for the hot hope that had filled me at the thought of our having found a way of escape had vanished as I perceived that from this chamber there was no outlet save the hole in the roof; which hole also accounted for the current of air whereby my hope had been inspired. Therefore, when Young spoke in this extravagant fashion, the dread came over me that he was going mad.

"How?" he answered, "why, through that Jack Mullins, of course. He *is* th' tippin' kind. I was just tryin' him, while you was pokin' 'round in that old rubbish, when I happened t' ketch sight of our guns; an' seein' them, you bet, made me bounce. Here goes for another shot at him! Stick somethin' under him t' keep him up when I heave."

I was so dazed by the stunning wonder and by the joy that Young's words carried with them, that I obeyed his order mechanically. With a grave seriousness he seated himself upon the head of the idol; and as the figure and the stone base upon which it rested settled down at the end upon which he sat, and its other end correspondingly swung upward, showing beneath it a dark opening, I wedged up the mass with a heavy plate of gold that served as the lid of one of the boxes ranged upon the shelves.

"It won't do for us both together t' go down there," Young said, as he rose from his seat and we peered into the dark cavity. "Mullins might take 't into his fool head t' shut himself up while we was down there, an' that ud mean cold weather for Rayburn an' Pablo. I'll just jump down them steps an' prospect a little, while you look after him t' see that he keeps steady;" and with these words down he went into the hole.

In five minutes or so he joined me again. "It don't look like th' nicest place I ever got into," he said, "but I guess we'll have t' take th' chances on it. There's a little room down there, an' out o' that a kind of a back entry leads into an everlastin' big cave. But there seems t' be a sort of a path runnin' along in the cave—it's all as dark as th' devil—an' as paths mostly have two ends to 'em, I guess if we keep on long enough we'll get somewhere. We can't stay here, that's sure, so we've just got t' risk it, an' th' sooner we get Rayburn down there th' better. When he's solidly safe, then we can do some prospectin'— by good-luck we've got lots o' matches—an' see where that path goes to. Just sling on your guns, Professor, an' let's mosey back an' get th' percession started. It's hard lines on Rayburn t' tumble him into a hole like that when he's feelin' so bad; but I guess it's better t' take th' chances o' killin' him that way ourselves than it is t' let these devils do it for sure. Come on!"

While he was speaking, Young had buckled his revolvers about his waist and had slung his rifle over his shoulder, and I also in like manner had armed myself—whereby was restored to me a most comforting feeling of strength. As for Young, the recovery of his weapons seemed to make him grow two inches taller, and he swaggered in his walk.

CHAPTER XXXVI

THE VENGEANCE OF THE GODS

Almost in the moment that we thus found ourselves in condition to show fight again, the need for fighting seemed like to be forced upon us; for as we turned to leave the treasure-chamber we were startled by hearing a creaking sound that we knew came from the sliding upward of the grating in its metal grooves wherewith the entrance to our prison was made fast.

We paused for a moment, and then Young motioned to me to follow him, stepping lightly; and as we came out into the oratory we heard a fresh creaking, by which we knew that the grating had been closed.

"I guess it's only th' fellow puttin' in th' grub," Young whispered. "But go easy, Professor, an' have your guns all handy, so's you can shoot. If anybody *has* come in it won't do t' let 'em get out again. Only mind you don't shoot unless you really have to. If there's only two or three of 'em we'd better try t' club 'em with our Winchesters, so's not t' bring all hands down on us with a rush before we can get Rayburn away."

As he spoke, we were assured that some one had entered when the grating was raised and had remained on our side of the grating when it was closed again, for we heard footsteps in the room where we ordinarily lay; and then the footsteps drew nearer, as though the unseen person were examining the other rooms in search of us, and we knew that in another moment or two this person would enter the chamber wherein we were. Rayburn was lying so quietly that it seemed as though he had fallen into a swoon again; and Pablo, as we could tell by hearing his sobs, had betaken himself to the room in which El Sabio was tethered in search of solacing companionship. Young motioned me to stand on one side of the entrance to the oratory, and himself stood on the other; and thus we waited, while the footsteps rapidly drew nearer, in readiness most effectually to cut off the retreat of whoever might enter the room.

The man who did enter, passing between us, was the Priest Captain. As he saw the wreck of the idol, and the opening in the wall behind where the idol had stood, he uttered an exclamation of alarm and rage; and in the same moment some instinctive dread of the danger that menaced him caused him to turn suddenly around. So, for an instant, he confronted us—and never shall I forget the look of malignant hatred that was in his face as in that instant he regarded us, nor his quick despairing gesture at sight of Young standing there with his rifle raised. Even as he opened his mouth to cry out, before any sound came from his lips, the heavy barrel of Young's rifle swept downward, and with a groan he fell.

Had the blow struck fairly it could not but have split the man's skull open; but he swerved aside a little as the rifle came down, and the weight of the stroke, glancing from his head, fell upon his shoulder. In an instant, dropping the rifle, Young was kneeling on his breast with a hand buried in the flabby flesh of his old throat, holding tight-gripped his windpipe. Excepting only Rayburn, Young was the strongest man I ever knew (though, to be sure, at that time he was weakened by his then recent wound and by the privations of his imprisonment), yet it was all that he could do to hold that old man down and to maintain his choking grasp. With a most desperate energy and a fierce strength that seemed out of all nature in a creature so lean and old and shrivelled, the Priest Captain writhed and struggled in his efforts to throw Young off, and sought also to grasp Young's throat with his long bony hands—while foam gathered on his thin lips, and his withered brown face grew black with congested blood, and his black eyes protruded until the half of the eyeballs, bloody with bursting reins, showed around the black, dilated pupils. And then him struggles slowly grew less and less violent, his knotted muscles gradually relaxed, his mouth fell open so that his tongue lolled out hideously, his legs and arms twitched a little spasmodically—and then he lay quite still.

For a minute or two longer Young maintained his grasp. Then rising to his feet, breathing heavily, he wiped the sweat from his face as he exclaimed, at the same moment giving the dead body a vicious kick: "You black devil, take that! Now I've squared accounts with you for killin' th' Padre—and it's the best day's work I've ever done!"

Though the struggle between the two had been a very desperate one, there had been no noise about it. Through the whole fight Rayburn had remained buried in his death-like stupor; and Pablo, though so near to us, had heard no sound of it at all.

"Now, then, Professor," Young said, when he had got his wind back, "we've got t' bounce. Th' first thing t' do is t' fasten that gratin' on our side, so's nobody can get in here t' bother us while we're doin' our skippin'. I guess we can sort o' wedge it fast so's t' stand 'em off for an hour or two, anyway, an' that's time enough to give us a fair start."

"We can do something better than that, I think," I said, as we went together towards the grating. "Unless I am much mistaken, only the Priest Captain knew about this sliding door and the treasure-chamber beyond it. If we can restore to their places those three plates, and can close the door behind us, I am persuaded that so far as pursuit of us is concerned we shall be absolutely safe."

"Gosh!" Young exclaimed. "D' you know, Professor, I wouldn't 'a' given you credit for havin' that much common-sense. It's a big idea, that is, an' we'll try it on. But, all th' same, we've got t' make things as sure as we can, an' this little job must be attended to first."

As we approached the grating we saw two of the temple guard standing outside of it, apparently waiting for the Priest Captain's return; and these men looked at us with such evident suspicion that I feared for the success of our plans. "Just talk to 'em," Young said, hurriedly. "Talk to 'em about th' last election, or chicken-coops, or anything you please, while I take a look 'round an' see how we're goin' t' get this job done."

Young dropped behind me, and then aside and so out of sight, as I advanced to the grating and spoke to the men, whose faces somewhat cleared as I told them that the Priest Captain desired that they should wait there a little longer. And then I managed to hold their interest for some minutes while I spoke about the devil that was in El Sabio, and about other devils of a like sort whom I had known in my time. While I thus spoke I heard a little tinkling sound, as of metal striking against stone—but if the soldiers also heard it they paid no attention to it—and then Young whispered, "We're solid now; come on!" Whereupon I quickly ended my imaginative discourse upon demoniac donkeys, and with no appearance of haste we walked away.

"It was just as easy as rollin' off a log," Young said, jubilantly. "There was a big gold peg stickin' there all ready t' slide into a slot, so's t' hold th' gratin' down, an' all I had t' do was t' slide it. I guess, with a plug like that holdin' that gratin' fast, they'll need jacks t' open it. Th' only other way t' start it'll be rammin' it with a bit o' timber;

but bustin' it in that way'll take a lot o' time, an' half an hour's plenty for all we've got t' do. If you're straight in thinkin' nobody knows about that slidin' door we're solid."

I felt very sure in my own mind that I was right in believing that only the Priest Captain had known of this secret opening; for, after him, the most likely person to have knowledge of it was the keeper of the archives, and that he was altogether ignorant of it I was well assured. Therefore I most cheerfully helped Young, so far as my unskilful hands could be useful, in the work of restoring the gold plates to the places whence the lightning had wrenched them loose; and when this work was done, so cleverly did Young manage it, there was no possibility of distinguishing the door from any other portion of the wall; nor was there then a sign of any sort remaining to show that by the passage of a thunder-bolt the idol had been destroyed.

As we were finishing this piece of work we heard the soldiers at the grating calling to the Priest Captain—at first in low tones, and then more loudly; and then we heard them give a yell together, which convinced us that they had tried to raise the grating and had found that it was fastened down.

The ten minutes that followed was the most exciting time that I ever passed through. Notwithstanding the secure fashion in which the grating was fastened, we could not but dread that those outside had knowledge of some means whereby it could be loosened; and in any event there was no doubt but that they could force a way in upon us by beating it down. Therefore we knew that there was no safety for us until we were fairly out of the oratory, and had closed behind us the sliding door—and with such difficult material to deal with as Rayburn, who still lay in a heavy stupor, and Pablo, whom sorrow had wellnigh crazed, we found it hard to make such haste as the sharp exigency of our situation required. Pablo, indeed, was so lost in wonder at finding the broken idol, and the dead body of the Priest Captain, and a door open in the solid wall, that what little remained of his wits disappeared entirely; so that we had almost to carry him— while El Sabio most intelligently followed him—into the treasure-chamber, and there we left the two together while we returned for Rayburn. And as we lifted the stretcher our hearts bounded, for at that instant there was a tremendous crash at the grating; whereby we knew that those without had brought to bear against it some sort of a battering-ram that they might beat it in.

"It's a close call," Young said between his teeth; and added, as we rested the stretcher inside the passage while we closed behind us the sliding door: "If you're off your base, Professor, an' they do know th' trick o' this thing, it may be all day with us yet—but it's a comfort t' know that even if they do finish us we'll everlastin'ly salt 'em first with our guns."

We heard another great crash behind us, but faintly now that the sliding door was closed, as we went onward into the treasure-chamber; and here we heard the like sound again, more clearly, through the slits cut in the wall. As gently as our haste, and the awkwardness of that narrow way would permit, we lifted Rayburn from the stretcher, and so carried him down the short flight of stairs beneath the upraised statue to the little chamber that there was hollowed in the rock. Here we laid him upon the stretcher again; and then, without any ceremony whatever, we bundled Pablo and El Sabio down the hole. It was a smaller aperture, even, than that through which we had come forth from the Cave of the Dead, and how El Sabio was able to condense himself sufficiently to get through it will remain a puzzle to me to my dying day.

All this while we could hear plainly, through the slits in the wall, the crashing blows which every minute or so were delivered against the grating, together with a shrill roar of shouts and yells; and we knew that before this vigorous assault the grating must give way within a very brief period, and so let in the whole yelping pack. If I were right in my belief that the Priest Captain alone know of the secret outlet to the oratory, we still would be safe enough, and could make some preliminary examination of the cave before we closed the way behind us irrevocably by letting the statue fall back into its place; but if I were mistaken, then there was nothing for us but to take the chance of life and death by going on blindly into that black cavern, after wedging fast the under side of the statue in such a way that it no longer could be swung open from above.

It was most necessary, therefore, that we should see what course our enemies would take when they came into the oratory and found it empty of us, and the idol broken, and the Priest Captain lying dead there; and, that we might compass this end, Young and I returned into the treasure-chamber and mounted upon a ledge that seemed to have been provided for a standing-place—whence we had a clear view into the oratory through the slits in the wall. And at the very moment that we thus stationed ourselves there reverberated through those rock-hewn chambers a deafening crash and a jingling clang of metal and a rattle of falling stone; and with this came a yell of triumph and a rush of footsteps—and then, in an instant, the oratory was full of soldiers and priests, all yelling together like so many fiends.

But upon this violent hubbub there fell a hush of awe and wonder as those who had thus tumultuously entered the oratory saw the Priest Captain lying dead amid the fragments of the shattered idol, and perceived that the prisoners who had been shut within these seemingly solid walls had vanished utterly away; and then a sobbing murmur, that presently swelled into moans and cries of terror, arose from the throng; and in a moment more, seized by a common impulse, the whole company bowed downward, in suppliant dread of the gods by whom such direful wonders had been wrought.

Young gave a long sigh of relief, and with a most mouth-filling oath whispered in my ear, "They haven't tumbled to it, an' we're all right!"

As we gazed at these terror-stricken creatures, a thought occurred to me on which I promptly acted. "Get both of your revolvers pointed through that hole," I whispered to Young. "Point high, so that the balls will not hit anybody; and when I begin to shoot do you shoot also, and as quickly as you can. Mind, you are not to hit anybody," I added; for I saw by the look on Young's face that he longed to fire into the crowd point-blank. For answer he gave me a rather sulky nod of assent; but I saw by the way that he held his pistols that my order was obeyed. "Now," I said, "Fire!"—and as rapidly as self-acting revolvers would do it, we poured twenty-four shots through the slits in the wall. No doubt several people were hurt by balls bounding back from the rock, but I am confident that nobody was killed.

When we ceased firing it was impossible to see anything in the oratory, because of the dense cloud of sulphurous smoke wherewith it was filled; but such shrieks and yells of soul-racking terror as came from beneath that black canopy I hope I may never hear again. I waited a little, until this wild outburst had somewhat quieted, and then—placing my mouth close to one of the openings and speaking in a voice that I tried to make like that of Fray Antonio—I said, in deep and solemn tones, "Behold the vengeance of the strangers' God!"

What effect my words produced I cannot tell. Our firing must have loosened a fragment of rock between the gold plating that lined the oratory and the outer surface of the wall, and even as I spoke this fragment fell. With its fall the opening was irrevocably closed.

"That was a boss dodge," said Young, as he recharged his revolver. "Those fellows'll just think hell's broke loose in here, for sure; and I guess after they've onct fairly got outside they'll rather be skinned alive than come back again. But what did you say to 'em? Hearin' you talkin' like th' Padre, that way, gave me a regular jolt. Don't you think, though, maybe it was a little bit risky t' give ourselves away?"

But when I had repeated in English the words which I had spoken, Young very seriously shook hands with me. "Shake!" he said. "I've done you injustice, Professor. Sometimes I've thought that you was too much asleep for your own good—but if anybody ever did anything more wide awake than that, I'd like t' know *what* he did and who he was. Why, when those fellows tell about all that's been goin' on in here—about their busted idol, an' their dead Priest Captain, an' our skippin,' an' this row our shootin' has made, an' then about th' Padre's ghost talkin' to 'em that way—it's bound t' give 'em such a jolt that th' whole outfit'll slew smack round an' be Christians right off!"

Some such notion as this had been in my own mind as I executed the plan that on the spur of the moment I had formed. When, later, I thought about it more calmly, I could not but regret, for Fray Antonio's sake, my hasty action; for he would have been the very last man to approve of such stringent methods of advancing the Christian faith. If any result came from my demonstration, it certainly came through terror; and the essence of Fray Antonio's doctrine, as it was also of his own nature, was gentleness and love.

XXXVII.

THROUGH DARKNESS TO LIGHT.

"I guess we're solid now, as far as bein' bothered by those sacred devils goes," Young said, as we stepped down from the ledge of rock on which we had been standing; "but this ain't no time t' take no chances, an' th' sooner we see what show we've got for gettin' anywhere through that cave, th' better it'll be. An' we've got t' look after Rayburn. He's closter t' handin' in his checks t'-day than he's been at all. Just think o' him keepin' still through all that row, an lettin' himself be yanked around like a bag o' meal without takin' any notice of it! But there's just a squeal of a chance for him if we do get clear away. Knowin' that he's safe'll do him more good, even, than fresh air an' sunshine—an' oh Lord! how good fresh air an' sunshine'll be, if ever we do strike 'em again!"

When we descended the stair-way again to the little hollow in the rock where Rayburn was lying, we found that he still remained in his dull stupor and took no notice of our coming. Close beside were Pablo and El Sabio, huddled together for mutual support in this very trying passage of their lives. El Sabio, indeed, was a most melancholy and dejected creature, for his short commons and his long confine-ment had taken the spirit out of him pretty thoroughly; but for our purposes just then, when his tractability was very necessary to us, it was a piece of good-fortune that he had fallen into so low a way. As for Pablo, the boy was in so dazed a condition that I feared greatly he would wholly lose his wits.

There was only a faint suggestion of light in that deeply hidden place, and Young struck a match that he might see to begin his explo-rations. "Well, I'll be shot," he exclaimed, as the wax-taper shed its clear light around us, "if here ain't a conductor's lantern hangin' up all ready for us, an' a can o' kerosene oil!" As he lighted the lantern, and the letters F. C. C. showed clearly on the glass, he added, in a tone of still greater amazement: "Ferro-Carril Central! Why, it b'longs t' one o' th' boys on th' Central!—but how th' dickens did it ever get *here*? An' here's a lot of old clothes—th' sort o' rags th' low-down Greasers wear. An' I'm blest," he went on, as he picked up a scrap of paper from the floor, "if this ain't a Mexican Central ticket from Leon to Silao! It's dated last June, an' it's only punched once, so 't couldn't 'a' been used all the way. I say, Professor, am I asleep or awake?"

As I examined the several articles which we had come upon so strangely in this incongruous plate, a flood of light was let in upon my mind, and with this came also the glad certainty that the way before us to freedom was open and assured. My belief that the Priest Captain had been in communication with the outside world no longer admitted of a doubt, for here was absolute proof of it: the clothes which he wore when making his expeditions into the nineteenth century; the lantern that he had stolen in order the more easily to find his way through the cave; the railway ticket that he had but lately used. In an instant I had connected all this with what the guardian of the archives had told me concerning the Priest Captain's habit of retiring for long periods of time to one of the chambers in which we had been imprisoned, and the whole matter was as plain to me as day; and I knew now, that in order to guard against discovery, he, or one of his predecessors, to whom this secret way must also have been known, had caused to be set in place the fastening by which the grating could be secured upon its inner side; which fastening, within that very hour, had been the means of saving our lives.

"Well," said Young, dryly, when I had briefly explained these several matters, "I guess he won't pull th' wool over nobody's eyes any more! An' now you an' me'll do some prospectin'. We must go back upstairs, before we pull out for good, an' bag what there is there that's worth carryin' off; but th' first thing t' do is t' get Rayburn where he'll be comfortable an' safe. Until that's attended to we've got t' be careful an' go slow; so we'll rouse up this fool of a Pablo, an' get it into his head that if he hears anybody comin' he's t' knock th' plug from under Mullins an' let him down, an' then chock him fast with a rock underneath. It's not likely that anybody *will* come, an' even if they do, I don't think that they'll know th' trick about Mullins' tippin', for that's a point that I'll bet a whole kag o' beer th' Priest Captain didn't give away t' nobody. I tell you, Professor, there wasn't any flies on that old man, now was there? He was a wicked old devil, an' I'm glad I did for him; but he was just an everlastin' keen one, an' a rustler from th' word go!"

In the dazed condition in which he then was, we scarcely should have ventured to place Pablo in a position of such grave responsibility had there been any likelihood of his being called upon to perform the duty with which we charged him; but we were well satisfied that to the Priest Captain alone had been known the secret of the sliding door, and that, consequently, the need for closing the passage leading upward into the treasure-chamber would not arise. Without any fear for Rayburn's safety; therefore, we left him lying in the little room at the foot of the stair-way, and thence went forth through a cleft in the rock—that seemed to be a natural crevice, where the mountain was split apart—and so came into a natural cave of such great size that the light of the lantern was not sufficient to enable us to see its roof nor its farther wall. Save that the well-defined path that we followed was continuously steep, we did not find walking difficult, for the fragments of rock with which the floor of the cave everywhere was strewn had been lifted aside carefully, so as to make a smooth and easy way. And only in one place—where for a short distance the path skirted the edge of a black gulf, in the depths of which we could hear the rush of water—was any part of it dangerous.

For near an hour we went onward, all the while steadily ascending; and then, as we turned a corner, we saw a long way before us a faintly luminous haze. It was so very faint that only by holding the lantern behind us, and then closing our eyes for a moment, could we assure ourselves that what we saw really was light at all; but when we turned another corner, presently, the light, though still faint, was unmistakable; whereat Young gave a whoop of joy, and we quickened our steps in our eager longing to behold the sunshine that we knew could not be far away. Suddenly the path dipped downward, and then another turn brought us into light so strong that the lantern no longer was needed to show us where to tread; and by a common impulse we gave a great glad shout together and went onward at a run; and so, running and shouting like the crazy creatures that truly for the time being we were, we made one turn more, and then beheld before us, reaching away broadly and openly in a fashion to give one a sense of most glorious freedom, a vastly wide plain, over which everywhere the blessed sunshine blazed full and strong. As we stood together in the mouth of the cave for a moment in silence—for no words seemed strong enough to express the bursting gladness that was in our hearts—two short blasts of a whistle, wafted upward on the light breeze that was blowing towards us from the plain, sounded very faintly but clearly in our ears. Young started as he heard this sound, and as he turned towards me he held out his hand and said, in a voice that was husky and tremulous, "Professor, that's a locomotive whistle, an' th' damn fool is—is whistlin' 'down brakes'!" And in these curiously chosen, yet not unmeaning words, did we celebrate our deliverance.

When we returned to Rayburn—and as we now knew the way, and as almost the whole of it was downhill, our return was accomplished rapidly—some of the joyous strength that we had gained seemed to be imparted to him. He opened his eyes as we stooped over him, and there seemed to be more life in them than there had been through all that day.

"Rouse up, old man!" Young cried cheerily. "We've struck th' trail out o' this cussed hole at last, an' we're goin' t' hike you right along to where you'll get some of God's sunshine again, an' some air that's fit for a white man t' breathe;" which words brought still more light into Rayburn's eyes, and a little color came into his pale cheeks as we told him of the open way that we had found to light and life.

"Where's the Padre?" he asked, as we together raised the stretcher, while Pablo, holding the lantern and leading El Sabio, went on ahead of us. Fortunately Rayburn could not see Young's face as he answered: "Th' Padre's—well, th' Padre's just gone on up th' line. You've got t' hold your jaw, Rayburn. You ain't fit t' talk; an' while we're packin' you along we can't talk either. Come on, Professor; and you, Pablo," he added, in his jerky Spanish. "Be careful with that lamp or I'll break the head of you!"

Although a good third of his flesh had wasted away, Rayburn would have been a heavy load for us to carry over level ground, even had we been hale and strong. Worn as we then were by our prison-life, we found carrying him up that long steep path in the heart of the mountain a weary work that only the hope and joy that strengthened us enabled us to accomplish. As it was, we went so slowly, and made so many halts for rest, that the sun had sunk almost to the level of the distant mountains, wherewith that great plain was bordered to the westward, when at last our toilsome journey was at an end. But we thought nothing of the heaviness of our labor as we saw the glad look that came into his face when he gazed out over that broad expanse of sunlit landscape, and snuffed eagerly the sweet fresh air, and so felt his soul grow light within him as he realized that he once more was safe and free.

In the mouth of the cave—within its shelter, yet where he could see out freely, and so have constantly in his mind the comforting thought of his deliverance—we made a bed for him of soft pine-branches, which some near-by trees gave us; and we took care that this couch should be so thick and so evenly laid that he would lie easily upon it; for we knew that many days, perhaps even weeks, must pass before we could venture to put so heavy a strain upon his strength as would come when we carried him down that rough mountain-side, and so began our journey towards home.

Fortunately, a little spring came out from the rock, clear and cool, just inside the cave; and game was so abundant on that mountain-side that Young came back presently from a foraging expedition with half a dozen codornices, that he had come so close to as to shoot with his revolver, and a jack-rabbit that he actually had caught with his hands as it jumped up almost beneath his feet; which excellent fare made a most satisfying supper for all of us; and eating it so added to Rayburn's strength—as we could tell by the fuller tones of his voice, and by his being able to move a little on his bed without our helping him—as to rouse in us a warm hope that the death that seemed so near to him might yet be thrust away. Our chief concern, lest the shock that would come to him of knowing it should fairly kill him, was to hide from him for the present the knowledge that Fray Antonio was dead; and to compass this end we plumply told him the flat-footed lie that the monk had gone on in search of some town whence he might bring back horses and supplies; and so, for a time, we laid at rest his doubts.

In his own original way, also, Young tried to put heart into him. "You see, old man," he said, "you've just *got* t' pull through. Think how damned ashamed o' yourself you'd feel after you was dead when you had t' tell all th' folks in heaven that you was killed by nothin' better'n a mis'rable chump of an Injun! That was what bothered poor old Steve Hollis when he was handin' in *his* checks—'t least it was th' same general sort of idea. I guess you never knew Steve, did you, Rayburn? He was an old railroader—had been a-workin' on th' Old Colony one way and another for more'n twenty years. When I knowed him he used t' run th' steamboat express from Boston t' Fall River—their boss train on that blasted old road. Steve owned a house clost t' th' line just a little way out o' Braintree; an' when 't was his day off he'd mostly slide down from Fall River on No. 2, an' walk out home from Braintree along th' track. Nobody ever know'd just how 't happened—Steve was th' soberest man I ever knowed; never drunk a drop o' nothin'—but one day, as he was walkin' out home, No. 15, that was th' slow freight from Boston t' Newport, ketched him an' got in its work on him—an' that was th' end o' Steve. It didn't kill him right smack off, an' I went down t' see him; for I did think th' world of old Steve. He was a-layin' in his bed, an' I could see that he was a-most gone when I got there; but he chippered up a little for a minute as I shook hands with him and ast him how he was. He said he was poorly; an' then he kep' quiet for a while. Then he kind o' ketched his breath an' seemed t' want t' say somethin'. So I bent over him, an' he said, in a kind of a whisperin' groan: 'Jus' think of it, Seth, what did it was th' slow freight! That's what cuts me; that's what cuts me the worst kind. I wouldn't a-minded if 't had been th' express—them things will happen, an' they've got t' come. But here I've been a-railroadin' for more'n twenty year, an' t' think o' *me* bein' busted by that damn slow freight!' An' then he turned over, an' give a sort of a grunt, an' died."

I am not sure that I myself should have selected this particular story to tell to Rayburn just then; but the moral that it contained unquestionably was a sound one, and, in a way, was calculated to impress upon him strongly the conviction that his duty was to get well.

CHAPTER XXXVIII

KING CHALTZANTZIN'S TREASURE

Whether or not Young's story had this good effect upon Rayburn, I am not prepared to say; but it is certain that he slept well that night— his first good night's sleep for many weeks—and that when morning came he was so much stronger and brighter as to fill us with a still more earnest hope that he was well started on the way to recovery.

Young quickly brought in some birds for our breakfast, and when the meal was finished he took me aside and said: "Now, Professor, lets me an' you go back t' that hole an' bring away all there is there that's worth carryin'. It's not much, I guess, but it's better'n nothin'. It just makes me sick t' think of all that gold, that ud 'a' made our ever-lastin' fortunes if we'd only been able t' pack it along with us. There was millions an' millions there, I s'pose—an' it'll never do us any more good than if we'd never seen it at all!" and as Young spoke he heaved a very melancholy sigh. "But we may as well grab all we can get," he went on, more cheerfully. "There was a lot o' gold boxes an' jugs in th' room where Mullins is; an' maybe there's somethin' that's worth havin' in all them little pots. Let's go back an' see, anyway. Rayburn's lookin' almost all right this mornin'; and Pablo's got his wits back now, an' can give him anything he wants."

For my own part I did not desire, because of their money value, any of the articles which I had seen in the treasure-chamber; but I did very earnestly long to possess myself of that most curious arbalest, and I desired also to examine carefully—because of the discoveries of great archæological value which I hoped to make—the contents of the gold boxes and vases and earthen jars. Therefore, Rayburn having expressed his entire willingness that we should leave him, I assented readily to Young's proposition; whereupon Young lighted the lantern and we set off.

As we entered again the treasure-chamber there was within me a strong feeling of awe. During our hurried passage through it, the imminent danger in which we were, and then the excitement of the scene in the oratory, and then the joyfulness of our finding a way of escape, had prevented me from realizing how wonderful was the deposit that this room contained; a deposit that certainly had lain there for not less than a thousand years, and that unquestionably was the most perfect surviving trace of the most intelligent and most interesting people that in prehistoric times dwelt upon this continent. Which strange reflections, now that my mind was free to entertain them and to dwell upon them, aroused within me a feeling of such reverent wonder that I hesitated for some moments before I could bring myself to disturb what thus through so long a sweep of ages had remained sacredly inviolate.

But reverence, as he himself would have said, was not Young's strongest hold; in truth, I am persuaded that there was not an atom of it in his entire composition; and as I stood hesitating beside the statue of Chac-Mool he briskly called to me: "Come right along, Professor; there ain't nobody t' stop us now. We've got th' drop, you might say, on th' whole outfit, an' we can do just as we blame please. This looks like a badly kept drug store, don't it?" he went on, "with all these pots an' boxes an' little jars stuck round on th' shelves. Well, here goes t' see what's in 'em: not much o' nothin', I guess; but then it *might* be di'monds, an' that just would be gay!"

As Young spoke he thrust his hand into one of the earthen jars, and thereby set flying such a cloud of dust that for some seconds his violent sneezing prevented him from examining the small object that he had brought forth from the jar and held in his hand; and when he did examine this object an expression of intense disgust appeared upon his face, and he exclaimed, indignantly, "Why, it's nothin' but a fool arrow-head!"

I could not but laugh at Young as I took the arrow-head from him. For my purposes, this beautifully carved piece of obsidian was far more precious than a diamond would have been; and I tried—quite unsuccessfully, however—to arouse his interest in this proof of the high degree of skill to which the prehistoric races of America had attained in the manipulation of an exceedingly hard yet delicate variety of stone; and I added that not less interesting was the proof thus afforded us of the great value which these same races attached to implements of war.

"Oh, come off with your prehistoric races, Professor!" he growled. "A whole car-load o' rubbish like this wouldn't be worth a nickel t' anybody but a scientific crank like you. If this is th' sort o' stuff that that old king o' yours thought was worth hidin', I guess he must 'a' been off his head. But that pot may 'a' got in by mistake. Before I get too much down on him I'll give him another show." With which words, but cautiously, that the dust might not be disturbed, he thrust his hand into another jar, and was mightily resentful upon finding that what he brought forth from it was only the head of a lance. However, the determination to give King Chaltzantzin a chance to prove his sanity, together with the hope that something of real value might be found, led him to continue his investigations, and he presently had examined all the jars ranged on two sides of the room; and his grumbling curses increased constantly in vigor as jar after jar yielded only arrow-heads, and lance-heads, and chisel-shaped pieces of obsidian, that I perceived must have been intended for the making of the cutting edges of the maccahuitl, or Aztec sword; but, for my part, all of these things filled me with the liveliest pleasure as I took them from Young and attentively examined them; for the delicate and perfect workmanship that they exhibited showed them to have been made by a people that had reached the highest development of the Stone Age.

"This business is gettin' worse, instead o' better," Young said, gloomily, as he began his search on the third side of the room by opening one of the small gold boxes. "The stuff in here is nothin' but a mean sort o' wrappin'-paper with pictures on it—like that old map o' yours that got us started on this tomfoolin' treasure-hunt. I s'pose *you'll* just have a fit over it!" And as I uttered an eager cry of delight, and bent over this casket that contained such inestimable riches, he gave a sniff of contempt, and added: "There, I thought so. You think more o' that rotten old stuff than you would o' gold dollars. Well, there's no accountin' for tastes, and it takes all sorts o' people t' make th' world." But I paid no attention to him as I rapidly glanced over these priceless manuscripts; and then had my cup of happiness filled absolutely to overflowing by the glad discovery that in every one of the gold boxes, of which there were nine in all, treasures of a like sort were stored. In the supplemental volume (in elephant folio) to my *Pre-Columbian Conditions on the Continent of North America* these wonderful manuscripts are reproduced in fac-simile; and when that great work is published the surpassing value of my discovery will be at once recognized. It is sufficient to say here that these several codices together constituted a complete hieratic chronicle of the Aztec tribes; and that (herein lying the extraordinary value of the collection) the uncertain picture-writing was accompanied by a translation into the ideographic characters of later times, the meaning of which I was enabled, thanks to the instruction that my friend the guardian of the archives had given me, fully to understand. In short, my discovery precisely paralleled that of Boussard; for even as the Rosetta Stone gave the key to Egyptian hieroglyphics, so did this transliteration into intelligible characters make all Aztec picture-writing plain. As the full significance of my discovery burst upon me, my joy and the excitement of my splendid triumph so moved me that my hands trembled as I held these precious manuscripts, and I no longer could see clearly the painted characters because of the tears of happiness which filled my eyes.

Young, however, whose longing was only for material treasure, continued his investigations in anything but a thankful mood. "There ain't no doubt of it *now*," he said presently in a most melancholy tone. "That old king o' yours must 'a' been just as crazy as a loon. Look here: this thing ain't even a fool arrow-head; it's nothin' but a bit o' green glass! I reckon it's part o' th' bottom of a porter-bottle. Nice sort o' stuff this is t' call treasure, an' t' take such an all-fired lot o' trouble t' hide away! Why, I should jedge that that king must 'a' spent most of his time settin' up nights a-puzzlin' over plans for makin' sure that he was th' very damnedest biggest fool that ever lived!—an' that's just what he was, for sure! It's tough, gettin' left this way; but it wouldn't begin t' be as tough as 't is if 't wasn't for all them car-loads an' car-loads o' gold right clost by us here that we might 'a' got away with as easy as rollin' off a log if we'd only ketched on to this back-door racket in time. An' see here, Professor," he went on in a very earnest tone, "I don't believe there's anybody in there now; why shouldn't we just chance things a little an' go back an' get some of it? We've got our guns; an' even if we do strike a crowd too big for us t' tackle, an' have t' run for it, we won't be no worse off 'an we are now. Come, let's try it on!"

While Young spoke I had been looking closely at the object that so violently had excited his indignation, and instead of replying to him I asked, "Are there any more pieces of that porter-bottle in the jar?"

"It's full of 'em," he answered with a contemptuous brevity.

"And the next?"

"That's full of 'em too. All th' jars on this side o' th' room are full of 'em," he added, as he rapidly thrust his hand into one after another—and so set the dust to flying that we both fell to sneezing as though we would sneeze our heads off. "Oh come along, Professor: what's th' use o' foolin' over this rubbish; let's go for th' stuff that's good for its weight in spot cash every time!"

"Wait till we see what is in these gold vases over here," I answered, turning as I spoke to the side of the room that as yet we had not examined.

"What's th' good?" he asked, sulkily. But he lifted down one of the vases, and with his thumb and finger brought forth from it a little round black ball. "Worse an' worse," he said, as he handed the ball to me. "We've got down t' what looks like lumps o' shoemaker's wax now. That's about th' sickest lookin' thing t' call itself treasure I ever did see!"

It did not seem to me probable that the little ball was shoemaker's wax; but in order to settle this point experimentally I cut into it with my penknife. Under the gummy exterior I found a layer of cotton-wool, and enclosed in this a hard substance about the size of a hazel-nut. While I was making this examination, Young investigated into the contents of the remaining vases—which themselves were exceedingly interesting, being made of hammered gold and most curiously engraved.

"They're no good," he said, "except I s'pose th' mugs must be worth somethin'. Shoemaker's wax in 'em all! It's worse 'an th' porter-bottles—for what's th' use o' shoemaker's wax t' folks who don't rightly know what a shoe is? Come along, I say, Professor, an' let's have a whack at them piles o' gold. If we don't tackle 'em we might just as well never have come on this treasure-hunt at all. Some o' the stuff in here's worth havin'—th' gold mugs an' boxes, an' that old gold bow-gun that you're so busted about—but what does th' whole of it amount to, anyway, when you come t' divide it up among four men an' a jackass? I guess even th' jackass ud turn up his nose at it if he knowed what a lot more there was that was t' be had just for grabbin' it an' packin' it along. It's somethin', I s'pose, that we've pulled through without losin' our hair; but we *have* pulled through all right, an' now we want t' make this business pay; an' unless we go for that gold this business won't 'a' paid worth a cuss—an' instead o' comin' out on top we'll be left th' very worst kind!"

As Young was delivered of this dismal remonstrance I handed him the small object that I had extracted from the pitch-coated ball.

"Before you make up your mind that we are likely to be 'left,' as you term it, suppose you look at this," I said.

He held out his hand carelessly; but as he saw what I had placed in it his expression suddenly changed, and he burst forth excitedly: "Great Scott! where did this come from? Why—why, Professor, it *looks* like it was a pearl; but if 't truly is one it's about th' bustin'est biggest one that Godamighty ever made! Do you truly size it up for a pearl yourself?"

"Most assuredly," I answered. "And it is a fair assumption, I think, that there is a pearl in each one of all these little pitch-covered balls. As to what you called bits of green glass, they are neither more nor less than extraordinarily fine emeralds; I should say that the smallest of them must be worth more dollars than you could carry at a single load. Of course, all the emeralds and pearls together are not worth a single one of these manuscripts"—here Young gave a sceptical grunt—"but in the way of vulgar material riches I am confident that the value of what is in these jars is greater than that of all the gold together that we saw in the Valley of Aztlan. Without a shadow of doubt, you and I at this moment are standing in the midst of the most enormous treasure that ever has been brought together since the world was made!"

"Honest Injun, Professor?"

"Certainly," I answered; "and if this is your notion of getting 'left' on a treasure-hunt," I continued, "it assuredly is not mine."

"Left?" Young repeated after me, while his eyes ranged exultantly over the rows of jars in which this vast wealth was contained. "Well, I should smile! I take it all back about that old king bein' crazy. He was just as level-headed as George Washington an' Dan'l Webster rolled into one. These pots full of arrow-heads an' such stuff was only one of his little jokes, showin' that he must 'a' been a good-natured, comical old cuss, th' kind I always did like, anyway. Left? Not much we ain't left! We've just everlastin'ly got there with all four feet to onct! Professor, shake!"

EPILOGUE

Throughout my whole life I have been saddened, as each well-defined section of it has come to an end, by the thought that during the period that has then slipped away from me forever I have wasted more opportunities than I have improved. As I write these final lines, therefore, I feel a sorrowful regret, which, in a way, is akin to the regret that weighed upon me when Young and I, having carried into the cave the contents of the treasure-chamber, removed the prop wherewith was upheld the swinging statue, and so suffered to fall into place again that ponderous mass of stone. From below, where we were, lifting it was impossible; and by heaping fragments of rock under the forward end of it we presently made it equally immovable from above. Thus for outlet or for inlet that way was irrevocable barred; and as I write now I know that I am not less irrevocable severing myself from one portion of my past. For, says the Persian poet, "A finished book is a sealed casket. To it nothing can be added. From it nothing can be taken away. Therefore should we pray to Allah that its contents may be good."

The record that I am now ending was begun partly that I might find in the writing of it relief from the more serious work in which I have been engaged, and partly because I perceived that I could properly include in a personal narrative many matters which were too trivial or too entirely personal to be incorporated into my extended scientific treatise, but which, I was persuaded, were of a sufficient interest to be preserved. But I certainly should not have finished this history of our adventures nearly so expeditiously had not Rayburn and Young taken a very lively interest in it, and pressed me constantly to bring it to an end.

"You see, Professor," said Young, "I don't want t' say anything against that big book you're writin'. I don't doubt that in its way it'll be a daisy; but you know yourself there won't be more'n about three cranks in th' whole o' God's universe who'll ever read more'n about ten lines of it; an' that's why I want you t' rush ahead with th' little book—that stands some chance o' bein' read outside o' lunatic asylums—so's folks'll know what a powerful queer time we've had. Don't be too cussed particular t' say just where that valley is—for, while it's not likely, we might want t' take a fightin' crowd along an' dynamite our way back there some day after more cash; but, exceptin' that, just give 'em th' cold facts. I reckon they'll make some folks open their eyes."

From times to time, as my narrative has grown beneath my hand, I have read aloud to my fellow-adventurers what I have written, and have received from them suggestions in accordance with which it has been corrected or amended in its several parts; and it is but just to add, in this connection, that in every case where I have referred (as it seems to me now in words not nearly strong enough) to the loyalty to our common interests, and to the splendid bravery which Rayburn and Young constantly exhibited throughout that trying time, I have been compelled to exert the whole of my authority over them in order to win their grumbling permission that my words might stand. Even Pablo—for the love that there was between this boy and me was far too strong to permit me to leave him behind in Mexico, and we are like to live together as long as we live at all—has taken issue with me concerning what I have written of his steadfast faithfulness and courage; and this on the ground that he could not possibly be anything but faithful to those whom he loved, and that it is only natural for a man to fight for his own life, and for the lives of his friends. In thus applying the word *hombre* to himself Pablo spoke a little doubtfully, as though he feared that I might question his right to it; yet did he roll it so relishingly under his tongue, and so well had he proved his manliness, that I suffered it to pass.

In point of fact, the only member of our party who has accepted my just tribute of praise with entire equanimity has been El Sabio. It was Pablo's notion, of course, that El Sabio should hear what I had written about him. "Not the whole of it, you know, señor," the boy said, earnestly; "for some of what you have written—while I know that it is true, and therefore must be told—would hurt his tender heart. It was not his fault—the angel!—that he gave us so much trouble when we swung him across the cañon; and to tell him that there was even a thought of eating him, while we were in that dreadful valley where every one was dead, assuredly would turn him gray before his time. No; we will hide all such unpleasant parts of the book from him; but we will read to him what you have said concerning his beauty and his wisdom—and, surely, you might have said of those a great deal more; and also about his gallant fight with the priests, when, all alone, he slew so many of them with his heels. And it would have been fairer to

El Sabio, señor," Pablo added, a little reproachfully, as we walked out together to the paddock in which the ass, grown to be very fat, was living a life of most royal ease, "had you told in the book how well he served us in bringing all the treasure, in many weary journeys, out through that dismal cave; and also how carefully he carried the Señor Rayburn down that steep mountain-side, and so to the little town beside the railway, and never hurt his wound."

However, El Sabio did not seem to notice these omissions from my narrative, though he certainly did exhibit a most curious air of interest and understanding as I read to him those laudatory portions of it which Pablo desired that he should hear. According to Pablo's understanding of his language, he even thanked me for speaking well of him; for when the reading was ended he thrust his nose far forward, laid his long ears back upon his neck, planted his little legs firmly, and as he erected in triumph his scrag of a tail, he uttered a most thunderous bray. "And now, Wise One," Pablo said, tenderly, as he infolded the head of the ass in his arms and hugged it to his breast, "thou knowest that we not only love thee for thy goodness and thy wisdom, but that we also honor thee for thy noble deeds."

Rayburn's fancy was mightily tickled by this performance in which El Sabio and Pablo and I had engaged—though Young evidently thought it but another proof of the addled state of my brains—when I told about it that evening as we all sat smoking comfortably in my library before the open fire. This was to be our last meeting for some time to come; for Rayburn was to start the next day for Idaho to look after some mining matters, and Young suddenly had decided that he would accompany him. In truth, Young was rather at a loss to know what to do with himself; for his plan for buying the Old Colony Railroad, in order to be in a position to discharge its superintendent, had been abandoned. "I'd like t' do it, of course," he said. "Bouncin' that chump th' same way that he bounced me would do me a lot o' good; but I've made up my mind it wouldn't be th' square thing t' do, considerin' that if he hadn't bounced me I'd still be foolin' round on top o' freight-cars, in all sorts o' weather, handlin' brakes. So I've let up on him, an' he can stay. What I want now is t' do some good with this all-fired big pile o' money that I've got. That's one reason why I'm goin' out with Rayburn t' Idaho. Right straight along from here t' Boisé City I mean t' set up drinks for every railroader I meet. That'll be doin' good, for sure."

Rayburn and I laughed a little at this odd method for benefiting humanity that Young had got hold of; and then Rayburn's face grew grave as he said: "Well, we're doing a little good, I suppose, in putting that old church in Morelia in good shape. I'm glad you thought of that, Professor. I don't suppose that anything we could have done would have pleased the Padre more than to have that church, that he loved so much, made as handsome as money can make it all the way through."

"Yes," Young added, "an' I guess th' Professor's head was level in havin' all th' new stuff that we've put in it made t' look like 't was about two hundred years old. I did kick at that at first, I'll allow. What I wanted t' do was t' build a first-class new church, with a rattlin' tall steeple, an' steam heat, an' electric lights, an' an organ big enough t' bust the roof off every time she was played. But th' Padre was as keen as th' Professor, a'most, for old-fashioned things; an' so I guess we've done that job just about as he'd 'a' done it himself. It makes me feel queer, though, puttin' up money on a Catholic church that way; an' when I was tellin' an old aunt o' mine, down t' Milton, about it, she just riz up an' rared. An' she didn't feel a bit better when I told her that if I thought it ud please th' Padre t' have me do it, I'd go smack off t' Rome an' shake hands with th' Pope. And I truly would do that very same thing," Young continued, earnestly, while his voice trembled a little, "for this side o' heaven I never expect t' meet anybody that's so near t' bein' a first-class angel as th' Padre was. An' when I think how he saved our mis'rable lives for us, as he surely did, by givin' away his own—that was worth more'n all of ours put together, an' ten times over—I don't care a continental what his religious politics was; an' I'll punch th' head of anybody who don't say that he was th' pluckiest an' th' best man that ever lived!"

Pablo had caught the word Padre in Young's talk, and as the lad looked up from the corner in which he was sitting, I saw that his eyes were full of tears; Rayburn's eyes also had an odd glistening look about them as he turned away suddenly, and emptied the ashes from his pipe into the fire; and I know that I could not see very clearly just then, as very tender, yet very poignant memories surged suddenly into my heart.

And when the others left me—as they did presently, for we could not fall again into commonplace talk—I bade Pablo be off to bed, and so sat there for a while alone. What I had planned to do that night was to revise an address that I was shortly to deliver before the

Archæological Institute; but the pen that I had taken into my hand lay idle there, while my thoughts went backward through the channels of the past.

In that still season of darkness I seemed to live again through all the time that Fray Antonio and I had been together—from the moment when I first caught sight of him, as he knelt before the crucifix in the sacristy, to my last sad look at the dead body whence his soul had sped back again to God.

As my thoughts dwelt upon this most loving and most tender companionship, the like of which for perfectness I am confident was never known, and then upon the cruel violence that brought it to an end, so searching a pain went through my soul that I knew that either it must cease or I must die of it in a very little while. And then was borne in upon me the strong conviction—and so has it since been always, when thus my thoughts have been engaged—that because of my very love for Fray Antonio must I rejoice that he had died so savage a death; believing confidently that what he prayed for when first I found him in the Christian church of San Francisco was, in truth, that very crown of martyrdom that God granted to him when at last I lost him in the heathen city of Colhuacan. And with the pressing in upon me thus strangely of this strange thought, it seemed as though he himself said again to me, "I go to win the life, glorious and eternal, into which neither death nor sin nor sorrow evermore can come."